FIVE SIBLINGS AT 23

Paul Ilett

Five Siblings At 23

Copyright © *Paul Ilett, 2024*
All Rights Reserved

This book is subject to the condition that no part of this book is to be reproduced, transmitted in any form or means, electronic or mechanical, stored in a retrieval system, photocopied, recorded, scanned, or otherwise. Any of these actions require the proper written permission of the author.

For
Jan, Lynsey, Megan and Luke
with love x x x x

CHAPTER 1

11 March 2000

Charlie Fletcher stood outside the small Victorian manor, smartly dressed in his best navy suit and clutching a small bouquet of pink tulips. It was raining softly, a cold March breeze whistling across the grounds, but he barely noticed the weather. From the moment he'd arrived at the entrance, he had found himself unable to go inside, as if the longer he stayed in that moment, stood quietly in the rain, he could somehow hold time in its place. It was his birthday, his twenty-third, the last birthday he would ever share with his mother, and he did not want the day to end.

There was so much he wanted to talk to her about, so much that he wanted to share, things he'd never told her. He didn't want to spend the rest of his life believing his own mother had never truly known him. But the days had passed at such a cruel pace, and Charlie had never found the right moment to share with her the quiet truths about himself. Now she was receiving end-of-life care in a local hospice, and all he could do was stand in the rain and wish time would stop still so nothing bad could happen to his mum.

'Would you like to come in, my dear?'

It took a moment before Charlie registered that someone had spoken; he glanced to the entrance and saw a woman smiling at him, her hand held out in his direction. She was in her sixties, wearing a dark grey trouser suit and had the air of someone who had been through this process many times before. Charlie was not sure whether to take comfort in her demeanour or feel sad that his mother would soon become just another poor soul who would see out her life under that roof with so much time left unlived.

'Sorry,' he said. 'I just lost myself for a moment.'

'That's quite alright, dear. But do please come inside.'

Suddenly in motion, Charlie found himself walking next to her through the doors and into the quiet reception area.

'Susan Fletcher,' he said. 'She's my mother.'

The woman gestured for him to take a seat. 'I will go and check she's awake for you,' she replied. And once Charlie had sat down, she walked behind the reception desk, picked up the phone and proceeded to have a quiet conversation.

Charlie looked directly across the room and realised he could see himself reflected in the mirrored back of an empty display cabinet. Droplets of rain glistened in his dark hair, and he noticed his eyes – the same deep brown he had inherited from his mum – were glistening as well. He knew she would not want that. She would want him to be brave and to enjoy his birthday.

His younger sister and brother, Vicki and Billy, had wanted the same, to make the day as happy and as normal as possible, although he suspected that was as much for themselves as for him. There had been a homemade cake at breakfast, with a cheerful chorus of 'Happy Birthday to You', followed by cards and presents.

Billy had bought him a t-shirt with the slogan 'I Survived Y2K', and Vicki gave him a couple of CDs and a bottle of cava. His father had put in a brief appearance, but Charlie had noticed his dad's thick blonde hair was unbrushed, and his clothes were creased as though he had slept in them, which was unusual for a man who always took great pride in his appearance. He stayed just long enough to hand Charlie a £20 note and wish him a happy birthday before making his excuses and returning to his bedroom.

His mum's best friend, Carol, had popped in with birthday gifts she had bought on behalf of his mother. Her son Tyler was with her, just eight years old, but a thoughtful young boy who'd made Charlie a batch of chocolate brownies for his birthday and presented them proudly with a homemade card. Carol had spent a few moments upstairs, speaking with Charlie's dad. Charlie couldn't quite make out what they were discussing, but at one point, their voices had been raised, and after about five minutes, Carol returned to collect Tyler, and then they had left. No one mentioned the argument. Instead, they simply tidied the kitchen, after which Billy left for school, and Vicki made her way to the local bus stop to get to work.

Charlie had showered and dressed and driven himself to Southend Hospital to spend some time with his new baby sister Elizabeth; the family had already decided to call her Lizzie. The staff in the neonatal unit understood the very difficult circumstances into which Lizzie had been born, and so had been able to provide Charlie with some private time during his visit.

He picked up some flowers for his mum at a little florist shop before making the difficult journey to the hospice, where she had agreed to be transferred less than a day after giving birth. The previous few months had been unforgivably cruel to his mother. At first, she had been offered the joy of an unplanned pregnancy at the age of forty-six. But too soon after, there had been that awful day when something unexpected had shown up during her first prenatal appointment.

And then there had been all the terrible, dark days that had followed, where every glimmer of hope had been extinguished with brutal speed. Amidst all the anger and fear and loss, Charlie could only watch helplessly as his beloved mum tried to steer focus away from herself and make sure everyone remained excited at the imminent arrival of a little baby girl.

'Your mum's ready for you,' the woman said. 'It's Charles, isn't it?'

He stood. 'Everyone calls me Charlie,' he replied politely, following the woman from the reception area into a long corridor that contained half a dozen doors leading to private rooms, each of them with a sign naming the occupant.

'We have your father, Peter Fletcher, as the emergency contact,' she said. 'But we only have a home number for him. Is that right?'

'There's usually always someone there,' Charlie replied, 'so it is the best number to get us on.'

'And I hear you have a little sister now,' she said.

Charlie nodded. 'Little Lizzie. Six pounds and eight ounces. Quite a miracle, really. I have photographs for Mum. We bought one of those instant cameras. You know, like they used to have back in the eighties? So, we don't have to spend time getting them developed at the local chemist.'

3

The woman stopped outside one of the doors, which carried a small sign reading 'Susan Fletcher'. 'Sounds like your mum was quite a miracle,' she said.

And then, with a less jovial tone, she added, 'You know that she's been through a lot over the past week, and I think labour took the last of her strength. She's very frail now. She is not in any pain, but I do want to tell you, my dear, that I don't think we have much more time with her. There is a buzzer next to her bed, so please just press it if you are worried about anything.' And then, before she left, the woman gently held Charlie's arm. 'Are you OK?'

Charlie tried to reply, but a lump in his throat stopped any words coming out of his mouth. Instead, he just nodded. The woman offered him a reassuring smile and then left. Charlie took a moment to prepare himself, and then he opened the door to the room.

He could feel himself weighed down by his secret, wracked with uncertainty as to whether he should unburden himself. Would it be selfish, he wondered, or would his mother be pleased to hear of his happy life away from the family home? But as he stepped inside his mother's room, he had no idea she had a far greater secret she intended to share with him.

CHAPTER 2

Charlie was pleased he had brought the flowers. They offered him a moment of normality, a distraction from his mother's condition, as he arranged them in a glass vase, half filled with water, standing on a little table in front of the window. The room was far less clinical than he had expected, more like a small budget-hotel room. There were two comfortable armchairs on each side of the small table and a portable television on a wooden chest of drawers.

His mother's bed was the only item in the room that looked medical, with raised metal railings on each side and two handles at the foot, which he assumed were to lower or raise the frame.

'They're lovely,' she said, a little breathlessly, as she gazed at the flowers. 'Now, come and sit with me. Pull over a chair. I want us to talk.' She beamed him a smile, happy to see her son dressed so smartly, just for her.

She was resting under layers of sheets and blankets, with her arms above the covers and her hands resting on her chest. And for the first time, Charlie could see how thin she was, how frail. He leaned over the railings and kissed her forehead. He could still see her, his mother, but she was pale, and her eyes no longer sparkled. She was worn out and appeared quietly reconciled with whatever was going to happen next.

'Happy birthday, darling,' she said. 'Did Carol bring my gifts? She came to see me yesterday. She did my shopping for me.'

'Oh yes, yes. This morning, first thing,' he replied.

'Thank you.'

Charlie dragged an armchair closer to the bed, and lowered the railing so he could sit holding his mother's hand. He tried not to focus on how tired she looked, but it was difficult because she was so weak and never seemed to have quite caught her breath. He could not bear the thought of what might happen over the next few days. 'Vicki and Billy send their love,' he said, grasping at ordinary words and ordinary topics. 'They're coming to see you later today. I think Dad's bringing them.'

He reached inside his jacket and pulled out the photographs of Lizzie. Handing them to his mother, she looked silently at each one in turn. A picture of the baby with Charlie, and then one with Billy, and then Vicki. And then a group shot, of all the Fletcher children together, Lizzie wrapped in Vicki's arms. 'There are four of us now,' Charlie said.

'There was a picture of Peter with Lizzie, and that made Charlie chuckle. 'One of the nurses thought he was Lizzie's granddad,' he said. 'He was not impressed. But that's what happens when you become a dad again in your fifties.'

Next was a picture of Carol and her young son Tyler with Lizzie, and for some reason, it was that photograph that his mother looked at for the longest time. And then there was another photograph of Charlie and Lizzie, only this time with his friend, Jason, sitting next to him, both of them smiling at the camera.

'I thought you might bring Jason with you,' she said. 'I would like to see him. Are you both OK?'

'Yes, of course, he's fine,' Charlie replied. 'I'll bring him to see you tomorrow.'

Susan looked at the picture again with an obvious fondness. 'He grew into such a handsome young man,' she said, 'that scrawny little boy you brought home for tea after school all those years ago. How old were you both? Ten? Eleven?'

'About that,' Charlie replied. 'First year of senior school.'

'And then he came for tea the next day and the next. It didn't take long for your dad and me to work out that he didn't have a particularly nice home life, bless him.' She lay the photographs on the bed next to her. 'I'll keep them there so I can look at you all.'

Charlie wasn't sure how the conversation would progress, but he wanted to keep the focus on Jason in case he summoned enough courage to explain everything to his mother. 'He's never forgotten, you know. Everything you did for him. All the dinners and packed lunches, letting him stay for sleepovers pretty much all the time.'

Susan gave his hand a little squeeze. 'You didn't answer me,' she said, 'how are you both?'

Charlie paused because no one had asked after Jason before, at least not like that, with a tone so fond and familiar, and he wondered if he was misinterpreting the question or whether his mum just knew.

'It's alright,' she said when Charlie failed to respond to her question. 'You don't have to talk about it if you don't want to. I just wanted you to know that I love you both, and I am happy you have someone.'

This was the very conversation Charlie wished to have with his mother, to share the details of his secret happy life with Jason. But he suddenly found himself completely unprepared for it. Where would he even begin, he wondered, and how much did his mother already know? But as he looked at her face, her smile, he knew he might not have the chance again, and he did not want to spend the rest of his life regretting a missed opportunity.

'I developed a bit of a crush on him at sixth form,' he said. 'It just felt very strange that I had suddenly had feelings for my best friend.'

'And is that when you started dating?'

Charlie shook his head. 'No, I never told him. And then he was accepted by Leeds and disappeared for the next four years. We wrote to each other all the time, and his letters were just filled with so much... so much of everything. I was doing work placements with local estate agents, and his life seemed full and exciting. I thought he'd never come back. But then, last summer, he did.'

Charlie couldn't quite gauge his mother's reaction. She appeared content to just listen, perhaps pleased to finally hear about a part of her son's life he had kept hidden for so long. 'I hadn't seen him since college,' Charlie continued. 'I was sure he just thought of me as an old schoolmate, someone he wanted to catch up with, now he'd moved back to Southend. But after a few glasses of wine, he told me he'd been thinking about me the whole time he'd been away. Four years of wondering if I felt the same way about him. And after a few more glasses of wine, I finally plucked up the courage to tell him that I did. And that was pretty much it.'

Susan chuckled and then said, 'He's good for you. He looks after you. And you need that, Charlie. You spend too much time worrying about everything and everyone. I'm glad Jason's there. Thank you for telling me. I look forward to seeing him tomorrow.'

Feeling emboldened, Charlie continued to share little snippets of his secret life, with just enough detail to create a happy, colourful picture for Susan to enjoy. He spoke about Jason's flat, which had become his second home, and the holiday they had shared together in Spain. And with every word, with every little detail, Charlie felt he had finally let his mum into his world.

'And how is work?' Susan asked.

Jason had returned to Southend with a business degree, whilst Charlie had spent years working in the local real estate market, and with a loan from Charlie's grandmother, the two had started to renovate and then sell empty, dilapidated houses.

'Oh, really good,' Charlie replied. 'We're doing two at the moment. A couple of three-bed terrace houses in the town centre. We got one of them for just £30,000 at auction. But property prices are going up very quickly. We could probably make a good profit on both without even renovating.'

'But you *are* going to renovate?' Susan asked.

Charlie nodded, 'Oh yes, yes. Of course. That's our business model. Putting more family homes back into the community. We've even been able to finally repay Nan the money she lent us to start the business. So, she's happy too.'

'Oh, I bet she is,' his mum replied. And then she took a breath as though she were about to say something, but instead, she tutted and pursed her lips.

'You OK, mum?' Charlie asked. 'Do you want anything?'

Susan closed her eyes and withdrew her hand. 'No, no,' she replied. After a beat, she opened her eyes again and looked directly at him. 'I am guessing your father hasn't spoken to you.'

Charlie shrugged, 'What about?'

Susan rested back on her pillow and looked to the ceiling, muttering something under her breath. And then, more clearly, she said, 'No, of course he hasn't,' with a cross tone to her voice.

It was unusual for his mother to openly criticise her husband, even if only lightly. Many people spoke poorly of Charlie's father, including Charlie himself, but his mother had always been his greatest champion, someone who spoke up for him and defended him, even when he had done something which appeared indefensible.

Charlie had never understood her loyalty to his dad. Indeed, there were many things he did not understand about his parents and their marriage. But it was clear his father had failed to tell him something that his mother thought important, and he wondered what it could possibly be.

CHAPTER 3

Charlie waited for his mother to continue, hoping she might be about to share some of the many secrets he suspected she and Peter had kept from their children. But he also knew that if she did, it had to be her choice. She was drained, tired, and in no condition to be pestered for family gossip.

'Carol helped me put together a family album,' Susan said. 'It's in the top drawer of the dresser. Could we look through it together?'

It was an unexpected moment because, at the very least, Charlie had expected his mother to explain her oblique comment about Peter. But he did as he was asked and retrieved the album, which seemed new, with a shiny leather cover that was completely unblemished.

He retook his seat and glanced through a few pages, and he realised it was different to the other Fletcher family albums. All the others his mother had compiled over the years had been a snapshot of time, a collection of pictures all taken over a period of weeks or months, usually from the same roll of film. This album seemed more eclectic, with pictures from across the years, although they appeared to have been collated in order, like a story, from start to finish.

He leaned slightly onto the bed so his mother could see the pictures, too, and began to slowly move through the pages. The first images were of Susan and Peter, both so young; his mum pretty and curvaceous, with dark eyes and long dark hair, the same colourings Charlie and his siblings had each inherited from her. His dad tall and brawny, older than Susan, with thick blonde hair and blue eyes.

'I'll give you this,' Charlie said, 'you were a very handsome couple.'

'I remember the first time I saw your father,' Susan said wistfully, a smile on her face but a sad tone to her voice. 'That funny little record shop, up that road just off Southend High Street. I was about seventeen and had just popped in on my way home from school to see if I could get Carole King's new album. And there he was, standing behind the counter, smoking a cigarette. This beautiful, older boy. In his mid-twenties. He had long blonde hair down to his shoulders and sparkling

10

blue eyes. He was wearing a white t-shirt that showed off all his muscles and these tight blue jeans that showed off everything else.'

'Oh my god, mum,' Charlie said, appalled at the sexualised image of his father. 'Please, I don't need to hear any more.'

Susan snickered, and Charlie could tell she was enjoying the sensation of a more grown-up and honest relationship with him, sharing more than they ever had before. 'Oh, Charles, don't be so prudish,' she said. 'We were all young once. And your dad absolutely swept me off my feet. He was so handsome. Even now, sometimes, there are moments when I catch sight of him, and he's still that boy in the record shop. He still has that thick blonde hair and those cheeky blue eyes. And he might be fifty-three years old, but when he's walking around our bedroom in his pants, it's still *all* muscle.'

Charlie put his hand to his forehead and closed his eyes for a moment, 'Mum, please, I beg you, I cannot have images like that in my head.'

Susan summoned just enough energy to laugh, and for a moment, it was like they had both forgotten where they were. They were just a mother and son, having a funny conversation without a care in the world. Charlie turned the page, and there was a picture of his parents' wedding day, Susan in a traditional wedding dress and Peter in a smart black suit. Next to them, Dorothy and Stanley, his mum's parents, stony-faced, Dorothy holding baby Charlie in her arms.

His grandparents had always been deeply unhappy with the union. Susan was the only child of an old-money family, whilst Peter had been one of eight, raised by parents who'd always struggled to make ends meet. Dorothy and Stanley had always thought their daughter had married well beneath her station, something his grandmother still believed to that very day.

The next photographs moved their story forward to their family home, a huge six-bedroom detached house overlooking the estuary. It was a house Peter could never have dreamed of having, if not for the generosity of Susan's parents, a house he had named, rather grandly, as 'The Lodge'.

There were pictures to celebrate the arrival of baby Vicki and then baby Billy. There were photographs of Susan tending her garden, one of the great passions of her life, and Peter renovating the kitchen. And then a selection of pictures from the many dinner parties Susan and Peter had thrown over the years.

Charlie remembered those evenings clearly, often allowed to stay up for the first hour or so, and then he would secretly listen, cross-legged in his pyjamas, peering through the bannisters at the top of the stairs. He remembered how elegantly but unfussy his mother dressed on those evenings. She never sought unnecessary attention for her appearance, far happier with compliments for her hosting or her food. But Peter had a need to be centre of attention, and so always wore tight shirts and trousers, parading his looks and his muscles, flirting openly with the guests, often in front of his wife.

The next pages were a mixture of images from school concerts, family holidays, Christmases and birthdays. Many of those pictures included Carol and Jason and then Tyler, but Charlie noticed that fewer and fewer of them included Peter.

By that time, his father was often working away from home or drinking with his mates at a pub. For many years, it had felt as though his parents had little more than the pretence of a marriage because they spent so little time together. And even after the surprise news that baby Lizzie was on her way, it felt as though it was too little too late. He'd wondered if they had simply drifted apart or if something had happened, something that had driven a wedge between them.

'What was Dad supposed to talk to me about?' Charlie asked.

After a moment, his mother replied, 'About your brother.'

'Oh, good lord,' Charlie said. 'What's Billy done this time?'

Susan did not respond. Instead, she reached across, her hand shaking ever so slightly, and continued to turn the pages of the album. 'Your father is a good man,' she said. 'I know he's not perfect, and I do understand why you've grown apart. It doesn't help that he's so reticent when it comes to his feelings, but I do think it upsets him, Charlie, the distance between the two of you. He once said it's like he's always

12

walking on eggshells around you. That anything he says or does could set you off.'

There was so much Charlie had to say about his dad, all of it negative. But his mother was so weak, and there was nothing she could do about her life choices now. Charlie felt any attack on his father would feel like a criticism of her, too, and that was not how he wanted to leave things with his mother. That's not how he wanted to remember the final few days of her life, that he had been at odds with her.

'Mum, I will…. try to make things better with him,' Charlie said. 'So, go on. What has Billy done?'

Susan reached the final pages of her album. One of them had been left blank. 'Carol took some pictures of me with Lizzie, before I left the hospital' she said. 'When they're developed, could you pick a nice one and put it there?' She smiled and then, with a gentle nod, gestured for Charlie to look at the final picture, her hand resting on the page, covering part of the image. It was Carol with Tyler, wearing colourful paper hats, both with a full plate of food in front of them; the Fletcher's dinner table a few months earlier, Christmas Day. It was a nice image, but Charlie could not help but think it was an odd choice to finish the album.

'I wasn't talking about Billy,' Susan said. 'It's not about Billy.'

Charlie shook his head, a little bewildered at his mother's words, suddenly concerned that perhaps she had become confused. 'Mum, are you feeling OK? Do you want me to call for someone?'

But Susan just stared at her son directly in the eyes as though urging him to understand. 'Look at him,' she said, her voice weak, tired.

Charlie glanced at the photograph again, at Tyler, with his rosy cheeks, big blue eyes and blonde hair.

'Look at him. He's the image of his dad, isn't he?' Susan said. She moved her hand, exposing the full picture., and sat next to Tyler was Peter. 'You see,' Susan said, 'there's not four of you, sweetheart. You're one of five.'

13

CHAPTER 4

Charlie could not speak. He stood at the window, arms folded, looking out. The weather had grown worse. The rain was now torrential, and the trees were bending from side to side in the wind. He had been unable to find any words, or even to form an opinion, on the secret Susan had shared with him. His mind was racing through so many different events and conversations from the previous eight years of his life. There had been so many little things which had not made sense at the time but which now, suddenly, all linked neatly together into a clear narrative.

Of course, his father had a second family. All those 'work trips' he had taken over the years. *Of course,* he did. Peter was a man who could turn his hand to most manual work, whether it be carpentry, plumbing or bricklaying. He had always avoided full-time employment, preferring 'cash in hand' jobs that had meant he could work for a few weeks and then take a few weeks off. And much of that work involved regularly being away from home.

Charlie had never questioned any of his father's trips because, in truth, he enjoyed the house much more when Peter wasn't there. It had never occurred to him that his lack of interest in his dad's life might have enabled an eight-year affair and a secret love child; Peter had been able to enjoy a carefree life, happily coming and going between his two families whenever it suited him, leaving Charlie's hardworking mum to manage everything at The Lodge. And with that, Charlie finally found the words to reply to his mother.

'This is when he told you?' he said, his voice soft but angry. 'You're in a hospice, and this is the moment he decides to cleanse his conscience and admit he's been having an affair? After parading his mistress and his love child in front of you for all these years. Your best friend and her son.'

'Oh Charlie, don't,' his mum replied despondently, her voice increasingly quiet, tired. 'It isn't like that. Please. I asked you to listen to it all. Now come back and sit down.'

14

He looked at his mother and saw she was holding out her hand to him, her dark eyes pleading for him to keep his temper and listen to what she had to say. Reluctantly, he returned to the armchair and held his mother's hand, obediently doing as she had asked so as not to upset her.

'Your father is a complicated man,' Susan said.

'No, he's not,' Charlie snapped, his temper flaring up. 'He drinks too much and contributes next to nothing to our home. He's lazy, selfish, and entitled. That's all. That's as complicated as he gets. And the fact he's happily cheated on you, on *us*, his whole family, all these years. I just hate him, Mum. I hate him.'

Susan squeezed his hand with more strength than Charlie thought she could expend, and he instantly suffered a wave of terrible guilt. 'Sorry, mum,' he said. 'I won't interrupt.'

Slowly, pausing every now and again to manage her breathing, Susan began to explain. 'I have *always* known that he was Tyler's father,' she said. 'Carol and I, and your father, we made it work. And it is important that you understand that, Charlie. It is important that you embrace Carol and Tyler as family. Because that's what they are. That's how much they mean to me.'

Charlie looked down to avoid his mother's gaze for a moment, to try and navigate the swirl of confused thoughts and feelings rushing through his mind. All of a sudden, everything felt so messy, so untidy. There were so many loose ends and too many complications. Charlie liked everything in life to be well-ordered, and discovering he was part of some strange extended family did not fit into his very precise world.

Carol was the opposite of his mother in so many ways; tall and very slim, with a tendency to tell rude jokes and use coarse language in everyday conversation. Charlie was quite fond of her but had always found her close friendship with his mother a little odd. He was even more confused by their friendship now he knew she was also his father's mistress.

And then there was Tyler, a cheerful and thoughtful little boy, never happier than when he was outside with his Auntie Susan, learning about plants and how to make a garden flourish. A boy with blonde hair and blue eyes, who now, in retrospect, was so obviously the image of Peter but who, for so long, had been presented by Carol as the result of a brief and failed relationship.

There was something else, something that did not make sense, something that jarred with Susan's version of events. His parents' subterfuge had been perfect. He and his siblings had never suspected a thing, even after the endless Christmases when Carol and Tyler had joined the Fletchers at The Lodge because their Christmas plans *always* fell through at the last minute. Why was his mother letting him in on their big secret now, he wondered. Why now?

'I don't understand why you told me,' he said.

'You had to know,' Susan replied.

Charlie looked up, 'I would rather I hadn't been told. I would rather have continued not knowing.'

'And if it had been left to your father, I doubt you would have been told,' Susan replied. There was a hint of defeat in her voice, and Charlie realised his mother must have asked Peter, on that one occasion, to take responsibility for his actions and to be the one who told Charlie the truth. But it was no surprise to Charlie that, even in those awful circumstances, his father had still done what was best and easiest for himself and left it to his dying wife to break the news.

'And I am sorry, Charlie, but you do need to know,' she continued. 'Because I have made some decisions about Lizzie. And it is important you understand why I made those decisions.'

'What decisions?' Charlie asked. 'Lizzie's coming home, isn't she?' It felt close to being a rhetorical question because Charlie had never doubted his baby sister would grow up at The Lodge. He had imagined that he and his dad, and Vicki and Billy, would somehow pull together to look after her. He felt his heart skip a beat when his mother gently shook her head, tears forming in her eyes.

'She's going to live with Carol and Tyler,' she said. 'You'll see her all the time. But, darling, your father wouldn't have a clue what to do, and you have your own life to lead, with Jason. Vicki and Billy have their own lives, too. I cannot have you taking on a responsibility like this.'

'But I'm happy to,' Charlie said, blurting out the words without thinking. 'I want to. She belongs with us. We're her family.'

16

His mother closed her eyes, and a tear trickled down her cheek. 'So are Carol and Tyler,' she said, suddenly seeming exhausted. 'And I am sorry, sweetheart, but I think it is going to fall on you to tell Vicki and Billy. That's going to be a very hard conversation, I know. But please, please help them to embrace Carol and Tyler as part of our family, like I did. Like you must. I need you to be strong and brave, Charlie. Strong and brave.'

As she continued, her voice gradually became softer. 'I'm so sorry,' she whispered. 'There's so much more. I need to tell you everything. But I've worn myself out.'

Charlie removed the photo album and the photographs from the bed and placed them on the floor next to him. And then Susan closed her eyes and rolled slightly onto one side. 'I am going to nap for a bit,' she said. 'Can you sit with me, hold my hand? I will tell you everything when I wake up.'

Suddenly, none of it mattered. Charlie pushed everything to the back of his mind, all the insanity he was going to have to deal with at some point in the coming days. For now, he just wanted to look after his mum. And so, he settled into the armchair, held her hand, and watched as she began to fall asleep. 'I love you,' he whispered. 'You're the best mum in the world.' And he felt her gently squeeze his hand.

CHAPTER 5

'Dorothy is taking tea in her living room, Mr Fletcher,' said Louise, the manager of the retirement complex. It was still raining, so she offered to take Charlie's jacket to dry it before he left at the end of his visit.

'No, I'll keep it on, thank you,' Charlie replied politely.

Louise stared at him for a moment, and Charlie could see that she was trying to read his emotions, as though recognising something was wrong, that this was not the cheerful young man who had so often visited his grandmother over the years.

Around them, the sounds of quiet existence, the distant clink of spoons in teacups, and hushed voices, residents and visitors enjoying moments of normality, ordinary conversations. But Charlie knew he was to have a difficult meeting with his grandmother and was still trying to think what he was going to say.

'Would you like me to walk you through?' Louise asked.

Charlie shook his head, 'No, honestly, it's fine. I know the way.'

'Very good,' Louise replied.

Before he left her company, Charlie asked, 'How is my grandmother today?'

Over the years, he had grown quite fond of Louise, a middle-aged Irishwoman who was calm and darkly funny and ever so slightly world-weary but who always stuck to the formalities of her role and had repeatedly declined to refer to Charlie as anything other than Mr Fletcher. Charlie had learned to rely on her judgement, to offer him forewarning so he could prepare himself if his grandmother was in a bad mood.

'Oh, she's quiet today,' Louise said. 'I cannot quite judge how she's feeling. It's like she's waiting for something. The calm before the storm, perhaps.'

Charlie thanked Louise, inhaled deeply and made his way down the short corridor that led to his grandmother's room, a large self-contained suite between the entrance hall and the library. Usually, he would take time to enjoy the surroundings, the large landscape oil paintings on the walls, the marble statues and the crystal vases spilling over with freshly cut flowers, an interior designed to reflect the wealth of the people who had retired there. But that day, it all faded into the background, and all Charlie noticed was how short the distance was from the hall to his grandmother's door, and that he had no more time to decide what he was going to say to her.

He found his grandmother alone, reclined in her favourite seat, an old Chesterfield Queen Anne leather armchair, placed in front of the French doors which led from her living room onto a private lanai. She had always been very proud of her view across the gardens outside, sometimes bragging that she had secured the best rooms in the complex.

She was dressed in an elegant peach trouser suit and was smoking a cigarette, with an ashtray and a cup of tea on a small occasional table next to her. She was peering through the glass panels in the doors and seemed to be watching the rain with great intensity.

'Hi Nan,' he said.

She glanced over her shoulder in his direction and nodded to him. She looked so similar to his mother, but with lines on her face and grey in her hair, the signs of a long life that his mother would never have. 'Come and sit with me,' she said and waved her hand at some of the other chairs around the room.

Charlie picked up a wooden chair and carried it over to her. He placed it next to the occasional table, sat down, and smiled at her. 'You are looking well,' he said. 'How are you feeling?'

She did not answer. Instead, she avoided his eyes and focussed on the view of the rainswept grounds outside. She drew deeply on her cigarette and seemed to groan slightly as she exhaled the smoke into the room. 'Tell me, then,' she said curtly.

Charlie realised she had guessed why he had made his unexpected visit, and he knew there was no way to soften his news, so he simply told her as kindly as he could. 'Mum passed away this morning,' he said. 'I was with her when it happened, holding her hand. She was asleep. There was no pain, and she wasn't frightened. It was all very gentle.'

His grandmother nodded. 'Right,' she said. And then, choking slightly, she added, 'That's that, then.'

19

She glanced down, just for a moment, and Charlie could see she was desperately trying to hold herself together. But he knew not to embrace her or to offer his shoulder to cry on because she had never been tactile, not in the least, not even in that moment when she was grieving the loss of her only child.

With a deep sigh, she sat up and drew on her cigarette once more. 'Your father knows?'

Charlie nodded. 'I think so,' he said. 'The people at the hospice called The Lodge. Carol was there, dropping off some groceries. She's gone to pick up Billy and Vicki. Dad wasn't there, but she said she would track him down.'

'Pub, one assumes,' Dorothy muttered, only partly under her breath, and then she added, 'You need to take care of them, Charles. Your brother and sister. They're going to need their big brother now more than ever. It's not as if they have a father they can rely on.'

On a normal day, Charlie would have enthusiastically agreed with his grandmother's negative assessment of his father. But, in her dying moments, his mother had burdened him with a wish that he and his father try to get along, and that weighed heavily on his conscience.

'He's not getting a penny,' his grandmother said, an unexpected comment delivered with an obvious amount of spite. 'Your father. I've written a new will. He isn't getting a penny. It's all going direct to my grandchildren. You and Victoria, William, Elizabeth. The four of you.'

Charlie shrugged and gestured with his hand to the grandness of her living room, at all the antique chairs and tables, and at the shelves which were filled with dozens of leather-bound books. 'Nan, you are living in the world's most expensive retirement complex,' he replied. 'This is costing you thousands of pounds every week. By the time we get to your will, I seriously don't think there's going to be anything left.'

His grandmother chuckled to herself and then added, 'Oh, you would be surprised, Charles.'

He shook his head. 'Well, let's not talk about that,' he replied. Charlie knew his grandmother had an intense dislike for his father. It did not take much prompting for her to gladly share the many reasons she had always loathed him with anyone who would listen, including, on more than one occasion, with Peter himself.

From their very first meeting, Dorothy had assessed that Peter was a man who would not amount to anything. She acknowledged that he had been blessed with a handsome face and a certain amount of charm, and that he could have had his pick of the girls. But it had not been lost on Dorothy that the girl Peter had picked had been the girl with the wealthiest parents.

'My accountant tells me you have repaid my loan,' she said.

'Yes, as agreed,' Charlie replied. It was an unexpected segue in the conversation, but he knew his grandmother was trying to deal with all manner of repressed and difficult emotions, and so, out of pure kindness, he responded factually. 'I really cannot thank you enough, not just for the loan, but for the advice. The business is going well. Still early days, but property was definitely the right thing to invest in.'

Dorothy raised her eyebrow and smiled as though happy to have been listened to and proven right. 'Just don't fall out with Jason,' she said. 'You need him. He's a proper businessman. I can tell. And you've always been terrible with money. So, you stick with finding the properties and working out how to add value and leave Jason to do the finances.'

Charlie smiled, happy that his grandmother, who seemed to have spent most of her life finding reasons to dislike people, had something of a soft spot for his secret partner. And he almost continued the conversation, to probe a little further and to see if his grandmother, like his mother, had guessed the truth. But it suddenly occurred to him that there was another secret his grandmother might have known about, and before he could stop himself, he asked her; 'Did you know? About Tyler?'

His grandmother did not reply. She did not even acknowledge the question. Instead, after a moment, she stubbed out her cigarette in the ashtray and produced a bronze cigarette case from her pocket, engraved with an image of a flower and a matching lighter. With great efficiency, she was soon sat with a newly lit cigarette in her hand.

'I'm not going,' she said, 'To the funeral, I won't be going. I told your mother that, and she understood. It would finish me, Charles. Watching them put my daughter in the ground. It would finish me.'

'I completely understand, Nan,' Charlie said, his voice breaking slightly as he spoke, 'That's absolutely fine.'

'I'll ask Louise to sort flowers out for me, for the coffin. But that's all I can do.' And with that, the conversation seemed to have run its course. Dorothy sat quietly, smoking her cigarette and watching the rain, but out of the corner of her eye, she could see that her grandson had started to cry. He was quiet with his grief, dignified. Like his mother and grandmother, he did not wish to make a fuss.

He was leaning forward slightly, his face covered by his hands, trembling as he tried his hardest not to make a sound. And Dorothy wondered if her mention of the funeral had been the final straw, that his great effort to remain strong had finally been overwhelmed by the reality of his terrible loss. She balanced her cigarette on the ashtray, reached over to him, and squeezed his shoulder.

'You're a good boy, Charlie,' she said. 'Susan was always very proud of you.'

She retrieved her cigarette and returned her gaze to the grey and wet view outside the French doors. She could feel every moment of her grandson's grief, every single bit of it. Dorothy knew she would live out the rest of her years in those rooms, and her little girl would never visit her again, and the thought of that broke her heart.

CHAPTER 6

The drive home was lonely and difficult. On two occasions, Charlie's grief overwhelmed him, and he'd had to pull to the side of the road so that he could cry. On one occasion, a concerned woman, out walking her dog, tapped on the window to ask if he was OK. He wound down the window, thanked her and said he was fine, and so she left him with a little packet of tissues and a wish that he get home safely.

He parked his car on the gravel drive at the front of The Lodge and made his way inside. He carried the photograph album with him but didn't want anyone else in the family to see it, just yet, in case the final photograph resulted in questions he wasn't ready to answer. And so, he slotted it onto a shelf on the bookcase in the sitting room and left it there, hidden for the time being.

He then went to the kitchen at the back of the house, where he thought it most likely he would find the rest of the family. But instead, he just found his father sitting alone at the breakfast bar, nursing a whiskey in a crystal tumbler. Peter looked up and acknowledged his son with a nod but seemed either too upset or too apprehensive to say anything.

Charlie was clinging to his mother's words, that he should try to make things better with his dad, and so he opened one of the cupboards and took out a wine glass. He poured himself some red wine from a half-empty bottle which had been left on the kitchen counter next to the kettle and then walked over to the breakfast bar and raised his glass. Peter did the same.

'To mum,' he said quietly, and Peter responded with, 'Susan.'

They sipped their drinks and then his father stood and embraced him. It was an unexpected gesture, one Charlie had not prepared himself for, and he almost let the moment pass without reciprocating. But there was the promise he had made to his mother just hours earlier, and so he placed his glass on the countertop and wrapped his arms around his dad.

'I am so, so sorry,' Peter said and kissed Charlie roughly on the cheek. 'You shouldn't have been there on your own.'

They patted each other on the back, and Peter sat down again. Charlie pulled a stool to the other side of the breakfast bar so he could talk to his father face to face.

'None of us knew how much time mum had,' he said. 'But she knew you were going in to see her. You and Vicki and Billy. She knew.'

Peter nodded. 'And she was asleep?' he asked.

'Yes,' Charlie replied. 'It was all very quiet and peaceful.' He noticed how suddenly old his father looked, no longer the fifty-something who could pass for early-forties on a good day. Peter's face appeared lined, with dark rings around his tired eyes, and Charlie wondered what grief might feel like for a man who cared for no one but himself.

'The kids are upstairs,' Peter said. 'Carol collected them both. They've been crying all afternoon. I think they wanted some time alone. They'll be down later.'

Charlie knew they would want to hear what had happened, to know how their mum had died, to be reassured that she did not suffer. The events of the previous few months had been devastating for his brother and sister, but at their mother's request, they had all tried to carry on with their usual daily routines.

Susan had hoped the normality of everyday life might keep her children from falling apart, and so she had kept Billy in school, and made certain that Vicki kept going to work. Charlie had seen how hard his siblings had tried to keep themselves together for their mum, even when he knew they just wanted to break down and cry.

Vicki was only a couple of months shy of her 18th birthday and had spent the previous couple of years working at a large out-of-town supermarket. She looked so much like their mother and although not particularly academic, she had inherited many other qualities from Susan; she was hardworking and dependable and had great skill dealing with people. The store's HR manager had recognised someone with potential and quickly invested in her training and development. And even in the middle of everything that was going on at home, Vicki had continued to go to work every day, just as her mother had asked.

Things were different for Billy. Although he was still at school, he was already more than six feet tall, a skinny young man with dark hair, big brown eyes and a booming deep voice. For a few years, Charlie had worried that Billy would turn out like their father and would spend too much of his life relying on a handsome face and a bit of charm. But he had learned there was an honest simplicity to his little brother, a kindness that shone from within. Billy was not, in any way, sophisticated but he had a good heart and expected everyone around him to be good people, too. He was always left confused by anyone acting with meanness or rudeness.

Billy had particularly struggled with their mother's declining health, and his behaviour had taken an unexpected downward turn. Because of his height and deep voice, few people suspected he was only 14 years of age, and Billy had started to blag his way into the local pubs and bars. On more than one occasion, he had been delivered back to the house by the police, too drunk to stand and barely able to speak. Charlie was worried about how his little brother might behave under the stress and strain of the coming few days.

'Carol's gone to the hospital,' Peter said, as casually as he could, 'to see Lizzie.' Charlie could see his father was staring at him, trying to take a measure of him of what he might know, and he realised it was an opportunity to reach out to his father, to explain what he had been told.

But despite his mother's plea that he try to build a better relationship with Peter, in that moment, Charlie was just too angry, and he was in no mood to satisfy his father's curiosity. Instead, he chose to leave the topic hanging in the air and nonchalantly moved the conversation on. 'I saw Nan,' he said softly. 'She isn't coming to the funeral. She'll send flowers, and I promised we would put them in the hearse with mum.'

Peter nodded. 'Of course, of course,' he said, appearing somewhat agitated, and Charlie knew he was getting under his father's skin. In the middle of such a horrible dark day, he found he could still enjoy upsetting his dad.

'We're bringing Lizzie home tomorrow,' Peter added. 'Carol and Tyler are going to stay here until your mum's funeral. I've sorted out the two spare rooms for them. I've put the cot into Carol's room. She's going to look after the baby.' He sipped his whiskey and waited for his son to respond.

25

'Oh, lovely,' Charlie said. 'It will be good to have Lizzie home. We have a lot of adjusting to do, don't we?' He had chosen his words carefully, a vague sentence that would leave his father still none the wiser as to what he did or did not know. And Charlie liked that. He liked leaving his dad with the fear that perhaps, in her final moments, his dying wife had chosen not to take responsibility for telling their son about Peter's secret second family.

But it appeared his father wasn't willing to play along any further. He put down his glass and stared Charlie in the face. 'What did your mum tell you?' he asked bluntly.

Charlie was tempted to continue playing it innocent, just for a bit longer, but he felt his little ruse had come to an end. He folded his arms and, leaned forward onto the breakfast bar and stared his father directly in the eyes. 'Mum told me,' he said, but before he could continue, there was a noise from behind him which made Charlie turn.

There he found Billy, standing in the kitchen doorway looking at him, still in his school uniform, tears tumbling down his face. Charlie stood up. 'Oh, Billy,' he said and held out his arms as Billy rushed to embrace him. Charlie squeezed his younger brother tightly as he sobbed into Charlie's shoulder.

'We… we were going… we were going to see mum,' Billy cried, choking on his tears as he spoke. 'We were going. But we missed her. We missed her.'

Charlie kissed Billy on his tear-stained cheek, 'We didn't know how long she had, Billy. None of us did. Not even Mum.' And then he noticed that Vicki had joined them, her usually pale face red and glistening from an afternoon of crying. She stood in the doorway awkwardly, as though not sure what to do, so Charlie held out his hand to her. 'Come here,' he said. 'Come on, group hug. Group hug.'

Vicki hurried into his embrace, and the three of them stood there, for a long time, just holding each other. After a while, they sat down on the chairs overlooking their mum's garden, holding hands, sometimes crying, sometimes just talking, and occasionally laughing, although those brief moments of laughter would invariably lead them back to crying. Charlie told them about their mother's peaceful passing, of how proud

26

she had been of them all, and how she wanted them to be strong, and to live happy lives.

And all the time, Charlie could see his father loitering uncomfortably in the kitchen, wondering what Charlie knew and if he was going to say something.

CHAPTER 7

Charlie knew he would have to spend the night in his bedroom at The Lodge to be there in case Vicki or Billy woke and needed someone to talk to or cry with. But he needed some time away from the house, so when the moment felt right, he made a few excuses about the need to run some errands, and then he climbed into his car and started the four-mile drive along the esplanade to Jason's flat in Westcliff-on-Sea.

The pain of his grief swept to and fro like waves, offering moments of peace and then moments when all he could do was cry, and he wanted someone to take care of him for a while. There were more direct routes to the flat, but habit always took him along the seafront. The wet weather had kept people at home that night, and whilst the arcades and amusements were open and all brightly lit, they were mostly empty.

Despite the gloom, the journey offered Charlie some comfort and happy, sunny memories from his school years. He, Jason and their friends would often head to the seafront after class. They would play games in the arcades or enjoy the rides at Adventure Island. But mostly, they would simply buy a drink and some warm, fresh, sugary doughnuts to share and sit on the seawall, chatting about what they all wanted to do when they were grown up.

It was a small group of friends bonded through a mutual sense they didn't fit in anywhere else. And although Charlie was very fond of them all, his strongest attachment was always with Jason. In many ways, they were an odd pairing; Charlie was an anxious child, constantly worried about failing and getting poor marks or accidentally upsetting someone. Jason, by comparison, carried himself with a strange confidence that belied his age as though he had arrived with his character fully formed. And although he was young, Charlie was acutely aware of the great contradiction in Jason's life; the boy who was always so together, so organised and grown up, but whose home life was unstable, messy and chaotic. And knowing that had made Charlie even fonder of his young friend.

Almost from the first day they had met, it became routine for Charlie to invite Jason home for tea and often for sleepovers, too. It became so frequent that Susan always set an extra place at the dinner table and made sure the bed was made up in the guest room. By the time they were in sixth form, Charlie began to have other feelings for Jason and noticed things he had not noticed before. Jason was slightly taller than the other boys in their year, and he had a nice face, his features even and his complexion always clear. His auburn hair was always neatly trimmed to a number four, and his piercing grey eyes began to captivate Charlie whenever they were in conversation.

Jason kept himself immaculately clean and fresh, was slim and fit (Charlie grew to be particularly distracted by his thighs), and always appeared smartly dressed, even when he was wearing something casual. For Charlie, everything about him seemed perfect.

There had been times when just being physically close to Jason — sitting next to him at a burger bar or walking alongside him on the beach — would make his stomach churn with excitement. But he had never mentioned any of this, and Jason had certainly never said or done anything to indicate he might reciprocate. And by the time they had finished their A-Levels and Jason had relocated to Leeds for his degree, the subject had never been addressed. Charlie remained in Southend, fearing the love of his life had left him behind.

Jason's letters would occasionally imply he was enjoying some sort of love life in Leeds, but those sections were always slightly vague, leaving much for Charlie's imagination to fill. Too much, perhaps. Jealously, he would read and re-read those sections to try and establish exactly what was going on and who might be the subject of Jason's attention. And after his return to Southend, as they prepared to spend their first night together, Jason confirmed he'd had numerous sexual partners, whilst Charlie conceded he had remained a virgin.

And so, Jason had taken the lead. Quietly, intimately, he explained everything they were going to do and how it was going to work, and for those intense few hours, Jason made Charlie feel he was the absolute centre of his world. Charlie had never felt so loved, so cared for, or so important. And even after so many months visiting Jason's flat, Charlie still felt a little pop of excitement in his chest as he pulled into the road and parked his car.

The flat was on the middle floor of an old three-storey Victorian house, and, despite that terrible day, just walking up the flight of stairs to the front door somehow lessened the pain he was feeling. Jason was waiting for him, the small lounge gently lit by lamps and a glow from the little three-bar electric fire set into the wall. Charlie knew how deeply fond Jason had been of Susan for everything she had done for him, growing up. Even during all his years away, he never once forgotten her birthday and always sent an extra gift for her at Christmas, too. And Charlie could tell Jason had been crying, although he was clearly attempting to pretend he had not.

They embraced and as Jason held him tightly in his arms, Charlie's resolve evaporated again, and he began to sob as he remembered his mother, so happy to learn of their relationship. After a long while, Jason loosened his arms and stepped back.

'Will you tell me what happened?' he asked, and so they sat on the couch, and Charlie relayed the events of the day. He shared everything, every detail, every heartbreaking moment and every shocking revelation. When he had finished, Jason was quiet for a while, clearly trying to absorb everything Charlie had learned. And then he said, 'It's so bloody obvious, isn't it? I mean, now we know, it's like, how did we ever *not* know? He's the absolute image of your dad.' He put his arm around Charlie's shoulders, and they both settled back into the couch. 'And there's no animosity between your mum and Carol?'

'No,' Charlie replied, still a little mystified by the whole situation. 'And that's the bit I find hardest to understand. Why are they still best friends? Why didn't mum kick dad out of The Lodge the moment she found out Carol was pregnant?'

They rested their heads together, knowing there would be no answers that evening. And then Jason said, 'You need to tell Vicki and Billy. They need to understand why Lizzie is going to live with Carol rather than at The Lodge.'

Charlie sighed. 'I know.'

'I'm with you for all of this. You're not alone.' He gently squeezed Charlie's shoulders. 'How long do I have you for?'

'About an hour. I can't leave Vicki and Billy for too long.'

'Right,' Jason said, and then stood up. 'You haven't eaten, have you?'

Charlie shook his head. 'I don't think I could,' he replied.

'Well, I'll heat up some soup,' Jason said. 'You have to eat something.' He left the lounge, and Charlie could hear the clanking of pots and bowls in the kitchen at the end of the hall.

'I love you, Charlie Fletcher,' Jason called to him.

Charlie smiled. 'I love you, Jason Day.'

CHAPTER 8

Charlie found himself preoccupied throughout his mother's funeral. With great fascination he watched his father and Carol as they carefully navigated the service, barely ever acknowledging each other.

Carol held Lizzie throughout, with obvious tenderness and affection. She and Tyler had stayed at The Lodge ever since Lizzie had come home from the hospital, and the family had easily adjusted to Carol taking on the main responsibilities for her care during those difficult days. He hadn't spoken to either his father or Carol about what his mother had told him, but he knew that at some point, Carol and Tyler would go home, and when they did, they would take Lizzie with them. Vicki and Billy were still unaware that was going to happen; a difficult conversation Charlie would need to have with them.

As he watched Carol, he noticed there were moments during the service when the expression on her face suddenly changed, as though she were about to cry. But she didn't, not once. It was as if she did not wish to draw attention to herself, even though she had lost her best friend.

By comparison, Peter appeared to be gleaning some grim enjoyment from the event, taking pleasure in all the attention he was receiving, the hugs and the enquiries as to his wellbeing. He had made overly dramatic public gestures towards his children, embracing Vicki, clutching Billy's shoulder, and walking into the chapel holding Charlie's arm. It had annoyed Charlie as he could see what Peter was trying to prove to everyone in attendance: what a great dad he was, putting the emotional needs of his children first.

Charlie was thankful that his mother's funeral, in line with her wishes, was short and to the point. It was attended by a limited number of mourners who had all been personally invited in advance by Susan. The immediate family was joined by Carol, Tyler and Jason, and about a dozen people Susan had worked with over the years in various jobs. There were also a couple of nurses from the cancer ward at Southend

Hospital and Louise from her mother's care home. Dorothy did not attend.

Vicki had brought a man with her that Charlie had seen hanging around the house a few times before. He seemed older than Vicki, and Charlie was sure he could see arm and neck tattoos concealed just under his shirt collar and cuffs. The man had remained at the rear of the church during the service and stayed very much in the background throughout the burial. But Charlie noticed that Vicki would occasionally look at him as if to check he was still there, and he would return her gaze with a reassuring nod.

The service was brief, held at a small non-denominational chapel led by a funeral celebrant. Charlie suspected his mother had provided the celebrant with plenty of notes in advance, as he spoke with great knowledge of Susan and did a good job at explaining her life, her character and her passion for cooking and gardening.

The burial was equally short. Several days of rain had finally passed, and the sky had remained a clear blue. Sunlight poured through the trees at the cemetery, making the wet grass and foliage glisten and sparkle. Birdsong echoed all around the small group of mourners as the celebrant read the poem 'Immortality'. For a moment, Charlie was overwhelmed, a tingling sensation running through his veins as though something truly spiritual was happening. So many birds were singing, and the trees were glowing, and the celebrant delivered the words of the poem with great eloquence, a poem he knew his mother had grown to love.

But then, suddenly, it was all over. The mourners were shaking hands, mumbling directions to The Lodge, and walking back to their cars. Charlie found himself standing at the grave, realising his beautiful mother really had been placed into the ground, and there she would lay, forever more, on her own.

'Sweetheart, it's time to go,' Jason said. He checked no one was watching before squeezing Charlie's hand, 'Come on. I'll drive.'

Charlie blew his mother a kiss, and then he and Jason made their way to the car and drove to The Lodge. The back of the house had been laid out ready for the funeral reception, and Carol had worked tirelessly the day before to prepare a nice tea of sandwiches, quiches, and various nibbles.

Charlie knew he would have to do the rounds at the reception to speak to all the guests and thank them for coming. But by the time they were all back at The Lodge, he needed a moment on his own. He asked Jason to go ahead without him, and quietly took himself into the sitting room at the front of the house. It was a small room filled with display cabinets showing some of his mother's favourite things, such as an antique music box that had been in the family for generations, and an oddly shaped clay pot Billy had made for her in an art class when he was eight.

Charlie closed the door and walked over to the fireplace, the wooden mantle filled with his mother's favourite photographs, all displayed with an eclectic mix of metal, glass and wooden frames. Amid all the happy smiling faces, there was a photograph of Carol, holding baby Tyler, which had been added, so discreetly, to the collection of family pictures years earlier. He sighed and shook his head, feeling such a fool for not having put the pieces together himself. Now he knew the truth. It all seemed so obvious. How, he wondered, could he not have seen it?

'Do you mind if we talk?'

He turned and found that Carol had entered the room and was staring at him anxiously. 'Of course,' he replied, and so she closed the door and, with obvious trepidation, walked over to him. Charlie knew immediately what she wanted to talk to him about, and although it made him feel uncomfortable, he realised time was running out, and it was a conversation which needed to happen.

'I just wanted to check how you are,' she said, her voice deep. 'It's been a horrible few days, and we haven't really had the chance to talk.'

With all the will in the world, Charlie just couldn't bring himself to be angry with Carol or even dislike her. He had always liked her company, and although he could not understand the bizarre friendship she had enjoyed with his mother, he knew that his mother had genuinely loved her. He also knew his mother had wanted him to embrace Carol and Tyler as members of his family. 'Where's Lizzie?' he asked.

34

'Oh, she's doing the rounds with the guests,' she said. 'Everyone wants to hold her. If this were a religious family, she'd have no shortage of people wanting to be God parent.'

Charlie smiled, 'She's an absolute sweetheart.' After a pause, tentatively checking the waters, he added. 'I have had to assume that when you and Tyler go home today, you are taking her with you.'

Carol exhaled loudly, clearly relieved that Charlie knew what was going to happen. 'Yes,' she said. 'I know your useless father didn't tell you that, so I'm guessing it was Susan?'

'Yes. She told me everything.'

Carol nodded. 'Right,' she said. 'Right. OK. And I guess you have a lot of questions.'

Charlie knew he probably did have many questions, but the day had defeated him, and all he wanted at that moment was to sit down with Jason and have a glass of wine. 'What's happening with Dad? Is he moving in with you, too?'

Carol's expression changed slightly, puzzlement rather than anxiety, and she shook her head. 'Of course not,' she replied. 'Why would he do that?'

Charlie shrugged. 'Carol, look, at some point, you had an affair with Dad, you got pregnant, and for whatever reason, Mum forgave you both. That's really all I need to know.'

'Charlie, I didn't have an *affair* with Peter,' Carol said, with a clear emphasis on the word 'affair', as though it had no place in the conversation.

'Fling, one-night stand. Carol, I don't care what it was,' Charlie snapped, but then he caught himself, the tone of his voice becoming terse and critical, and he could see Carol beginning to shrink backwards as though under attack. And he knew that was not what his mother had wanted. He took a moment, a breath, and then, in a far more conciliatory tone, he said, 'Sorry. This is all new to me. I'm still processing.'

Carol didn't respond straight away, and it appeared to Charlie that she was processing something too, perhaps something he had said. And then she moved forward, slightly closer to him, and spoke. 'I'm not expecting you to be OK with... well... with what Susan told you. At least,

35

not straight away. But it's important we find a way to move on.' There was another odd lull in the conversation, and for a moment, Charlie felt Carol was going to continue to offer a little more information as to what had happened between her and Peter all those years ago. But she didn't, and he wondered if his ill-tempered response had persuaded her to keep quiet.

In truth, Charlie could feel an anger rising inside of him, but he knew it was misplaced. He was not angry with Carol, but he was angry with his father. 'Mum loved you and Tyler very much,' he said, his voice now smooth and calm. 'She told me that very clearly. The most important thing for her, in the end, was for me to promise that I would embrace you both as family. And I will do that, Carol. I know I will. I just need some time.'

'Really?' Carol asked quietly, tears forming in her eyes. 'That's what she said?'

Charlie nodded. 'I don't understand a lot of this, Carol, but it was important to her for me to promise that.'

'Oh,' Carol said and tried to say something else. But for a moment, she could not speak, and so she just nodded at Charlie and, with tears falling down her cheeks, offered him a grateful smile. 'But for now, Charlie. You and me,' Carol said, gesturing between the two of them with her hands, 'are we OK?'

And after a moment, Charlie nodded. 'You're about to spend the next 20 years of your life raising my little sister,' he said. 'So, we have to be alright, don't we?' And with those words, he was reminded that he had a task to perform. He still had to explain to Vicki and Billy that their baby sister would not be growing up at The Lodge. And he would need to explain to them why.

CHAPTER 9

Vicki and her friend had decided to sit outside in the garden, and Charlie and Jason were sat inside watching them through the patio doors. Charlie wondered if his sister was trying to avoid the rest of the people who had attended their mum's funeral for fear of being asked who her male companion was and how she knew him.

'I reckon he's at least 30,' Jason said. 'Look at those lines when he smiles.'

Charlie chuckled quietly. 'They're just laughter lines,' he said.

But Jason shook his head. '*Nothing* is that funny,' he replied.

Their exchange was unheard by everyone else, just another part of the low murmuring that passed as conversation at funeral receptions. Charlie leaned in against Jason, not enough to arouse suspicion but just enough that he could feel his partner's shoulder pressing against his own, and he let his gaze drift around the room to absorb the scene.

Carol was holding Lizzie once more. For the first time, she seemed to be interacting with Peter in an obvious manner, and Charlie wondered if she was gradually letting her guard down because she knew the great Fletcher family secret was finally about to be revealed.

Billy was sat at the breakfast bar sipping (what Charlie hoped) was a plain cola. He seemed to be enjoying a conversation with Louise, who was no doubt regaling him with hilarious tales of all the people who had quit the retirement complex because of their grandmother's terrible rudeness.

Charlie had already spoken to the two nurses who had cared for his mother during her pregnancy, and both had since left the reception to go back to work. Most of his mother's work friends had left, too. And as the numbers dwindled, Charlie knew they were approaching that moment in the day when Carol and Tyler would leave with Lizzie, and Charlie would have to explain to Vicki and Billy what was going on.

'I'll get us both a top-up,' Jason said. 'I assume we're leaving the car here and getting a taxi home?'

Charlie frowned. 'I'll see how things go with Vicki and Billy,' he said. 'I might have to stay here the night.'

Jason sighed and stared Charlie in the eyes. 'This isn't the day to talk about it, but I would like to get to a point where if you are staying here for the night,' he said, 'I can stay over with you, in the same room. You know, your mum guessed. It might not be as big a surprise for everyone else as you think.' With that, he took their glasses and wandered over to the kitchen to refill them.

Charlie sank back into the sofa and closed his eyes for a moment. He knew Jason was right, and in truth, it was not only Jason who wished to tell the rest of the family. Charlie had been trying to find the right moment, but he just did not know when the right moment would present itself or what it would feel like.

Somone tapped him on the knee and so opened his eyes, and found Tyler was stood in front of him, a little blonde boy in a smart black suit and tie. He was staring at Charlie and looked a little uneasy. 'You OK, sweetheart?' Charlie asked and offered him a friendly smile.

Tyler leaned forward and whispered to Charlie. 'Mummy said it was OK to talk to you. About being my half-brother.'

Charlie was thrown for a moment and did not know immediately how to respond. But Tyler's big blue eyes were filled with so much excitement and hope, that Charlie felt all his emotions fall into place, and for the first time, he had clarity as to what he should do.

'Well,' Charlie whispered back, 'we don't do things by half in this family, do we? So, let's not say half-brother. I'm your *brother*. How about that? Would you be happy with that?'

Tyler giggled, happy and relieved. 'Yes,' he said. Impulsively, Charlie reached out and swept Tyler up onto his lap, and the two sat there for a moment, happily hugging each other. Charlie kissed Tyler on the forehead. 'Mum loved you,' he said. 'She loved spending time with you in the garden. Her little helper.'

Tyler sat forward slightly so that he could look Charlie in the face. 'I told Auntie Susan I would look after her garden for her. If she wasn't here to do it herself. Would that be OK? May I still help with her garden?'

Charlie nodded. 'I think that would be super,' he said, and then glanced to the kitchen and saw that Carol was watching them with a huge smile on her face. Peter, who seemed oblivious to what was going on, whispered something into Carol's ear and took Lizzie from her. Carol looked back to Charlie and gestured to her watch, and Charlie realised it was almost time for her to go.

'I think your mum's ready to take you home,' he whispered to Tyler, who gave him one last squeeze before climbing off his lap and hurrying back to Carol, cheekily grabbing a mini quiche from the dining table as he went.

For a moment, Carol, Peter, Tyler and Lizzie were framed together in front of Charlie, like a family portrait, one that could easily have been on the mantle in the sitting room, amongst all the other photographs. And despite his best efforts, Charlie could not help but feel envious, perhaps even a little resentful, towards them. He wondered if this was the new normal, that Carol, Peter, Tyler and Lizzie would become a family, leaving Lizzie, Billy and Charlie as his father's 'other kids'.

He saw Louise was approaching to say goodbye, and he stood and gently hugged her. 'Thank you for coming,' he said.

'That's quite alright, young man,' she replied. 'I will let your nan know how the day went. She's told me she doesn't want to hear about it, but I know she does, so I'll tell her anyway.'

'Can you let her know I'm coming to see her tomorrow? Probably about midday? Vicki and Billy are coming with me.'

'Yes, of course,' Louise said. She took Charlie's arm and squeezed it, 'I am truly sorry for your loss, Charlie. I know that's the sort of trite thing people always say at a funeral. But I got to know your mother very well over the years, and she was one of the good ones. She had a lot to give this world, a lot of life to live, and that truly is a loss.'

With those words, she leaned in and kissed him on the cheek before making her way out, whispering goodbye to Billy as she went, and he thought how nice it was that she had finally called him Charlie.

As his gaze fell on his little brother, he suddenly remembered he had a job to do. Carol was about to leave the house with Lizzie, and it was down to him to break the news to Vicki and Billy that their baby sister

39

was not going to grow up at The Lodge. He gestured to his brother to follow him, and they stepped through the patio doors and into the garden, where Vicki was sitting with her friend.

'Sorry, Vicki, but I need to talk to you and Billy on your own for a moment,' he said, and then he looked to her friend. 'Would you mind giving us five minutes?'

The man stood and buttoned his jacket. 'It's fine, I have to go anyway,' he said, and then he shook Charlie's hand. 'I'm Nate, by the way,' he said, 'and I'm really sorry about your mum.'

'Thank you, Nate,' Charlie said, and took an instant dislike to him.

Nate kissed Vicki on the cheek. They made arrangements to speak on the phone later that day, and then he walked into the house. Charlie quietly slid the patio doors shut so he could speak privately, and he and Billy joined Vicki on the patio chairs. Three siblings, huddled together, with secrets to be shared.

CHAPTER 10

'I have something to tell you both, and it's going to be quite a surprise. But just try to stay calm. You see, there's something that you don't know.'

Before Charlie could continue, he noticed an odd exchange between Vicki and Billy. They looked at each other, smiling slightly as if they already knew something. 'What was that?' he asked. 'What was that look?'

Vicki smiled at him. 'It's about you and Jason, isn't it?' she asked, almost groaning as she spoke, and then she and Billy grinned at each other.

'No,' Charlie replied abruptly, frustrated by the distraction, because he knew he was on a deadline. Very soon, Carol would appear, with Lizzie in her carrycot, to say goodbye to them all, and Vicki and Billy had to know the full story before that happened. And so, he took a deep breath and readied himself to break the news.

But then his sister's words repeated in his head, and he realised the significance of her question and the meaning behind the knowing looks she and Billy had exchanged. 'Wait. What? Me and Jason?' he asked, wondering if perhaps he had misunderstood.

'It's OK,' Billy said reassuringly and patted him on the leg. 'We really like him. He's basically family already. We always thought you two would end up together.'

'Did you honestly think we wouldn't guess?' Vicki asked. 'Jason, your business partner, who always seems to be your plus-one?' She made air bracket gestures with her hands as she spoke the words 'business partner'.

Charlie suddenly felt exposed, as though his greatest secret had just been snatched away from him. His immediate instinct was to say it was not true, that they had got it completely and utterly wrong. And that denial was on the tip of his tongue, but he just managed to stop himself, realising that would have been the very worst thing he could have done.

41

Vicki and Billy were clearly reaching out to him, hoping he would let them into his secret life, just as their mother had done.

And so, instead, he paused for a moment and reset the conversation in his head; he would explain about Jason first, and then he would move onto the rest of the family business. 'I'm glad you know,' he said, his heart pounding in his chest, unable to quite believe he was finally coming out to them. 'Jason will be too. He's been wanting to tell you for ages. We both have. But with everything going on—'

'So, were you going out with each other at school?' Vicki interrupted.

Charlie shook his head. 'Oh, good lord, no,' he said. 'Absolutely nothing happened until he got back from Leeds after his degree. We really were just friends up until then. Mum had guessed, too. She told me that the last time I saw her. She said she was really pleased.' And then his voice trailed off, and he looked to the ground and tutted. 'I wish I had told her sooner,' he said quietly. 'I wish I'd been braver.'

In unison, Vicki and Billy leaned forward and put their arms around their older brother. 'At least she knew, at the end,' Vicki said. 'And she was happy for you.'

Charlie smiled and then hugged them both.

'So,' Vicki continued, 'that wasn't quite the shock you thought it was going to be.'

And with those words, Charlie suddenly realised that he had not done what he had set out to do. Vicki and Billy still did not know about Carol and Tyler, so he ended the embrace, sat back in his seat and looked at his sister and brother. 'Vicki, the problem is… that isn't what I was going to tell you,' he said. 'There's something else.'

Before he could continue, the patio door slid open. Peter stepped through the opening holding a carrycot, and Carol joined him, baby Lizzie swaddled in her arms. Tyler stayed just behind them, in the doorway, not sure if this was a conversation for a child to attend.

'So, we're off,' Carol said cautiously, not quite certain what conversation she had interrupted but hoping everyone was on the same page.

Suddenly confused, Vicki and Billy looked at each other, and then at Charlie, and then at Carol and their father.

42

'What do you mean?' Billy asked. 'Off where?'

Carol immediately looked to the floor as though wishing the ground would simply open and swallow her, and Peter frowned, then glared at Charlie, immediately apportioning the blame for the awkward moment to his eldest son.

Charlie sighed, stood up, and walked over to Tyler. He crouched down so he could whisper into his little brother's ear and said, 'Could you give us a few minutes, sweetheart? You can go and put the television on in the sitting room if you like.'

Tyler did as he was asked, and then Charlie pulled the patio door closed once more. He stood next to Carol and began to speak. 'Mum made arrangements for Lizzie,' he said, 'to make sure she was well cared for without her becoming any sort of a burden to her three other children.'

'Burden?' Billy said, unhappy at the use of the word to describe his baby sister.

Charlie shook his head. 'No, not a burden,' he said. 'Sorry, not a burden. But Mum wanted us to be free to live our own lives and looking after a baby… well… that's a big job. So, she and Dad agreed that Lizzie would live with Carol and Tyler.'

'You'll see her every day,' Carol interceded, looking at Vicki and Billy, her face pleading for their support and understanding. 'She's going to be a big part of your life. I promise. She will live at my house, but we're only a 10-minute drive away.'

Vicki grew teary and looked aside, away from the group, so they would not see. But Billy continued to challenge the situation, completely bemused by the whole suggestion that his baby sister was moving out.

'But she won't be with family,' he said. 'Carol, you're lovely and all that. But you're not family.'

And with those words, Charlie realised he had to tell the whole story. So, he retook his seat next to his siblings and quietly explained. 'Billy, she will be with family,' he said. 'She'll be with Tyler. And Tyler's our brother too.'

Billy continued to look confused, but Charlie noticed his sister suddenly go rigid, clearly registering what he had said. With tears in her eyes, she turned her face, now flushed and angry, and glared at him.

'He's *what*?' she snapped.

Charlie looked to his father, a silent invitation for him to intervene. But Peter simply stood and waited, and Charlie recognised that expression, an entitled man happy for someone else to sort the problem out. And so, Charlie turned back to Vicki and Billy. 'Tyler is dad's son,' he said. 'Mum knew all about it. She knew right from the start. And she was cool with it. The last time I saw her, she told me that she loved Carol and Tyler, and she wanted us to make them part of the family. In all honesty, that was her dying wish.'

Believing the conversation had run its course, Peter chose that moment to interject. 'So, I hope everyone is OK with this,' he said, 'because this is your mum's funeral, and this is what she wanted.' He thought that would be the end of the matter, but his daughter quickly set him right.

'Oh, did she?' Vicki asked angrily, and she stood up. 'My mum wanted you to have an affair, did she, Dad? She wanted you to father an illegitimate son? Did she, Dad? When she married you, this is what she always dreamed of? A cheating husband?'

Charlie knew his father. He knew if things got too difficult, he would simply chuck in the towel and leave. More than that, he knew his father wanted to get Carol, Tyler and Lizzie settled at Carol's house so he could spend the rest of the day at the pub, drinking. But Charlie wanted him to remain until the matter had been resolved or, at the very least, smoothed over for the time being. Before he could speak, the patio door was slid open once again and Jason stepped out, frowning at everyone, trying to gauge the situation. 'I wondered where everyone had gone to,' he said. 'What's everyone talking about?'

Carol sighed and turned to him. 'It's OK, Jason,' she said fondly. 'Everyone knows.'

And with that, Jason exhaled loudly and grinned. 'Oh, thank goodness,' he said cheerfully. 'This probably wasn't the right day, but I'm so glad he finally told you all.'

Jason had misunderstood Carol's comment and believed everyone on the patio now knew he and Charlie were a couple. Charlie was not prepared to share that secret with his father, particularly on that day, but it was all too late. He watched helplessly as his carefully constructed web of excuses and misdirections suddenly unravelled in front of him. It was as though it was all playing out in slow motion, and he was a reluctant bystander, fixed to his seat, unable to stop it or say anything.

Jason was walking towards him, smiling at him, his arms outstretched. He took Charlie's hands and pulled him to his feet, and then he cupped Charlie's face gently in his hands, kissed him on the lips, and embraced him tightly. Over his shoulder, Charlie could see the others. Vicki was still angry and frustrated, but her emotions just tempered enough to find the situation amusing. Billy just looked at the two of them, happy that on such a sad day, something nice had happened, while Carol was smiling as if, perhaps, a long-held suspicion had finally been proven correct. But his father was just staring at them, a deeply puzzled and unhappy expression on his face.

'That was lovely,' Charlie whispered into Jason's ear. 'But that wasn't what I told them.'

'Oh,' Jason said, and his embrace tightened a little as he tried to calculate what to do next. And then he released Charlie, turned and faced everyone else. 'Sorry,' he said. 'I appear to have misunderstood.' But Jason was not going to let the moment pass, left as an awkward funeral faux pas, and so he looked at Charlie with an expression that clearly indicated he wanted his partner to elaborate.

Defeated, Charlie threw his hands up. 'Right,' he snapped. 'For those here who do not know, Jason is the love of my life. We've been together nine months since he got back from Leeds. Mum knew, and she was very happy for us. We're both very happy. And we hope you're happy for us.'

He turned, very specifically, and looked at his father, a man he knew had mostly abysmal views on many subjects. Peter said nothing. He simply stood, staring ahead, as though he had not acknowledged anything that had just happened. And Charlie suddenly found himself filling with rage, at a man who was expecting his eldest son to do his

45

dirty work, but in return could not bring himself to even pretend to be happy for him.

'Yes, we are,' Vicki interceded, 'of course we are. We're very happy for you both.' She stood and gave Jason a hug which was brief and perfunctory, her mind elsewhere. And then she stepped back and looked at Charlie, her face dark and serious. 'But I am really sorry, you're going to have to explain to me again what the hell is going on with Lizzie.'

Charlie realised this is what his grandmother had alluded to, that he would have to step-up, to help and support his sister and brother in the absence of any help or support from their father. And he remembered his mother, lying in her bed, so tired and thin, enduring the final moments of her life, whilst her entire focus was not on herself but the people she was leaving behind, and her request that Charlie be the one to guide them all to a new way of living together, a different type of family.

'Vicki, I promise you, this is what Mum wanted,' he said. 'She put a lot of thought into this and decided it was the best for everyone, but especially for Lizzie. All the arrangements were agreed months ago.'

'But I thought we were all going to help out,' Vicki said, the anger in her voice now replaced with a great sadness. 'I thought that's what Mum would have wanted. All of us, bringing up our little sister together.'

'Vicki, sweetheart,' Carol said, intervening when it was clear Peter was going to say nothing. 'I know you're in a state of shock, and I can only imagine how you must feel about me right now. And I honestly don't blame you. But Susan and your dad and me... we talked all of this through. Over and over again. And Susan, she just didn't want you and Charlie and Billy to have to put your lives on hold. You're all so young still. That's just not what she wanted for you.'

Vicki stared at Carol, holding her baby sister in her arms, and her face suddenly crumpled, and she began to cry. Billy leapt up immediately and tried to console her. 'But couldn't you live here?' he asked Carol, looking at her over Vicki's shoulder. 'I mean, if you and Dad are already together. Why can't you just live here?'

In unison, Carol and Peter shook their heads. 'No, no, that wouldn't work,' Peter said.

46

'And we're not together,' Carol insisted, 'we are absolutely not together.'

'This isn't just about Lizzie,' Charlie added. 'It's about Tyler, too. He's our little brother, and Mum was very clear that she expects us all to treat him as such. There are five of us, not four. Those were her words.'

Vicki stepped back from Billy, and the two of them looked at Charlie, and he could tell they were both trying to organise their thoughts and their feelings now they had discovered they had an extra sibling.

'Look, this has been a tough day for all of us,' Charlie said. 'And I think we're going to end up just talking around in circles.' He looked to Carol and his father and said, 'So, you two should head off with Tyler and Lizzie, and we can start to tidy up.'

There was a moment when everyone seemed to silently agree with him. But before he left, Peter looked at Jason and appeared to nod at him as though to quietly acknowledge his relationship with Charlie, and then he and Carol departed.

'So,' Jason said and grinned at Charlie. 'I'm the love of your life, am I?'

Charlie rolled his eyes and shook his head. 'Oh my god, the moment those words came out of my mouth, I knew I would never hear the end of it.'

Jason paused for a moment, and then he looked at Vicki and Billy, and he realised things between the siblings were far from resolved. 'Look, I'll start cleaning up the kitchen,' he said. 'You three have stuff to talk about.' And then quietly, he added, 'They need their big brother, Charlie.' He gave both Billy and Vicki a hug and then disappeared back into the house, and with the gentle sound of the patio door being closed once more, Vicki sat down.

'I thought losing mum was bad enough,' she said quietly. 'Now this. How could Mum have allowed this to happen? How could she have stayed with Dad or stayed friends with Carol?'

Charlie sat down next to her, and Billy joined them.

'Mum said she made a decision that she thought was best for everyone, including for us,' Charlie said. 'And then, I don't know, she and Dad and Carol, they just somehow made it all work. And Mum was

47

clearly very fond of Tyler. She really wants us... *wanted* us... to embrace him as our little brother.'

Billy sat silently pondering the situation as though he had not quite determined how he felt or how he *should* feel. But Vicki's face crumpled once more, and she began to cry.

'But mum didn't think I could help with Lizzie,' she said. 'She didn't trust me with my own little sister.'

'No, no, no,' Charlie said. 'That's not it at all. She just wanted us to be able to enjoy our lives but also see Lizzie all the time too. And Carol's doing an amazing thing. She's raising her best friend's child. This really is going to be OK, I promise you. Once we've all gotten used to it, everything will be OK.'

Charlie thought he had been persuasive, but the moment he stopped talking, Vicki looked at him and shook her head.

'It's not going to be OK,' she said, tears tumbling down her face. 'Mum didn't even want me to just help out with Lizzie. She didn't think I was up to it. How would she have felt if she knew I was going to have a baby of my own?' With those words, Vicki covered her face and sobbed.

Charlie and Billy, at first, said nothing, too shocked by Vicki's words to respond. And then, instinctively, Billy reached forward and began to gently stroke his sister's shoulder. 'Vicki, are you pregnant?' he asked.

Vicki blurted out a word, but she was crying so hard that neither of her brothers could quite work out what she had said, although both assumed it had been 'yes'. They looked at each other, Charlie and Billy, both wide-eyed and a little frightened. This was most definitely a situation where they needed their mum, and they needed her calmness, her organisational skills, and her kindness.

But Susan wasn't there anymore. Apart from Jason busily cleaning up the kitchen, their house was empty, and it was just the three of them.

Gently, Charlie nudged Vicki's hands away from her face until she was looking at them both once more, tears falling down her cheeks. 'Every child is a blessing,' he said. 'And this little one is going to be a blessing too. They're going to be born into a family that's filled with happiness, laughter and love. And everything is going to be OK.

Everything is going to be wonderful. And, hey, Billy and me. We're going to be uncles.'

Through her tears, Vicki just about managed to offer him a smile. 'Really?' she asked, her voice trembling. 'You really think so?'

'I promise,' he said. But the moment he had spoken, Charlie could feel how completely hollow those reassuring words had been. He had no idea what the months or years ahead would hold for the three of them.

Their mother, the heart and soul of their family, was gone, and he had no doubt their father would continue to be mostly absent from their lives. And for the first time, he understood why his mother had made such drastic arrangements for Lizzie, to live with Carol and not at The Lodge. Because apart from Jason, and whoever Nate was, it seemed to Charlie that he, Vicki and Billy would be on their own, trying to raise a baby. And the thought of that, of the responsibility they were each taking on, truly frightened him.

CHAPTER 11

Five years later

As Vicki parked her car outside the community centre, she could feel her emotions running away from her, a confusing mix of excitement and dread. The community centre had become grimly familiar over the previous couple of years, a place Vicki would visit once a month, where she got to be a mum again and see her son Jack for a couple of hours. He had grown into an adorable little boy, an excited bundle of questions and giggles, with deep brown eyes and dark hair, just like his mother.

But whenever she saw him, she knew his social worker was just a few tables away, a woman called Lydia who, for some reason, always looked exhausted. Lydia was very good at fading into the background during contact, but Vicki never forgot that she was there. She suspected everything she did for those two hours was monitored by Lydia, and then assessed and put into a report. And that report, she feared, could be used to justify Jack's care order being continued.

She hated feeling like that. She wanted to enjoy every second of contact and needed to have much more to do with his life. Later in the year, in the autumn, he would start at infant school, and Vicki was keen to start the arrangements for that. But at every contact, in the back of her mind, was the worry she might say or do something that Lydia would assess as inappropriate.

Vicki spent a moment checking her reflection in the mirror in the sun visor, then she took a deep breath and climbed out of the car, a little red hatchback her family had bought for her 21st birthday two years earlier. It was a warm sunny day, and so she had dressed simply in her blue jeans with a light cotton blouse and sandals. She had pulled her long dark hair into a ponytail and carried a large fabric bag over her shoulder.

The bag contained gifts, photographs, and a few packets of sweets. Everyone had contributed. Billy had autographed a flyer of a recent am-dram production of 'Anything Goes', which had played at The Cliffs Pavilion, in which he had been in the chorus. There was also an invitation to Charlie's civil partnership ceremony, although Vicki knew she would have to double-check the invitation with Lydia before she handed it over to Jack's foster carers. It was a family event that sat outside the agreed arrangements for contact, and she knew she would need to get Lydia's agreement for Jack to attend.

Just as she was about to step forward, she suffered a wave of terrible panic, a fear she was going to get something wrong. She paused, closed her eyes and visualised her mother, remembering how she had always carried herself. In every situation, Susan had behaved as though she owned the room, always polite and quietly assured but never particularly impressed by anyone and certainly never intimidated. All Vicki hoped for was that she could channel the same energy, even if only for the next two hours. 'Right,' she said aloud, then opened her eyes and walked inside, trembling with nerves.

Contact was always held at the little café just inside the entrance, and as she walked through the doors, she immediately saw Jack's foster carers, Debbie and Kim, sitting at one of the plastic tables by the large full-height windows overlooking the road. Just the sight of them made her relax a little: two older women with years of childcare experience who had done so much over the previous 24 months to make sure Vicki remained an important part of Jack's life, even though she barely ever saw him.

Vicki knew Debbie and Kim had been a couple for about 20 years and had assumed they were in their early forties, although it was tricky to work out their exact age. They were both prematurely grey and kept their hair short, sometimes cropped. They always wore t-shirts and jeans and brought a kind, humorous energy to each contact, an energy that somehow lifted Vicki's spirits, even on some of her darker days.

'There she is,' Debbie said, 'Jack, look, there's Mummy.' The little boy sitting on Debbie's lap turned to see Vicki, clapped his hands with excitement, jumped to the floor and hurried over to her. As he fell into Vicki's arms, and she could feel his hot breath on her neck and smell his cleanly washed hair, everything in her troubled world fell into place, and all she could feel was happiness.

'Hello, Jack darling,' she said. 'Mummy's missed you so much. I have so much to tell you.'

She picked him up and carried him back to the table, noticing that Lydia was sitting in the corner, quietly reading a book. They exchanged a polite, low-key wave as Vicki joined Debbie and Kim.

'I'm just getting the teas in,' Kim said, 'maybe a bit of cake?' Kim looked at Debbie for approval, but Debbie shook her head. 'We don't need a cake,' she said. 'Tea will do. I did you a full English this morning. That'll see you through until lunchtime.'

Kim shrugged. 'Just tea then,' she said disappointedly, then headed off to the counter.

'How are you, Vicki?' Debbie asked.

Vicki gave Jack another hug and smiled. 'I just live for this moment,' she said. 'It's still so hard.'

Debbie nodded. 'You know, we've been fostering for a lot of years now, and there have been many times we've been sat here, with a child, waiting to see their parents, and they just don't show up. Sometimes, it's even been the child's birthday. But you always do, every time without fail.'

Vicki took the compliment with great pride. 'And what have you been up to, you little rascal?' she asked Jack.

The following two hours passed too quickly. Kim and Debbie shared photographs of some of the places they had taken Jack over the previous month, which included Colchester Zoo and the London Eye. They also gave Vicki some pictures Jack had drawn, especially for his mum. Vicki did the same in return, sharing the contents of her bag, apart from the invitation to her brother's ceremony.

And before Vicki even thought of the time, Lydia was standing at the door gesturing to her watch that contact was over. Vicki's heart sank; it would be another month before she got to see her little boy again. She gave him a big hug and kiss and told him how much she loved him. Reluctantly, she stepped away from Jack to give both Debbie and Kim a hug, thanking them for all they were doing before making her way outside.

52

It was a routine they had all adopted over the course of the previous year. Vicki always left first, as it meant there would be a quiet and organised goodbye in the café rather than something awkward and unstructured in the car park. It seemed to make a difference to Jack, who was far less likely to cry if he said goodbye to his mum inside the café rather than if he saw her climb into her car and drive away without him.

As Vicki stepped through the door, she found Lydia waiting outside for her. Vicki's heart skipped a beat.

'How did that go?' Lydia asked and started to walk with Vicki towards her car.

'Lovely,' Vicki said. 'Do you know how much longer this is going on for? Jack starts infant school in September, and I need to start thinking about getting him enrolled, and I can't do that until he's back home.'

Lydia stopped walking, and instinctively, so did Vicki.

'Vicki,' Lydia said, with a softness that indicated she was about to deliver some unhappy news. 'We are working with Debbie and Kim to find a school for Jack near to their home.'

Vicki felt her stomach churn. She knew, immediately, what that meant, but she didn't want to accept it, to acknowledge it, and so carried on speaking as though she had not understood. 'But they live in Westcliff,' she said. 'That's miles away. When he moves back home, there's no way I can get him there and back every day. I'll have to change his school. That seems a bit unfair on him.'

Lydia did not say anything immediately. Instead, she just stared at Vicki with an expression that suggested she had missed the point. 'There are no plans for Jack to move home with you,' she said abruptly. 'We have asked Debbie and Kim to provide him with a home, longer term, and so we need to make school arrangements that are close to where they live.'

Vicki felt her blood run cold. Everything she had done since Jack had been taken into care, everything, had been built around the idea he would eventually come back to live with her and Nate. She had no idea there were plans to keep him in care for longer, and especially not for years.

53

'I don't understand,' she said. 'I've been working so hard.' She could feel tears building in her eyes, and as much as she tried to fight them, she suddenly found herself sobbing. Gently, Lydia took Vicki by the arm and led her to a bench at the side of the car park, overlooking the playing field behind the community centre. Lydia sat her down and held her hand.

'Vicki, listen,' she said, 'You see Jack for two hours once a month.'

Vicki managed to utter a few words in response. 'And I'm always here,' she said.

'Yes, you are. But where's Nate? This is the fourth contact in a row he's not attended. And even before that, he didn't attend regularly.'

'He's working. He can't always get the time off.'

Lydia reached into her handbag and found a plastic packet of paper tissues and offered them to Vicki, who took one and started to dry her eyes.

'So, he has a job, you say. And is he still clean?' Lydia asked.

Vicki nodded.

'And the drinking?'

'He only drinks socially. With me.'

'And have there been any further incidents involving the police?'

Vicki shrugged, and Lydia tutted and sighed. 'Well, perhaps I should tell you that we are aware of two more incidents, both recent.'

Vicki had spent years making excuses for Nate, explaining to other people that all the trouble he got into regularly was never his fault. It was always *other people*; he had been sacked because a boss had it in for him. He had been carrying drugs because he had put on a mate's jacket by accident. He had been charged with drunk driving because someone had swapped his alcohol-free lager at the pub for real lager without his knowledge.

At every stage, with every incident, Vicki had an excuse for Nate. But as she sat on the park bench, the custody of her son having been so cruelly snatched away from her, she knew Lydia wouldn't believe a word of it, and so she remained silent.

'Vicki, you have been trying to regain custody of your son by building a stable home life for him with his father,' Lydia said. 'And I do believe

54

you are doing all you can to achieve that. But Nate isn't. And the way things stand right now, our view is that the best thing for Jack, the safest thing, is the status quo.'

Vicki clutched the paper tissue in her hand and looked to the ground. 'I just can't go on like this,' she said, feeling as though every ounce of energy was being drained from her. 'He's growing up so quickly. And I am missing it all. It's torture.'

'I understand that. So, perhaps at our next placement planning meeting, we can revisit contact. Debbie and Kim are very committed to helping parents see as much of their kids as they can, so I am sure we can come up with an arrangement you will find... less unbearable. How does that sound?'

Vicki took a deep breath. 'It's him, isn't it?' she asked. 'Nate. You consider him a risk. To Jack's welfare.'

Lydia paused before answering, her mind trying to negotiate a minefield of professional boundaries and confidentiality issues. But she liked Vicki, and she had seen how much effort she had put into trying to regain custody of her son. She had certainly seen how much she loved him. She decided, on that one occasion, to offer some personal rather than professional advice.

'Vicki, I am going to say this to you off the record, which I never do, but I hope you will take this advice in the spirit with which I am giving it.'

Vicki looked up, intrigued and immediately a little apprehensive. 'I will.'

'There are plenty of single parents out there, raising their kids and doing a brilliant job,' Lydia said. 'If your arrangements at home were to change, and you presented yourself as a single mother, living in a stable environment, with a good support network around you... like your family... then I am sure that is something we would have to seriously consider.'

With heart-breaking clarity, Vicki understood exactly what Lydia was saying. After five tumultuous years with Nate, after all his lies and deceits, the thieving and the court appearances, and even after their little boy had been taken into care, she had never, not once, considered ending

55

their relationship. Everything in her heart and her head had centred on the fantasy that Jack would be returned, and she and Nate would raise him happily together. But she had spent so much time and energy chasing after Nate, trying to help him be the good man she believed he could be, that she had never stopped and considered all that he had cost her.

She reached into her bag and plucked out the invitation to Charlie's civil partnership. 'I don't know if you saw my email,' she said. 'About my brother's wedding? He and Jason were hoping Jack could be there as a page boy. I didn't know if you had been able to consider that?'

Lydia nodded. 'I think the wedding reception might be too much for him,' she said, 'A lot of people he doesn't really know, all at the same time. I think that would be too much at this point. But it is being held at Southend Registry Office, isn't it?'

Vicki nodded.

'Well, Debbie and Kim are happy to take him along. They can sit in their car outside during the ceremony, and then you can take all the pictures, and then they can just take him home again. How about that? He can skip the party but be there for the ceremony and the pictures.'

It was both less and more than Vicki had hoped for, but in the middle of such a horrible moment, she took it as a small win and said thank you. After their conversation, Vicki remained on the bench for a while, alone. From a distance, she watched as Debbie and Kim walked from the community centre, Jack between them, merrily holding hands with them both. Once at their car, they strapped Jack into his child seat and then they drove away, and Vicki knew it would be another month before she would see him again.

Lydia's advice had been hard to hear, and it had left Vicki with the most terrible choice, one she did not know she had the strength to make. Because she knew, she finally understood, that she would never regain custody of her son if she continued to be with his father. Lydia had made it clear; Vicki had to choose between either Jack or Nate.

CHAPTER 12

Vicki drove straight home, to her little one-bedroom ground-floor flat in Shoeburyness, close to the high street. It was pleasant enough, with a parking space at the front and a small garden at the rear that she shared with the tenants in the flat above. She remembered how excited she had been when the housing association had first offered it to her, a place of her own where she and Nate could raise Jack, away from all the arguments at The Lodge.

She thought it would be a new start, a chance for Nate to fulfil his promises to get a job and stay out of trouble so they could give their son the best start in life. But his promises came to nothing, and he continued to make money as and when opportunities arose, even if those opportunities were somewhat nefarious.

Within months of moving in, her little home was being raided by the police on a regular basis, often in the middle of the night. Nate always had an excuse: someone else to blame, a mistake, the police picking on him. Vicki loyally parroted every word of his excuses to anyone who would listen. And mostly, other people would react as though they believed her, that Nate was the victim of circumstance.

But then a team of social workers visited, following a concern raised by the police. Vicki told those same stories to the social workers, that it was all a mistake, that Nate had done nothing wrong. But the social workers had heard it all before.

They had assembled a file of criminal offences and serious child welfare concerns, and Jack was taken into care. Vicki had genuinely believed it would be for just a few weeks, a month at most. But two years had passed, and despite her best efforts, it seemed as though Jack's return home was further away than ever.

She let herself in the front door and could hear the television was on. She dropped her bag on the hall floor and opened the door to find Nate lounging on the couch, stripped down to his boxer shorts and a t-shirt, which was riding up to expose his belly. He was watching a live feed from the Big Brother house.

At the back of the room, a depressing reminder of her birthday from the week before, were two large helium balloons, one was the number two, and the other a three, but both heavily wrinkled and dishevelled and barely floating off the floor.

'What the hell are you doing?' she asked.

Nate looked up and grimaced at her as though her question was completely unreasonable. 'I just got back,' he said defensively. 'I just wanted to chill for a bit.'

'What do you mean you just got back? You were supposed to meet me at the community centre. We had contact with Jack. You missed it again. It was noticed that you missed it again.'

'Oh, I'm sorry love,' Nate said, his gaze focussing back onto the television. 'But you're the one who keeps telling me I need to get a job. So that's what I was doing.'

Vicki frowned, puzzled by his response, 'So… you have a job?'

Nate waved his hand in the air, 'It's looking good. With Simon and Diane's firm. Delivery driver.'

Vicki placed her hands on her hips and glared at him, 'But you're still banned. You've got, what, seven months to go? How's that going to work?'

Nate shrugged, 'They're happy to hold it open for me.'

'Right. And what are you going to do until then?'

Nate looked at her accusingly, 'I'm going to have to sit it out, aren't I? You know it's not my fault I lost my licence. But I can't get a driving job until I get it back.'

Vicki tried to hold onto her anger, hoping it might help her focus, to decide what to do. But Nate's manner always had a disarming effect on her, and she could already feel her anger draining away. She still loved him and all his silly nonsense. She loved their evenings together, tucked up in bed in front of their wall-mounted TV, gossiping maliciously about all the people on the various TV shows they watched. She loved the romantic gestures he would sometimes make, an unexpected bunch of flowers or a surprise takeaway so she didn't have to cook. And she loved how safe he could make her feel when he just held her in his arms and told her everything would work out.

58

And for far too long, that had been the only route to happiness for Vicki; at some point, Nate would turn his messy life around and then everything would work out. But now Lydia had given her a different route, a new option that meant Vicki's happiness was no longer dependent on Nate. And as she stood looking at her boyfriend, spending another lazy, pointless afternoon on her couch, she realised that no matter how much she loved him, no matter how it might hurt, she had to make a change.

Without saying a word, she walked from the lounge to her bedroom at the back of the flat and closed the door. She sat on the unmade bed, the floor mostly covered with Nate's discarded clothing and dirty laundry, and she took a moment, just for herself, to catch a breath and really think about what she should do next. Without a shadow of a doubt, she did not want her little boy to spend the rest of his childhood in foster care, but the way things were, she knew she would never get him back. And the thought of that, the permanency of it, made her feel nauseous.

But she could tell exactly how the next few days would play out if she asked Nate to leave; they would have a big fight, he would blame everyone else, try to persuade her that he would change, that he was turning his life around. And even if, on that one day, she found the strength to stand her ground and force him to go, she knew he would be back within a day, all flowers and apologies and promises. And she knew her resolve would evaporate, and she would be back to square one.

She realised there was only one other option, one other route for her to take, that would break her free from Nate, a clean break that would prevent a reconciliation. And then, as if on autopilot, she packed a couple of suitcases, walked them to her car and loaded them into the boot. She then walked back into her flat one last time.

'I'm moving back to The Lodge,' she said calmly.

Suddenly, Nate was paying attention. He switched off the television with the remote control and sat up, 'Why are we doing that?'

'I didn't say "we". I said that I am moving back. I will be letting the housing association know I am giving up the lease on this flat. So, you have about a month to find somewhere to live.'

Nate stood up, suddenly alert to everything Vicki was saying and the great impact it would have on his quality of life, 'But I'll have to move to The Lodge with you, won't I? How can we get Jack back if we're not living together?'

Vicki shook her head, 'You know my family won't have you set foot in that house again. And it was made clear to me today that I stand a much better chance of getting Jack back if I am not with you.'

She could see Nate was getting agitated, his easy life quickly disappearing with every word from Vicki's lips. 'No, no,' he said loudly. 'All that trouble with your family at the Lodge, you know that was all Charlie's fault. He couldn't help himself, could he? He had to interfere in our relationship. And there is no way you can get Jack back unless we are together, his mum *and* his dad. You know that. They have told us that.'

Vicki knew no one in social services had ever said such a thing. Nate was twisting multiple conversations and letters and court judgements into a narrative that suited him. It was a narrative Vicki had bought into for far too long. But after her horrible morning at the community centre, she knew Nate's version of events was a complete lie. And as much as she could feel her heart aching at the thought of leaving him behind, as much as she wanted to agree she was just being silly and should get her belongings back in from the car, she knew she couldn't.

'I'm sorry, Nate,' she said. 'But I am going to get my son back, and I will do that without you.'

She turned to walk away, but Nate grabbed her arm and tried to pull her back. 'No, you're not,' he growled. 'You are not leaving.'

Vicki stood still, looking towards the door, unable to move. 'Let go of my arm, Nate,' she said calmly, without looking back at him. 'I will not ask you a second time.'

Nate paused, trying to weigh up his options, to think what he could do next. But then he noticed, in her free hand, that Vicki had made a fist around her car keys, with one of the keys sticking through her clenched fingers. It suddenly felt as though a decision had been made, and nothing he could do would change that. He released his grip on Vicki's arm. After a moment, and without looking at him again, she left.

60

Nate heard the car door slam, and then the engine start, and then the noise of Vicki's car driving away. He stood in the empty flat, in his boxer shorts and vest, and wondered who in social services was to blame for this, which one of those bloody social workers had ruined his life.

CHAPTER 13

Vicki arrived at The Lodge and quietly let herself in. She took her suitcases up to her old bedroom and unpacked as quickly as she could. She put out a few photographs of Jack and some old family pictures which included her mum. She was surprised how quickly it felt like she was home again, as though a great pressure had just been removed, a great weight that she hadn't been aware of until it was no longer there.

She wasn't like Charlie. He could stay angry for weeks and hold a grudge forever. But Vicki knew she was different. She could go to bed furious but wake up filled with regret and a need to apologise, even if she knew she had been in the right. And that frightened her, the thought that she might wake up, having lost all her resolve, and re-pack her bags and move back to the flat and to Nate.

She needed to put some boundaries in place. She picked up her shoulder bag and rummaged through the contents until she found her mobile phone, a little silver Nokia that flipped open to reveal the keyboard and screen. Billy had always laughed when she used it and would sit in the background, making references to Star Trek whenever she was making a call. But the conversation she was about to have was no laughing matter. She called her support officer at the housing association to cancel her lease of the flat and to explain her reasons for moving back to The Lodge.

After a long and detailed conversation where her support officer expressed clear surprise and concern at her decision, and explained the repercussions of giving up her lease, it was agreed, and the paperwork was underway. Next, Vicki sent a curt text message to Nate. *'Notice handed in. I have agreed to vacate in 14 days. You need to find somewhere else to live.'* Immediately after that, she blocked his number, switched off her phone, dropped it into her bag, and went downstairs.

At the back of the house, she found Jason and Billy playing Jenga with Lizzie, sitting on the couches by the newly installed French doors, which were open, allowing a cool breeze into the space. The little tower of wooden blocks collapsed just as she entered the kitchen, and the room

62

was filled with cheering and laughter, and the sound of Lizzie giggling with joy, sat on Billy's lap.

Jason noticed her first. Vicki had grown very fond of him over the years. He was calm and warm and always the first to offer to help if someone was in need. He had completely embraced being one of the Fletchers and never allowed any family disputes to dictate what he should think or how he should behave towards anybody else. He had also proven an interesting foil for Charlie, tempering her brother's tendency to quickly lose his temper. And, as always, he immediately stood and walked over to embrace her. 'Vicki, what a lovely surprise,' he said. 'You look fabulous.'

'Oh, thank you,' she replied and kissed him on the cheek.

Jason continued past her into the kitchen. 'I'll make a brew,' he said and started clanking around with the kettle and teacups.

'Hello, Vicki,' Lizzie yelled loudly, clapping her hands with delight at the sight of her older sister, before jumping from Billy's lap and running over to give Vicki a kiss and a hug. Vicki picked her up and noticed how much heavier she was than Jack, even though she was only six months older. Lizzie was a sturdy little girl with rosy cheeks, dark eyes and curly brown hair, who always seemed to be in pretty pinafore dresses with matching tights and shoes, as if she already had a signature look.

Vicki lowered Lizzie onto the floor by the coffee table. 'How about you start to put the Jenga bricks back in the box?' she asked, and happily, Lizzie immediately set to work. Vicki sat next to Billy and ruffled his hair, 'You OK, bruv? How's work?'

'Good, good,' he said. 'I think they've realised I'm not the super smart employee my sister was, but they seem to like me, and, you know, no one's complained or anything.'

Vicki sat back and grinned. 'Well, you did have a lot to live up to,' she said as she pretended to blow her fingernails dry.

Billy's expression darkened for a moment, and he leaned forward. 'Can I grab you before you go?' he said in a low voice. 'I just need to ask your advice about something. It's… well… it's really a bit embarrassing, but I don't know who else to ask.'

63

'Yes, of course,' Vicki said, intrigued as to what Billy had gotten himself into this time. He had grown into an undeniably tall and handsome young man, six-foot-four and slim, with a deep voice and an appealingly innocent nature. Older women, in particular, seemed attracted to him, to his height, good looks and his impeccable manners. But many of those women turned out to be married, and Billy would often only find out when an angry husband was banging on the front door of The Lodge, wanting a word. Vicki wondered if Billy needed advice about one of those older women. She only hoped he hadn't left anyone pregnant.

Jason re-joined them, carrying a tea tray. 'There we are,' he said, sitting down and handing out the drinks: milky without sugar for Vicki, strong with two sugars for Billy, and a sugar-free squash for Lizzie. Lizzie finished what she was doing, climbed onto the couch next to Jason, and took her drink. 'Thank you, Jason,' she said, and before she started to drink from her plastic cup, she looked at Vicki and smiled. 'Did you know I'm going to be a bridesmaid at Charlie and Jason's wedding?'

'I did,' Vicki replied brightly. 'And little Jack's going to be a page boy with you,' she said and looked at Jason and smiled.

'Is he?' Jason asked. 'They said yes?'

'Only for the service and the pictures. Not the party, but at least he'll be there.'

'Oh, that's marvellous! I can't wait to tell Charlie.'

Vicki leaned back on the couch, holding her hot cup in both hands. 'Also,' she said, 'Big announcement. I've moved back into my room upstairs. I'm giving up the flat.'

She noticed a concerned exchange between Jason and Billy and knew exactly what they were both thinking.

'Vicki,' Billy said, 'you know you can't do that. Dad and Charlie have both said Nate isn't setting foot in this house again. It's quite literally the only thing they agree on.'

Vicki rolled her eyes at the mention of Charlie's name. 'Well, Nate isn't moving in. It's just me. He and I are no longer living together.'

'Oh,' Billy said, and immediately felt the conversation had moved beyond his comfort zone and wasn't sure what to say.

64

She looked at Jason to see how he had reacted. She knew he, like Charlie, had always disliked Nate, although he had been far less vocal about his feelings than her brother. Jason had trod a very careful middle ground and had often tried to be a peacemaker between Vicki and Charlie. She watched as he put down his cup of tea and then asked, simply, 'Are you OK?'

Vicki shrugged. 'I have a horrible feeling I am going to wake up in the morning, alone in my old bed, in my old room, and regret everything I did today. But, right now, I know I have to do this. Social Services made it clear today that I'd never get Jack back if I was living with Nate. So, I have to get my priorities in order.'

'Well, that's good, then,' Billy said. 'If you are living here, hopefully, they will see you are part of a big family. You know, stable. Like it was before you and Nate moved out.'

For a moment, Vicki felt spiteful. It was just fleeting, but she remembered the way she and Nate had left The Lodge, and before she could re-think her words, she said, 'Well, none of this would have happened if Charlie hadn't kicked us out in the first place.'

Jason sat back, his concerned expression replaced with a deeply furrowed brow. 'Oh, no, no, no,' he said quietly, and then he looked to Lizzie and said softly, 'Sweetheart, do you want to go and tidy up your sand pit at the end of the garden? Just collect your bucket and spade and bring them back onto the patio?'

Lizzie put her plastic cup onto the coffee table. 'OK,' she said happily and then hurried out through the French doors.

'None of that, Vicki,' Jason said calmly. 'Come on. You know that isn't fair. Charlie could no more kick you out of this house than you could kick him out. That is not at all what happened.'

Vicki scowled at him, unexpectedly feeling defensive, and as if she needed to deflect some of the blame from Nate, 'Charlie made it impossible for us to stay.'

'Did he?' Jason asked. 'Sweetheart, I know you've had a horrible day, but honestly, you are being very unfair to your brother, and I think you know that.'

Vicki placed her teacup firmly onto the coffee table and sat back with her arms folded, 'He made it impossible for us to live here. He didn't stop having a go at Nate. Every opportunity he had.'

'All he did, which was fair, was tell Nate that if he was going to live in this house, he had to get a job and start paying towards the bills,' Jason replied assertively. 'Everyone else contributed. Your dad, you, Billy. Even Charlie and I put money towards the bills, and we only stay here a couple of nights a week. But we still contributed. The only person who didn't was your boyfriend.'

'But he *wasn't* living here,' Vicki snapped.

'And you know what, Vicki,' Jason continued, 'I think that is what upset Charlie the most. That you moved your boyfriend into this house and then pretended he was just staying over every now and again when he was clearly living here full time. And it wasn't just that he slept here every night. It was when he started hanging about here during the day. Lounging about on the furniture, smoking roll-ups, watching the TV. Eating the food. Using the hot water. Making himself cups of tea. When everyone else was going to work so we could all earn money to pay the bills, Nate was here treating it like he owned the place, without paying a penny towards any of it.'

Jason had never spoken so critically of Nate before, at least not to her face, and Vicki did not like it at all. She pursed her lips, angrily trying to think of a retort, but her mind was blank. All she had was an overwhelming feeling she had been wronged and that her older brother should be blamed for something. But she knew Jason's retelling of events had been annoyingly precise and accurate. Desperate not to let go of her version of events, she glared at Billy, expecting him to step up to defend her honour. But, instead, quietly and politely, he agreed with Jason.

'And to be fair, Vicki, it wasn't just about the bills, was it?' Billy asked, his voice calm and deep. 'I mean, be honest, you know it wasn't just about the bills. It was when the police started coming around, interviewing him in Mum's sitting room. Asking him about break-ins and stolen goods. And then that time they came and searched the house in the middle of the night, looking for a gun.'

66

'None of that was Nate's fault,' Vicki insisted. 'And they didn't find a thing because it had nothing to do with Nate.' But she knew her words would fall on deaf ears. No one in the family believed for a moment that Nate was an innocent victim of police harassment.'

'But then it happened again,' Billy said. 'And that second time, Lizzie and Jack were both here, and the police frightened them. And they were screaming and crying at three in the morning. And that's when Dad and Charlie both told Nate to get out.'

'That's right, Billy,' she snapped. 'They kicked us out in the middle of the night.'

Jason sighed. 'Vicki, look, I am sorry,' he said, trying to take a kinder tone with his words. 'We all want what's best for you and little Jack. And we want to help you get him back. But you know that the problems with the police and with Nate they continued long after you moved out of here. And to be fair to Charlie and, to be honest, your dad, they didn't tell you and Jack to go. They just said that Nate couldn't stay here anymore. It was your choice to go with him.'

Vicki closed her eyes and tried to make sense of the anger she was feeling. She knew, to some degree, she had always blamed Charlie because he had never liked Nate, not from day one, and had taken every opportunity to belittle him or criticise him. But she also knew everything Jason and Billy had said was true.

And then she remembered Lydia explaining in no uncertain terms that Nate was the reason Jack was staying in care, and she realised how misplaced her anger was. It all felt very real and very raw, but she knew she had to reset her thinking and put the blame where it really belonged. 'Sorry,' she whispered and opened her eyes. 'Sorry, both of you.'

Billy immediately put an arm around her and kissed her on the forehead. Jason leaned forward and squeezed her hand.

'When you tell Charlie… about me and Nate,' she said to Jason, 'please make sure I'm not there. I really don't want to see him punch the air.' And then she chuckled.

Jason shook his head. 'First and foremost, he'll want to know if you are OK,' he said, knowing Charlie was far more likely to jump up and down cheering than punch the air.

67

'You can't help loving someone,' Billy said. 'And you did love Nate. He just couldn't love you back, not in the same way at least.'

Vicki rested her head on Billy's shoulder and closed her eyes. She remembered the miserable, tiring months after she left The Lodge and the sacrifices she had made in order to be housed, sacrifices that Nate had declined to make. To prove she and Jack were homeless, she had moved them both into a bedsit, a single room in a dark little four-bedroom terrace house a few roads back from the seafront. The landlady was strict and would not let them stay in the house between nine and five, so every day after breakfast, regardless of the weather, Vicki would have to leave her room and walk around Southend with Jack in a pushchair until they could return to the house at teatime. And that had been her life for six months, even at weekends.

But Nate had suffered no such ignominies because he knew only Vicki and Jack needed to be homeless for them to be housed. It wasn't necessary for him to go through it with them, so he moved back in with his parents. While Vicki and Jack were walking the streets, Nate was sleeping-in or lounging around on his parent's settee, drinking their coffee and watching daytime TV. Yet the moment Vicki was given the keys to her flat, Nate moved in and acted like the place was his. And Vicki had let him.

'I've been such an idiot,' she said. 'All these years, an absolute idiot.' Vicki suddenly felt calm and enjoyed that moment, surrounded by love, her brother cuddling her and her brother-in-law to be holding her hand. 'Sorry I was so cross,' she said. 'I am just angry at myself. And blaming Charlie's just become second nature for me.'

It ran deep, though, her feelings of blame towards her older brother. And even though, in those calm moments when common sense briefly prevailed, and she could see he was not responsible for what had happened to her, to Jack, she still could not rid herself of an anger, a spitefulness, towards him, and a grinding sense that he should take at least some portion of the blame.

CHAPTER 14

Just before she went to bed, Vicki recalled Billy asking for her help. Apart from the intriguing nature of his request, Vicki needed something to take her mind off her own problems. She made two mugs of hot chocolate, turned off all the downstairs lights, walked up to his bedroom and called his name gently through the closed door.

'Come in,' he said.

Vicki used her elbow to press down on the handle. Billy's bedroom, as always, was immaculately clean and tidy. The bed was neatly made, there were no stinking stray socks on the floor, and the room smelt of vanilla from a candle he had burning on the mantle above a small metal ornamental fireplace. Billy was in his pyjamas, with slippers and a cotton dressing gown. He was sitting at his desk in front of his home PC, a matching black set of keyboard, monitor, tower, mouse and webcam. The screen was on, and he appeared to be reviewing a Word document.

'Hot chocolate,' Vicki said, 'made from steamed full-fat milk.'

'Lovely,' Billy said.

Vicki closed the door behind her with her foot, handed him his drink, and perched on the edge of his bed with her mug gently held between both hands. 'So,' she said, with some trepidation, 'what was this issue you wanted to talk to me about?'

It was clear from Billy's face that he had momentarily forgotten their earlier conversation. But then his expression changed, and he uttered the words, 'Oh… yes… that.' And his tone was difficult to judge. Perhaps, Vicki pondered, it was embarrassment or possibly dread.

'Come on,' she said lightly, trying to keep her kid brother from crawling back into his shell and keeping his story a secret. 'It can't be that bad. What have you done this time? Or should I ask, *who* have you done this time?'

Billy shook his head, 'No, no. Nothing like that. I haven't done anything wrong.' He opened his desk drawer and took out a coaster, which he placed on the desk for his mug. From the same drawer, he retrieved a few sheets of paper which appeared to have some emails printed on them.

'I've been put in touch with a casting agent. For my acting,' he said.

Vicki raised her brow, 'Oh! So, you are really going to try and go professional. Good for you.'

Billy looked at the sheets of paper he was holding in his hand and then back to Vicki. 'She specialises in independent movies. You know, art house stuff. She says it's where a lot of actors get their big break. The films get seen at places like Cannes. They don't make much money, but they get seen by the right people, critics, and producers looking for a rising star. It's a really great stepping stone.'

Vicki just nodded. She knew next to nothing about the film industry, and so was taking everything her brother was saying at face value, 'OK. Well, it sounds exciting. So, what's the problem?'

But Billy remained hesitant, and Vicki could tell he was getting increasingly embarrassed. 'She's based in LA. In America,' he said, 'and so we've been talking by email, and she's sent me sections from some scripts that she wants me to read through on camera.'

Vicki assumed he wanted her to read the emails and was puzzled as to why he still had not handed them over. She could only assume that the contents of those emails were troubling her brother. And so, rather than forcing him to say anymore, she leaned down, placed her mug on the carpet, and held out her hand. After a moment, Billy handed her the emails, and she read the first.

Billy

I am excited to be representing you. Thank you for sending me your head shots. For the producers here in the US, I will be referring to you by your proper name, William Fletcher. This will go down better with the Americans.

I am currently working with a number of producers who will be shooting in the UK later in the year.

The scripts are challenging for both the actor and the audience, as you will see from the sections I have sent you. The producers are happy to see pre-recorded readings, rather than live, which is becoming the

70

norm in the industry. If you do not have any digital recording equipment, then your webcam will do.

Film the sections, email them to me, and I will edit them together into a showreel for you. The showreel is what I then use to generate interest in you. There is no charge for any of this.

Where the scenes call for nudity, you will need to be seen fully nude. There is one scene which includes masturbation. Again, you will need to be seen masturbating on camera, not acting it.

Please remember these are producers who need to trust that their actors are willing to be challenged and pushed to the extreme. I urge you as strongly as I can to step out of your comfort zone, and film these scenes explicitly, exactly as they are written. If you do this, I guarantee you will be called for at least two formal, face to face shortlist auditions here in LA, but only if you give the producers the courage, the vulnerability and the honesty they are looking for.

I look forward to working with you. Caroline.

Vicki skim-read the scripts, five short scenes with plenty of stage direction but little by way of dialogue. Each involved a single male character, starting naked and getting dressed, or fully clothed and getting undressed, and one scene which involved a male character masturbating whilst staring at the camera, as though;

'looking directly into the eyes of a lover'

She placed the emails onto the bed next to her, picked up her mug and looked at Billy with a concerned frown. 'You haven't filmed any of this yet, have you?'

'No, no,' Billy said and shook his head. 'I have been trying to pluck up the courage, but I just keep feeling… you know… just really—'

'Embarrassed.'

'Well, yes. But also, I just don't know what my motivation is in any of these scripts. The one where the guy is getting undressed and ready for bed. What's he been doing all day? Is he tired, upset, happy to be home? How can I act it when the script doesn't give me any context?'

Vicki shook her head and released a sigh that had a hint of a laugh to it, as it appeared her younger brother was feeling troubled by the wrong issue. 'Billy, who is this woman? How did she find you?'

71

'Oh, one of the managers at the supermarket. He's been to quite a few of my shows. He's always been really supportive. Great bloke, actually. His nephew is an actor, too, and Caroline is his agent. Apparently, she got his nephew some great roles.'

As Billy spoke, everything about the story began to fall apart in Vicki's head. It all sounded phoney, and quickly Vicki became certain 'Caroline' did not exist, that there was no 'nephew' and no producers in LA desperate to see 'honest and vulnerable' showreels of her brother wanking.

'Billy, I need you to promise me that you won't do any of this. Is that understood? I need you to promise me.'

'But she's emailed me a few times over the past week. She keeps telling me the casting window for these parts is closing.'

'OK, OK,' Vicki tried to sound reasonable, 'can you give me 24 hours? Just until this time tomorrow. Can you promise me that?' She pointed at him, 'No wanking on your webcam tonight,' she said strictly.

Billy chuckled awkwardly and agreed. Then blushed.

'And, just out of interest,' Vicki said, 'What's the name of the manager who's helping you? Is it someone I would know?'

72

CHAPTER 15

It was 10pm, and Charlie was standing in his kitchen wearing his pyjamas, slippers, and dressing gown. He was waiting for the kettle to boil so he could make two cups of tea and take them back to bed with him. He was exhausted after another 12-hour day sorting out a whole range of issues at one of the properties he and Jason were renovating. He had bathed, eaten dinner, had a couple of glasses of wine, and was now relaxed and ready for bed.

The kitchen was gently lit by hidden LED lights positioned under the newly fitted wall cupboards. Everything in the kitchen was new: the cabinets and work surface, the appliances, the shiny new wooden floor, and the little breakfast table by the back door. After years of flipping houses and then selling them, mostly for small profits, he and Jason had flipped a property and decided to move in.

Over the previous six years, Charlie and Jason had bought, renovated, and sold twenty houses in all and were currently renovating two more. But that house was different. It was his home, his very own home. And as he looked around his new kitchen, Charlie felt a sense of great pride.

It was nothing fancy, certainly nothing like The Lodge. A simple three-bedroom mid-terrace in the town centre, a minute's walk from the high street, that they'd bought at auction. It had required a full renovation, including the wiring and the plumbing, new windows and exterior doors, a new kitchen and bathroom, new flooring throughout and every wall and ceiling had needed to be re-plastered.

The small garden had been piled high with rubbish, and so Charlie and Jason had to arrange several skips to clear it, and the front of the house had received a pleasant facelift, too. Charlie had been particularly pleased with the new front door, which he had painted a deep green, an easy way to recognise his house if he and Jason were ever stumbling home late at night, a little worse for wear.

The neighbours had been thrilled to see a long-standing eyesore finally given some love and attention. Indeed, the response from the

73

neighbours had been one of the main reasons Charlie and Jason had decided this would be the first house they would keep, as a home. They wanted to be part of a friendly community where people said hello to each other in the street and would occasionally stop for a chat.

The kettle boiled, and Charlie quickly made two cups of strong tea. He switched off the kitchen light and walked carefully up the stairs, enjoying the smell of 'new carpet' as he did. Their room was painted a deep red, lit by the lamps on either side of the bed. It was quiet and cosy, a perfect sanctuary after a tiring day. Jason was sat up, reading through several spreadsheets, so Charlie walked around his side of the bed, placed his mug of tea onto a gold coaster neatly positioned next to the lamp, and kissed him on the lips.

'Thank you,' Jason said.

Charlie climbed under the covers on his side and resumed his review of properties that were for sale or up for auction. After a few moments of thoughtful silence, Jason rested his spreadsheets on his lap. He sighed loudly and then turned to Charlie and groaned. 'God, I'm bored.'

Charlie rolled his eyes, smiled, and put down the papers he was reading, 'I'm not surprised. You've had your nose buried in those spreadsheets since I got home. I was bored just watching you.'

'No, it's not that. I'm bored with what we are doing. We've been doing the same thing over and over again. We buy a property. We do it up. We sell it. We buy a property. We do it up. We sell it.'

'Well, that is what property developers do, sweetheart. And we make a reasonably good living out of it.'

Jason frowned, and Charlie realised his partner wanted a serious conversation, not some glib response that was an obvious attempt to quickly draw a line under the topic.

In truth, Charlie knew exactly how Jason felt. Their business model was quite specific, which meant their work was repetitive. They renovated mostly dilapidated buildings and returned them to use as family homes. They then sold them with a small profit margin to enable young families a chance to get on the housing ladder. That was one aspect of their work which gave them both great satisfaction: the knowledge they had helped couples and families in an environment where property prices were rising so quickly.

They had also gained a small amount of fame in the local area. They had been interviewed on the BBC Essex breakfast show and had a two-page spread dedicated to them in the Southend Echo. 'Gay couple flips houses to help Southend families', the headline had stated. It had also become routine for local residents to send them unsolicited emails asking, sometimes pleading, for them to renovate an empty, run-down house that was ruining the look of a local neighbourhood.

Charlie and Jason's commitment to providing affordable housing meant they had not made much by way of profit. They both knew they could have easily sold those houses at much higher prices and potentially doubled their income. But they had stuck to their original philanthropic ideals and still been able to eke out a comfortable standard of living, which meant their new home had come with a relatively small mortgage.

Regardless of the pros and cons of their business model, Charlie knew the main reason he had never considered a change was the dread that it would lead him back into full-time employment, the dreary routine of Monday to Friday, nine to five, and having to report to a boss again. As exhausting and repetitive as house flipping had become, he still thought it far preferable to the alternative.

But he knew he should not dismiss the conversation or persuade Jason he'd simply had a bad day or that they were both going through a bit of a funk. He knew Jason would only have raised the issue if it had become a genuine burden to him. So, he decided to open the conversation up, 'OK, so, what would we do instead? What *could* we do? And please keep in mind that my skill set is very narrow.'

Jason flashed his eyebrows at Charlie, which was usually a sign that he was in the mood for something romantic. But, on that occasion, he simply dropped the spreadsheets onto the floor, opened a drawer on his bedside table, and pulled out a small pile of paper. Charlie glanced at the top sheet, and at first sight, it appeared to be the details of a property for sale. But there was something odd about the main image; the sky above the property seemed a little too blue, and the greenery outside seemed a little too colourful.

'What's that?' he asked.

Slowly, Jason handed the documents to Charlie, 'I don't want you to just say no; I know what you can be like. You like to stick with things as they are. But I want you to just think about this. I don't even want you to tell me what you think tonight. Mull it over.'

Intrigued, Charlie took the papers and began to look through them. Immediately, he realised where Jason was going with his idea. None of the properties were in Southend. They weren't even in the UK. Instead, they were houses and apartments in Torremolinos, Fuengirola, Benalmádena and a few on Gran Canaria. Mostly two or three-bed, many in complexes with shared facilities like swimming pools or access to a golf course.

'You want to start flipping properties in Spain?' Charlie looked at Jason quizzically.

But Jason shook his head. 'No, not flip. Something different entirely. I want us to buy properties that only need a little amount of work, and then we rent them out. Long-term or holiday lets. I'm not sure which yet. I am still running the numbers. But I think we can make a good income, at least match what we are currently making each year. And, you know... we'd be flying off to Spain pretty regularly.'

It all sounded terribly risky, Charlie thought. But he knew Jason was extremely skilled with money and would not be recommending something that posed any serious threat to their finances. And even if they only did it for a couple of years, just to test the waters, it might make a nice change from what they were currently doing. But there was still that nagging at the back of his head, a feeling that it would be safer to just stay with what they knew.

'Fine. I'll mull it over,' he said after some thought. 'I suppose if the worst happens, we will just have to rent out this place and move in at The Lodge for a while.' He handed the papers back to Jason, who returned them to his bedside table and closed the drawer.

Jason picked up his spreadsheets and, focusing his gaze on the papers rather than Charlie, said, 'We could, although it's getting a little crowded there now that Vicki has moved back.' Immediately, he felt

76

Charlie shift slightly next to him, and he realised it was not a piece of news he should have revealed so casually.

'What?' Charlie snapped.

Jason put the spreadsheets down and turned to look at Charlie. 'Do not overreact,' he said. 'Your sister has moved back into the Fletcher family home. As she has every right to do.'

'We made it very clear that lazy, scrounging criminal she's attached herself to was never to set foot in that house again.'

'And he isn't. Vicki left him. She has given up the flat and moved back to The Lodge. On her own.'

'Oh.' Charlie felt as though the rug had been pulled from under his moment of self-righteous anger. 'Oh, well, that's... that's...'

'That's very sad, isn't it? For your sister,' Jason said, providing his angry partner with some guidance as to how he should actually be reacting to the news. 'Because, like it or not, she was in love with Nate. And it has taken every ounce of strength for her to finally walk away from him. And I hope you realise that and remember that the next time you see her.'

Charlie grimaced and tried to think of a reason he could disagree with Jason. The mere mention of Nate always made his blood boil. And even though Charlie had quickly realised he had no reason to be cross, the misunderstanding had left him with some residual rage that was difficult to diffuse. But he knew Jason was right. Vicki would be devastated, and as frustrated as he often found himself with the way his sister led her life, he still only wanted the best for her. 'Yes,' he said a little petulantly. 'I don't know why you're getting so uppity about it though.'

'Because,' Jason said, 'I don't have brothers or sisters, and I haven't spoken to my parents in years. I just have you and your family. I've known Vicki since she was a little girl, and Billy was just a baby. They're a big part of my life, and I care about them very much. And this is the perfect opportunity for you to make up with your sister.'

Feeling suitably chastised and a little humbled, Charlie gently nudged Jason with his elbow. 'It must be so hard being completely right all the time,' he said, smiling.

'With great power comes great responsibility. But also, and this should be good news for you. Your nephew Jack is going to be a page boy. Vicki's agreed it with social services.'

'Oh, how lovely!' Charlie suddenly felt uplifted and genuinely happy.

'He's allowed at the ceremony and the photographs, but his foster carers are taking him home before the party.'

'Oh, OK.' Charlie felt deflated. 'I guess that's still good.'

'Oh,' Jason continued hesitantly, 'this is something else I wanted to talk to you about. Jack's foster carers are going to drop him off and then just sit in their car for the whole ceremony in the car park. How might you feel about asking Vicki to invite them?'

'Why would we do that?'

'They are raising our nephew,' Jason replied, his voice a little tense. 'In a way, they are part of our family. They will always be a big part of Jack's life. I just think it would be a nice memory for him that his gay uncles welcomed his two foster mums to their wedding ceremony. It would join up both parts of Jack's life. And you know, with some of the people who declined to come, for whatever reason, I think it would be nice to have another same-sex couple there.'

Charlie could see the logic behind Jason's argument. They had both been disappointed, in truth, very hurt, that a few of their school friends had declined invitations to their civil partnership because of their religious beliefs. They had wished Charlie and Jason well but could not overcome the idea that a civil partnership was the same as a marriage and, in their view, a marriage could only be between one man and one woman.

And as heart-breaking as it had been for the whole family that Jack had been taken into foster care, Charlie had found some consolation in knowing his nephew was being raised in an inclusive environment. 'Yes,' he said. 'Absolutely. Ask Vicki to invite them. I think that sounds like a lovely idea.'

CHAPTER 16

As Vicki stepped through the entrance to the busy supermarket, she had an odd sense of being home. She had not been inside the store for years, since the day she had left on maternity leave. Her intention had always been to return to work someday, but that day had never come. She had eventually handed in her notice by mail and quietly left her job without the chance to say goodbye to her colleagues.

After that, she had never felt able to return, even to do her shopping, for fear of bumping into someone she used to work with and being asked how she was doing or, even worse, how Jack was doing. But on that day, her concern about Billy was too great, and she needed to speak to someone high up.

After what seemed like a lifetime away, she could see little had changed. It still looked the same, sounded the same, and offered the same overwhelming smell of clean floors and fresh fruit and veg. Vicki just hoped there would be a least one former colleague who could point her in the direction of the new store manager.

'Vicki?'

She turned at the sound of a familiar voice and found herself face to face with a young man in a suit with bright red hair and a pale complexion. She recognised him immediately but simply could not remember his name. She decided to bluff it.

'Oh, my goodness, hello,' she said and moved in for an embrace, quickly scanning his name badge as she did: *Rupert*. Yes, of course, she thought. Rupert. She had trained him on the till, she recalled, a nice young man. They had chatted quite a few times.

'Well, Rupert, you've done well for yourself,' she said and stepped back to look at him.

'I'm only acting up,' he said, 'but it's a good experience. Anyway, how are you? You look really good.'

With those words, Vicki recalled that during their time working together, Rupert had developed something of a crush on her and had appeared to be a little bit devastated when she had told him she was

79

leaving to have a baby. 'Thank you,' she said. 'I finally got rid of the baby weight, but it took a few years.'

She could tell he was immediately falling into old habits as he stared at her with a vacant, happy expression, as though all his old feelings were rushing back. But Vicki didn't have time to break his heart all over again, so she quickly moved the conversation on.

'Who's the store manager these days? I really need to have a quick chat with them.'

'Oh, he's not here today. Training, or area conference, or something'

Vicki groaned and looked to her feet, 'Oh, no. I really needed to see him.'

After a moment, Rupert said, 'But do you remember Mandy? Our old HR manager? She's the regional HR director now. And she's in today looking over our staff training records. She always liked you. I know she'd love to see you.'

Vicki lifted her head and smiled, 'Oh, yes, that would be great.' Vicki remembered Mandy very well, indeed. She had been a tough boss, and quite intimidating for many young members of staff at the store. But Vicki had taken an instant liking to her 'firm but fair' management style and had been particularly impressed with Mandy's unwavering commitment to the company's equality and diversity programme.

Vicki had also recognised that, amongst a sea of young white male managers, Mandy – a middle-aged black woman – had probably had to work twice as hard as her peers to get where she was. And hard work was certainly an attribute Vicki had always respected in a colleague. Mandy had also been the first person to notice Vicki's potential and had found the money to send Vicki on numerous development programmes that were rarely offered to other members of staff.

But even though Vicki had a clear memory of Mandy, she did not assume Mandy would remember her. Surely, she thought, from Mandy's point of view, Vicki had been one of hundreds, if not thousands, of staff Mandy had dealt with over the years. Before she could worry any further, Rupert had hurried her through a door leading to the staff-only staircase, which took them to the first floor.

At the top of the stairs was a viewing gallery, with small round windows overlooking the entrance and the nearby fresh produce area. Vicki stopped for a moment, 'God, this takes me back.' Rupert joined her and together they looked down at the customers and staff, briskly going about their business, the noise from the shop floor almost eliminated by the thick glass.

Vicki was about to take advantage of the moment to casually ask about the manager who had been assisting Billy with his search for an agent, but before she could ask her question, a man's voice interrupted her.

'Is everything alright, Rupert?'

Vicki looked to where the voice had come from. It was another man in a suit, but this time older, in his early forties, she guessed, overweight and balding with spectacles and a goatee beard.

'Oh, hello, Mr Croker,' Rupert replied. 'Yes, all is good. This is Vicki Fletcher, and she used to work here. I was just taking her to see Mandy.'

Croker was the surname Billy had given her, but Vicki needed to be sure this was the same man who was trying to coerce her brother into emailing sex tapes of himself. 'Oh,' she said, a huge fake smile on her face. 'Are you *Neil* Croker?' she asked and stepped towards him.

He returned her smile, although his was genuine. 'Yes, that's me. Guilty as charged.'

Vicki held out her hand, and he gently shook it. 'Oh, how lovely to meet you. Billy Fletcher's my brother,' she said, and she noticed his smile lessen ever so slightly; he subtly withdrew his hand. 'He speaks ever so highly of you, Mr Croker, he really does,' she added quickly, feeling a need to reassure him so her scheme would not immediately unravel. 'Is he doing OK, though?'

Mr Croker nodded. 'Oh, yes, Billy. Of course. Tall lad? Yes, yes. He's doing well. Reliable, honest. The customers like him.'

The moment he pretended that he only had a vague recollection of Billy, Vicki knew she had been right about Neil Croker. She smiled at him again and said, 'Well, again, thank you for all you are doing.'

'Absolutely my pleasure,' Mr Croker replied, then he turned and headed down the stairs to the shop floor.

Rupert and Vicki continued through several short corridors until they reached the management suite, which, in Vicki's day, had often been referred to as 'the purple palace' by staff: four offices, all fitted out with purple carpets and colour-matched furniture.

Before she could catch her breath, Rupert escorted her into one of the offices, and she was face-to-face with Mandy once more. Mandy looked up from her desk, almost hidden behind a tall pile of folders, and it only took a moment before she recognised Vicki and a huge smile crossed her face.

'Vicki Fletcher, after all these years,' she said and stood up to embrace her. 'I hope you are here to ask for a job,' she said, stepping back to get a good look at Vicki. 'Well, motherhood obviously suits you, my dear. You are positively glowing.'

'Thank you, Mandy,' Vicki said brightly, all the while knowing that she was going to lie about Jack and spin all sorts of fanciful tales about her busy life as a mum. The truth would be too humiliating. She glanced back awkwardly at Rupert and said, 'I was hoping to have a private conversation with Mandy, Rupert. Would that be OK?'

'Yes, of course,' Rupert replied and looked to Mandy. 'Just call me when Vicki's ready to go, and I can show her out.'

But Mandy shook her head. 'Thank you, Rupert, but I can do that myself, now off you go,' she replied with an obviously dismissive tone. She saw him from the office and closed the door behind him. 'Oh, dear. Something tells me Rupert never did get over his little crush.'

Mandy smiled knowingly at Vicki, who suddenly recalled that Mandy had once spoken to her formally about Rupert. Vicki had always considered his crush to be a bit silly and harmless. But Mandy had spotted that Rupert had repeatedly requested shift changes and had eventually worked out that he had been trying to align his entire work pattern with Vicki's. She had spoken privately to Vicki to check if Rupert had been doing anything to make her feel uncomfortable. The two had agreed to keep an eye on things just in case Rupert needed to be reprimanded. Considering the reason Vicki was at the store that morning, that memory was a reassuring indicator that her concerns about Neil Croker would be handled seriously.

82

'Anyway, come and sit down,' Mandy said as she moved most of the files from her desk onto a nearby meeting table. She and Vicki sat down opposite each other. 'If you are looking at a return to work, I wouldn't want to put you back to the level you were at. I would look at something more senior for you. If that helps sweeten the pot?'

'I am very flattered, but I am actually here to talk about my younger brother. Billy.'

'Oh yes,' Mandy's eyes twinkled, 'our very own Casanova. He's certainly popular with some of the older ladies who work in the store. You know, he tried to chat me up once.'

Vicki's heart sank. 'Oh no,' she said. 'What did you say?'

Mandy laughed. 'I gave him five hours of mandatory training.'

Although her brother had clearly fallen foul of Mandy's quick, no-nonsense disposition, it was exactly that disposition she hoped Mandy would bring to the fore now to keep Billy safe. 'On this occasion, it's not the older *ladies* I am concerned about,' she said, and immediately, the atmosphere in the office changed as it became apparent to Mandy that Vicki's visit was far from light-hearted.

For the next few minutes, Vicki repeated the story Billy had told her the night before. She reached into her shoulder bag and produced the emails Billy had given her. Mandy read them closely, every now and again muttering under her breath. 'Oh, dearie me,' or 'Oh, no, no, no.'

'Neil Croker?' Mandy asked as she placed the emails flatly onto her desk.

'Yes. I just met him, actually, on the way in.'

Mandy knitted her fingers together and stared upwards, thinking. 'There is a chance that Neil is completely innocent. That he is genuinely just trying to help launch your brother's acting career and has no idea what this agent is asking Billy to do. But,' she added, and then looked directly at Vicki, 'this does not feel right. I have a nagging sensation that you might be correct, my dear.'

'Is there anything you can do? Talk to Neil perhaps?'

'Oh, no, no, no. He would just deny it. And then I'd have to walk away from the store later today knowing I was leaving your brother and other staff at risk from a… what… a sexual predator. I cannot have that.

83

No, Vicki, if this is true, then we need to catch him red-handed. And I think I know exactly how we can do that.'

CHAPTER 17

Charlie had better things to do than chase around after his father. Jason was out of town, and Charlie was battling multiple deadlines to get a house ready for sale. And amidst all the chaos of a particularly challenging flip, their electrician had started ghosting him. But Charlie couldn't ignore a plea for help from Carol, and he didn't feel it fair to leave her alone to collect Peter from yet another local pub where he had drunk himself into a stupor in the middle of the day.

He knew why she always called him for help rather than Vicki or Billy. They would likely handle the situation with too much concern or empathy and inadvertently give Peter exactly the sort of attention he was seeking. Charlie knew, by comparison, he would be openly indifferent and matter of fact, robbing Peter of his self-indulgent drama.

Jason had the car, and so Charlie locked up the house and caught a taxi to The Bell pub, where he found Carol waiting for him. She stood outside on the busy intersection, obvious relief on her face when she saw him hurrying towards her in black overalls splattered with paint and covered in dust.

Out of sheer relief, Carol threw her arms around him and squeezed. 'I'm sorry to call you again,' she said. 'But I am so glad you are here.' She took a step back and gestured to the pub entrance. 'He's in there.'

'And how bad is he?'

'I think we might have to add this to the list of local pubs your father is barred from.'

'Oh great,' Charlie visibly slumped. 'I'm sorry that it's always you who gets the call. It's not right, Carol. He's not your responsibility.'

Carol looked thoroughly despondent. 'He's the father of my two kids,' she replied, exasperated. 'Tyler and Lizzie deserve better than to hear from some stupid schoolkid that their dad was banged up in prison for the night.'

Charlie had grown fond of Carol over the years. She had dutifully, perhaps even lovingly, fulfilled every promise she had made to Susan. She had raised Lizzie as her own, but also made sure Lizzie remained an important person in the lives of her older siblings. 'I'd best go in then,' he said.

Carol nodded, 'I'll bring my car around.'

Charlie had only been inside The Bell once when he was about seven or eight years old. His parents had taken him for a New Year's Eve party, and he had a vague memory of it being small and dark and crowded, with people smoking, laughing, and spilling drinks all around him. The building had been much smaller back then, just a bar and some tables and chairs. In the intervening years, it had been expanded to provide a large carvery restaurant at the rear. As he walked through the door, he realised there was not a single part of the pub that was as he remembered.

He could hear people talking at the back of the building, the restaurant clearly doing a busy lunchtime trade. But the bar area was mostly empty, apart from a slightly portly blonde man slumped over the bar, talking earnestly to one of the bar staff about something that seemed terribly important, at least to him. Charlie groaned as he realised it was Peter.

The woman behind the bar was undoubtedly attractive, slender with a pretty face, small features, and shoulder length red hair. She was exactly the sort of person Charlie knew his dad would feel a need to impress. But the woman, Charlie judged, was probably in her early fifties and was staring at his rambling, mostly incoherent father with a tired expression that suggested too many years of dealing with drunkards.

He approached his father briskly and slapped him gently on the shoulder. 'Dad,' he said assertively, 'Carol's outside. She's going to give you a lift back to The Lodge.'

Without looking to see who was speaking to him, Peter raised a finger in the air. 'Attitude!' he said loudly, 'Attitude.'

'Oh, be quiet, you old fool,' Charlie replied, immediately irritated. He looked at the woman behind the bar. 'Sorry, has he been a real pain?'

'Oh, don't worry about it, darling,' she said, her voice smooth and deep. She reached over and squeezed Charlie's arm, an act he found somewhat overfamiliar. 'I've had to deal with much worse. But I can't serve him when he's like this. And he was happy to give us a contact number, for someone to call. So, no harm done.'

86

'Well, I am sorry,' he replied. 'I'll just get him home.'

The door to the pub swung open, and Carol appeared, gesturing to Charlie that her car was just outside.

'I feel like I know your father very well,' the woman continued, her tone unexpectedly cheerful. 'He said he lives in one of those big houses on the seafront, overlooking the estuary. And that his son is a famous property developer. Are you him? He said you'd been in the local papers.'

Charlie rolled his eyes. Of course, he thought, that's exactly the sort of thing his dad would tell a woman he was trying to impress. He would brag about his big house overlooking the sea. He probably even told her its market value. And then he would brag about a son who had a fancy-sounding job without admitting that the same son had almost nothing to do with him. With that, Charlie pushed Peter's shoulder more forcibly. 'Dad, get up,' he said, his patience quickly running out. 'I am taking you home.'

With that, Peter turned and looked at his son and seemed to recognise him, and then he smiled. 'This is him, Angel,' he said and looked at the woman behind the bar. 'This is my son. I told you. The queer one who does up houses.'

'Oh, Dad, I swear to god....' Charlie muttered under his breath, and then he looked to the woman behind the bar. 'Sorry about calling you angel. He gets a little over-familiar when he's had a few.'

'Oh no, that's my name, darling,' the woman replied and pointed to her name badge.

'Oh,' Charlie said. 'That's... unusual.'

'Well, I was christened Abigail, but I'm always doing kind things for other people. Makes my day if I can do nice things for other people. It gives me real pleasure. And after a while, other people just started calling me Angel, so I stuck with it.'

Charlie realised that in a very short space of time, he had grown to dislike Angel very much.

'Angel,' Peter said, 'like she fell from heaven.' He raised his hands as though praying to God.

Charlie's patience was at an end. He leaned forward and whispered angrily into his father's ear. 'You are absolutely shaming yourself,' he said. 'What do you think mum would say if she could see you like this. Drunk, again, in another pub, making a scene. She would be ashamed of you.'

Peter turned his head and stared Charlie in the face as though suddenly sober and aware. 'Oh, son, I could tell you a few things about your sainted mother,' he said, his voice filled with contempt. His eyes rolled, and then he focussed on the figure over Charlie's shoulder. Carol. And he grimaced at her. 'Couldn't I, Carol? I could tell Charlie a few home truths about Saint Susan.'

Carol, angry, shook her head. 'Shut your fucking mouth, Peter.'

But Peter was clearly gleaning some enjoyment from the moment. He grasped Charlie's shoulder, levered himself up, and began to speak. Even though he was speaking directly to his son, he maintained his eye contact with Carol as though daring her to intervene. 'So, let me tell you, Charlie, about one night at The Lodge. When I arrived home after working away in Norwich.'

In a flash, Carol shot forward, her arm outstretched, screaming. She brought her hand crashing down against Peter's face, and a loud slap echoed around the empty bar. Peter, liquid squirting from his mouth, flew from the bar stool, falling backwards, his feet above his head. He landed on the sticky, carpeted floor with a loud thud. And there he stayed.

'Oy, that's it. All of you out,' Angel shouted. 'Out now, or I'm calling the police.'

Charlie, shocked by Carol's actions, bent down and heaved his father back to his feet. With Peter's arm wrapped around his shoulders, Charlie led him from the pub.

He and Carol managed to get Peter home. They lay him out on the couch in the sitting room, with a washing-up basin on the floor next to him, in case he was sick. And then they retreated to the kitchen. Charlie made them both a coffee, and they sat together at the breakfast bar.

There was an awkwardness between them, Carol was embarrassed by her actions, and Charlie was perplexed by them. But before he could ask Carol if she could explain what had just happened, she spoke.

'I'm sorry, Charlie. I don't care how drunk your dad is, but he is not going to speak badly of your mother. Whatever crap he was coming up with, he will never speak badly of Susan in front of me.'

Charlie could tell she was still very upset, more upset than he had seen her in a long time. 'That's OK,' he replied, and then he attempted to reduce the tension with some humour. 'I've wanted to give him a good slap on more than one occasion. Let's be honest, who hasn't?'

Carol sipped her coffee and seemed genuinely regretful for what had happened. 'I know he's always been a drinker, but he's really spiralling out of control,' she said. 'I think, when your mum was alive, she helped him keep a lid on it. But now, he has too much freedom. Your mum's gone. If he wants to drink himself to death, there's no one to stop him.'

Most of Charlie's childhood memories of his father involved the stink of beer or whiskey. He had not known, as a kid, what those smells were or what they meant. But as a grown man, so many of his childhood memories had taken on a completely different context. And he wondered if, perhaps, his father's drinking had been one of the reasons Susan had turned a blind eye to whatever sort of relationship had developed between Peter and Carol, that she had, on some level, felt it gave her a break from her efforts to manage Peter's drinking.

'Mum used to find empty bottles,' he said. 'In the guttering above the back door. Mostly whiskey, sometimes cheap brandy. But mostly whiskey. I think he had a little routine. He would hide the empties up there, and when mum was out of the house, he would put them into a carrier bag and drive to the shops on the pretext of getting groceries, where he'd pile all the empties into the bottle bank in the car park at the supermarket.

'But mum cottoned on, at some point, and started to dispose of the bottles for him. She didn't say anything. But you could tell how anxious he would get when he would hang around the back door, and he could see the gutters were clear when he knew there should be empty bottles there.'

Carol placed her mug on the breakfast bar and groaned, 'There was one night he was supposed to be having dinner with Tyler and Lizzie. I'd cooked a lasagne or something, one of Susan's recipes. I can't remember which. But it was something I knew he liked. He was sitting there in my lounge at six o'clock on a Tuesday evening. And he had a dozen cans of lager on the floor next to him, his drinks for the night. I just wanted one dinner with Peter and the kids, where he was in the room, not slurring his words or telling everyone how much he loved them.

'So, I asked him, said to him, that if he loved the kids at all, he would have one night, one single night, where he wouldn't drink. And you know what he said? He said he loved the drink more. He looked me in the eyes and told me that alcohol was more important. If he had to make a choice, he would always choose the drink.'

It was a story Charlie had not heard before. He couldn't pretend to be surprised, but he still felt terribly sad for Carol. Because in the middle of the strange life she had carved out for herself, he knew how badly she wanted Peter to be a good father to her children. 'I'm sorry,' he said. 'You deserve better.'

Affectionately, Carol squeezed his arm. 'Oh, it's not about me, Charlie. It's about you kids. You all deserve better than this.'

In the five years since Susan had died, Charlie had never found the right moment to have a conversation with Carol about her relationship with his father, and there was still so much that did not make sense. Tyler had shared with him many happy stories of life at Carol's house when he was a kid. He'd painted a colourful picture of warmth, laughter, and fun. But what Charlie had found most unexpected was that Peter had hardly featured in those stories. His visits to see Tyler had been infrequent and the only times he had stayed over was when he'd passed out on Carol's couch.

But there was another detail Tyler had shared about his childhood, something Charlie knew might be considered small, inconsequential, but a detail that had stuck in his head, for some reason. Tyler had always spoken with great fondness of his Auntie Susan and how often she had visited for meals, movies, or games nights. And as he heard Carol describe Peter's failure to show up for Tyler, he wondered if his mother had tried to compensate, to be there for Tyler in a way she knew her husband never would.

And then Charlie could feel it again, that familiar niggling at the back of his mind, a need to know more, to understand exactly how Carol's relationship with Peter had begun, how his mother had found out, and how the three of them had made the whole complex situation work for so many years. But it didn't feel like it was the right time. For Charlie, for some reason, it never felt the right time. And so he just quietly sipped his coffee and decided to leave his questions for another day.

CHAPTER 18

Vicki and Mandy sat together in a small, dark office, a rarely used part of the building directly beneath the purple palace. It was where the IT team had set up Mandy's surveillance area as part of her plan to discover whether one of the store managers was trying to take advantage of a junior employee.

The entire operation had been quickly arranged by Mandy, an urgent and highly confidential response to what she considered to be a serious staff safety issue and Vicki felt she had certainly pulled out all the stops.

Neil Croker's office had been fitted with a hidden camera, placed behind his desk with a clear view of his computer screen. The camera fed directly to the computer monitor in front of Mandy and Vicki. Vicki knew she should not be in the room, but Mandy had agreed that her presence was something she would simply omit to mention if she needed to file a report.

The video feed showed an empty office, the only thing of note was Neil's screensaver, a rotating montage of photographs of his wife and two young children, an uncomfortable reminder for both Vicki and Mandy of how much was at stake. If they were wrong, then all was well and good in the world. But if they were right, Neil's career was over, and Mandy would likely have to hand information over to the police should Billy wish to press charges. And that would likely rob two children of their father for several months if not years.

Much of the success of the operation was dependent on Billy and whether he was able to give a believable performance. Vicki had told him what to do; he would have to seek out Neil in the store, thank him again for putting him in touch with Caroline, and claim that he had finally sent her the videos.

Mandy suspected that if Neil was, indeed, a sexual predator, he would not wait until he got home that night to view Billy's videos. He wouldn't be able to help himself. He would have an impossible urge to view them straight away, even if that meant taking a risk by viewing them on his work computer.

92

As they sat and watched the empty office on the video screen, Vicki's mobile phone vibrated in her hand. She lifted it up and flipped it open. On the small screen, there was an SMS message from Billy which simply stated: 'I just told him'.

'Billy?' Mandy asked.

'Yes, he's done his bit,' Vicki replied. 'I guess we just have to sit and wait to see-'

Before she could finish her sentence, there was a sound from the computer. They both looked at the screen and saw that Neil had entered his office. His movement was odd. He seemed furtive, perhaps even slightly panicked. He spent a moment peering through a crack in the door to see if anyone was in the lobby outside, and then he quietly closed the door and locked it.

He hurried over to his computer and sat down, clearly excited, his breathing so heavy it was clearly audible. He typed in his password and then immediately opened his browser window. He appeared to click on a bookmark on the main browser bar, which took him to the login page for an email account.

'Oh,' Vicki said, 'that's Hotmail. Caroline uses Hotmail for her emails.'

Mandy raised her hand, an indication they both needed to be silent. She leaned closer to the screen so she could hear clearly what happened next. And after a few moments, Billy's clear, deep voice filled the air.

'Hello, Caroline. This is William Fletcher. I'm afraid my webcam isn't working at the moment. Until I get it fixed, I thought I would send you an audio file of me reading some classics, which I hope will do for now. I thought I would begin with Tom Wingfield from The Glass Menagerie.'

'Oh, what?' Neil said loudly, angrily. He closed down the audio file, 'Absolute bloody waste of my time. What the hell are you playing at, Billy?'

Without speaking, Mandy stood and left the room. Alone in front of the monitor, Vicki watched as Neil logged out of his email account and closed the browser window. He stood and began to pace around the room, looking perplexed and frustrated. Vicki wondered what was going

93

on in his head. Why had he responded with anger toward Billy, she wondered; did Neil actually feel entitled to naked videos of her brother?

And then it was all over. There was a knock at the door. Neil quietly unlocked it, and Mandy entered the office, flanked by two of the store's uniformed security guards. Neil started saying something about not understanding how the door had become locked, his voice trembling, clearly terrified that he had been rumbled.

'Neil, I am suspending you with immediate effect,' she said, her voice calm but firm. 'You will be escorted from the premises, and you will not be allowed back. I have evidence that you have committed gross misconduct, and I will be submitting a formal report with the recommendation you be dismissed.'

Vicki noticed that Neil was gazing towards his computer and that he was unable to see the screen. She wondered if he was trying to remember if he had logged out of his fake email account, closed the browser window, or locked the screen.

'I have no idea what you are talking about,' he said, trying to sound strong, but his rebuttal came out high-pitched, the shock of being caught.

'You also need to know that Billy Fletcher is aware of your actions and may consider reporting you to the police,' Mandy continued. 'If that is the case, we will fully cooperate with any criminal investigation.'

With that, Neil dropped his head. His entire world had just collapsed on top of him as he realised just how much trouble he was in. 'I was just… I was just trying to help him…' he said quietly, hoping to find some way to lessen the impact of his behaviour.

But Mandy was having none of it. 'You need to leave, now,' she said and gestured towards the security guards. 'Keith and Jodie will see you out. You are not to speak to any staff on your way out of the building. You are not to make any attempts to contact any members of staff during the course of our investigation, and, in particular, you are not to contact Billy Fletcher. Is that clear?'

Without looking up, Neil grunted his assent as he was escorted from the room. Once they were gone, the door opened once more, and a smartly dressed young woman entered Neil's office. 'All done?' she asked.

'Yes, all done,' Mandy replied. 'Thank you so much for everything you did and for your discretion.'

The young woman nodded, 'No problem. The camera feed has been digitally recorded, so I can give you access to that file. And my colleagues and I will review Mr Croker's hard drive and internet history. I will give you a full report on that, too.'

The young woman left, leaving Mandy alone in the room. Forgetting Vicki could still see her, she perched on the corner of the desk and put her hands over her face as though she were about to cry. Vicki suddenly felt she was intruding on a private moment, so she switched off the computer screen.

She understood how conflicted Mandy was and knew what she was thinking, not of Neil and how he had just ruined his career and probably his entire life. Mandy was thinking of his family, his wife and kids and what this would mean for them, the financial impact, the emotional repercussions, the shame. Vicki wondered what Neil's wife would do, whether she would leave him or stand by his side regardless and tell everyone the accusations were a lie, a mistake, or a conspiracy against her husband.

Vicki knew what that was like to remain steadfastly loyal to a man whose actions did nothing but ruin the lives of his family. For the first time, she understood what everyone else must have seen when she had walked out of The Lodge with Nate, taking Jack with her. She could even begin to sympathise with Charlie, with how he must have felt, seeing his sister make such a devastating mistake, and how it must have all played out from his perspective, how grimly predictable it must have been for him.

But he had never said it to her, not once in all that time. He had never said 'I told you so', even in the middle of a fight, when she had so angrily blamed him. She could finally see that all he had ever shown was concern and that his 'interfering' had just been well-meant advice. If only she had been prepared to listen. Vicki began to collect her things, and as

95

she did, she promised herself that the next time she saw Charlie, she would make things right with him.

CHAPTER 19

'Shop boss fired for sex tape plot. Exclusive by Colin Merroney.'

His bedroom dimly lit by the low, morning sun, Billy slowly read through the article in the newspaper, laid out in front of him, the page illuminated by the lamp on his desk. He could feel his face burning with shame as he absorbed every salacious word. He had been warned the story was coming, but he was still completely bewildered at how the details of such an embarrassing episode in his life had made their way into the pages of a scandalous national tabloid newspaper.

The leak couldn't have come from the store because none of his colleagues knew what had happened. Mandy had made a few subtle enquiries to see if anyone else had been targeted by Neil Croker, but beyond that, everyone had been told he'd chosen to leave the company to pursue new career opportunities elsewhere. Vicki had suggested the story might have been sold to the paper by someone at head office, possibly someone who believed Neil should be publicly shamed for what he had done or, alternatively, someone who just wanted to make some quick cash. But Billy doubted he would ever know the truth.

Married dad-of-two demanded male worker perform on camera – naked!

The article was illustrated with a large picture of Neil, caught outside his house by a paparazzi photographer. He looked frightened, wide-eyed, his hand raised as though trying to shield his face from the camera. There was an image of Billy, too, a professional head and shoulders shot, lifted from the website of the local amateur dramatics group he belonged to. By comparison, a good picture, one that Billy had previously been quite pleased with. But now, set in an entirely different context, it just added to his humiliation. Not only would people know his name, but they would also know his face.

When the company's communications team had first contacted him to let him know they had received a press enquiry, they had agreed with his manager to give him paid leave to keep him safe, out of the way of any press who might turn up at the store. Mandy had also been in touch

97

to see if he wanted counselling and to offer support when he was ready to return to work. Within the company, at least, Billy felt he was being treated as the victim of a terrible incident.

But the newspaper story portrayed Billy in a different light; a fame-hungry dimwit, willing to do almost anything to get a big break. That was the part that upset Billy the most, the suggestion that, in some way, he had brought this on himself, that his desperate pursuit of an acting career had made him easy pickings for a predatory older man like Neil.

He heard his name spoken gently from the other side of his bedroom door. He called, 'Come in', and Jason entered, carrying a mug of tea and a plate with a bacon sandwich on it made with thick, sliced white bread.

'I'm heading back to work,' he said. 'But I thought I'd make you a bite to eat before I went.'

Billy quickly produced a coaster from his drawer, and Jason put the mug and plate onto the desk, and then he perched on the edge of the bed, ready for a chat.

'I'm beginning to think I shouldn't have brought that,' he said, gesturing to the paper. 'I'm worried you're going to sit and just obsess about it all morning.'

'I needed to see it,' Billy replied glumly. 'At least I know what they've said about me.'

Jason sighed, clearly unhappy that he had to leave Billy alone and get back to one of the houses he and Charlie were in the middle of renovating. But he'd made plans for the day and so relayed them to Billy. 'Charlie's dropping in this afternoon,' he said. 'And don't worry about dinner tonight because Vicki's getting a takeaway, and it sounds like Carol and Tyler will be joining you.'

Billy knew all those arrangements would have been made by Jason, diligently organising the entire family to ensure Billy would have plenty of company that day. And he was grateful for that because, left to his own devices, Billy knew Jason was right; he would most definitely just sit and obsess about the article, about the millions of people who must have seen it, and what they must all now think of him.

He was pleased to have started the day in Jason's company, a man who always managed to bring a little commonsense and sunshine to even the darkest of situations. Billy couldn't remember a time when Jason hadn't been a part of his life. When Charlie had first started bringing him home from school, Billy had been just a baby, and throughout all the years that followed, Jason had quietly become a comfortable part of their family, long before he and Charlie had become a couple. And during that time, Billy had grown deeply fond of him. For Billy, it was like having two older brothers rather than just one.

'I promise you, Billy, this will all be old news this time next week,' Jason said. 'Don't let it upset you.'

Billy folded the paper closed. 'I'm so embarrassed,' he said. 'I don't want to go outside. I don't want anyone to see me.'

Jason nodded. 'I understand how you must feel,' he said. 'But please remember, Billy, whatever that paper says, you did the right thing. You helped catch a bad guy. That's a good thing.'

Billy had spent the morning trying to convince himself of exactly that point, that he hadn't done anything wrong, and everything that happened was entirely Neil Croker's fault. But the newspaper story had been written in such a cruelly persuasive manner that even Billy had been left feeling he was in some way culpable for Neil's actions. Suddenly overwhelmed by the whole horrible situation, Billy crumpled forward with his head in his hand and instantly, Jason leaned over to him and gently rubbed his shoulder.

'Hey, Billy, none of that. Come on, come on,' he said softly. 'That man will have to take responsibility for what he did. That's not your fault. And to be honest, Billy, if you hadn't helped catch him, he may have done it again to someone else. I think you did a very brave thing. It's just a shame rags like that don't see that,' And with those words, Jason took the newspaper, rolled it up, and then slotted it firmly into the wastepaper bin under the desk. Next, he placed his hands on Billy's shoulders and gently coaxed him back into an upright position until he could see his face again.

'There, that's better,' Jason said and sat back on the edge of the bed again.

'Do you want to know the worst thing? The very worst thing of all?' Billy replied despondently, his eyes glistening. 'I know it all got really weird, really quickly. But when Mr Croker first put me in touch with Caroline, I had a few days when I really thought that might be my lucky break. I was lying in bed at night, thinking how proud Mum would have been if I got to be in a movie. But the whole thing was fake. Caroline wasn't even real. It's all been snatched away. I'm 19 years old, Jason. I've got two GCSEs. Everyone thinks I'm a bit thick. And I'm working in a supermarket. I'm going to be stuck there forever.'

Jason offered him a reassuring smile. 'Your mum was plenty proud of you, Billy,' he said. 'She was proud of the boy you were. And she was proud of the man she knew you would grow up to be. And I think you're looking at this all wrong. You say you're 19. I say you're *only* 19. You have everything ahead of you. You're kind and thoughtful. Funny. You're tall and handsome, and all the ladies notice you the moment you walk into any room. And don't forget that you have a lovely home and a family that adores you.

'You've got the world at your fingertips. This thing with the newspaper it is horrible, I know, but it will be over much more quickly than you realise. And you can still follow your dream. You just have to keep working at it. And one day, you'll be the star of the show. And I'll be sat there, front row, cheering the loudest.'

Jason picked up the plate from the desk and handed it to Billy. 'Now, get this down you before it goes cold,' he said, and then he stood and gently ruffled Billy's hair before heading to the door.

There was something in Jason's manner, his calmness, which had helped ease Billy's frayed nerves. He could begin to believe that everything *would* be OK, that the salacious newspaper story would soon be forgotten, eclipsed by whatever scandals came next. And Jason was right, Billy thought; he shouldn't give up on his dream.

He looked up and, with a smile, said, 'I'll hold you to that, Jason. One day, front row ticket. I promise.'

CHAPTER 20

Vicki stood patiently at the entrance to the car park, waiting for Kim and Debbie to arrive with Jack. She knew how conspicuous she must look stood next to the entrance barrier wearing a bright pink dress with a white and pink fascinator weaved into her hair. But Charlie and Jason had given their wedding a pink theme, and everyone had worked hard to observe the dress code. And at her brother's wedding, in front of all the family, she wanted to arrive hand in hand with her son. It was important for Vicki that she and Jack be seen arriving together.

After anxiously watching about a dozen cars go through the barrier, Kim and Debbie finally arrived, and Jack waved excitedly to her as the car passed by. They parked quickly and climbed from the car, Jack in his cute little pink pageboy outfit and Kim and Debbie in fitted black suits with pink shirts and ties, and both with a splash of pink in their hair to match.

They walked Jack across the car park to Vicki, who lowered herself so he could hug her. 'Don't you look handsome,' she said. He kissed her on the cheek and squeezed her tightly. Vicki then stood up and kissed both his foster parents on the cheek. 'And loving the suits, ladies,' she said, hoping she had not been overly familiar.

'We look like a couple of giant liquorice allsorts,' Debbie replied, smiling. 'Pink's not our usual choice, but, you know, when in Rome.'

'And we were both so flattered that your brother thought to invite us,' Kim added. 'It does beat sitting in the car for an hour. And we did double-check with Lydia yesterday, about the party, but she still says no. Sorry.'

Vicki sighed. 'I'm just glad he's going to be in the pictures,' she said. And then she took Jack by the hand and proudly walked with him up the car park to the entrance of the registry office. Kim and Debbie followed but made a point of leaving a respectful distance so the other guests would very much focus on Vicki arriving with her son.

A small group of friends and family had already gathered, all dressed in various hues of pink, rubbing arms and stamping feet to stay warm on the chilly winter day. And everyone turned and reacted with great joy, seeing little Jack hand in hand with his mother. Billy immediately swept his nephew into his arms and hugged him, and Jack laughed with delight. Then Billy carried him over to say hello to Carol and Tyler and lowered him to the ground next to Lizzie, who was in a pink bridesmaid's outfit. The two children proceeded to compare clothes and talk about the colour pink.

Vicki could not take the smile off her face, so proud that her little boy was part of a family wedding. And then she noticed, at the edge of the group, her grandmother in a wheelchair, with Louise standing behind her. Louise was wearing a pink dress, but Dorothy was dressed in green, a large camellia pinned to her lapel the only suggestion of the 'pink' theme. Her grandmother was thin frail, her mind still sharp but her body failing her. She would never admit to it, but she had become almost completely dependent on the staff at her retirement complex and, in particular, on Louise.

Vicki walked over and kissed her grandmother on the cheek. 'Hi Nan,' she said and noticed her grandmother flinch slightly, unhappy at having been touched. 'This is a lovely day, isn't it?' Vicki gestured to Louise, 'Very pink!'

'Well, I wanted to respect the wishes of the grooms,' Louise said. 'Of course, your grandmother flatly refused.' She leaned closer to Vicki and whispered, 'I pinned a pink camellia to her jacket as a compromise. But don't tell her. I don't think she's made the connection.'

Dorothy indicated to the children in front of her, 'That boy with the brown hair and brown eyes. Is that your boy, Victoria?'

'Yes, that's Jack,' Vicki replied, thrilled that her grandmother had noticed her arrive with him.

'Oh,' Dorothy nodded agreeably. 'He's a good-looking lad. You can tell he's one of us.'

Vicki chuckled, 'I'll bring him over to say hello in a minute. He's just talking to Lizzie.'

As she glanced over, she could see Lizzie and Jack were having an animated conversation, Jack frowning as Lizzie pointed at him, telling him something he clearly did not like.

'No, you're not,' Jack said.

'I am,' Lizzie said crossly. 'And so you must call me Auntie Lizzie.'

'I don't have any aunties,' Jack replied, frustrated. 'I only have uncles.'

Carol bent down and said something in Lizzie's ear, which made Lizzie look to the floor and fall silent.

Tyler, twice as tall as Lizzie and Jack, was smartly dressed in a pink three-piece suit. It didn't appear as though he had paid much attention to the exchange between the two children in front of him, but the moment he saw Lizzie was upset, he took her by the hand, and she quickly moved next to him, cuddling into his side.

Carol saw that Vicki had witnessed the exchange, and she simply smiled and shrugged; Vicki did the same in return. But the scene had taken the shine from Vicki's happy moment. She had hoped Jack would just fit in, that his familial relationship with Lizzie and Tyler would give him a natural connection to them and make up for all the time he had been absent from their lives. But she could see how close Lizzie and Tyler had grown, and, standing in front of them, Jack looked like an outsider. All Vicki could do was hope that in the months ahead, she would be able to bring Jack closer into the heart of their family.

As she gazed at the group of wedding guests, she could see how people had naturally gravitated to different spaces. Carol had positioned herself a respectful distance from Dorothy whilst Peter was stood by the entrance to the registry office, a perfect spot where he could give a wide berth to both Dorothy and Carol.

Billy was chatting warmly with Kim and Debbie, clearly making great efforts to ensure they felt a part of the day. There were a few other people, some of whom were vaguely familiar, school friends of the two grooms she had probably met over the years. But Charlie and Jason had made a point of keeping the guest list small; they had wanted something intimate and meaningful, with just the most important people in their lives.

She knew Jason had not invited his parents, and there had been a few friends who had declined to attend due to their personal beliefs. The invitation to the civil partnership had prompted a number of unexpected conversations for Charlie and Jason, with people they had known since they were school kids. Most of their friends had been delighted, but a few had surprised them by expressing strict views about what did and did not constitute a marriage. Vicki knew Charlie and Jason would have handled those situations politely and sensitively, but she also wondered if they would have any interest in continuing with those friendships once they were married.

The door to the registry office opened, and a woman stepped out with straight blonde hair and wearing a smart grey suit, 'Hello, everyone. Are you all here for Jason and Charlie?'

The group responded with a most definite 'yes'.

'My name is Margaret. I am a registrar with Southend-on-Sea Borough Council, and I will be conducting the service here today. I do appreciate it is chilly, so I will be asking you all to come inside shortly. For now, though, I am looking for Tyler, Lizzie and Jack.'

Carol began to manoeuvre the children to the door, but Vicki very much wanted to be seen as Jack's mum that day. She hurried over, took his hand and led him to the door, with Carol following behind with Lizzie and Tyler.

'Well,' Margaret said, 'you really have thrown yourselves into the pink theme, haven't you? You all look lovely.' And with that, she took the children into the registry office and closed the door behind her.

With Margaret and the children gone, Carol found herself standing awkwardly with Peter, but she was having none of it. She immediately took herself over to Billy to be introduced to Kim and Debbie.

However, Vicki remained with her father. He looked out of place, stood alone, almost like an afterthought, someone from a wedding guest backup list who had only been invited when other people fell through. Up until that morning, she hadn't been entirely sure if he would attend. She knew, on so many levels, he still struggled with having a gay son and had repeatedly questioned why Charlie and Jason felt the need to 'make a big show of it' by holding a civil ceremony. She also knew he would leave as soon as he could to get to a bar or a pub and start drinking.

But she wanted to ask if he had seen her arrive with Jack and if he would like his grandson to sit next to him during the service once he had completed his page boy duties. As she went to chat with him, she could smell alcohol on his breath. 'Oh, Dad, you've been drinking already,' she said quietly, her disappointment clear in her voice. 'We haven't even had the ceremony yet.'

Peter shook his head as though annoyed at the implication in her comment. 'I haven't drunk today,' he said. 'I had a bit of a night with my mates. But I have not drunk today.'

Vicki sighed, wondering where in her father's mind 'the night before' ended and 'the morning' began. 'Please remember it's Charlie's wedding. And it's going to be a long day.'

'Wedding,' he said dismissively, as though sneering at the whole idea of it.

'Yes,' Vicki replied, finding herself quite irritated by him. 'Whatever they call it legally, this is your son's wedding day. So, stay off the drink and keep sober.'

Peter looked to his side, and Vicki could tell he was thinking something over. After a moment, and still without looking at her, he walked away. 'I didn't want to come, anyway,' he said.

Vicki gasped, 'No, Dad. You get back here. Dad! Come back.'

But it was too late. Inadvertently, Vicki had handed Peter an excuse to leave. He had spotted a taxi pulling up, delivering a couple of belated wedding guests, and the moment they were out of the vehicle, Peter jumped in and was driven away. Vicki watched in dismay as he left, an awful feeling she may have just ruined her brother's big day. Quickly, Carol was at her side, rubbing her back gently.

'Take a deep breath, Vicki,' she said. 'Whatever just happened, take a deep breath. I guarantee it wasn't your fault.'

'I didn't mean this to happen,' Vicki said, her heart breaking at the thought of Charlie entering the registry office and seeing his father was not there. 'I was just asking him not to drink.'

'It's fine,' Carol said quietly. 'Honestly, it's fine. I spoke to Charlie last night, and I told him this might happen. He and Jason are quite prepared for Peter to miss their wedding. If anything, to be honest, I think they would both be a little relieved. They don't want anything to happen that might ruin the day. So, don't you blame yourself. It's all fine.

105

All Charlie wants is for three kids to be there as the page boys and bridesmaid. And for you and Billy to be their witnesses. Anything else is just gravy.'

Despite Carol's reassuring words, Peter's abrupt departure had robbed Vicki of almost all the joy she had hoped to glean from the day. She looked past Carol and realised most of the guests were staring at her, some perhaps wondering what had happened, whilst others wore expressions which suggested they had probably guessed.

Billy excused himself from Kim and Debbie and stepped over to her, a half-smile on his handsome face. 'Dad off to a pub?' he asked. 'To be fair, I'm surprised he showed up at all.'

And then, guided by Louise, her grandmother joined them, her desire to speak badly of Peter clearly sufficient for her to tolerate Carol's presence for a few moments. 'I saw your father leave, Victoria. He has gone to get drunk, one assumes.'

Vicki nodded.

'But it wasn't Vicki's fault, Dorothy,' Carol interceded.

Dorothy raised her brow. 'Well, of course, it wasn't, you stupid woman,' she said sharply. 'That sorry excuse for a man is always in some pub or bar. He wasn't present at the birth of any of his children. He didn't turn up to my husband's funeral, even though he was supposed to be one of the pallbearers. He wasn't there when Susan passed away. The only time he ever turned up, unsurprisingly, was for his own wedding. And even then, he got so drunk at the wedding breakfast and couldn't stand up for their first dance. I said the very first time I saw him that he was a complete waste of space, and I stand by that assessment to this very day.'

'Dorothy!' Louise snapped. 'Whatever you think, he is still their father. Show some respect to your grandchildren.'

Vicki clutched Louise's arm, 'No, honestly, it's fine Louise.' Taking a step back, she adjusted her fascinator using her reflection in the windows of the registry office. Her grandmother was still such a powerful presence, even though she was now so physically frail that she needed the use of a wheelchair. Her condemnation of Peter's character was all Vicki needed at that moment to reassure her that she was not

106

responsible for his departure. 'Nan, I don't agree with most of what you have said about Dad over the years, but you are right about that. We have got to stop talking about him as though he's a 'bit of a drinker'. He's not. He's an alcoholic. He's also lazy and he's selfish, and always puts himself before everyone else. And it has to stop. For me, walking out on Charlie and Jason's wedding is the final straw.'

She looked at Billy, who had a faint hint of a smile on his face as though acknowledging and agreeing with her. 'What do you think we should do?' he asked.

'We'll wait until Charlie and Jason are back from their honeymoon, and then we'll have a family meeting,' her eyes rested on Carol to silently communicate she was including her in the family meeting. 'But, for now, let's just enjoy our brother's big, pink wedding day.'

CHAPTER 21

The ceremony lasted less than half an hour, but Charlie and Jason had managed to weave in just enough elements of a traditional wedding service, to make it feel more than a simple signing of a legal document. Tyler escorted Lizzie and Jack down the little aisle which had been created in the centre of the chairs. Tyler looked mortified to be the centre of attention whilst Lizzie and Jack held hands and giggled all the way to the front of the room.

When Charlie and Jason entered, it was instantly clear they had completely ignored their own 'pink theme', both wearing matching navy three-piece suits. Everyone stood, as they walked hand in hand towards the registrar stood behind a desk at the front of the room. They were both smiling and did not appear to notice anyone was missing.

Once at the front, before Margaret spoke, Jason turned dramatically and said, 'Thank you all for being here and for throwing yourself into our pink theme. And may I just say, you all look really, *really* gay.' His comment received a ripple of laughter and even Dorothy, who had a dislike for jokes during solemn moments, could not help but smile.

Although there was no legal requirement for either of them to speak during the ceremony, they had each chosen some simple vows from the internet: short statements of their love and commitment to each other, their happiness at spending the rest of their lives together, and the great adventures that were to come. After they had signed the civil partnership contract, Vicki and Billy were called to sign as witnesses, and both gave Charlie and Jason a hug before returning to their seats.

And with that, the ceremony was over.

Jason and Charlie posed for some 'signing the contract' photographs and then led their guests to a nearby ornamental garden, a pretty and secluded refuge in the middle of a busy town centre that not many people knew about. And there, in front of a stream, they posed for their official wedding photographs.

Vicki noticed an elderly couple out walking their dog, who stopped and at first appeared puzzled by what was going on. She assumed the very noticeable absence of a bride had confused them, but after a few moments of deep discussion, it seemed the penny had dropped, and they waved happily at the two grooms and called, 'Congratulations' before heading off with their dog.

Once the photographer had all the official pictures she needed, the party returned to the car park, ready to head off to one of the hotels along the seafront for Jason and Charlie's wedding breakfast.

Vicki had been enjoying the day so much and was taking such great pride in showing her son off to the family that she had forgotten he was only there for the ceremony and the pictures. But then she noticed Debbie and Kim waiting quietly, some metres away, and her heart sank as she realised it was time for Jack to go. And she knew her sudden sadness wasn't just because he wouldn't be a part of the rest of the day. She knew it would be many weeks before she saw him again.

She picked him up and gave him a hug. 'It has been lovely,' she said, and then she looked her son in the eyes. 'I am so proud of you. You looked so handsome, and you were so well-behaved.'

The little boy hugged his mother, and then she put him on the ground. Kim returned to the car with him, where she carefully strapped him into his car seat. But Debbie remained, and it appeared she wanted to talk to Vicki about something. Vicki's delicately balanced composure immediately shifted to anxiety, and she wondered if, at some point during the day, she had done something terribly wrong, and Debbie was about to make her aware of it.

'I just wanted to let you know,' Debbie said, 'that we have been talking to Jack's social worker, Lydia, and our own social worker, too, about Jack. And you.'

'Oh?' Vicki said, hoping she was not about to receive any bad news.

'Kim and I have both said that we want to facilitate more contact for you and Jack and that we think it's time, now you are back at your family home, that he should be able to have sleepovers with you. I hope you don't think we overstepped, but-'

'No, no, of course I don't,' Vicki blurted out, her anxiety immediately dispelled. 'I would love that.'

109

Debbie's happy expression changed slightly as she continued to speak. 'And I hope you don't feel I am speaking out of turn, Vicki, but our concern was never you. You must know, it was never you. It was always Jack's dad. And that was always the concern for social services as well.'

'I know,' Vicki replied softly. 'Jack's social worker said something along those lines back in the summer.' And as she recalled that moment, that awful conversation with Lydia in the community centre car park, she found herself feeling the same terrible pain she had suffered when she had been told there was no chance that her little boy was returning to live with her. 'To be honest, Debbie, that was the day it all ended for me and Nate. I realised how stupid I had been, wasting so many years, fooling myself, that the three of us could end up in a happy home together. It was never going to happen.'

Debbie didn't reply immediately, but after a moment of thought, she said, 'I imagine it took a lot for you to walk away from him, to give up your home, and move back in with your family. But I think you have made all the right choices, and Kim and I are both going to support you as much as we can so you and Jack get to see a lot more of each other.'

Debbie's reassuring words were almost enough to take the edge off the sadness of Jack leaving the wedding and being taken home. Without saying anything else, Vicki gave Debbie a hug, and then she waved as Debbie got back into the car, and she, Kim and Jack drove away.

And then, all the noise was gone, the chatting and the laughter, the giggling of her young son. Vicki stood alone, an aching quietness all around, but left with a hope that things might finally start to go right for her. Even if she did not gain full custody of Jack, just seeing him more often having sleepovers with him, would be more than enough for the time being. And that thought offered her hope for the future.

'You OK?'

She turned and found Charlie standing behind her. 'Carol told me what happened with Dad. I hope you aren't upset about it. Jason and I really aren't upset. We're just surprised he turned up at all.'

'I just felt so guilty,' she said, closing her eyes for a moment. 'Funny. I'm feeling guilty about a lot of things today.'

'Well, you shouldn't, Vicki, not at all,' Charlie said and then, to further their conciliatory moment, he added, 'and I am sorry if I ever made you feel that way.'

Vicki had tried so hard over the previous few months to rewire her brain, to repeatedly remind herself, reinforce to herself, that Charlie was not to blame for the way things had played out with Nate and Jack. But, for some reason, she still felt some resentment towards him, and she still struggled to look at him without feeling any bitterness, even though, in her head, she knew that was wrong.

'You are a complete bastard,' she said.

'Oh, what have I done now, Vicki?' Charlie asked, frustrated that his attempt to reach out to his sister appeared to have been so quickly rejected.

Vicki took his lapel between her fingers. 'Navy,' she said. 'Absolute tools, both of you. Everyone else is in pink, including me, and you know I have always hated pink. And the two of you swan into your big pink wedding, both wearing navy blue. Oh, I could just strangle the pair of you.'

And then she put her arms around Charlie and hugged him, and she could feel him doing the same in return.

'I blamed you, you know,' Vicki said quietly, as if she wanted finally to speak the truth to her brother but hoped he might not hear it. 'For a long time. I think it was easier for me to blame you for what happened with Jack. And Nate.'

Charlie sighed and then released Vicki from his embrace and stepped back. 'I know,' he said. 'Believe it or not, there have been plenty of moments when I thought I could have... should have... handled things differently.'

'Well, you aren't the most subtle person with your emotions,' Vicki replied, chuckling slightly as she spoke.

Charlie's expression was suddenly that of someone with great regrets, a sadness and a darkness etched on his face. 'I know I didn't ever make the situation better,' he said.

But Vicki did not want him to feel like that, not on such a happy day. And so, she shook her head and said, 'Nope, not today, Charlie Fletcher.

This is your wedding. And today, you get a free pass. I have a beautiful son because of Nate, but everything else that went wrong, all of it, including Jack going into foster care. That's on me. You are, as of now, fully and completely pardoned.' And as she spoke the words, she hoped her heart would eventually forgive her brother, too.

She took his hand, and they began to walk back to the wedding party, stood at the top of the car park outside the registry office, everyone waiting for a sign they should head off to the wedding reception. 'We need to have a proper grown-up conversation about Dad at some point,' she said. 'You and Jason and me. And Carol. We can't let this go on.'

Charlie agreed, 'Perhaps in a couple of weeks when Jason and I get back from Spain. We can all sit down and see what we can do about it.'

'Oh yes, honeymoon! Although it sounds more like a busman's holiday. Are you seriously scouting for investment properties while you are there?'

'Oh yes. It's all Jason's idea. But the more we talk about it, the more we think that's where the future of our business lies. And, you know, if it works out, there will be plenty of free Spanish holidays for you and Billy. And, you know, hopefully, perhaps even Jack, one day.'

'Yes,' Vicki replied confidently. 'One day. With Jack.' She squeezed her brother's hand, and for the first time in far too long, she had hope for the future; hope that Jack would be spending more time with her and the family, and hope that, perhaps one day, he would come back to The Lodge to live with her.

She knew, without a doubt, that leaving Nate behind had been the right thing to do. But she'd heard all sorts of rumours, through friends and mutual acquaintances, that his life was spiralling out of control. And that frightened her because she knew he blamed her and Charlie for everything that had gone wrong in his life. And she was never quite sure what Nate might do next.

CHAPTER 22

Four years later

There was a stink of burning in the air, and the noises around him were loud and chaotic; a man shouting, someone else, a woman, reassuring, saying not to worry, that help was on the way. There was a metallic taste in his mouth, and his head hurt as though something was pushing down on him. He realised he couldn't move, everything was closing in around him, stealing the air from his lungs. He blinked and opened his eyes, and at first, nothing he could see made sense. He was inside something, a car, but there was something padded pushing into his face, and the inside of the car was dark, even though he was sure there should be daylight.

He tried to turn his head, but he felt as though he were somehow jammed against the roof, his neck at a strange angle, and as he gazed through the shattered windows, he realised he could see people's feet rushing around the vehicle, the whole world upside down.

'They're on their way,' a woman said, 'just hang on, they're on their way. They'll get you out.'

He tried to reply, to ask what was going on, to ask for help, but it was as though he had forgotten how to speak.

'What's your name? Can you tell me your name?'

But he couldn't. He couldn't remember his own name.

And suddenly, the world flipped over in his head, and it made sense. He was upside down, the roof of the car resting on the ground, the seat belt tightly gripping him, his legs stuck under his seat, and an airbag pushed into his face. There were tiny shards of glass sprinkled around him, and someone was next to him, suspended upside down as well, jammed between the steering wheel and the seat. It was a man with blonde hair, but not moving, not awake like him.

Someone reached into the car through the broken passenger window and held his hand. 'It's OK. The fire brigade is coming, and an ambulance. They'll get you all out. Just stay still for now and try not to be frightened. Can you tell me your name?'

And then he remembered his name. He opened his mouth to speak, but first, he coughed, and he felt a warm liquid spray out, downwards, into his eyes. 'Oh god,' he said. 'Oh god.'

'No, don't panic. You aren't alone. I'm here. I'm Emma. And I'm going to stay right here until you are out of the car.'

'Billy,' he said.

'Is that your name?'

'Yes, Billy,' he said, breathless, feeling a panic quickly building in his gut. 'Billy Fletcher.' Within that small, confined space, Billy's mind was overwhelmed by too much sensory information, too many smells and tastes and sounds and pains. His head was throbbing as his memory, still a jumble of confusion and missing pieces, began to slowly return, and he began to recall what had happened and how he got there.

His dad. Peter. His dad had been driving the car.

Billy moved his head as much as he could, looking to his right at the driver's seat. There was a figure, unmoving, upside down like him, trapped at the wheel. 'Dad?' he said quietly. 'Dad, are you OK?'

'It's OK, Billy. They're on their way,' Emma said.

'It's my dad,' Billy replied. 'He's not moving. He's not moving. Oh god. I think he's dead.' And then Billy started to cry.

CHAPTER 23

The train to Southend Victoria rail station was surprisingly busy, and Charlie could not help but gaze around the carriage at all the grey-faced commuters travelling home late from the city. And those sad, tired expressions offered him some reassurance because although he was looking forward to a short break from the busy world of Spanish holiday rentals, he could appreciate that he had been successful in his efforts to avoid the daily grind of a nine-to-five.

He was travelling light, a shoulder bag without any luggage, but his flight had been delayed by hours, and he knew he would have missed most of Billy's birthday celebrations. One consolation was that he was going to be home for a few days, and so would have plenty of time to catch up with everyone, although he wished he and Jason could have more than a couple of days together.

For eighteen long, hot months, Charlie had been in Maspalomas, running the five apartments they had purchased, and for most of that time, he had been alone; eighteen months of marketing and customer relations, bookings, occasional transfers (if he was in a good mood), ensuring the flats were cleaned, and sometimes managing complaints.

Jason had joined him as regularly as he could, but his visits had always been necessarily short because he had his own responsibilities back in Southend, where he was leading the house-flipping side of their business. For the most part, their marriage had been little more than a stream of funny text messages, frequent missed phone calls, daily business emails with 'I miss you' tagged at the end and, occasionally, a late-night webcam rendezvous.

Charlie knew it wasn't working, and he guessed Jason had come to the same conclusion. At some point, they were going to have to make a choice on which part of the business they would close down; house renovations in Southend or holiday rentals on Gran Canaria.

In his heart, he knew which he wanted to keep because, as busy as he was and as lonely as he had often been, he enjoyed a great quality of life in Maspalomas. Despite the hustle and bustle of the business, he had

115

managed to get into a pleasant routine. Each morning, before he started work, he went for a quiet swim in a nearby communal pool. He always went early because he knew he would likely have the pool to himself, and so he could enjoy a leisurely swim and not have to participate in a conversation with anyone else.

Throughout the rest of each day, he wore shorts, a t-shirt and sandals and even took a well-earned siesta each afternoon. After that, he would work for a further two or three hours and then take himself out for dinner and a few beers, a short five-minute walk from his apartment to the Yumbo Centre and all its bars and restaurants.

He had begun to make friends among the local ex-pat community, a small eclectic group from a range of backgrounds, and so it was unusual for Charlie to dine alone in the evening. There was always someone to chat to. The only downside were the lonely nights, lying in bed, aching for Jason to find a break in his workload so he could join him.

The flight from Gran Canaria had been quiet and given him plenty of time to review some of the upcoming reservations and read a book about how to effectively use the internet to market a business. And after several hours engrossed in 'Simple Online Marketing Hacks to Boost Your Business', Charlie wondered if he and Jason should shift their business model and only target older couples and gay couples or whether it was far too early to go down that route. He looked forward to spending a boozy night with Jason in their little terrace house in Southend town centre, going over the data and getting the clarity of his husband's financial expertise.

It was only as the train passed Prittlewell, the final station before Southend Victoria, that Charlie suddenly realised his phone was still in 'flight mode' and that none of the messages he had sent to Jason since he had landed would have been received. The moment he restored his phone to normal operation, text messages began to arrive. The first was a text from Jason, sent at about midday.

'Billy loved the book. Says Tennessee Williams is his favourite playwright. Sorry. He couldn't wait to open his presents! '

And then another a few minutes later.

116

'Your dad's already drunk. Sorry. We tried to keep him off the drink. Can't wait to see you xx'

And then another.

'Oh, forgot. Don't panic when you see the back garden. It's a work in progress x x x'

'Oh my god,' Charlie thought. 'What's he up to now?'

And then there appeared to have been a gap of a couple of hours before any other texts had been sent to him. But they all arrived instantly, at the same time as the messages from Jason. But all the later texts were from Carol, the same message, over and over again, each sent 15 or 20 minutes apart.

'The moment you land, call me.'

'Call me.'

'Charlie, as soon as you get this, call me.'

'Check your messages. I have left you a voice mail.'

'Call me.'

'Check your messages.'

Quickly, Charlie dialled into his voice mail, where a computer voice told him he had one message received that day at 4.07pm.

'It's Carol. Charlie, we're all at Southend Hospital. A&E. Get a taxi straight here from the station. There's been a car accident. Your dad was driving, drunk. Billy's recovering, we think he's going to be OK. We know your dad's in surgery, but they won't tell us anything-'

Panicked, Charlie hung up on the call and shot to his feet. He rushed to the train door but then had to wait, breathless, his heart pounding, as the train slowly pulled into the station.

'Come on, come one, come on, come on,' he whispered to himself, his mind churning over so many different images and scenarios, the horrible idea of his kid brother lying in a hospital bed, injured.

The train stopped, and there was a pause before the doors opened that felt like forever, but finally, they were released. He jumped from the train and onto the platform and then rushed towards the ticket barrier, weaving between the other passengers, trying to get outside first before all the taxi cabs were taken.

'Hospital,' he repeated to himself. 'Southend Hospital.'

117

CHAPTER 24

Vicki looked at the people taking up seats in the waiting area, and she felt like screaming at them all: one with a bandaged finger, another with a cough, someone with a bee sting who appeared to have brought their entire family along for emotional support. The waiting area was small, with only about 20 seats, and a queue had formed at the reception desk.

Over the previous five hours, she had veered between anxiety, sobbing, and fleeting moments of hope. She had watched countless individuals being booked in but did not believe a single one of them had a genuine reason to be there, selfishly absorbing valuable attention from doctors and nurses when there was a genuine emergency to deal with.

'I am going to say something,' she said angrily, partially covering her mouth with her hand. 'These absolute trolls. My family's in there, and God knows what's happening to them. And all these idiots are sat here, with paper cuts and bee stings, expecting the same attention as people who've been in an actual car crash.'

Wearily, Carol put her arm around Vicki's shoulders. 'Just focus,' she said softly. 'Ignore them all and focus on good thoughts. We need good thoughts right now.' She then withdrew her arm and checked her phone. 'Message from Tyler,' she said. 'He says the kids have gone to bed. They don't know anything. Just think we've taken Billy out for drinks.' And then she sighed, helpless. 'He wants an update. What do I say? Nothing. There is still no update.' She texted, 'No news yet xx' and put her phone back in her jacket pocket.

Vicki rested back in her seat and looked at the ceiling. She wished she could take that day back and start it again. She wished she had kept tabs on how much her father had been drinking. She wished she had taken his car keys off the holder by the front door. She wished she had remembered to buy the frozen pizzas so he'd have no excuse to rush out. And she wished he had driven away on his own, without anyone else in the car.

118

A doctor approached them, a young woman in a white coat, her long dark hair tied behind her head. She had been very helpful when they had first arrived and had promised to keep them informed, but she had then disappeared for hours. Vicki could see her, looking at them, about to deliver news, and her heart began to pound heavily in her chest, fearful of what she was about to say to them.

The doctor knelt in front of them and spoke quietly. 'Your father is out of surgery,' she said and gently held Vicki's arm. 'He's a few broken bones, and he's going to be very bruised, but it seems his injuries were mostly minor. And your brother, likewise, battered and bruised but OK. There was some blood in his mouth where he bit his tongue, so he's had a few stitches, but that's all.'

Vicki began to cry, overwhelmed, relieved to finally have some news, to have so many terrifying thoughts dispelled. 'Can I see them?' she asked tearfully, her hands shaking.

'Not your father, just yet, but your brother is back in one of the cubicles. We're keeping him overnight, to monitor him because he did have a knock to his head. We're just trying to find him a bed. He's very tired, but he asked to see you. I will walk you to him."

Vicki glanced at Carol, who shook her head. 'You go, sweetheart. I'll wait here for Charlie. And I need to send an update to Tyler. Give Billy my love.' As she spoke, Carol's voice broke, just for a moment, and Vicki realised she was trying not to cry. And in an unexpected gesture which surprised them both, Vicki kissed her on the cheek.

She then stood and followed the doctor from the waiting area into a part of the A&E department that most people don't get to see. They passed several clinical staff, stood in small groups, having quiet discussions, and a cleaner, mopping the floor, a strong smell of disinfectant in the air. Soon, they were in a row of curtained cubicles, and the doctor entered one. Vicki could hear her speaking to the patient inside, and then she appeared again. 'Your brother's here,' she said and gestured for Vicki to go inside. 'But not too long, now.'

The doctor left, and Vicki gently stroked the curtain aside and stepped forward. At first, she thought she had been led into the wrong space. The man on the bed was a stranger, his shirt untucked and

119

unbuttoned, with plasters and bandages on his head and hands, his face bruised. But then he held out his hand, tears streaming down his swollen cheeks, and suddenly, she could see it was her brother.

'Oh, Billy,' Vicki whispered, and she stepped towards him, gently taking his hand, and she kissed him on his palm, worried she might hurt him if she kissed him on the head. She pulled up a plastic chair from the side of the cubicle, and sat with him, so happy to see him, to see his face, even though he looked so different.

Billy pointed to his mouth, and said something, and she realised he was saying that his tongue was swollen and was struggling to make words.

'You don't have to say anything,' she said. 'They tell me dad's going to be OK. He's out of surgery. Carol sends her love. She's outside, waiting for Charlie to get here.'

Billy stared at Vicki, his big brown eyes wide, filled with both fear and hope, and she knew exactly what he wanted to ask. But she did not have an answer for him, and so she simply said, 'We don't know. They won't tell us anything.'

CHAPTER 25

The taxi journey to the hospital seemed to take forever. Silent, Charlie sent a single text message to Jason, informing him he was heading straight to A&E and he would see him there. He then put his phone away, too scared to check for any further messages in case Jason sent him a terrible update on Billy's condition. Or his dad. And Charlie didn't want to find out anything bad while he was stuck in traffic, unable to do anything.

The taxi driver had tried to be chatty at the beginning of the journey but had quickly put two and two together when Charlie had asked for the accident and emergency department and then proven to be so reticent afterwards. And so, he had let his passenger just be, a look of fear so clearly etched on his pale face.

When the cab pulled up outside the A&E main entrance, Charlie jumped straight out, his bag over his shoulder. He handed the driver a £20 note and rushed away before it was even suggested there was change.

Through the automatic doors, he found a queue of people waiting in front of him, all in a line for the reception staff. He was panicking and didn't have the time or patience to wait. But before he could begin to push his way to the front, he saw Carol standing a few metres away, her arms outstretched towards him. He hurried to her.

'My stupid phone was on airplane mode,' he said. 'I only switched it on when I got to Southend Victoria. I didn't see any of your messages until then.'

Gently, Carol manoeuvred him onto a seat and sat with him. 'Vicki's with Billy. He's fine. Battered and bruised. They're keeping him in to keep an eye on him, but he seems OK.'

'Dad?'

'He's out of surgery. No other updates, but we're told he's going to be OK too.'

Before Carol could continue, Charlie produced his mobile phone and started to check through the messages. 'I thought Jason would be

121

here,' he said. 'He hasn't gone to the station to pick me up, has he? He hasn't replied to my texts, but maybe he's driving.'

Suddenly, Carol clutched Charlie's hand. 'Did you listen to my message?' she asked, an urgency to her voice that Charlie found unsettling.

'Yes,' he replied. 'I mean, I was on the move, so I might not have heard the whole thing, but-'

'Oh my god, Charlie. Jason's here,' she said, her eyes wide with a shock that he did not know. 'They brought him in. He was in the car.'

Charlie looked at her blankly as though her words simply did not make sense.

'When your dad got in the car, he jumped in the back seat. Jason was the only person who hadn't been drinking, so he was going to try and persuade your dad to let him drive. But then your dad just drove off with both Jason and Billy in the car.'

Charlie's blood ran cold. 'How... how is he?' Charlie asked.

'They won't tell us anything,' Carol replied. 'They say we're not family.'

Without saying a word, Charlie abandoned Carol, desperate to find someone who could tell him about his husband. A man was walking by in a white coat, possibly younger than Charlie, but he seemed clinical, a doctor. Charlie grabbed his arm, and he swung around and stared at Charlie crossly.

'Excuse me, sir,' the doctor protested and tried to pull himself free.

But Charlie was terrified, unable to think of anything but finding Jason. 'Please, my husband,' he said, 'he was in a car accident. I just need to find out what happened to him. Where you've put him. I just need to see him.'

The doctor looked exasperated, busy, and unhappy at having been grabbed. But then his expression changed, as though he remembered himself, what he was there to do, and he could see how much Charlie needed his help. 'Yes, of course, sir. I will check for you. Can you tell me your husband's name?'

'Jason Day,' he said. 'Date of birth 11th November 1976.' With that, Charlie released the doctor's arm and followed him behind the reception desk to one of the reception staff, a woman in her fifties who was busily typing on a computer keyboard.

'Margaret, I just need to find out where we've put a patient, can you have a look for me?'

'Yes, Doctor,' she said without looking up, a weariness in her voice.

'Jason Day,' the doctor said, his glance flicking briefly at Charlie to check he had the name correct. 'He was brought in following a road traffic accident.'

Charlie stood behind the doctor, silently, waiting to be told which cubicle Jason was in, wanting to just see him, hold him, tell him everything was going to be OK. The receptionist was quickly typing, swiftly navigating whichever computer system the hospital used, and then she said, 'Oh, he's not here.'

'He's been moved?' the doctor asked.

'No, he was the fatality,' she said. 'He was taken to the mortuary.'

Everything stopped. Charlie's entire world just stopped, and the air rushed from his lungs. Everything around him seemed to fall silent, the only sound the pounding of his own heart. And suddenly, he was alone, completely alone. Jason wasn't there. Jason would never be there again.

'What?' he said, the word blurted out, a plea for help, to erase those few moments, live them again, for the woman to say something else, that Jason was alive.

The doctor spun around and looked at him, his expression one of horror. Finally, the receptionist looked up and, seeing Charlie for the first time, she immediately realised what she had done. 'Oh god,' she said, her hands over her face. 'Oh, I'm so sorry. I'm so sorry.'

'Jason Day,' Charlie said, his voice growing louder. 'I was asking about Jason Day.'

But then he was moving quickly. The doctor had grabbed him and was rushing him from the reception desk into a small room, poorly lit, with lockers and plastic chairs, coats on hooks. 'Just wait here,' he said and pushed Charlie down onto one of the chairs. 'I am so sorry you found out like that. But I will get all the information for you. Please just stay here, and I will be back.' And then he left Charlie alone, struggling to catch his breath.

123

Outside in the waiting area, Carol had watched, confused by what she had witnessed, unable to understand why Charlie had been so quickly and so forcefully rushed away. But then she heard him, his voice, howling, crying out in pain, in so much pain, and she jumped to her feet and ran to him.

'Oh my god, Charlie,' she yelled, 'Charlie!' She found him on the floor, on his knees, his arms wrapped around his waist, crying uncontrollably. She dropped to the floor and grabbed him, letting him cry onto her shoulder. Instinctively, she understood what had happened and why the hospital had refused to release any information about Jason until Charlie had arrived. 'I'm so sorry,' she said, tears tumbling down her cheeks. 'Oh my god, I am so, so sorry.'

For a moment, the whole waiting area fell silent. Every conversation paused. A short distance away, in one of the cubicles, Billy sat up on his bed, Vicki next to him, now on her feet. They could hear someone crying, and they heard Carol shout Charlie's name.

'Is... is that Charlie? Is he here?' Vicki said, trembling. 'Why's he making that noise?'. But then she saw that Billy had tears in his eyes, that he had understood what was happening, and all of a sudden, Vicki understood too. She understood why their brother was in such pain. 'Oh no,' she whispered. Billy put his arm around her, and the two gently held each other, crying.

Charlie had just lost his everything.

CHAPTER 26

It seemed so ordinary, the place where it happened. A small junction with a mini roundabout just next to the beach. It was not even particularly busy. Months had passed, and there was almost no sign it had been the location of a devastating accident. People had even stopped laying flowers at the scene.

It was a balmy evening, early autumn, and a few people were out and about. A jogger, a couple walking their dog, a group of kids on bikes. Billy was sitting on the sea wall and noticed a few young women smiling at him as they passed. He realised he must have looked like he was waiting on a date. He was wearing a crisp white shirt with black trousers and neatly polished black leather shoes. He was holding a bouquet of sunflowers and dahlias, wrapped in brown paper and tied with string. But his rendezvous was most definitely not a date.

He was staring at a deep fracture that ran from the curb and across part of the walkway and was wondering if that was the exact spot where the car had overturned and crashed against the pavement. The exact spot where his brother-in-law had died. Even in that moment, so many days and weeks later, he still remembered the accident as if it had just happened. He remembered the sounds, and the smells, the taste of blood in his mouth. But most of all, he remembered the hospital, the horror of hearing his brother's grief, cried out across the emergency room. A grief so terrible that he sometimes wondered if Charlie would ever be able to move past it.

'Billy?'

A voice interrupted his thoughts, and he turned to see who had spoken his name. A black woman with short hair stood a few feet away in jeans and a leather-style t-shirt. She seemed about the same age as Billy, and she smiled at him as though she were meeting an old friend. 'I'm Emma. It's nice to see you,' she said, her voice clear and smooth.

Billy attempted to smile, but for a moment, good manners escaped him, and he found himself unable to even pretend to be pleased to meet

125

her. He stood, impulsively thrusting the bouquet towards her. 'This is for you,' he said, 'just to say thank you for coming.'

'Oh, these are lovely,' she replied, admiring the flowers. 'And not shop-bought, either.'

'No, they're from our garden. My mum was quite passionate about gardening, so we've tried to keep up her good work over the years. I planted the sunflowers myself.'

'Well, that's very thoughtful. And I know exactly where I will put them when I get home.'

Billy sat down on the seawall again, and Emma joined him. 'I was surprised you wanted to meet here,' she said. 'I honestly thought this was the last place you would want to be. Would you like to go for a walk, perhaps a little further down the beach?'

'No, honestly, its fine. I come here quite a bit. I am still trying to piece everything together. If you don't mind, I would like to sit here for a while.'

Emma smiled at him and nodded. 'Thank you for your lovely letter,' she said. 'The reporter at *The Echo* passed it onto me. She asked if we were to meet up, could she come along with a photographer, but I said a very definite no.'

Billy finally managed to smile, 'Good call. To be honest, I just wanted the chance to see you face to face, to say thank you,' he said. 'It was very brave, to reach into an upturned car, to hold my hand until the fire brigade arrived. But you stayed, and you talked to me and reassured me. And that really made a difference.'

Emma shrugged as though uncomfortable with the compliment, 'It was all a bit of a blur, wasn't it? How are you now?'

'A few scars. A couple of small breaks. But nothing major. I was lucky.'

'Oh yes, of course.' She paused, 'I'm so sorry about your brother-in-law. Jason, wasn't it? The local papers did quite a few stories about him, afterwards. Lots of people came forward to say lovely things about him. There were quite a few families who bought houses from him, who said how he helped them get on the property ladder.'

126

Billy nodded. 'I'd known him since I was a baby,' he said. 'He was always round our house, part of the family before he… you know… became an official part of the family. I still can't believe he's gone. And that's one of the bits I don't remember. What happened to him. After the accident, I remember being in the car, and dad was next to me. And he was unconscious. And I remember the doors being cut away so they could get us out. But I don't remember them getting Jason out. I would like to think they tried, that they at least tried to help him.'

Emma hesitated before answering, unsure how her words would be received. But Billy appeared desperate to know the details, everything that had happened, and so cautiously, she began to speak. 'He wasn't in the car, Billy,' she said.

Billy frowned, unsure what she meant.

'He… he was on the road. Quite a distance from the car. I think the impact threw him out the back window.'

Billy closed his eyes, overwhelmed at the thought of Jason, poor Jason, lying on the ground, alone, dying, possibly frightened, without Charlie to hold his hand.

For a few moments, neither of them spoke. The only sounds were those of seagulls crying overhead and waves loudly rolling onto the beach behind them.

'Billy, it would have been instantaneous,' Emma said softly. 'He wouldn't have felt anything or known anything. I promise you.' She waited for him to reply, but he sat with his eyes closed and seemed unable to speak. 'Did your brother ask what happened? Is that why you wanted to meet me? To ask on his behalf?'

Billy looked at her, flushed with sadness, 'Charlie doesn't want to know anything. He's not even going to be there when Dad's in court. Every time the topic comes up, he just walks away. He can't talk about it.'

'I can understand that. But I haven't been asked to give evidence. I didn't know if that might be why you asked to meet me, to find out what I was going to say. But I'm not in court.'

Billy shook his head and raised his hands, 'Oh, no, no, not at all. Honestly, I just had this voice in my head. Your voice. Talking to me.

127

Telling me everything was going to be OK. It was the most frightening moment of my life, and you were there. And I just didn't ever get to see you, your face, or to say thank you. I give you my word; that is the only reason I asked to meet you.'

Emma reached over and squeezed Billy's arm, 'Well, I'm glad you did.' She sat back and smiled at him, 'What do you do for a living?'

He sighed, 'I'm trying to be an actor, but for now, I'm still working in a supermarket. I've only just gone back to work. I had to take some time off. You know.'

'Of course.'

'What about you?'

Emma stretched out her arms and wriggled her fingers, 'Well, my mother is a barrister, and my father is a corporate lawyer, and both my brothers are solicitors. So, of course, I went into barbering.'

Billy cocked his head and stared at Emma. 'You're a barber?' he asked incredulously, and for the first time, he found himself able to smile. 'Wow, you must really hate your parents.'

Emma laughed, a lovely sound, Billy thought, honest and warm.

'My parents are very cool. They always wanted me to find my own happiness and have been very supportive.'

'Why barbering, though?' Billy asked.

Emma shrugged, 'I did hairdressing for a few years, but I found I enjoyed barbering more. I have my own shop in Southchurch Village. I do the whole thing, you know. Wet shaves, threading, hot towels, ear singing. You name it. I do it.'

The more Billy listened to Emma talk, the more he noticed how well-spoken she was. And he wondered if she had grown up, like him, in a moneyed family. She seemed incredibly familiar, like someone whose parents might have been in his mother's circle of old money friends. He also knew there were aspects of his father's character that would have made it unlikely a black family would have been involved socially with the Fletchers. But as she spoke, Billy realised he wanted more from their chat than to say thank you. He wanted to find out all about her. 'Would you mind if I bought you a drink?' he asked. 'Just a little 'thank you' beer, or whatever you fancy.'

128

Emma looked conflicted, as though weighing up the pros and cons of the situation, and Billy imagined she was trying to consider if the two of them having a beer together was wildly inappropriate, bearing in mind how they had met. But after a few moments, she'd made her decision. 'Why not?' she said as she pointed across the road at some of the grander properties with views across the estuary. 'That hotel has a lovely bar overlooking the sea.'

Billy released the breath he hadn't realised he'd been holding, 'That hotel it is then.'

CHAPTER 27

In the nine years since her mother's death, Vicki had always arranged a celebration for Susan's birthday. Typically, it was something small, a few drinks and a meal, an almost-birthday party to remember someone taken too soon. And that year, it felt even more important to mark that day.

The previous few months had been unbearable, as she had watched her whole family going through the motions of life, but only the bare minimum, the bits that needed to be done. It was as if The Lodge, usually filled with music and laughter and sunlight, had fallen into a deep sleep.

Charlie had kept away. He would not face their father to be so cruelly reminded of what he had lost at the hands of his own parent. Vicki, Billy and Carol visited Charlie's house regularly, trying to offer their love and support, all of them so frightened the darkness that had enveloped his life might try to steal him away from them completely. They had created an unofficial rota, nothing too obvious, but enough that Charlie was seen and spoken to several times each day. And then they would check in with each other, the three of them, just a quick call or text message in the evening, to make sure they were happy he was OK.

Peter, so defensive and so angry that the blame for the accident rested solely on his shoulders, had little to do with anyone. He was seen coming and going from the house, mostly leaving a stink of alcohol in his wake. His regular nights away from the house had left Vicki, Billy and Carol suspicious that he had found himself a new partner, but no one was willing to speak to him about it. They just let him be, knowing the approaching court case would likely rob him of his freedom for several years.

With such dark days behind them and many more to come, Vicki had been left with an overwhelming need to do something normal and routine, traditional even, and Susan's birthday felt like something that might anchor them all, help them find their way back to a normal life once more.

And so, she arranged a small group, just with Billy, Carol, Lizzie and Jack. Tyler had promised he would pop in on his way home from work and might possibly bring someone with him. Vicki needed everything to be perfect. Everything. And so, as she had dressed the metal patio table in a patterned cloth and furnished it with napkins, glasses, cutlery, plates, and various condiments, she could feel her hands trembling and her heart racing. It all needed to be perfect.

There were two covered bowls, one containing a chopped salad in a Caesar dressing and the other containing lightly spiced vegetable rice. She had burgers and spicy chicken portions cooking in the oven, and a few halloumi and vegetable kebabs so Tyler would have something to eat if he showed up.

There were a few bottles of sparkling wine cooling in the fridge, along with a dozen bottles of lager and soft drinks for Lizzie and Jack. She had slotted her portable media player into its speaker, hoping to create some ambience with a playlist of Carole King songs, her mum's favourite singer. The only thing she'd forgotten was the burger baps, but Carol was collecting Billy from work and had agreed to pick some up at the supermarket while she was there.

'It looks really lovely, mum,' Jack said, squeezing Vicki's hand as he joined her in the garden.

'Thank you, sweetheart.' Vicki brushed Jack's thick brown hair from his face, cupped his cheeks in both hands and kissed him on the forehead, 'I know your Nanny would be very happy that you are here to celebrate her birthday.' She hugged him before heading back into the kitchen to check on the food.

'Is Uncle Charlie going to be here?' Jack asked as he followed his mother back into the house.

The question took Vicki by surprise, so she busied herself for a moment, checking the chicken portions in the top oven, a few moments to gather her thoughts before responding. 'No, sweetheart, Uncle Charlie isn't coming,' she said softly, closing the oven door. But before she could say anything further, Jack spoke again.

'Is he still sad about Uncle Jason?'

Vicki stopped what she was doing and looked at her young son, who was so desperate to understand why he hadn't seen his Uncle Charlie in such a long time. 'You have to understand,' Vicki replied, 'that he is *always* going to be sad about that. Sometimes, it might not be so obvious, but it will always be there. He loved your Uncle Jason with all his heart, and he's always going to miss him. And we have to give him a lot of time and a lot of love.'

Jack nodded, a sad frown on his face, and so Vicki walked over and cuddled him. She had longed to have him back home for so long and had been elated when the social services department finally conceded they no longer had a case for keeping Jack in care. But Jack's return to the family had been happy only for a brief few months, before the accident, and then his young heart had been forced to deal with so much loss that in some moments Vicki had wondered if it would have been kinder on him to stay with his foster mums.

There was a noise from the front of the house. The door to the kitchen opened, and Billy walked in, carrying a bag of shopping, followed by Carol, and an unhappy-looking Lizzie after her. Vicki walked over and took the shopping bag from Billy, kissed him on the cheek, and did the same to Carol. But before she could even say hello to Lizzie, her little sister stomped past her to the kitchen table, pulled out a chair and sat down, arms folded, lip curled, not saying a thing.

Vicki looked at Carol and quietly asked, 'Everything OK?'

Carol rolled her eyes, 'I wouldn't buy her sweets. I told her there would be plenty of food here, but she wanted Haribo's. I said no.'

'Oh, dear,' Vicki gave a little chuckle. She glanced over to the table and saw that Jack had attended to Lizzie and was stroking her arm and quietly talking to her. There were six months between them, and they were about the same height, Lizzie possibly a little taller. Jack had always been thin, a little streak of lightning, bombing around on his bike or rushing from one friend's house to another after school.

But Lizzie had grown into something of a homebody, mostly hanging around Carol's kitchen and enjoying the endless supply of home-cooked meals and puddings that always seemed available. Vicki had begun to worry about her little sister's weight, but she didn't know

132

how to address the issue with Carol or even if she should. Food seemed to be one of the ways Carol expressed her love, but Vicki was concerned that love had left Lizzie several stones heavier than Jack.

'Right,' Carol said. 'Vicki, you have done everything so far. So how about if you and Billy put your feet up in the garden and have a glass of wine together, and I'll take it from here?'

Vicki would usually decline such an offer and insist she be allowed to finish cooking and serving her meal, but over the years, she had seen how important Susan's birthday was to Carol and how important it was for Carol to feel she had a role on those occasions, that she wasn't just a guest, that she was contributing in some way.

'Oh, Carol, that would be lovely if you don't mind,' Vicki said. Billy had pre-empted her answer and quickly removed a bottle of sparkling wine from the fridge and wandered off to the garden, calling, 'Sounds like a plan!' as he went.

'Leave the kids in here,' Carol said. 'I'll get them a squash, and it will give Lizzie a chance to calm down. You and Billy catch up.'

As Vicki left the kitchen, she noticed that Jack was now sitting on a chair next to Lizzie, and the two appeared to be chatting more amiably about something. She kissed Jack on the head as she walked past, and she did the same to Lizzie, who then offered her a smile, a good sign that her sister was getting over her sweets-related tantrum.

Vicki was pleased to have a moment alone with Billy. She suspected something was going on, something he was keeping secret from her. She could sometimes hear him, late at night, in his room, having whispered conversations on his mobile, and then there were times during the day when he would disappear for hours on end and then have no credible explanation as to where he had been. And even though he was usually clean and smartly dressed, she had noticed he appeared to be taking particular care with his appearance of late. Vicki was almost certain that he was hiding a secret, and she wanted to know what it was.

CHAPTER 28

By the time Vicki reached the patio, Billy had already sat down and was pouring two glasses of sparkling wine. As she joined him, they raised their drinks, saying, 'Happy Birthday, Mum,' before clinking their glasses together.

'Everything looks amazing, Vicki,' Billy said. 'You've done mum proud.'

'Thank you,' she replied, but she had already decided the nature of the conversation she wanted to have with her brother, and so she simply said, 'You were out late again last night. Are you seeing someone?'

Billy smiled but, yet again, seemed reluctant to say anything. It was a new sensation for Vicki. Billy had always shared with her, including things most young men would want to keep private. She was not used to him being so evasive.

'Are we going to meet her?' Vicki asked, hoping to glean even the tiniest of details from him.

Billy huffed, 'It's early days. I don't want to jinx it.'

Vicki put her glass onto the table and frowned quizzically. 'Can I at least ask her age? Is this one under forty?'

'Yes,' Billy laughed. 'She's the same age as me, pretty much.'

Vicki shrugged. 'Well, you did go through that whole MILF phase, so I had to ask.'

Billy chuckled, but his expression quickly grew pensive, 'To be honest, Vicki, it's just a bit complicated. The way we met... I'm not sure how everyone will react. Especially Charlie.' He downed his glass of wine and immediately poured himself another.

Vicki was perplexed. She could not imagine what could be so bad that Billy would hesitate to share the details of how he met a new girlfriend. 'I don't understand,' she replied, feeling a little anxious.

Billy went to drink from his glass, but Vicki placed her fingers over the rim, gently pushing his hand down until the glass rested on the table. 'Who is she?' Vicki asked.

'Her name's Emma,' Billy replied slowly. 'We've been seeing each other for about a month.'

'And how *did* you meet her?'

Billy paused, clearly unsure how his sister was going to react to his news. 'She's the one from the day of the accident,' he said. 'You know, the woman who reached into the car and held my hand until the fire brigade and the ambulance arrived.'

'Oh,' Vicki was unable to hide her surprise. She quickly lifted her own glass of wine and took several large gulps from it.

'Do you… do you think this is wrong?'

For a moment, Vicki did not have a clue what to say. Everything in her head was screaming that it was wrong, that there was no way she could welcome someone into the family, no matter how kind or brave that person might be if they were so cruelly connected to the horrible dark day when Jason had died.

But, in her heart, she just wanted her little brother to be happy. He had suffered, too, losing his mother at such a young age, and the accident had left him with such deep scars. Not scars that could be seen, but she had heard him, so many times, crying in the middle of the night or yelling in his sleep. That seemed to have subsided over recent weeks, and she wondered if, perhaps, his secret nighttime phone calls with Emma had something to do with that.

'It's just that I don't know how Charlie will react,' Billy continued. 'And he will ask one day, won't he, how we met?'

Vicki sighed, 'You really like her?'

'Yes. I wouldn't be pursuing anything with her if it didn't feel… you know… special. And she is really special.'

'Then I think you just continue as you are. We can deal with the Charlie situation when we have to. But, for now, I don't think he's going to be asking any questions.'

They were distracted by Lizzie and Jack, who both appeared from the French doors carrying plates of food, burgers and chicken, two large plates for the adults and two small ones for the kids.

'Oh, that looks good,' Billy said, then enthused about their waitering skills.

135

The children placed the plates at the far end of the table, and then Lizzie sent Jack back inside for the final plate.

'Mum, which one's mine?' Lizzie called.

'They're both the same,' Carol replied, her voice carrying through the warm air from the kitchen.

'So, I can have any of them?'

'Yes, they're both the same,' Carol said again.

And then there was a pause, and Lizzie stood, staring at food in front of her, and Vicki suddenly realised what her little sister was doing; she was calculating, in her head, whether there had been enough vagueness in Carol's instructions, that she could take one of the adult plates, and pretend it was a misunderstanding. Vicki watched, fascinated, as Lizzie slowly stroked her finger along the edge of the table, lost in thought, completely focussed on the food.

'Sweetheart, could you hand me and Billy our meals,' Vicki said, hoping to quickly resolve the issue without making her little sister feel embarrassed or uncomfortable.

Lizzie, a flash of anger across her face, gave Vicki a hard stare as she realised her sneaky plan had unravelled. With a sullen expression, she stomped over and handed Vicki and Billy the two larger meals. She then took her own plate, and sat down directly next to the bowls and began to help herself, piling it high with rice.

'Oy, you want to leave some for us?' Billy said, laughing.

Carol and Jack appeared from the kitchen, Jack carrying a large plastic bottle of diet lemonade and Carol a plate of food for herself. She immediately scalded Lizzie. 'Put some of that back, Lizzie, right now.'

Lizzie looked at Carol as though betrayed, apparently not used to being challenged on how much she ate. But she did as she was told, and then sat moodily for the rest of the meal, unhappy with how she had been treated.

Carol poured wine for herself, topped up Vicki and Billy's drinks, and gave lemonade to each of the kids. She raised her glass and, with unexpected emotion, said, 'To Susan, who I miss so much.' And then she looked to the sky and added, 'Happy Birthday, darling.' And

136

everyone at the table, even Lizzie who was still sulking, raised their glass too.

Over the next hour, the clouds dissipated, and the evening sun turned the sky a burnt red. Carol, Billy and Vicki all told stories of Susan, most of them funny, and a few tears were cried, but there was so much laughter that the tears did not hurt so much. The kids left the table and barrelled to the sitting room to watch a Disney DVD Billy had bought for them at his store. Billy stayed in the kitchen to wash up, leaving Carol and Vicki in the garden together, drinking coffee.

'I popped in to see Charlie this morning,' Carol said. 'I think it will be suspicious if I call later, so are you or Billy OK to do that?'

'I'll do it,' Vicki volunteered. 'I need to chat to him about the weekend, anyway. Kim and Debbie are having Jack for a few days, so I thought I would stay at Charlie's. He said he needs to start going through Jason's stuff, and I know it will be too tough for him to do it alone.'

There were voices from the kitchen, Billy excitedly talking to someone. Through the French doors, Vicki could see Tyler had arrived and was talking in an animated fashion to Billy. He was the only kid in the family who looked like Peter, with his blonde hair and blue eyes. He hadn't inherited their father's height and was the shortest of the boys and, standing next to Billy, he looked tiny. But he had a handsome face and always looked effortlessly stylish, as though he could just roll out of bed, throw a load of clothes together, and still end up looking like someone from the cover of a magazine. That day, he had pulled his long blonde hair into a ponytail and was wearing stonewashed ripped jeans, black boots and a tight grey t-shirt.

Billy handed Tyler a beer, and then another young man stepped into view with a very similar appearance to Tyler, and Billy handed him a beer, too.

'Ooh. Tyler's brought a friend,' Vicki said to Carol.

'Boyfriend,' Carol corrected her.

Vicki sipped her coffee and carefully studied the new arrival. 'Did Tyler just want to date someone who looked exactly like himself?' she grinned.

Carol laughed, 'They met at work, at the Council. He's a nice boy.'

'What happened to Alison? She seemed quite sweet.'

'Oh, she was lovely. But you know Tyler's life plan is to work for a couple of years, save up some money, and then go travelling. And, very specifically, to go travelling on his own. Well, Alison started to talk about going with him, which just isn't what Tyler wants. He's only seventeen, and he's just not interested in anything serious. So, he said they should go back to just being friends. And then, a few days later, he brought Jonathan home for dinner. And, after dinner, Jonathan... you know... he stayed over.' Carol flashed her eyebrows at Vicki, and they both collapsed into laughter.

Vicki was very fond of Tyler. He had worked so hard over the years, even as a young boy, to help maintain her mother's garden. He had shown a real passion for it and a great fondness for the memory of his Auntie Susan. She liked the young man he had become, how calm and laid back he was, a good listener, an 'old soul in a young body' as Carol once called him. Sometimes, he seemed older than Billy, even though he was years younger. And he was certainly calmer than Charlie.

Vicki remembered Charlie at seventeen, how stressed and anxious he was about money, about the rising costs of houses, and worrying whether he would ever be able to afford a place of his own. But Tyler had no such worries; settling down or buying a house were not on his list of priorities. Tyler wanted to wander, see things, and experience the world. And Vicki wondered how long it would be, before her youngest brother jumped on a plane and headed off for his great adventure.

glass and stood up. 'Right, everyone,' he bellowed, 'I'll be back in a moment, but please continue to enjoy yourself. This is my home, and you are all very welcome here.'

There was a small cheer from the party guests.

Peter strode over to Billy. 'We need to have a talk,' he said, 'in the sitting room.'

'Dad, Vicki and Jack are asleep upstairs,' he said. 'You need to tell all these people to go home. It's after one in the morning.'

Peter stared at Billy with a look of resentment that Billy had not seen before.

'I've got a gay son who grew up thinking he could speak to me like a piece of crap,' Peter said. 'Don't think for a moment I'm going to tolerate you doing the same. Now. Sitting room.'

Peter opened the kitchen door and walked down the hallway to the room at the front of the house. Billy realised he would get no peace that night unless his father got his way, so dutifully, he followed and closed the kitchen door behind him.

He entered the sitting room, the noise of the storm growing even louder, and found Peter had already turned on two of the standing lamps and taken the seat by the fireplace, Susan's favourite chair. Peter gestured to the couch, so Billy closed the door and took a seat.

Resting his elbows on his knees, Peter stared directly into his son's face, 'It's time we talked about the court hearing.'

'Dad, I don't think we're supposed to.'

'Well, we need to. Because I am very concerned that you are not going to tell the truth about what happened. And if you don't tell the truth, I will end up going to prison. For a long time. And that will be your fault.'

Perplexed, Billy shook his head and momentarily closed his eyes. 'Sorry?' he said and blinked several times, frowning at his father. 'I have done nothing but tell the truth all along. Why would I lie?'

Peter sat back, curled his lip and raised his hand in the air as though confused. 'I didn't accuse you of lying,' he said. 'I just said you haven't told the truth. I didn't use the word lie.'

'But that's the same thing.'

141

'No, it isn't. You just haven't remembered what really happened, yet. And I understand that, son. I really do.' With a more genial manner, Peter reached forward and gently squeezed his son's knee. 'I was unconscious. The first I knew about the accident was after I woke up in the ambulance. But you... you were in the car. Trapped. It must have been terrifying. I'm not surprised you've tried to block so much of what really happened.'

'I remember it all clearly.'

Peter shook his head. 'Billy, you don't. Because you don't remember what he did, do you? You've never mentioned what he did.'

Billy had a growing unease that is father was about to say something terrible. 'What, who did?' he asked.

There was a pause as though Peter was suddenly uncertain about what he had planned to say. But then he took a deep breath and spoke. 'Jason,' he said. 'Jason caused the accident. And you've never mentioned that. You've never mentioned what he did.'

Billy fell silent, a swirling, sickening sensation in his stomach as he began to realise what his dad was saying, what he was trying to persuade Billy to do.

'Jason was shouting at me to stop driving, to pull over,' Peter said. 'You remember? And when I didn't, he jumped forward from the back seat, grabbed the steering wheel, and tried to push me aside. That's why I lost control of the car. It wasn't me. It was Jason.'

Around him, Billy could feel the details of the room begin to vanish, disappearing into the darkness beyond the reach of the light from the two lamps. The noise from the party in the kitchen and the thunderstorm outside dissolved into silence, and all that was left was a terrible, frightening realisation of the person his father had become.

Billy knew that nothing Peter had said was true. Jason had remained calm throughout that terrible car journey. He had coolly, even good-humouredly, tried to persuade Peter to pull over and swap seats with him so he could take the wheel. It was Peter who had started shouting, yelling, not paying attention to the road or the speed at which he was driving. And now here was his father, trying to blame a dead man, a man Billy had loved like a brother, for the accident.

142

The door to the sitting room opened, and the noise from the party breezed into the room for a moment. Angel walked in and gently closed the door behind her before taking a seat on the arm of the chair next to Peter. She ran her fingers through his hair and kissed him on the forehead. 'How are you both doing?' she asked, her words soft and a little slurred.

Peter nodded and smiled slightly. 'I think my son's memory loss might be at an end,' he said and looked to Billy, expecting some sign of agreement. But Billy simply stared at them both, his face still and expressionless.

Angel brushed her long hair behind her shoulders before folding her arms and focusing on Billy. 'Sweetheart,' she said, 'all your father and I are asking of you is that you tell the truth in court. Exactly as your father has just told you. Because if you stick to your old story, now that you know it's not true, that means you will be lying in court. And that's really serious, Billy. It's called perjury, and it's a criminal offence. Your father and I are just trying to stop you from getting into trouble. That's all.'

Sat alone, browbeaten, knowing he was being coerced into doing something very wrong, Billy again wished Charlie were in the room. He'd always had a quiet respect for his brother's ability, indeed willingness, to say exactly what needed to be said, no matter how he might upset others. And Billy knew that was exactly what the conversation needed; someone to articulate clearly, angrily even, why Peter and Angel were so very wrong.

But Billy was nothing like that. He was shy, didn't like to cause a fuss, often unable to raise his voice, even when he felt he should. So, instead, without speaking, he simply stood and went to leave. But something caught his eye on the mantle, just over Angel's shoulder. The collection of family pictures had remained the same since his mother's death, but he noticed it had been added to. There, placed partly in front of a framed photograph of his parents on their wedding day, was a photograph of Peter with Angel, laughing, holding drinks, possibly at a party or in a pub. The photograph wasn't in a frame; it had just been casually added to the display of family memories as though it was of equal importance.

143

'It's lovely, isn't it?' Angel said, noticing where Billy's line of vision had settled. 'I just thought it was a fun memory, my first date with your father. One for the Fletcher hall of fame.'

But Billy didn't agree. It just wasn't right, that photograph, added with such arrogance, placed partly over an image of his late mother. He knew he could not let it stay there, not for another second. And even though he was usually so reticent, so keen to steer clear of confrontation, on that one occasion, he found the courage to say something.

'It shouldn't be there,' he said quietly. 'You need to remove it.' Then he turned and started to walk from the room, but he could hear Angel speaking to him as he left.

'I thought you would all enjoy seeing it,' she said. 'I am going to get it framed. Perhaps you can help me rearrange all the family pictures and find a good spot for it.'

But Billy did not turn. He did not acknowledge that Angel was speaking. He left the room, closed the door behind him, and went back to bed.

CHAPTER 30

'So, the electrics. The finishing touches for the en suite and the walk-in. And the garden, but that's mostly about the pool, now, to be honest. The landscaping's almost done. And then I just need to have the buyers approve everything, and that's it. I can come home.'

Charlie was sat on the floor, in the middle of his darkened house, all the curtains drawn and none of the lights on. Rain was chattering against the windows, and a loud wind was howling around the walls. Charlie's face was partly illuminated by the screen of his mobile phone, held just in front of his mouth as he spoke, and the occasional flash of lightning would partly illuminate the thick curtains.

His daily phone call from Blanche, one of the friends he'd made on Gran Canaria, had become an important part of his routine, a reminder that he had somewhere to go to when his time in Southend was finally done and friends who were waiting for him.

'A pool?' Blanche asked, her smooth voice filling the room. 'Sorry, you are putting a swimming pool into the garden of a house... in Southend-on-Sea?'

Charlie chuckled. 'I have buyers. And we've negotiated the price to include the installation of a pool. Don't ask. It's what they want, and at this price point, I'm not going to argue.'

He could hear Blanche tutting and huffing at the end of the line, exasperated at the whole idea that a house in Essex would ever have enough good weather to justify the running costs of an outside swimming pool.

'And is it covered, or heated?'

'No,' Charlie laughed. 'It's a bog-standard swimming pool. Although right now it's just a huge hole that is rapidly filling with rainwater. Look, this is a big house, a stone's throw from Southend Golf Course. We're pushing a million here. I'm not in a position to argue.'

'And that's another thing I don't understand, my darling,' Blanche said. 'How does this fit into your business model? You know, providing affordable housing for new families. Helping people get on the housing ladder?'

'Well, it doesn't,' Charlie said. And then he felt a pang in the pit of his stomach as he remembered the reason he and Jason had bought the property. 'This one… well… this was purely business,' he said. 'We… I mean, Jason and I… we needed a bigger cash injection to help us get things up and running with our rental properties in Maspalomas. So, this was our final flip. It was Jason's idea. One last renovation, but one that would actually yield a decent profit. This house… it feels like it's his final gift to me. But he was always the one who was good with money, and I just want to make sure I get it right.'

There was a pause at the end of the line, and then Blanche replied, 'You'll do him proud, my darling. And if you need any financial advice, please give me a call.'

'Oh, of course. You're running a dozen successful businesses simultaneously; of course I would come to you for advice.'

Blanche laughed. 'Oh no, Charlie. I'm terrible with money, but I have a very, very good accountant. I can put you in touch with her.'

Charlie grinned. 'That sounds great too.'

'And, have you told your family about your decision yet?'

Charlie paused, feeling suddenly weighed down, as he was reminded of a difficult conversation he had yet to have. 'No. I'm waiting for the right moment. Dad's trial begins next week. I want to get that out of the way first.'

'I understand,' Blanche said fondly. 'Listen, Martin and Peggy send their love. Everyone at Ricky's too. We're all looking forward to having you come back to us, back home. And whatever happens, my darling, we'll all be here for you. We all love you, and we'll be here for you.'

'I love you all too,' Charlie said, and then he added, 'Four weeks. All things considered, I should be home in four weeks.'

'Good. I'll call you tomorrow, same time. Love you.'

The call ended, and for a moment, Charlie just stayed where he was, on the floor of his lounge. He hadn't felt the need to put any lights on. It made no difference to him whether the room was lit or immersed in

146

darkness. Very little in his life mattered anymore. None of it felt particularly real.

Whenever he joined a conversation, or laughed, or bought something in a shop, he had to remind himself how to act as though everything was normal and not as if his entire life had been destroyed. There were still mornings when he awoke, and forgot Jason was gone, and for a few moments was puzzled why the bed was empty. There were still moments when he boiled the kettle to make tea and automatically put out two mugs rather than just one. And moments when he was alone, when he would just cry uncontrollably.

He closed his eyes and, for a while, just listened to the sound of the storm outside, thrashing so vigorously against the exterior of the house. He could easily just stay there, on the lounge floor, all night, listening to the wind and the rain whilst staying dry and warm inside. But he knew he would eventually fall asleep and didn't want to wake up sprawled out across the floor.

He stood and made his way to the kitchen, the room gently illuminated by a small, digital panel at the front of the oven, just bright enough to allow Charlie to manoeuvre to the countertop by the hob, on which was a bottle of whiskey and a single crystal tumbler. It had been a gift from the couple buying the house he was renovating. They considered themselves to be whiskey connoisseurs. Charlie wasn't much of a whiskey drinker, but he felt he needed something to take the edge off his mood. He poured himself a half glass and sat down at the kitchen table.

Then, unexpectedly, he began to feel uneasy, as though he were not alone. He placed the tumbler onto the table and cocked his head, wondering if there had been a sound from outside, something he'd noticed, perhaps just subconsciously, but enough to make him feel troubled. And as he listened, he realised there was something within the noise of the rain and the wind; something quiet but close by, a scratching, perhaps something metal.

The house was mid-terrace, with no access to the garden from the street. But there was a side return next to the kitchen, bordered by a six-foot fence, and Charlie began to sense that someone was there. He heard

147

the noise again, only now a little louder. Suddenly, the thick wooden back door shook as if something had slammed against it from outside, and Charlie realised someone was trying to break into his home.

He stood, and strode to the back door, his anxiety disappearing, replaced with a rapidly building sense of annoyance. How dare they, he thought. How dare they try and break into his house. Instinctively, he opened the cutlery drawer and took out a large chef's knife, and then he switched on the exterior light, quickly unlocked the door, opened it, and stepped outside into the rain.

Within the gently illuminated space, he could immediately see the cause of the disturbance: a figure, just a few metres from him, in a black raincoat with the hood up, their arms slightly raised, surprised to have been caught, exposed, and their head tilted downwards, staring at the weapon in Charlie's hand.

'What the fuck?' Charlie shouted loudly, making sure he could be heard over the noise of the rainstorm. He could tell how shocked they were, the intruder, clearly having believed the house was empty. 'What are you doing in my garden?'

'Charlie,' the intruder said. A man's voice, panicked but familiar.

Charlie narrowed his eyes, trying to see if he could recognise him from the glimpses he could see below the hood.

'It's OK, it's me, I just came to talk to you.' Again, that voice; something so familiar, Charlie thought. Someone that he knew.

Despite the rain and the wind, Charlie did not feel cold. The moment had sent blood pumping through his veins, and he felt nothing but anger. Something about that man, that voice, immediately enraged him. The man reached for his hood and slowly pulled it down. And there was Nate, so many years since Charlie had last seen him or heard anything about him, suddenly and unexpectedly in front of him.

The exterior light, shining onto him from above, did him no favours, Charlie thought, amplifying the lines in his face and his thinning hair. His teeth had deteriorated further; he now had obvious gaps that could be seen when he spoke.

'What the hell are you doing here?' Charlie asked, in no mood for any of his nonsense.

148

Nate paused for a moment, his eyes wide as though trying to think what to say. 'I came to talk to you,' he said. 'Vicki told me you would be here.'

'Bullshit.'

'She did.'

'There is absolutely no reason Vicki would ever give you my home address,' Charlie snapped. 'You were trying to break in. Burglary now, is it? What, did you just make your way along the back alley until you found a house with all the lights off, and thought you'd give it a go?'

'I came to talk to you.'

'And you thought bunking over my back fence made more sense than knocking at the front door? Fuck you, Nate. I'm calling the police.'

Nate threw his arms up, exasperated. 'Oh yes, there it is. That Charlie Fletcher arrogance. Looking down on everyone else. Always making accusations, never thinking how lucky you had it, born with a silver spoon in your mouth. Like all you Fletchers, thinking you're so much better than everyone else. Better than me.'

'And yet I'm the one working 12-hour days, seven days a week,' Charlie shouted angrily. 'Vicki, a single mum, still works part-time. Billy stacks shelves in a supermarket. Tyler's only 17, and he's already got a full-time job. Funny, isn't it, Nate? That the kids you say were born into privilege are all working. And what do you do? Well, let me guess. You sit on your arse all day long, lounging around on other people's furniture, watching their TV, eating their food, using their hot water, not paying a penny towards any of it.'

Nate, rainwater dribbling down his face, scowled at Charlie. 'I'm homeless because your sister made me homeless,' he said. 'She's fine, of course, living in that big house of yours. I'm the one who ended up with nowhere to live.'

'My sister's twenty-seven. You're, what, fifty?'

'I'm thirty-nine,' Nate snapped.

'Well, you look a fucking state. Regardless, you're a grown man. My sister broke up with you years ago. She is not responsible for you or for putting a roof over your head. None of us is responsible for you, Nate. So, get the hell out of my garden.'

149

Nate stood for a moment, his lip slightly curled, and then, with an unpleasant smile, he enquired, 'How's your dad?'

Charlie's grip tightened on the handle of the knife.

'Oh, that's right,' Nate continued sarcastically. 'He killed your boyfriend, didn't he? I bet that makes family dinners awkward. You think you can look down your nose at the likes of me? When your own father's going to get banged up for killing someone. You Fletchers are such hypocrites. You're no better than the rest of us.'

A barrage of lightning momentarily lit the area as brightly as though it were the middle of the day, and Charlie noticed something behind Nate, beyond the side return, in the garden itself. Something was moving, up and down and side to side. And in the moments between the lightning and a loud roll of thunder which followed, he could hear something too, a whooshing and swooping. He realised it was the plastic sheeting, which covered a deep trench Jason had dug for a koi pond. It was weighted down by heavy cement tyles, but one corner had come loose and was now being tossed around in the wind. And that infuriated Charlie even more, that he had something he needed to fix, and Nate was getting in his way.

'I'm in touch with Vicki again,' Nate said.

And those words stopped Charlie in his tracks.

'She's sorting out access for me, to see my son, so he can get to know me,' Nate said, with a tone filled with malice and conceit. 'You know, if things go well, I could imagine us getting back together again. Perhaps I'll even move back into The Lodge, to be with her and Jack.'

Charlie began to move his fingers, turning the knife around and around in his hand as though preparing it for use. 'My nephew spent years in a foster home because of you,' he said. 'Vicki has only just got custody of him again. Do you honestly think she would risk that, over the likes of you?'

'What, and miss the chance for us to live as a happy family, Charlie? A normal, happy family. I always wondered if that was why you took such a dislike to me. Because Vicki and me could have what you and your boyfriend could never have.' And then Nate smirked. 'Well, especially not now.'

150

Charlie didn't reply. His expression dark, his soul emptied of all compassion, he held Nate in a fixed stare and wished him dead. He stepped forward, only slightly, but enough for Nate to instinctively take a step back. And when Charlie did speak, his words were slow and precise. 'Do not say his name,' he said. 'You say his name, and I swear, I will kill you.'

Nate, cowardly in so many ways, could see how the conversation might progress, and he did not like his chances against a young man like Charlie, so quietly angry, a weapon in his hand, so happy to cause genuine harm.

'Fine, I'll go,' Nate said, his voice trembling. 'But if you phone the police, I'll just deny I was here. There are a dozen people who will say I was with them all evening.'

Charlie said nothing. He simply stepped forward again, but this time Nate hurried from the side return and disappeared into the darkness beyond. The moment he was gone, Charlie stepped from the rain and back into his house. He locked the back door and then, out of pure spite, he switched off the outside light, leaving Nate to find his way from the garden in the dark.

He stood for a moment, almost certain he had heard his name being called from outside. Then he heard it again; Nate yelling for him. Charlie had a terrible urge to return to the rain and the storm, to find out why Nate was goading him, to see if he had one last spiteful comment to make. As the darkness in the house enveloped him, Charlie felt nothing but rage for the man who had ruined so many lives, a man who had just stood in front of him and mocked Jason's death.

The knife turning in his hand, Charlie waited, listening intently, as the rain rattled against the windows and the wind screamed around his house. But it wasn't the weather he was listening to. He was listening for Nate, wishing and daring him to call out again, one final time.

151

CHAPTER 31

As Debbie and Kim fussed about their kitchen, preparing a pot of tea and organising a plate of chocolate biscuits for their guest, Vicki sat quietly at the table and remembered the many times over the years she had visited their home. It had been different back then when Jack had been in foster care. Her visits had always been for a formal social services meeting, where she would join Jack, Debbie, Kim and a small group of professionals to discuss how the placement was going, how he was doing at school, and if he was happy with how contact with his mother was being arranged.

Vicki had always felt those meetings were some sort of judgement on her, on her failure as a parent. Sometimes, when her self-esteem was particularly low, she had even felt as though she didn't deserve to be in the room. And as lovely as it was to see her son, those meetings always left her feeling empty, hopeless, and with a sense of shame.

Debbie and Kim had been the source of conflict for her, too, because even though she had quickly grown very fond of them both, Vicki had always felt a deep imbalance in her relationship with them; they were the foster carers, part of a social services team keeping Jack in care, and Vicki was the young single mum, desperately trying to prove she was worthy of having her son's custody returned to her. Rightly or wrongly, she had always felt they had power, whilst she had none.

Her dream had always been that one day, Jack would be returned to her, and she could close the door on that whole part of his life and just be his mum, with no further interference from anyone. But when that day finally presented itself, Jack had sobbed uncontrollably. It was such a confusing time for him to be so happy at the thought of moving home with his mum but so devastated at the loss of two women who had been his parents for most of his childhood.

After several discussions with Jack's social worker, Vicki agreed the kindest thing to do was to allow her son to continue seeing Debbie and Kim. At first, she had believed this would just be in the short term, that as time went by, she would be able to wean her son from his emotional need to see his former foster carers.

But as the months passed, she found her own dynamic with Debbie and Kim changed, and she decided they should continue to be a part of his life, and she did not mind that at all. At some point in time, Vicki realised that Debbie and Kim had become her friends, and she did not want to lose them from her own life either.

Over the previous few months, since the day of the accident, Vicki had relied on them even more, to have Jack for sleepovers and occasionally for a few days at a time while things were going on at The Lodge that made it an unpleasant environment for a nine-year-old boy. And now, sat happily in their kitchen, having brought her son to stay with them for the weekend, she allowed herself to feel some pride in how settled she was with her own emotions and how she could leave her son with his former foster mums without any trepidation or envy.

'He was worried you'd given his old bedroom away,' Vicki said as Debbie and Kim joined her at the kitchen table. Debbie poured her a cup of tea, and Kim wedged two chocolate digestives onto the saucer and slid it over to her, 'when I told him you had a girl staying here too.'

'Oh, dear lord, no,' Debbie replied. 'Honestly, Vicki, his bedroom will be his bedroom until he doesn't want it anymore. That really isn't a problem.'

Vicki smiled, sipped her tea and then asked, 'What's she like, the girl you have now?'

Kim and Debbie glanced at each other, a silent but solemn exchange that suggested things were not going well.

'Actually, we do need to talk to you about that,' Debbie said, 'just so you understand the situation.'

'Oh, OK,' Vicki replied. 'Is everything working out?'

'Her name's Rose,' Debbie said. 'She's been here two weeks. We took her as an emergency placement. Her previous placement broke down very suddenly, so we literally got a call from the out-of-hours team at 11pm one night, asking if we could take her for a few days.'

'Oh, my goodness,' Vicki said, 'Eleven o'clock at night?'

153

Debbie nodded. 'She turned up with most of her stuff piled into bin bags, and the social worker could only offer vague comments about why the placement broke down.'

'And that's a bad sign,' Kim added quietly, as though sharing a secret. 'When the social workers are vague. That's always a bad sign.'

'So, we had a couple of days when she mostly behaved herself,' Debbie continued, 'but after a very, very short honeymoon period, everything just exploded. Dinners were thrown on the floor, her bedroom was trashed. The tiniest thing sends her spiralling into a rage.'

Vicki sipped her tea and listened intently. She recalled that Kim and Debbie had taken a number of short-term placements when Jack had lived with them, but Jack had always been quite happy about the other kids and young people who had come into his home. There had never been any stories like this one. 'And there's no sign as to what triggers her temper?' she asked.

Debbie and Kim both shrugged.

'She threw her dinner on the floor last night because I had given her chicken dippers instead of chicken nuggets,' Kim said. 'She screamed for about ten minutes and then trashed her bedroom. Again.'

Vicki frowned. 'Aren't dippers and nuggets the same thing?'

'You'd think, wouldn't you,' Kim replied, an unusual hint of irritation in her usually calm voice. 'Honestly, anything, and I mean anything, can set her off.'

'Where is she now?' Vicki asked.

'She's out with her social worker,' Debbie replied. 'I can't imagine what the poor child's been through in her life to have so much anger, to be ready to explode like that, all the time.'

'Are you sure you are still OK to have Jack this weekend?' Vicki asked, 'Honestly, it sounds like you have enough on your hands.'

Kim and Debbie both reassured Vicki that everything was fine. 'We just need to have a chat with Jack so he's aware of what might happen,' Debbie said. 'But, no, absolutely, he can stay this weekend. We'd love to have him. And you need the time with your brother.'

The doorbell chimed, and Debbie reached across the table and squeezed Vicki's wrist. 'Brave heart,' she said wryly, 'sounds like she's home.'

She then disappeared from the kitchen, and Vicki could hear a man's voice, the girl's social worker, she assumed, and then there was the sound of the front door being closed. Moments later, Debbie reappeared with Rose, who was not at all what Vicki had been expecting. From the description, Vicki had pictured a big, brooding teenager, chewing gum and looking disinterested in everything. Instead, she was presented with a short, skinny child, probably only about seven years old, with long brown hair, pale skin and grey eyes. She stared coldly at Vicki as though taking a measure of the new adult in the kitchen.

'This is Rose,' Debbie said. 'Rose, this is Vicki, Jack's mum. Jack's in the front room playing with the Wii. You remember? He's staying with us for the weekend.'

'Hello,' Rose said and unexpectedly waved at Vicki.

'Hello Rose,' Vicki replied. 'Did you have a nice time with your social worker?'

Rose nodded. 'He took me to KFC for lunch,' she said. 'I had nuggets.' And then she glared at Kim as though she had proven a point.

'Right, you need to go and tidy your bedroom,' Debbie said, 'and then we'll introduce you to Jack. Kim's making cottage pie for dinner. Would you like to help her make it?'

Rose frowned, 'What's cottage pie?'

'Oh, it's a lovely meal of minced beef and onion topped with mashed potato,' Kim replied and then paused, waiting for Rose to state whether or not she liked the sound of it. But Rose didn't say anything. She scowled at Kim and then simply turned, marched from the kitchen, stormed up the stairs, and seconds later, the sound of her bedroom door being slammed could be clearly heard. After that, they could hear her wailing and screaming in her room.

'I didn't think my cottage pie sounded that bad,' Kim said glumly.

'Should she be in foster care?' Vicki asked delicately. 'It seems a lot to ask you to deal with.'

155

Debbie sighed, then shrugged, 'She's only here until Wednesday, and then she's moving to a new foster family.'

'Oh yes,' Kim said, rolling her eyes, 'apparently they've been specially trained to deal with children with more extreme behaviours.' And then she whispered the words 'specially trained' whilst miming air brackets with her hands.

'To be honest, this is what we do now,' Debbie said. 'We don't do long-term placements anymore. We just do short-term respite placements and emergencies. We're winding down to retirement.' She sipped her tea just as there was a scream and a loud crash from Rose's bedroom. 'If you can call this winding down,' she added, only partly muttered under her breath.

Kim groaned and stood up. 'I'll go and see what the little madam is doing,' she said and quickly exited the kitchen.

'It's not as bad as it seems,' Debbie said. 'She has moments when she's quite sweet.' And then she placed her teacup back onto its saucer and settled back in her chair as though there had been a step-change in the conversation. 'May I ask how things are at home? Since the accident?'

'Oh, Debbie, it's a bloody shit show,' Vicki replied. 'We're really worried about Charlie. We lost Jason that day, but it feels like we lost Charlie too, in many ways. And then there's Dad, out getting pissed all the time, pretending like everything's going to be fine when it's clearly not. Billy's been called as a prosecution witness, and he's so stressed about that. He hasn't talked about it, which is unlike Billy because he usually talks to me about everything. But I can see how worried he is; he knows what he says in court will likely send Dad to prison, for years.'

Debbie reached over and gently patted Vicki's hand, 'But what about you? How are you coping?'

Vicki suddenly realised how exhausted she was, 'I feel like I'm in the middle of it all. I want to be there for Charlie, but he's so distant with me, and I know part of that is that I'm still living with Dad. I know what that must be like for him, how much it must hurt, to see that I still have a relationship with our dad. Billy just needs protecting from everything, from the world, he always has, bless him. But this time, I just don't feel I can do anything for him. And then there's dad. And I can see how scared he is. Just moments, fleeting, in his eyes or in his voice. And when that happens, it's like I can't be angry with him. I just want to give him a hug. Because even though he did a terrible, horrible thing, he's still my dad, and I can't help but love him.'

As Vicki finished speaking, she could feel tears pouring down her cheeks, and she was suddenly very embarrassed as she realised, she had started to cry. Debbie opened a nearby drawer, produced a box of tissues, and handed them to Vicki, who quickly took one and began to dry her eyes. 'Sorry,' she said, 'I'm so sorry.'

'I'll have none of that,' Debbie replied. 'You ever need a good cry, you come here. We always have tissues, and we always have wine.'

Vicki let out a laugh, then, 'Oh. A glass of wine.' And before she could say anything else, the cups of tea and plate of biscuits had been nimbly replaced with three large glasses of pinot and a bowl of savoury nibbles.

Kim re-joined them and closed the kitchen door slightly as she did. 'Rose is going to help me make the cottage pie,' she said, 'and if she doesn't like the look of it, I said she could have fish fingers and beans instead, which she does like. The fish fingers will be Captain Birdseye, and the beans will be Heinz. She was very prescriptive about that.' She joined them at the table and sipped her wine, 'Some people might accuse me of caving into the unreasonable demands of a badly behaved seven-year-old. But I say we found a compromise that works for everyone.'

And all three of them raised their glasses as though in a toast.

'Vicki, may I offer you one piece of advice?' Debbie said, and Vicki quickly responded by urging her to do exactly that. 'Have you considered buying your own place?'

Vicki shook her head. 'I haven't,' she said. 'I mean, moving back to The Lodge was such a big part of the court order being removed. You know, Jack coming to live with me. I haven't really thought of anything else.'

'Look, it's none of our business,' Debbie continued, 'it really isn't. But you have Jack now, and you said your grandmother left you some money in her will. Was that enough for a deposit on a place of your own?'

157

Dorothy had bequeathed £55,000 to each of her four grandchildren, money Vicki had left in a savings account because the idea of buying a house had simply not occurred to her. But she also had a relatively good income from some part-time HR work she had taken on, for the supermarket she used to work at. 'It would be enough for a deposit, but I'd have to think if I could afford the repayments. Perhaps I might need to up my hours at work,' she said. 'Mind you, that wouldn't be a bad thing. Jack's nine. I'm sure he can cope with the idea of a working mum.'

'And we're always here,' Kim said. 'And you've got Billy and Charlie too. And your dad's ex-partner.'

'Carol,' Vicki said, and it suddenly felt so strange to hear Carol described like that. Even though she and Peter had a child together, Vicki had seen little evidence of an actual relationship between the two of them. 'Yes, and there's Carol,' she said.

'And to be honest,' Debbie said, 'the way house prices are going up, I would say it's a good time to get on the property ladder. You know, we bought this house in 1988 for about £50,000. A house two doors down was sold last year, pretty much the same property as this, four-bed semi-detached. They got more than three hundred grand for it. Honestly, Vicki. Now's the time to buy.'

Vicki could feel herself being persuaded that buying her own house was a good idea. Her return to The Lodge had been a means to an end, a way to create a stable home life for herself so that Jack could live with her again. But ever since she'd regained custody of her son, she had found herself increasingly less satisfied with life at the house. She knew how lucky she was, to have a family that was so supportive, so readily available to offer help whenever she needed it. But she had begun to yearn for her own space, and suddenly, the prospect of buying her first house seemed completely within her reach. All she needed to do was find the perfect property.

CHAPTER 32

Billy spoke slowly and clearly, his deep voice filling the courtroom as he described the moment his father lost control of the car. He spoke of the terrible noise as the vehicle crashed into a lamppost and bollards at the centre of a mini roundabout, the fright of an airbag bursting from the dashboard, and the sensation of the car taking to the air as it flipped upside down, before skidding across the road on its roof, coming to a stop only when it collided with metal railings.

As he conveyed his story he looked straight ahead, as he had been told to do by the witness support team, to direct his words to the jury. And he was grateful for that advice, as it meant he did not have to look at his father, who was sat some distance away, to his left, in the dock.

Every now and again, he would glance to the back of the court, behind the lawyers, to the public benches, and he could see Vicki, Carol and Tyler, all dressed in formal dark clothes, as though attending a funeral, but all there to support him. A few seats away from them, he could see Angel, sat with her arms folded, staring at him as though waiting for him to say something different. But Billy did as he knew he should and just recounted the events exactly as he remembered them.

'Mr Fletcher, thank you for your very clear and precise testimony. I appreciate these must be deeply unpleasant memories for you.' With those words, Billy knew the defence lawyer wanted to present herself as a friend, someone concerned for his wellbeing. But he also knew what she was likely to ask him and that the conversation might grow unpleasant.

'Am I right in thinking that you first gave that account of this accident to the police, shortly after the accident itself occurred?'

'Yes,' Billy replied.

'And you have repeated, pretty much word for word, that version of the accident here today?'

'Yes.'

The defence lawyer paused and appeared to rifle through some papers on the table in front of her. Billy watched, nervous and trembling

159

slightly, worried she may have something in that stack of papers that would cast doubt on his story. Or, perhaps, he wondered, it was some sort of legal grandstanding to give the impression she had some important documents to refer to when, in fact, she had nothing.

'One of the reasons your injuries turned out to be relatively minor is because you remembered to put your seatbelt on when you got into the front passenger seat next to your father. Is that correct?'

Billy nodded, 'I... I suppose so.'

'But Mr Day, the man who died, your brother-in-law, he was thrown from the vehicle because he was not wearing a seatbelt.'

Billy did not reply, believing the question to be rhetorical. But then the Lawyer gestured to him, with her hand, to answer, and so he said, 'I don't know. I couldn't see Jason. He was sat behind me.'

'But it is true, is it not, that if Mr Day was not wearing a seatbelt, he had freedom of movement? He was not constrained to his seat, as presumably you were?'

Billy shrugged, 'He was sat behind me, so I couldn't see him.'

The lawyer paused and tilted her head as though pondering his reply. 'You were unconscious for a while, weren't you? Immediately after the collision. You spoke about awakening and, at first, being confused as to where you were, what had happened.'

'Yes. I think I was out for just a few moments. Seconds.'

'But despite your confusion and your injuries, when you spoke to the police, later that day, you were able to give an account of the accident that you have stuck to ever since.'

'Yes.'

'Is it possible, Mr Fletcher, that you didn't get all the details exactly right?'

Billy shook his head, 'I've told you what happened, exactly as I remember it.'

'Yes, yes, and that is my point,' the lawyer replied sharply. 'This was a very traumatic experience. Terrifying, I would suggest. And one that left your family, your brother, in particular, trying to come to terms with a devastating loss.'

'Yes.'

Billy glanced over to his family and could see them all staring at him, each of them utterly baffled as to where the line of questioning was leading. For a moment, he wished he had told them of the conversation in the sitting room with his father and Angel. He wished he had prepared them for what Peter and Peter's defence lawyer were going to claim in court. And he was so pleased that Charlie had not attended the hearing. He did not know how his brother would possibly cope with what was about to happen.

'It is unusual when someone had been through such a frightening and traumatic experience, for that person to have such a clear and detailed memory of it. By your own admission, at some point, you lost consciousness. And yet, at no point over the past months have you suggested that your recollection of the accident might not be totally accurate or complete. Nor have you suggested that you have remembered any additional details to add to your account. You gave a version of events to the police the day of the accident, and you have recounted exactly the same story here today.'

'That is because what I said is what happened. I don't have anything to add.'

The lawyer raised her brow and inhaled loudly as though getting irritated with him. And then she exhaled as she fiddled with the papers in front of her. 'We have established that Mr Day was not wearing his seatbelt,' she stated and looked at Billy. 'And therefore, he could move about relatively freely on the back seat. You have also, in your own words, recounted that he and your father were arguing just before the accident, raised voices, shouting at each other.'

'No,' Billy said abruptly.

'I beg your pardon?'

'I didn't say that,' Billy insisted. 'I didn't say that Jason was arguing or shouting. He was calm and polite the whole time.'

'But, steadfastly, he was attempting to persuade your father to pull over and let him take the wheel.'

'Yes, but he didn't shout or raise his voice.'

The lawyer nodded. 'Is it possible that your recollection of this accident is not correct, Mr Fletcher, or at least it is not complete?'

161

Billy shook his head, 'I remember it clearly, still.'

'But surely you must admit it is possible that you do not remember every detail, that something quite significant could have happened during the final few moments of that ill-fated car journey, and you simply do not remember it. Perhaps because of the head injury you suffered, being knocked unconscious. Perhaps you simply glanced in another direction, out of the window, for a moment.'

Billy said nothing. He simply stared at her, knowing exactly what she was going to suggest.

'Let me propose that at some point in the final seconds of that car journey, Jason Day lurched forward, through the gaps in the seats, and attempted to grab the steering wheel. He tried to force your father to pull over by physically taking control of the car. If we take into account the speed at which all of these events happened, your head injury, the fact that you were unconscious for a period of time, not forgetting the terrible mental and emotional trauma that this accident must have caused you. If we take all of that into account, can you honestly say, one hundred percent, without a shadow of a doubt, that your recollection of this accident is absolutely correct? Can you honestly tell this court that the events I have just described definitely did not happen?'

And there it was. The opportunity to keep his father out of jail without telling a lie. Because Billy knew he simply had to agree with the point that it was hypothetically possible his memory of the accident might not be complete. And he knew that was all the defence lawyer needed, the suggestion that his dad might be innocent. Because to convict, the jury must have no doubt of Peter's guilt, and the defence lawyer was trying to cast doubt on Peter's guilt by making them question Billy's version of events.

Billy glanced over to look at Vicki to see if he could glean some idea of what to do from the expression on her face. But someone else was there, next to Vicki, and Billy's heart missed a beat as he realised it was Charlie, who must have quietly slipped into the public benches a few moments earlier. And Billy knew how hard that would be for Charlie to have to listen to the details of his husband's death just so he could be in that court to support his younger brother.

162

Charlie's face was pale and thin, and Billy realised he had been there just long enough to hear the discussion with Peter's defence lawyer and the claim that Jason had caused the accident. And he could see how scared Charlie was, his eyes wide, panicked, so frightened that the next words from Billy's mouth would allow the blame to be placed with Jason.

Billy knew what that would mean for Charlie, that there would be no justice for Jason, and the grief Charlie was carrying would be never-ending, that it would consume him entirely. And then Billy's gaze wandered slightly, to the left, and there was Angel, glaring at him, not speaking, but raising her brow and nodding her head, willing him to agree with the defence lawyer.

For a moment, Billy found the silence in the court overwhelming, as though it were trying to press the oxygen from his lungs to force him to fill the air with noise, with words, to either confirm or deny what the defence lawyer had said. But then there was a whisper, a familiar voice from so very long ago, at the back of his mind, nudging him forward, comforting him, reminding him how important it was to tell the truth. Billy wrapped himself in the love and reassurance that voice offered him, and as his emotions settled down, he knew what he had to do.

'Yes, I can,' he said softly, tears beginning to well up in his eyes.

The defence lawyer gesticulated, 'Pardon? Can you speak more loudly, Mr Fletcher?'

Billy stared directly at the jury once more as a tear tumbled down his cheek. 'Yes. I can say, one hundred percent, that my memory of the accident is correct and complete. Jason did not try to grab the steering wheel. He remained in the back seat, talking to Dad calmly, just trying to persuade him to pull over.'

'Mr Fletcher—' the lawyer attempted to interject, but Billy continued speaking.

'The accident happened because my father was driving whilst he was very drunk. He was angry and frustrated, shouting and yelling that he could do whatever he wanted. He was speeding and not paying attention to the road. The accident was entirely my dad's fault. It is not right to try and blame Jason just because he's not here to defend himself.'

163

And then he faced the dock, where Peter was staring at him, an expression of absolute loss on his face. 'You shouldn't have tried to blame Jason, Dad,' Billy said. 'That was a really wicked thing to do.'

CHAPTER 33

Vicki wondered how long she would have to sit there, at the table in Charlie's kitchen, before her brother would ask about their father's sentencing. She had never seen him like this before, avoiding eye contact with her, so agitated and distracted.

From the moment she had arrived, Charlie had busied himself; he made a pot of tea, and wiped down all the kitchen surfaces, and had been talking about the weather and how bad the wind and the rain had been over the previous few days. And then he had gone into a protracted story about the final house he and Jason had bought to flip, a large six-bedroom detached house near a golf course, a property which had been empty for years.

'We had that whole philanthropic business model,' he said, 'renovating houses and then selling them as cheaply as we could to help local people to get onto the housing ladder. We know we helped lots of people, but always small profits. And Jason wanted us to balance that with the occasional renovation where we would make some proper money.' Charlie loaded a few plates and cups into the dishwasher as he spoke. 'We weren't even half done with the renovations and Jason found some buyers. Can you believe they've negotiated the price with Jason to include the installation of an exterior swimming pool, in their garden? Here in Southend. An outside pool?'

Vicki was used to this, Charlie slipping between past and present tense when speaking of Jason. It was as if, all these months later, his mind still struggled to acknowledge that Jason was gone. And she knew what he was trying to do; avoid the conversation Vicki was there to have with him, the news from the final day of their father's court case. She allowed him a few more moments of procrastination before she drained her teacup, placed it back onto the saucer, and interrupted.

'Dad got six years,' she said before he had the chance to find something else to speak about. 'The judge made a point of criticising him for trying to blame the accident on Jason. He said it showed Dad had no remorse for what he did. We think that's why he got a worse sentence than we'd been told to expect.'

She paused, waiting to see how Charlie would react. Throughout her life, she had been able to read Charlie, because he was so obvious with his feelings. But in that moment, she had no idea what he was going to say or do, and that left her feeling anxious.

Charlie stood still, leaning against the sink and staring out through the kitchen window. When he didn't respond, Vicki stood and joined him but was immediately distracted by the view, which was not what she had expected. Jason had been busy in the garden in the weeks before he died and had numerous projects underway, and Charlie appeared to have erased them all.

'The storm, last week, it left quite a mess,' he said, and it was clear to Vicki that he had noticed her surprise and felt a need to explain what he had done. 'But it made me realise I had to sort out everything in the garden and decide what I wanted to do. So, I got rid of all the wood for the pergola. I've no idea how to build a pergola. Jason was the handy one.

'Same with the raised planters he was going to build for his vegetable garden. And I filled that deep trench where he was going to install the koi pond. Six feet deep. Took bloody ages, but I don't know the first thing about fish, either. So, I've got a team coming tomorrow to lay a cement foundation where it would have been, and then they're installing a cabin.'

'A cabin?' Vicki asked.

'It's quite big. Four metres by three. They're becoming very popular. People can use them as a place to work or a clubhouse for their kids, or teenagers. Or a summer house.' He pointed to the rear of the garden. 'Can you see those? The row of bamboo canes arranged along the back fence,' he said. 'Bizarrely, the only thing the storm didn't touch. They were another of Jason's ideas, back in the spring. He wanted to grow runner beans. He sent me pictures, him in his T-shirt and shorts, using a wooden ruler to place them in the exact positions he had found in a gardening book. And they're the one thing I can't get rid of. I don't know why because he didn't get the chance to plant the seeds, so there's nothing growing there. It's just a row of bamboo canes.'

'Charlie, Dad's gone to prison for six years,' Vicki said, 'because he is responsible for what happened to Jason. You must feel something about that.' Vicki tried to remain sensitive and kind, but her brother's behaviour was wrong, alien. She couldn't leave his house until she felt he had at least responded to her news. She needed to have something more from him, a raised voice or some tears. She just needed something to show that he was still there, somewhere, her brother, the real Charlie, and not this other person, a man who was so distant from her.

'I'm empty,' he replied, eventually. 'And I don't know what you want me to say.' He did not sound cross or angry. At the very most, perhaps, a little exasperated. 'I'm running on empty, sweetheart,' he said. 'It sounds like a just outcome. Dad killed Jason, and now he's gone to jail. That sounds just.' He moved away from her and started to rifle through the kitchen cupboards.

'But Charlie—'

'Vicki, I don't love Dad,' he said. He stopped what he was doing and looked at his sister, his expression cold, without warmth or even familiarity. 'I don't even like him. If I'm honest, I don't think I ever have. Dad going to jail isn't a problem for me. But this isn't about me. It's about you and Billy. And Tyler and Lizzie. He's your dad too, and you all need to sort out, in your own heads, how this affects you.'

'So, you wouldn't care if Dad had been found not guilty?' Vicki asked, struggling to believe her brother's lack of interest. 'If he was at home right now, celebrating. You wouldn't care?'

'Oh no, no, no,' Charlie replied. 'If Dad had managed to get himself acquitted by blaming Jason for what happened, I'd kill him.'

Vicki stood quietly, not sure how to respond. She had seen her brother lose his temper many times over the years, but he had always been articulate, clever, funny even. She had never, not once, heard him threaten violence, and the sound of those words coming from his mouth, delivered so calmly and so coldly, frightened her.

They were silent for a few moments, and then Charlie found a bottle of wine in one of the cupboards. He opened it, poured two glasses and then emptied a bag of savoury snacks into a bowl. He took them to the kitchen table and sat down. Vicki joined him.

'Sorry,' he said. 'That was a bit brutal, wasn't it?'

Vicki quickly took a sip from her glass, 'I've not heard you speak like that before,' she said. 'You didn't mean it?'

Charlie shrugged. 'What hurts,' he said, 'is that you still love him. All of you. He killed Jason, and you're all still running around after him. And at some point, I'll see you and Billy getting ready to visit Dad in prison, and I know it will feel like a betrayal. I'm not saying that's right, Vicki, right or fair. But I know how it will make me feel.'

Vicki bowed her head and sighed. She could feel the distance between her and Charlie so powerfully, and every time he spoke, the feeling intensified.

'I am not asking you to make a choice,' Charlie said. 'I'm not asking any of you to make a choice. I'm just explaining what this feels like for me. So, perhaps you will understand what I've decided to do.'

Vicki looked up and stared at him, worried she already knew what he was about to say.

'When Jason and I bought this house, it was going to be a flip, but we decided to move in, make it our home,' Charlie said. 'Five years. Five happy years.' He looked around the kitchen, and Vicki could only imagine how many memories he had in that house, the joyful life he'd had with Jason.

'Once we became homeowners, Jason wanted a proper grown-up conversation,' Charlie continued. 'About what would happen if one of us were to die. And it wasn't just about writing wills. It was about what happened next. He said being widowed wasn't about a funeral, or settling an estate, or the visits from well-meaning loved ones, and the endless casseroles. It was about what happened after that, when no one was visiting anymore, and it was time to go back to work. Paying the bills, doing the weekly shop. All those everyday events that you're suddenly having to do on your own.'

'Sounds a pretty grim conversation,' Vicki said.

And then Charlie smiled; for the first time in what seemed like forever, Vicki saw her brother smile. 'It was an undeniably grim

168

conversation,' Charlie said. 'But Jason is... Jason was the most practical person I ever knew. And he didn't want me to get stuck, to be unable to move on with my life, if I ever lost him. He made me promise that I would do whatever I needed to do to find happiness again. Sell this house, marry again. Whatever it took. And that's the problem, Vicki. Every part of the house is filled with Jason, little moments of his life, mostly silly or mundane things. The time he dropped a cup of tea on our newly fitted lounge carpet. Or his unsuccessful first attempt at poached eggs. Or the day he arrived home with great excitement because he had found the first season of "The Golden Girls" on DVD in a local charity shop.'

Vicki chuckled and then slid her hand over Charlie's. 'You're selling the house,' she said.

Charlie nodded. 'I have too,' he replied. 'I know if I stay, my happy memories will overwhelm me, and one day I might wake up, an old man, who's been alone for too many years. A half-life of wishing things had been different. That's why I'm sorting out the back garden, trying to make it appeal to buyers.'

Vicki sat back in her seat and sipped her wine again. 'Are you moving back to the Lodge?' she said. 'You know we'd all love to have you there.'

But Charlie shook his head. 'No,' he said. 'You're all keeping the house ready for Dad, for whenever he comes out of prison. And that's fine. I understand entirely why you are doing that. But the Lodge isn't my home anymore. It hasn't been for a long time.'

'So, what sort of place are you looking for? Same as this?' Vicki asked.

There was a long pause before her brother answered, and Vicki could tell he was about to share some upsetting news.

169

CHAPTER 34

The Lodge should have been empty, Billy was sure of it. He knew Charlie was at home, and Vicki had taken Jack away for a few days, down to Kent, to stay with an old school friend. Carol and Tyler would both be at work. Neither of them had mentioned they were planning to visit The Lodge, and even though they could both come and go freely, they always made a point of saying in advance if they were dropping in.

So, as he closed the front door behind him and placed his bags of shopping onto the hall carpet, he could not understand why he could clearly hear voices coming from the rear of the house. He marched forward, opened the door to the kitchen, and found the room filled with people he didn't know, all women, about a dozen of them, standing in the kitchen area or sitting at the breakfast bar, music playing in the background, all of them with a glass of wine in hand, chatting.

Billy looked around the space, trying to locate someone he recognised, someone whose presence would immediately make sense of the scene in front of him. But there was no one, not a soul. He hurried over to Vicki's portable media player, and, clearly irritated, he switched it off. A couple of the women turned and stared at him, scowling, but at least they acknowledged him. Everyone else carried on as though passive-aggressively ignoring him.

'I'm sorry,' Billy said loudly to no one in particular. 'Who are you all, and what are you doing in my house?'

One of the women leaned over and switched the music back on; there was a little cheer, and the conversation resumed as before. In retaliation, Billy removed Vicki's media player from its speaker and dropped it into his trouser pocket. He clapped his hands and projected his voice as strongly as he could, over the chatter and laughter that appeared to have grown even louder since he had entered the kitchen.

'I'm Billy. I live here. Would one of you please explain who you all are and what you are doing in my house?'

From the other side of the room, he heard a familiar voice, 'It's OK Billy, sweetheart, it's just me. I'm having a few friends over.' Angel

170

walked towards him, a friendly smile on her face, 'Perhaps you could put the music back on?'

But Billy did no such thing. He simply stared at her and wondered what on earth she was doing at The Lodge, with a load of her friends, in the middle of the day. Or, indeed, why she was at The Lodge at all. Angel appeared to recognise the puzzled expression on his face, so she grasped him by the elbow and walked with him back into the hall, where she closed the kitchen door behind them.

'Is there a problem?' she asked, sounding slightly irritated by him.

'Well, yes of course there is,' Billy replied. 'I don't understand why you and your friends are in my home?'

'Oh, I see. I guess your father didn't speak to you about this?'

Billy lowered his brow, unable to prevent an unfriendly grimace appearing on his face, 'I haven't spoken to him since the trial. None of us has.'

Angel looked as though something had suddenly made sense. 'Right,' she said. 'I'm your dad's partner, Billy, and he wants me to keep an eye on The Lodge, and all of you kids, while he's in prison. He gave me his house keys and told me to come and go as I please. To use it as a second home. I'm going to be moving some of my things into his bedroom, and I'll be here regularly. Pretty much all the time, as per your father's request. Keeping an eye on this house and all of you, too. So, I hope that's understood, Billy. Even though your dad is in prison, he's still thinking about you all, and wants to know you are all OK. Are there any other questions, because I need to get back to my friends?'

'Angel, we're all adults. We don't need you here, looking after us, or keeping an eye on our home.'

'Your father disagrees,' Angel replied.

Billy paused and felt a deep need to be very rude to Angel, but it simply was not in his nature to be offensive or ill-mannered. 'And you agreed this with Charlie, or Vicki, or Carol?' he asked. 'Because I knew nothing about this.'

'I don't see why your father would need to agree this with any of you,' Angel replied, her tone soft, puzzled. 'It's what he wants, and this is his home, after all.' She then held out her hand, an indication that she expected Billy to return the media player.

Billy had no intention of entering a discussion with Angel about whether she had a right to The Lodge, and he knew that was not the moment where the situation was going to be resolved. Angel had the upper hand; a key to the house and a kitchen filled with her friends. Begrudgingly, he handed the media player back to her before collecting his grocery shopping from the front door and walking back towards the kitchen.

'Oh, don't worry about my mates,' Angel said, introducing a more friendly tone to her voice. 'I've warned them the Fletcher boys are all very handsome, but they know to keep their hands to themselves.' She then opened the door for him, and Billy re-entered the kitchen.

Swiftly, Angel had the music playing once more, and some of her friends vacated the kitchen area to give Billy room to unpack his groceries.

'It's a lovely place you have here,' one of them shouted to Angel.

'Thank you, darling,' she simpered. 'I think we're going to have a lot of fun times in this house.'

Billy could tell the conversation was not natural, it sounded rehearsed, a way for Angel and her friends to lay claim to his home as their domain. He wasn't having it. Not one bit. He retreated to the sitting room, only to find further evidence of Angel's influence; furniture moved, pictures added to the mantel again, and some oddly patterned cushions scattered on his mother's couch.

He wondered what he should do next; this was more than just an inconvenience. This was an invasion of his personal space, of his family home, by someone who had absolutely no right to be there. His immediate impulse was to call Vicki, to ask her advice. But he knew how conflicted she would be; she would want to protect The Lodge as their family home, but she would also want to respect her father's wishes.

And then there was Charlie. Billy had seen him in such a dark place, for so many months, that he didn't want to add to his brother's distress. And as for Carol, who had been so bereft and so angry, in equal measure, since Jason's death, as though the terrible events of that day had in some way been a personal failure. Billy could imagine she would very likely just punch Angel in the face. And Billy had an impression that Angel would like nothing more than that, to present herself as the victim of a crime, to have Carol issued with a court order, banning her from The Lodge.

And he wondered if that was Angel's long game, that over time, she would gradually make life at the house so unbearable that eventually, all the Fletchers would leave. And that, he knew, was not what his mother would have wanted. And so, he took it upon himself to resolve the issue. Billy would not allow Angel to move into his family home. He would make it his personal responsibility to make sure of it. He just needed to work out what to do next.

CHAPTER 35

Over the following few days, Billy carefully executed a secret plan, one which involved a degree of subterfuge and perfect timing. The timing was critical because he was throwing a dinner party to introduce Emma to his family, and he certainly didn't want the evening ruined by any unexpected visitors.

It was also the first time, in far too long, that all the Fletchers were going to be together. Even Charlie had agreed to attend. Billy did not want anything to spoil the meal. He was already more than a little nervous, not because of anything to do with Emma. He knew everyone would all fall in love with her. But apart from Vicki, no one knew the story of how they had met, and he was worried how that information would land with his family, and in particular with Charlie.

He had found a way to deal with some of his anxiety by using his mum's personal recipe file. He knew the moment the kitchen filled with all those familiar aromas, it would immediately make him feel like Susan was there, helping to keep things calm. He and Emma had spent a busy afternoon in the kitchen preparing some of his mum's favourite meals; a boozy white wine, garlic and mushroom risotto as a starter, slow-cooked beef and ale stew with mashed potatoes and minted peas as the main, and a marsala-soaked tiramisu for pudding. It wasn't until Billy had looked through his mother's recipe cards that he had realised why so many of his parents' dinner parties had ended so late in the evening and so merrily.

Billy was desperate for Emma to like his family, for each of them to make a good first impression on her. Likewise, Emma was excited about finally meeting the Fletchers and wanted to make a good impression in return. She had decided to dress more formally than usual and so had coloured her hair a light brown and wore a fitted deep blue midi-dress with long sleeves. Billy had told her to just come as herself, but Emma knew there were going to be some difficult conversations that evening, and she wanted to present herself in a way that reflected that.

174

She helped Billy set out the dining table for nine, using the best cutlery, napkins and crystal wine glasses and tumblers. She then decorated the centre of the table with flowers she and Billy had cut from the garden, pink chrysanthemums mixed with yellow roses.

'Mum loved that, you know,' Billy said with great fondness in his voice. 'Even in the middle of November, she could still find colour in her garden.' He smiled as he thought of Tyler and all the hours his kid brother spent each week maintaining his Auntie Susan's garden and how skilfully and passionately he had managed to keep it the same whilst also occasionally making small changes but only changes they all knew Susan would have approved of.

Emma slipped an arm around his waist, and as he put his arm around her in return, she leaned against him. 'I think we've done a great job,' she said. 'Nervous?'

Billy sighed, 'I am,' he replied. 'You?'

'A little,' she said. 'It's Charlie, isn't it, mostly. You are worried how he is going to react.'

Billy didn't respond, but Emma knew it was true, and so she rested her head on his shoulder. 'I honestly don't have to be here if you think it's a conversation that would be easier if I wasn't.'

'Oh, you're not going anywhere,' Billy replied and then kissed her on the cheek. 'Besides, I need someone to help with the washing up.' He turned, wrapped both arms around her, and kissed her on the lips, 'I'm so lucky to have you.'

Emma gazed upwards into his deep brown eyes and suddenly felt a little overwhelmed that such a tall, handsome man, a man with such an unusually kind soul, was looking at her with such adoration. She had an incredible urge to take him to bed, but she knew they didn't have time. Their lovemaking was never brief; typically, it lasted several hours. And she knew the Fletchers would begin to arrive in the next thirty minutes.

'I look forward to later,' she said and allowed her hands to slide down Billy's back until she was able to hold his muscular rear in her hands. She could feel how aroused he was, pushing against her, a happy smile on his face.

'I look forward to that too,' he replied quietly. He leaned in to kiss her but was interrupted by the sound of the doorbell ringing repeatedly, almost angrily.

'Sounds like our first dinner guests are here,' Emma said. 'A bit early, though.'

Billy released her, 'No. I think that's someone else. You OK to keep an eye on the food?'

Emma, surrounded by pots and pans that were all gently steaming and bubbling, nodded, and so Billy made his way through the dark hallway to the front door. He tried to adjust himself as he walked to minimise the appearance of the bulge in the crotch of his jeans. After a brief detour to the sitting room, he switched on the exterior light and opened the door, but only partially. He kept his foot wedged behind it to prevent it from being forced and used himself to block the narrow opening.

Angel was on the doorstep waving her key towards Billy. 'There's a problem with the lock,' she said crossly.

'No there isn't.'

'My key doesn't work.'

'I had the locks changed. All of them.'

Angel lowered her hand and took a small step backwards, as though trying to get a proper view of Billy, of what he was playing at. 'That's fine,' she said. Placing her key into her pocket, she held out her hand, 'I'll have my copy of the new key.'

Billy frowned. 'Why would I give you a key?' he asked politely.

'I need to come in and start setting up,' she said. 'I've friends coming over for drinks.' Angel tried to remain matter-of-fact, refusing to engage with the point Billy was obviously making.

'Not here you don't. We're having a family dinner.'

'Oh. I must have missed my invitation.'

'I didn't send you one. It's for family.'

Angel's expression darkened, and then she spoke with obvious spite in her voice. 'You listen to me, Billy Fletcher. Your father—'

'Is in prison for the next six years, Abigail,' Billy interjected.

176

Her eyes widened at the sound of her real name, used as a clear rejection of 'Angel', of her pretence of being kind or good.

'When Dad's out of prison,' he continued, 'in six years' time and comes home, we'll have a family discussion. Dad, and me, and Charlie, and Vicki, and Carol. The family. We will agree who does and does not have a key to The Lodge. But, as I say, that will be in six years' time. Abigail.'

'I'll be speaking to your father about this,' Angel said with a threatening tone.

But Billy did not rise to it. 'Please do,' he replied lightly. 'And please make it clear to Dad that as long as he's in prison, he will not be handing keys to my home to complete strangers.'

He then reached through the gap in the door and held out the photographs Angel had added to the mantel, 'These belong to you.'

Silent, powerless, Angel snatched the photographs from Billy's hand and stared at him like she did not recognise him.

'Do not come here again. This is not your home.' And with that, Billy closed the door on her.

177

CHAPTER 36

For a while, it felt like old times. Familiar food, lots of wine, everyone talking, animated and happy. Just for those few hours, the Fletcher family was together again, and the terrible events of the previous months seemed to fade into the background, at least for that evening. Peter and Jason were present but not mentioned. Billy and Emma were the perfect hosts, making sure everyone had a full glass and graciously praising Susan's recipes when anyone commented on the delicious food.

They had placed Charlie at the head of the table, and as the evening progressed, he was inundated with hugs, everyone so pleased, so relieved, to have him home once more. Lizzie was told off by Carol for trying to have a third bread roll with her starter, and she sulked for a while until the main course arrived. Tyler regaled Vicki and Jack with stories of his planned travels through Europe whilst Jonathan sat next to him, a little forlorn, knowing those travels would not involve him.

As the evening continued and the meal concluded, Billy and Emma began to clear the table and load the dishwasher. They were soon joined in the kitchen by Charlie, helping to clear some of the plates. Billy had watched Charlie throughout the evening. He had seen his brother trying so hard to be present, to be a part of the conversations, but he had struggled to interact with everyone and had hardly spoken to Emma. And Billy guessed Charlie wished to correct that discourtesy, and properly introduce himself.

'The food could not have been better,' Charlie said. 'Honestly, Mum would be so thrilled. You both absolutely nailed it.'

Emma, a little tipsy, immediately hugged him and said thank you. 'I had no idea how strong your family genes were until I met you all,' she said, taking a step back and gesturing towards the dining table. 'The dark hair and the brown eyes. I've got two brothers, and we all look completely different.'

'Well, Billy got the height,' Charlie said.

'And the charm,' Billy added.

Charlie found three wine glasses on the counter, none of them used, and filled them from a bottle of red that was open on the side. Billy was crouching, continuing to fill the dishwasher, and so Charlie handed a glass to Emma.

'But I'm guessing you get your colourings from one of your parents?' she asked. 'Is it the Fletcher genes?'

'Actually, it's Mum's side of the family,' Charlie replied. 'The Morgans. I think that's why Tyler's the only one of us with blonde hair and blue eyes.'

Emma glanced over at Tyler and recalled Billy explaining that they had different mums. 'But Vicki and Lizzie?'

'Oh, one hundred percent Morgan,' Charlie said. 'And Jack, by the looks of things. But then, our Nan insisted on it.' And then he and Billy both laughed again at the thought of Dorothy insisting her grandchildren inherit her dark hair and brown eyes, because they knew, if it were possible, that is exactly what she would have done.

'Anyway, how's it going with you two?' Charlie asked. 'It's been quite a few months now. All going OK?'

'Oh, yes,' Emma replied. 'I'm very lucky. He's a lovely guy, your brother.'

'You're making me blush,' Billy said as he continued to load plates and cutlery.

'I haven't asked,' Charlie said, 'how did you meet?'

Billy stood up, and he and Emma looked at each other, realising the moment they had been so anxious about had finally arrived.

'Well, that's a bit of a story,' Emma said uneasily, unsure how to take the conversation forward.

'Oh, intrigue,' Charlie said, leaning back onto the breakfast bar and sipping his wine as if waiting for some salacious tale.

Billy could sense something was wrong. It was as if Charlie were acting, just pretending that he was enjoying the evening or even participating in the conversation. But he knew it was time to tell his brother the truth and, his heart suddenly pounding in his chest, he began to explain. 'It's a bit of a tough one, Charlie,' he said. 'You remember the day of the accident. I told you there was a woman, who reached into the car and held my hand until the emergency services arrived?'

Charlie's face was blank. He just looked at Billy and Emma as though waiting for the story to be completed. Billy could not read him at all.

'Well, that was Emma,' Billy said, and he took her hand. 'We met up, months later. I just wanted to say thank you, for everything she did that day. But then we just really got on.'

'It was completely unexpected,' Emma interceded. 'We didn't meet for a date or anything.'

'It really was meant to just be a chance for me to say thank you to her,' Billy added, and then he ran out of words. He glanced at Emma, but she was staring directly at Charlie, trying to assess how the news was being received. For a moment, it was not clear if Charlie had even realised what had been said. Perhaps, Billy wondered, Charlie had drunk a little too much, and his mind was slowly phasing out of the conversation. But then Charlie placed his wine glass back onto the counter and looked directly at Emma.

'I think that was an incredibly brave thing that you did,' he said. 'My brother was trapped inside a car, on its roof. You had no idea if it was safe. But you still climbed down onto the road, reached in through the window, all that broken glass and twisted metal. You held his hand. A complete stranger. I am very grateful to you, for doing that. And I hope you know we're all delighted to finally meet you.'

Emma, a little tearful, reached over and hugged him. And then Billy did the same, his long arms embracing them both, so relieved that his secret was finally out.

'Love you, bruv,' he whispered into Charlie's ear and then kissed him on the forehead. He knew his brother's feelings could not possibly be that simple. He guessed there was probably a storm of conflicting emotions swirling inside Charlie's mind now that he knew the only reason Billy and Emma had met was because of the accident that had claimed Jason's life. But he also knew Charlie loved him and had urged him to settle down for many years, and Billy hoped that would be enough for Charlie to accept Emma into the Fletcher family.

'I know this is your evening,' Charlie said as the long embrace ended, 'but I have some news I want to share with everyone. Do you mind if we reconvene at the table?'

'Yes, of course,' Billy said. 'We're just about to bring coffee in, so would that be OK?'

Charlie nodded. 'And maybe, later on,' he said quietly to Billy, as though sharing a secret, 'you can explain why you gave us all new house keys?'

Billy shrugged and grinned. 'Maybe,' he said.

CHAPTER 37

As the family assembled at the table once more, Charlie gently tapped his coffee cup with a teaspoon, the sound a familiar precursor to some sort of speech. He paused for a moment and looked around the room at his family, and he wondered how long it would be before they would all be together again.

He knew each of them had suffered in their own way, and each carried scars that might never heal, not completely. But he also remembered what his mother had asked of him all those years earlier. To be brave and strong. And on that day, that day of all days, he knew that being brave and strong meant being honest.

'I appreciate I am not hosting,' he said, taking to his feet. 'But I did want to say a huge thank you to Billy and Emma for bringing us all together this evening and providing such an amazing meal.'

There was an enthusiastic round of applause.

'I also wanted to say how lovely it has been to finally meet you, Emma, and to welcome you into the family.' There was a murmur from the table, everyone agreeing, and then Charlie smirked and pointed at his brother. 'So, Billy, don't cock it up.'

There was laughter, and Billy put his arm around Emma's shoulder and shook his head. 'No chance,' he replied, grinning.

The room fell silent again, and all eyes fell on Charlie. As he took a deep breath, it became clear to everyone in the room that he was nervous, about to say something important.

'I really appreciate what you've all done for me over the past few months,' he continued. 'Carol, and Vicki and Billy. All your visits, and phone calls, and text messages. All the grocery shopping you've done for me. And just being there, to be honest. In the house, having a cup of tea with me. It made a huge difference.'

'You're welcome sweetheart,' Carol said and raised a glass of wine in his direction, having declined the offer of a coffee.

'So,' Charlie continued, and his manner changed, becoming more serious, and it was obvious to everyone in the room that this was the

182

important part of Charlie's speech. 'Jason and I spent years flipping properties in Southend, and then, more recently, we started a holiday rental business on Gran Canaria. After Jason died, I eventually managed to take a good, hard look at the business, and it was obvious that I can't possibly manage it on my own. And so, I have decided to focus just on the holiday rentals. I won't be flipping any more properties in Southend.'

There was not an immediate reaction from around the table. Everyone remained silent. Glances were exchanged, but, mostly, no one quite understood why Charlie was ending the evening with an announcement about his business. Only Carol seemed to understand what he was alluding to, and she immediately covered her mouth with her hand, and stared at him, as though hoping she might be wrong.

'And in order to properly focus on that part of the business,' Charlie said, 'I'm selling my house. I'm going to move to Maspalomas. Permanently.'

The room remained silent, but Charlie could feel a change in the atmosphere, as though all the happiness and good humour had evaporated. He saw Billy's head drop, and then Emma, concerned, whispered something to him and stroked his shoulder. Tyler had a strange expression on his face, neither happy nor sad, and Charlie wondered if his youngest brother, of all the people in the family, might appreciate why someone would wish to move abroad.

Lizzie and Jack sat next to each other, not saying a word, feeling they were in the middle of a grown-up conversation and shouldn't really speak. And then there was Vicki, a calm expression on her face, her emotions settled, having known in advance of his announcement and the luxury of a few days to accept his decision.

After a few moments, Carol was the first to speak, 'Charlie, look, I may be out of turn here, but have you really thought this through? I mean, to move abroad, right now, so soon after... after...'

'I know,' Charlie said, acknowledging the point that Carol could not bring herself to say out loud. 'But if I stay, at some point, the pieces of my life are going to fall back into place, and when that happens, I'm going to really feel how many pieces are missing. I need a complete change, something big, and this is what I have decided to do.'

183

Again, there was a pause, and then Tyler asked, 'We can all visit, though, right? Free holidays and all that?'

'Oh yes, yes. One hundred per cent, yes,' Charlie replied enthusiastically. 'And we can web chat too, in between. And I'll come back to visit.'

Charlie could see the news had impacted everyone more than he had anticipated, and he suddenly felt terribly upset that he may have ruined the evening Billy and Emma's evening.

But then, Tyler spoke again. 'It's only four hours on a plane,' he said lightly. 'And you never know, they might start flying from Southend Airport one day. We could catch a plane from just down the road.' And with that, Charlie felt the mood shift slightly.

'Charlie, you have to do what's right for you,' Carol said, finally finding the right words and saying what she knew Charlie desperately wanted to hear. She stood, walked to him, and threw her arms around him. 'We all want the best for you, sweetheart,' she said. 'And if this is what you need to do, then you bloody well do it with our blessing.' She kissed him on the cheek and then returned to her chair, 'I guess you'll need to get your house on the market. But I can't see that being difficult to shift.'

Charlie sat down and glanced at Vicki, who nodded at him. 'Actually, I already have a buyer,' he replied.

'What?' Billy asked and looked up suddenly. 'You've already sold it?' He stared at Charlie, a look of despair on his face, unable to pretend he was happy.

Charlie reached over and held Billy's hand. 'Yes, but it's staying in the family,' he replied. And Billy looked at him, utterly perplexed.

'I'm buying it,' Vicki said. As everyone's attention fell on her, she smiled, 'I'm using the money Nan left me as the deposit, and Charlie's sorted me out with a really good mortgage advisor for the rest, and I've taken on some extra HR work at the supermarket. I've always loved Charlie and Jason's house; you all know that. I always said if I bought a place, I'd want a house just like it. So, once I'd stopped trying to talk Charlie into staying, I talked him into selling his house to me.'

184

The conversations which followed were quieter and more mellow, and Charlie could feel that his and Vicki's announcements had drained away much of the fun and energy from the evening. As the dinner party began to draw to a conclusion, he noticed Billy was missing from the room, so he took himself to the sitting room at the front of the house, where he found his brother alone. He was stood in front of the fireplace, looking at all the family photographs that he had so lovingly and precisely returned to their correct positions earlier that day.

'It's been quite the dinner party, hasn't it?' Charlie said calmly as he walked over to Billy and gently rubbed his back. 'You OK?'

Billy turned and looked at him, a sadness on his face that Charlie found unsettling. It was not how he had wanted the evening to end.

'It's like you are leaving me behind,' Billy said. 'I know I shouldn't feel like that. I should be pleased for you and Vicki. And I am. Or, I will be, I hope to be. But right now, it just feels really crappy.'

From the mantel, Billy picked up a photograph in a silver frame, a picture of the three of them as kids in the old kitchen before the renovation, making a huge mess with flour and eggs as they tried to bake a cake with their mother. 'Dad took this,' he said. 'He's not in it, but I remember him being behind the camera, and so it feels like all five of us are in the photograph.'

Charlie took the photograph from him and studied it. 'Funny,' he said. 'All these pictures, they've been on the mantel for years, but I think at some point I just stopped looking at them. I would see them every time I was in this room, but I just don't look at them.'

He placed the picture back on the mantel, and then Billy picked up another. This time, a photograph taken in the garden at a family barbecue. Susan was cooking the food, proudly wearing a 'kiss the cook' apron. Carol was next to her, behind a little plastic fold-up table on which she was slicing open the bread rolls. They were looking at each other, caught mid-conversation, both roaring with laughter.

To the edge of the picture, Charlie was sat at the patio table, probably about fifteen years old, gesturing the 'peace' sign with his hand. Tyler, just a baby, was in a buggy next to him and sat on his other side, tucking into a burger, was Jason, completely oblivious that a photograph was

185

being taken. Billy handed it to Charlie, who held it in both hands and, intuitively, gently stroked with his thumb the part of the image that contained Jason.

'Do you remember how busy this house used to be,' Billy said. 'This great big house. And now it's just going to be me living here. For the next six years, until Dad comes home.'

Charlie returned the picture to the mantel. 'Jack and Vicki will be here all the time,' he said, trying to sound enthusiastic. 'And Carol, Tyler and Lizzie. They'll all be coming and going, staying over. And when they're not, you and Emma will have somewhere to be on your own. And you've got friends, Billy. You've got lots of friends. Invite them round. Enjoy this big house. Let your am-dram group use it as a rehearsal space or something. Fill it with noise.'

The door opened, and Vicki appeared. 'All OK?' she asked and walked over to them. And then, just behind her, Tyler leaned into the room, his long blonde hair falling partly over his face as he did.

'May I join you?' he asked.

'Yes of course Tyler,' Charlie replied. 'This is your home too. You don't have to ask.'

As Tyler closed the door and joined the little group of siblings, Charlie noticed that Billy was already reorganising the pictures on the mantel, making sure they were exactly where they were supposed to be. Once finished, Billy looked at his brothers and sister.

'I'm fine,' he said. 'I just had a moment.' And then Vicki gave him a quick hug.

'Listen, I hope you don't think this is going to sound opportunistic,' Tyler said, 'but if you're moving abroad, Charlie, and you and Jack are moving to your own place, Vicki, well, I wondered how you might all feel about me moving into The Lodge?'

No one replied, because everyone was thinking the same thing; what would Carol say?

'I'm nearly eighteen,' Tyler continued. 'I have a good job with Southend Council, so I can pay towards the bills and everything else. I'm not expecting a freebie. And it's not long term, because you know I want to go travelling at some point, too.'

186

'Have you spoken to your mum about this, Tyler?' Charlie asked.

'No, not yet,' he admitted. 'I thought I'd test the waters with you lot first. The truth is, Mum's great about everything, but I feel a bit uncomfortable bringing Jonathan back to the house. You know, to stay over. It was the same when Alison stayed over. It just gets a bit awkward, with Lizzie in the next room. I just want to be somewhere I don't feel I need to creep about quite so much.'

He paused, and looked at his siblings, his big blue eyes filled with either hope they would say yes or fear they might reject him. And that was a new feeling for Charlie, because Tyler had always carried himself with such an unusual amount of confidence. He wasn't used to him looking so vulnerable.

'Tyler, you know this is your home just as much as it is ours,' Charlie said. 'It always has been. The only thing is, I'm not going to be here. And Vicki and Jack are moving out. But assuming Billy agrees, I think that sounds like a great idea. But honestly, Tyler, your mum has to give it the thumbs up first.'

'Oh yes,' Vicki interjected. 'It's got to be OK with Carol. But I think it sounds great.'

The three of them looked to Billy, who was suddenly grinning. 'I think it sounds great, too,' he said. 'We'll have a right laugh. And I'm happy to come up with a new housework schedule.'

'Oh my god,' Vicki grumbled good-naturedly. 'You and that bloody schedule.'

'We've got to keep the house clean and tidy,' Billy said. 'Mum always did, so we should too.'

'Absolutely,' Tyler replied. 'Look, I'll talk to mum. And Lizzie. I think she might be a bit upset. But I think Mum will be OK. Maybe we could look at me moving in this weekend?'

There was an exchange of looks and shrugs and agreeable noises.

'That's settled then,' Billy said and clapped his hands together before pulling Tyler into a sideways hug. 'Well, little brother, we just need to pick a room for you.'

For a moment, Charlie felt as though he wasn't actually there with them, his siblings. It was as if he were watching from afar, at Tyler, so young, so excited about his life and the months and years ahead. Tyler had so much time, Charlie thought, so much life to live and so many bright days to come. And shamefully, he realised he was envious of Tyler because he knew his own life was now shrouded in so much darkness, so much he wanted to run away from. All Charlie wanted was to jump on a plane, flee to his Spanish island, and never return.

'My room,' he said decisively. 'You can have my old room.'

And with those words, Charlie felt a sudden release because he knew he was breaking his final tie with The Lodge, and that made him feel safe.

CHAPTER 38

Six Years Later

Tyler wasn't accustomed to the quiet. For so many years, he'd woken to noise coming from all sides; Carol busy downstairs, making breakfast and shouting at Lizzie to get up and dressed and Lizzie, in the bedroom next to his, banging about, always annoyed that her sleep pattern had been interrupted by school. And underneath all of that, another layer of noise, the endless roar of the busy road outside their house.

And then, during all the years he had lived at The Lodge, there had been just as much disturbance; Billy and Emma and their marathon, morning love-making sessions in the room next door, or Vicki and Jack arriving to cook up a family breakfast for everyone, or Carol popping in before work to do some of Tyler's chores from Billy's housework schedule.

But now, each day, he woke to the peaceful sound of a warm morning breeze blowing through the trees, and birds singing happily as the first rays of sunshine reached across the sky. After so many years dreaming about travelling round Europe, he was finally doing it, and he had never felt so comfortable, so centred.

He sat up in his bed, a large wooden double with elaborately carved bed posts, and happily surveyed the space around him. His room had plain white walls and a tiled floor, and there were three sets of carved wooden doors. One gave access to the rest of the villa, another opened into a deep-set wardrobe, and the third led to a private bathroom. His room at the villa had French doors leading directly to a courtyard and pool. He had left the doors slightly ajar, the thickly lined curtains moving gently in the breeze, letting little snippets of daylight into the room.

He slipped from beneath the white linen sheets and walked to the bathroom, where he brushed his teeth and showered. His morning routine was much swifter than it used to be. Before he had started his travels, he'd asked Emma to give him a number four crop, so he now spent far less time drying and styling his hair.

189

He walked, naked, from his room into the courtyard, a large, mostly private area bordered on one side by the villa and encircled by a stone wall overflowing with bougainvillaea on the other. The air carried the sweet aroma of honeysuckle, and at the centre of the courtyard was the pool, its clear water sparkling as rays of sunshine reached down from the bright blue morning sky.

He took a deep breath and dived in, enjoying the refreshing rush of cold water against his skin. After a few lengths, he pulled himself up onto the side of the pool, his legs in the water, gazing at the early morning sun. It was exactly as he had always dreamed it would be. He was travelling alone, and it felt as though the whole world was just there, waiting to be discovered by him.

'Tyler, mate, for god's sake, how many times do I have to tell you about skinny dipping?'

Tyler smiled at the sound of a familiar voice and turned his head to see Charlie stood at the entrance to the kitchen, neatly dressed in pyjamas, a dressing gown and slippers.

'I know it feels private, but all the neighbours can see over that wall,' Charlie said. 'There's probably a dozen of them, with binoculars, watching you right now.'

Tyler shrugged, 'I'm offended you think they would need binoculars.'

'No more skinning dipping,' Charlie replied, a slight chuckle to his voice. 'Now, I've got the kettle on. Cup of tea?'

Tyler weighed up the pros and cons of the offer, 'Does that cup of tea come with a bacon sandwich by any chance?'

'The bacon's already in the oven,' Charlie said with faux exasperation. 'Go on, get dressed. I'll bring it out onto the terrace.'

Tyler returned to his room, dried himself with a thick cotton towel, and then went into his bathroom to complete his morning rituals. When he had finished, he paused for a moment and stared at his reflection in the bathroom mirror. He knew that, as he continued his travels, his own face would be the only familiar face he would see. His life would be filled with new people, strangers, every single day, and as much as that excited him, it worried him a little too.

190

People had always judged him solely on his looks. As a child, he had been routinely praised for his thick blonde hair, his bright blue eyes, his lovely smile. And as he had grown older, even though he was considered short for a man, he was aware that he was often treated more favourably, perhaps even reverentially, just because he was handsome. Sometimes, complete strangers had stopped him, in the street or in a shop, just to comment on his appearance, as though compelled to tell him he was beautiful.

But he had found there was also a downside to a handsome face. People often made assumptions about him too: that perhaps he coasted through life because of his looks, that he had never really focussed on his education. During the years he had worked for the parks team at Southend Council, he had noticed some of the managers would often speak slowly to him, as if they presumed he had chosen a manual job because he was good-looking but possibly a bit dim.

Over time, he was able to change those attitudes, by developing all sorts of programmes to increase awareness of the borough's parks and how people used them; from dog walking days, to gardening lessons for school kids, and horticultural fairs. Tyler became known as something of an ideas man and was rapidly promoted through the ranks. And, for many years, he postponed his plans to travel because he enjoyed his work so much and had an equally enjoyable home life at The Lodge too.

But his itchy feet eventually got the better of him, and he decided to take a long sabbatical from work and begin his quest across Europe with a visit to Charlie's villa in Maspalomas. Carol had suggested it, thinking it would be a good first stop, a gradual way for Tyler to adjust to travelling alone. And skinny dipping aside, Charlie had been thrilled to have him visit.

In the bedroom, Tyler put on a linen shirt, a pair of blue denim shorts cut at the thigh, and brown sandals. He walked across the courtyard where he found Charlie at the breakfast table under the covered terrace. He was diligently worked on his laptop, a pot of tea and two plates of bacon sandwiches in front of him. There was also a small package in brown paper, tied with string. The package had 'To Tyler, Love Charlie x x' written in pen on it.

Tyler sat down and smiled, 'This for me?'

Charlie closed his laptop and put it to one side before pouring the tea. 'It is,' he said. 'A little gift for you.'

Almost knowing what to expect, Tyler unwrapped the paper to reveal a pair of black swimming shorts.

'I thought they'd be good for your morning dip,' Charlie said and started laughing.

Tyler chuckled, 'But what about my fans? You know, all the perverts with binoculars?'

'I'm sure they'll survive.' Charlie handed Tyler his cup of tea and nudged one of the plates towards him. 'So, what are your plans today?' he asked. 'I'm popping to the Yumbo Centre later, if you want to come with me? We could have lunch out.'

'I'd love to, but I've been here three days, and I have got to look for a job. My whole plan was to work my way around Europe, not sponge off my big brother.'

'You are most certainly not sponging,' Charlie replied, sounding a little cross. 'You spent most of the weekend clearing up the courtyard, getting rid of all the weeds, repointing some of the stones. It was a complete mess before, and now it looks amazing.'

Tyler took a big mouthful of his bacon sandwich and washed it down with some tea. 'Well, thank you,' he said. 'But the point remains, I need to get a job because if I am going to be here for a while, I do want to pay my way. And I know you said you wouldn't take any money off me, but perhaps I could do the grocery shopping, for instance, and pay for that?'

Charlie knew Tyler had a streak of pride running through his veins, but he was thrilled to have his little brother finally visit him, and he had no intention of charging him a penny during his stay. But he also had to respect that such an arrangement would not work for Tyler. 'OK,' he conceded. 'The grocery shopping. I think that sounds fair. And, listen, I've got lots of contacts, particularly among the local ex-pats here. Any idea what sort of work you would want to do?'

'Well, obviously I can garden. But I pick things up quickly. I'm sure I could learn to wait tables or answer phones. Honestly, I'll have a punt at pretty much anything.'

Charlie thought for a moment and then began to list some of his local contacts who might have some work Tyler could do. 'I mean, everyone's desperate to meet you, so it will be a good opportunity to introduce you to the gang,' he said. 'There's Martin. Has his own salon. Great big gay guy, an absolute hoot, and by all accounts a fantastic hairdresser. He might need someone to help. And then there's Peggy. She owns a small caravan park. She used to do it all herself, but she's a bit older now, and I know she's struggling with some of the maintenance. We could pop and meet her today if you like? And... let's think, who else? Oh, and then there's Blanche. She owns a few bars in the area, one in the Yumbo Centre. She might need someone.'

'Perfect,' Tyler said. 'Sounds like a great start.'

For the next half hour, the two brothers sat happily drinking tea and chatting. They discussed Tyler's plans for the rest of the year and what he might do when he eventually returned to the UK. They spoke about Charlie's holiday rental business and some of the more difficult customers he had dealt with over the years. But, on some level, Tyler knew the conversation was defined not by what they talked about but by what was left unmentioned.

He was desperate to know if Charlie had met anyone special or, at the very least, was going out on dates. But that part of his brother's life had felt like a closed book to the whole family ever since Jason had died. And now, it was simply a topic that no one discussed, and Charlie appeared happy to leave it that way. Tyler also noticed that, since he had arrived, Charlie had enquired after everyone in the family: was Vicki's job going well? How were Carol's retirement plans going? Did it look like Billy and Emma might get married? How's Jack doing at school? Was Lizzie still learning social media?

Questions, so many questions, but not a single mention of Peter. At no point during the previous few days had Charlie enquired after their father or asked how he was managing his life, back at The Lodge, after being released from jail. It didn't feel as though Charlie was making some passive-aggressive point or deliberately ignoring the elephant in the room. Tyler could tell that, even after all those years, it was simply a topic that was just too painful for Charlie to confront. Tyler realised that the kindest thing he could do for his big brother was to remain silent. Peter would not be spoken about.

CHAPTER 39

It was only a short walk to the Yumbo Centre, less than fifteen minutes, but just long enough for Tyler to enjoy all the sights and sounds along the way; the glorious colourful gardens of the houses and villas, the bars that were closed but busy with staff sweeping floors and wiping down counters, and the scattering of shops and restaurants that would be extremely busy later in the day.

And then there were the people, some obviously residents, out walking their dogs, others more likely holiday makers, many with kids carrying inflatables, off to the beach or a communal pool. And throughout the journey, he noticed the rainbow flag, repeated so many times, attached to homes, hotels, shops and bars. He recalled Charlie and Jason, so many years earlier, explaining to the family that they had chosen Maspalomas for their business because it was so LGBTQ-friendly. And walking through the streets with his older brother, Tyler could see why Charlie felt so comfortable here.

The route to the Yumbo took them through a long alley, past a sex shop, and down a flight of stone steps to an open terrace on the top floor of the centre. Swiftly, Charlie led his brother through a maze of shops and restaurants before coming out on the other side of the centre to a hairdressing salon, under a large sign that read 'Hair by Martin'.

'This is him,' Charlie said, knocking on the glass front door. Inside, Tyler could see a tall, middle-aged man, quite overweight, wearing a gold vest and matching shorts, sweeping the floor. He looked up and immediately dropped the broom and clapped his hands with glee as he saw who was outside waiting for him.

'Come in, come in, it's open,' he yelled.

Charlie walked in and he and Martin hugged, laughing and smiling. Martin looked over to Tyler. 'And this must be Carol's boy?' he said, and before Tyler could move, Martin flung his arms around him. 'Oh, my goodness,' Martin said, 'your mother and me, we've had some fun nights out,' he said, and released Tyler from his embrace. 'Don't ask me for

195

details, but there's a couple of drag queens who know better than to invite your mother on stage again.'

Tyler roared with laughter, and immediately understood Charlie's earlier description of Martin as 'an absolute hoot'.

'Now,' Martin said, 'can I get you a cup of tea? Or something a bit more grown-up?'

'Only if you have time,' Charlie replied. 'Cup of tea would be great.'

Martin vanished into a back room and the sound of the kettle filled the air. Tyler looked around the salon, at its gold fittings, velvet seats and art deco standing lamps, and was struck by how stylish it was, glamourous but not vulgar. 'It's a lovely place you have here, Martin,' he called.

'Thank you, my love,' Martin called back, and then reappeared. 'Tea in a few minutes,' he said, ushering them towards the salon chairs. 'Now, to what do I owe the honour of this visit? We've all been waiting to meet you, Tyler. We thought Charlie was hiding you from us.'

'Oh, I was just settling in,' Tyler began. 'I'm going to be staying for a while, and I am looking for some work, to be honest. I didn't know if you needed someone here. I can sweep floors, make tea, answer the phone. I'm happy to do pretty much anything.'

Martin thought for a moment, 'I could definitely offer a few hours each week. Possibly even a day.' Addressing Charlie, he said, 'Have you spoken to Peggy, though?'

'I haven't, but she was on my list too.'

'Oh, well,' Martin said, sitting back in his chair and crossing his legs. 'I spoke to her last night. She won't admit it, but I can tell she's desperate for help. Everything's overgrown, things need to be painted, the pool needs to be cleaned. It's just getting too much for her, the poor love.'

There was a loud 'click' and the sound of the kettle stopped. Martin hurried into the backroom while continuing to talk, 'Well, Tyler, I can offer you a day each week. And I am sure your brother can persuade Peggy to give you a couple of days on top of that.'

'Honestly, I am grateful for anything.'

Martin returned with a shiny gold tray carrying a blue willow patterned tea pot and three matching teacups, a small milk jug, and a bowl piled high with sugar cubes. He set down the tray on one of the counters and poured each of them a cup. For the next few minutes, Tyler sat and watched cheerfully as Martin and Charlie caught up on all the gossip from around the Yumbo Centre and their community of expats. And it offered Tyler further reassurance that his brother was truly happy with his life there.

After a while, Charlie said they should leave so Martin could get ready for his customers, but he went to use the bathroom first and left Martin and Tyler alone in the salon.

'Now, let's be honest,' Martin said with a cheeky, conspiratorial tone to his voice. 'You want to know how your brother's doing, don't you? I mean, *really* doing.'

Tyler chuckled. 'Am I that obvious?'

'I understand entirely. So, let me just tell you that Charlie is very much loved here, by all of us. He's been a good and genuine friend to many people, including me, and we all absolutely adore him. He is most definitely not alone, and he leads a very full and happy life.'

'Thank you.' Tyler sat back in his chair, 'Did you ever meet him? Jason, I mean.'

'Oh yes, yes. Most of us did. Lovely young man. Very articulate. And practical, as I recall. Always coming up with solutions to problems.'

'Yes, that's very much Jason,' Tyler said fondly.

'We didn't get to know him as well as Charlie, because Jason was back in England, most of the time,' Martin continued. 'But, still, absolutely devastating when we heard the news. And devastated for poor Charlie, of course, knowing how much he loved him.'

Jason felt such a long time ago, for Tyler, someone who had gradually faded into a fond memory. But every now and again, Tyler would have a conversation with someone, like the conversation he was having with Martin, and suddenly, it would feel like Jason was in the room once more, a familiar presence; the clever man who used to help him with his maths homework, and who'd taken him to see *Attack of the Clones* and *Revenge of the Sith* when no one else in the family would go. And it was in moments like that when Tyler realised he missed Jason too.

'When Charlie first came home, after the funeral, he was in a terrible place, for a long time,' Martin continued. 'He's never struck me as being the religious type, but he started talking about heaven, and he wanted to know if Jason was there. He kept looking for signs, for something to show him that Jason's spirit was safe. It felt, for a while, like he was quite obsessed with it.

'And then, one day, we were having lunch in our favourite restaurant, the whole gang. And completely out of the blue, it started to rain. Not heavily, just a light shower, but enough that everyone was looking confused, all the waiters and the other customers. Because the sun was still shining, and it looked like the sky was blue and cloudless. To be honest, I thought a pipe had sprung a leak or something.

'We all stood up and leaned over the balcony to see what was going on. And it was the oddest thing. There was this little black rain cloud, hovering just over that building. I've never seen anything like it before. And Charlie started to cry, but like, a happy cry. He was smiling and crying, his arms stretched out, so he could feel the rain on his hands. And that was the sign he'd been looking for, to show him that Jason was in heaven, and he was happy. And after that, he seemed much more settled. It really helped him to begin to deal with his grief.'

Tyler knew his brother was not religious. None of the Fletchers were. But he could understand how the shock of losing Jason, and in such terrible circumstances, had left Charlie in such a dark place, searching for answers and reassurances.

'And, I am guessing that you are all wondering whether he's met anyone,' Martin said, grinning.

Tyler leaned forward in his chair, as if expecting to hear a deeply held secret. 'It just feels like it's a topic that's off the table,' he said. 'It's six years since Jason died. And we all want Charlie to be happy, to meet someone new, but we just… we honestly just don't know where Charlie is, emotionally.'

And in that moment, for the first time, Martin seemed less happy with what he was about to say. 'He hasn't met anyone,' he said, a little glumly. 'Not that he hasn't had offers. A good-looking lad like that, living in one of the gayest places on the planet? Of course, he's had offers. But, no, he's not interested. Not even once. And I promise you, if it had happened, even just once, one of us would know about it.'

Tyler sighed, 'Has he ever talked about it, to you, or anyone?'

'We've teased him a few times, when we've all been out, and he's had a waiter obviously flirt with him, or some guy has sent him a drink from the bar. But he just closes it down, straight away. To be honest, when he came home, after Jason had died, it was like… I don't know. It was like he didn't want anyone to get close to him again.'

CHAPTER 40

After a visit to Peggy's caravan park, followed by a slightly boozy lunch and a siesta, Charlie relaxed in his bath, knowing he had a good hour before he and Tyler were due to meet his friends at his favourite drag cabaret bar in the Yumbo Centre. He lay looking up at the ceiling, happy that he was finally getting to spend some proper time with Tyler.

The rest of the Fletchers had all stayed with Charlie at the villa many times, often for extended periods of time. Vicki and Jack had spent many long summer holidays with him, and once even brought Debbie and Kim with them too. Billy and Emma visited whenever they could, while Carol and Lizzie made sure they holidayed with Charlie for at least a couple of weeks each year.

Tyler, however, had never visited. He had been too busy, all that time, working and saving, ready for the day when he could jump on a plane and travel. And, likewise, Charlie had failed to keep his promise to regularly visit home. He hadn't returned once, in all those years.

Tyler and Charlie had kept in touch regularly, by text messages and through video chats and, more recently, by WhatsApp. But now they were spending time together, proper quality time, and Charlie had found Tyler to be particularly good company. If Charlie was honest with himself, he was a little in awe of his kid brother's natural self-confidence and hassle-free approach to life, qualities Charlie knew he lacked.

He had certainly felt proud introducing him to his friends. He had a nice speaking voice, good manners, and some of their father's charm. Also, he had noticed that Tyler truly listened when other people were speaking, a quality Charlie admired.

Tyler and Martin had clearly hit it off. By the time they had finished at the salon, the two seemed as thick as thieves. Martin had been the first friend he and Jason had made when they had started to visit Maspalomas, and Charlie had always treasured Martin's courage, that he never allowed himself to be anything other than exactly who he was: a great big camp gay guy who completely owned himself wherever he was and no matter who he was with.

And there was Peggy, who had been quick to offer Tyler a job the moment she had realised that was the reason he and Charlie had visited her. Peggy had moved to the island fifteen years earlier with her husband, but their new life together in the sun had been cut tragically short when he died of a heart attack not long after they had purchased the caravan park. Charlie envied Peggy so much, the comfortable way she carried her grief. She could speak about her late husband with such tenderness and happiness, and it never seemed to hurt. It was as if his memory only ever brought her joy, and Charlie wished he could remember Jason in the same way. But even after so many years, the thought of Jason, of how he died, how he was stolen away, it still caused him too much pain.

Blanche had also been one of the original gang, married and divorced multiple times and with an endless stream of hilarious stories about each husband, their many foibles, and how each marriage had eventually ended. She didn't have children, never wanted them, but had built a happy life for herself on Gran Canaria and owned many successful bars. She had helped Charlie and Jason start their business on the island by sharing several of her useful contacts. She had also been an enormous source of support and strength in those terrible months after Jason had died. She had called Charlie every single day, without fail, and often just sat at the end of the phone while Charlie had cried, understanding that there was nothing she could say to make him feel better.

And then there was Alan, a tall, bald, lanky divorcee who had arrived in Maspalomas a few years earlier after what had clearly been an acrimonious separation which had left him virtually penniless. Charlie had misjudged Alan when they first met. With his gruff voice and blokeish demeanour, Charlie had made a terrible assumption that Alan would be casually racist and homophobic. Instead, Alan had proven himself to be very politically correct. In fact, he had often schooled Charlie on many social issues, from trans rights to the demonisation of asylum seekers. Charlie had quickly realised he could learn a lot from Alan, and had grown quite fond of him.

Alan was a proud man, too proud to let anyone visit the 'shithole' he called home on the island, which was apparently a 'crappy one-bedroom flat above a stinking fish restaurant'. He entertained the group with stories about how his ex-wife had gotten the house and the money, and he'd ended up with the clothes on his back and nothing else. He was clearly a workhorse, always rushing off to drive a van for someone or help build something, or deliver something. But, despite his financial shortcomings, Alan was always generous with his friends and always bought rounds of drinks and sometimes he paid for everyone's meals too.

Charlie, lying naked in his bath, found himself growing aroused at the thought of Alan. It was something quite new for Charlie to have those thoughts of intimacy again, after all those years, for his heart to beat a little faster, to have the desire to be touched, held, and kissed. But a few months earlier, the two had spent a fun evening bar hopping for Alan's fiftieth birthday. In the early hours of the morning, after everyone else had gone home, Charlie and Alan had been staggering around Maspalomas, trying to find somewhere to get a coffee. At some point, Alan had put his arm around Charlie's waist, and the two had continued walking together, happily talking nonsense. And it had been in that moment, with Alan holding him so close and so firmly, that something had reawakened in Charlie.

Ever since that night, he had looked at Alan completely differently, and that was the source of great frustration for Charlie because he knew, from Alan's perspective, there had been nothing to it. In truth, Alan had probably just been leaning on him to stay upright. But Charlie could not help himself, and now, fully aroused, he realised he would need to extend his time in the bath by a few minutes to work it out of his system.

Afterwards, hot and flustered, he dried himself and then dressed in blue linen trousers, a blue polo shirt and brown moccasins. He checked his thick dark hair in the mirror and realised it was getting a little long; he'd make an appointment with Martin when he saw him that night.

He made his way to the other side of the villa and knocked on Tyler's door to check he had not overslept. He could hear voices, and then Tyler called for him to enter. Charlie opened the door and found Tyler sat on his bed, undressed apart from a cotton towel wrapped around his waist, facetiming someone on his phone. 'Oh, sorry, shall I come back?' Charlie asked.

'No, no, it's just Mum. Come and say hi.'

Charlie sat on the side of the bed and Tyler turned his phone sideways, landscape, so his mum could see them both. Carol's face was large on the screen.

'I hope you two are having fun. But not too much fun,' Carol laughed.

'We're going out for drinks tonight with the gang,' Charlie said, 'so I'm making no promises.'

'Oh, I wish I was there,' Carol said, fondly. 'Give Martin a big kiss from me, won't you?'

'I will,' Charlie said. During her many visits to the villa, Carol had struck up quite a friendship with Martin, and there had even been nights when Charlie had stayed home with Lizzie while the pair had gone out bar hopping.

'Listen,' Carol's tone turned serious. 'I'm glad you're both there because I have to tell you something about your dad.'

Her words filled the room, and the brothers sensed it was not good news. For Charlie, it was a subject that felt distant from him, a man he had not seen or spoken to in more than six years, someone he had pushed to the back of his mind, who barely existed for him anymore. But it was different for his brother, and he could feel Tyler shift slightly on the bed next to him, sitting up a little straighter in preparation for whatever news was to come.

'He's back in hospital,' Carol said. 'He collapsed yesterday evening, at The Lodge. It's all to do with his liver again. The hospital has said if he doesn't stop drinking, there's not much more they can do.'

Charlie remained silent, feeling as though it was not his place to express any opinion. Tyler sat quietly for a moment, then said, 'What's *she* doing about it?'

'Oh, she's walking around, soaking up all the attention. Playing the victim of course. She's doing nothing to help Peter manage his drinking. If anything, she's enabling it. Her and their drunken friends. I know it's not her fault. Peter's a grown man. But she is his wife, and—'

'Sorry? What?' Charlie interrupted, suddenly confused. 'Wife?'

Carol's expression froze in horror as she realised there was a critical piece of information that no one in the family had shared with Charlie. 'Oh, sweetheart, I thought someone would have told you.'

Charlie glanced at Tyler, who was biting his lip, awkward and guilty.

'I thought you knew, too,' Tyler said, 'but we never talk about dad, so it never came up.'

'Who? When?'

Tyler handed his phone to Charlie so he could speak directly to Carol.

'Abigail,' she said. 'You know. She calls herself Angel. They got married a few weeks ago, we think. Registry office. Just Peter and Angel, and some of her friends. Peter didn't tell anyone. We only found out a few days ago when Angel moved into The Lodge. Apparently, she visited him all the time when he was in prison.'

Charlie pondered the situation for a moment, and tried to understand the nature of the relationship between his father and Angel, and Angel's reason for marrying him, but none of it made any sense to him. 'I can't really see what she thinks is going to come from marrying an unemployed, alcoholic ex-convict. But, you know, if that's what she wants to do.'

Gently, Tyler leaned towards the phone and looked at his mother, 'Are Billy and Emma still at the house?'

Carol tutted, 'Not sure,' she replied. 'Haven't seen them for a few days.'

'Were they planning to move out?' Charlie asked.

Carol's expression changed, and she appeared suddenly quite cross. 'Has anyone told you what has happened, Charlie, since Peter was released from prison and moved home?'

'No,' Charlie replied, and experienced a pang of shame. 'But that's not their fault. I... I sort of make a point of not asking after him. I can understand why these things aren't mentioned to me.' Charlie could feel Tyler lean against his shoulder, a small gesture to show he understood how his brother felt.

'Well, it wasn't good,' Carol continued. 'He just completely blanked everyone. Barely spoke. Completely ignored Billy, Emma and Tyler

204

around the house. Acted like they weren't even there. Wouldn't speak to Vicki or Jack either, completely blanked me and Lizzie whenever we visited. He just drank and spent time with Angel and her weird friends. He's made life at The Lodge completely unbearable for everyone else. Making noise and playing music into the early hours. And I think he's done that on purpose.'

Charlie could easily imagine that Peter had whiled away his years in prison, bitterly blaming everyone in the family for what had happened to him rather than taking any responsibility himself. He could also imagine his father's resentment had been aggravated further by Angel, whispering in his ear each time she visited.

'But what's happening at the house, now?' Tyler asked.

'I honestly don't know, Tyler. You need to call Billy,' Carol replied. 'He and Emma were already spending a lot more time at Emma's parents just because of your dad's behaviour. I'm not sure what they're doing now Angel's moved in too.'

Tyler looked at Charlie, 'Billy absolutely hates her. She is the only person I've ever heard Billy really slag off. He doesn't have a good word to say about her.'

Charlie was surprised to hear Billy's name linked with such negative behaviour, and he wondered what Angel had done to create such an unpleasant reaction from his kind-hearted brother. And then there was Tyler, his usually cheerful expression gone. Now he looked pensive, perhaps even a little lost; his kid brother was now effectively homeless, The Lodge no longer a place he could return to when his travels ended.

'Perhaps we need to have a family discussion, about the house,' Charlie said. 'It's our family home. We can't have Dad and his wife think they can just take over and drive the family out.' He could see Carol was already shaking her head.

'It's Peter's home, sweetheart, you know that,' she said and paused, as though trying to find the courage to speak. 'Boys, look, there's something else. Peter's not talking to anyone, but I popped to the hospital today and spoke to one of the nurses on the ward. I told her a bit of a fib and said I was his partner and that I needed to know how to care for him when he got home. It turns out your dad's condition... it is

205

much worse than any of us realised. And the way he is carrying on, well...
the next time I call, I can't promise I'm going to have good news for
you.'

Tyler's head dropped, and instinctively, Charlie put his arm around
his brother's shoulders and kissed him on the forehead. On the tiny
screen, he could see Carol's expression: bereft, a mother thousands of
miles away from her child, worried that she wasn't there to look after
him.

'I'm here,' he said to her, quietly. 'We'll be fine.'

Carol mouthed the words 'thank you' to him and blew him a kiss.

CHAPTER 41

Charlie had learned to accept that his brothers and sisters had all maintained, or at least attempted to maintain, some sort of relationship with their father, despite all the terrible things he had done. For Charlie, it had been easy to close the door on Peter and erase him from his life. But he understood that for the others, it had been different, and they had not been able to untangle themselves from those strong emotional ties.

Mostly, the family simply did not speak about Peter when Charlie was around, but the events of the previous day had changed that. Tyler needed to talk about their father, he needed to be able to express his feelings, his anxieties and his anger, and Charlie knew it was important that he accommodate those needs.

The previous evening had been entertaining enough: the two of them with the usual gang, a few beers at one of Blanche's bars and then the cabaret show at Ricky's. But Charlie could tell Tyler's heart wasn't in it. He had been polite and cheerful, but there were moments when Charlie caught him zoning out, looking into empty space, his smile gone, and he realised his brother needed to go home and sleep, so they made their excuses and left before the end of the evening.

By the time Charlie had risen from his bed and gone for his morning swim, Tyler had already left the villa and headed to the caravan park for his first day working for Peggy. He'd left Charlie a note, thanking him for a fun night out and promising to be home by mid-afternoon. Charlie was pleased Tyler had a job. He hoped it would keep his mind busy so he wouldn't spend the day anxiously waiting for news. And Charlie had a feeling that news would come soon, a grinding sense that history was about to repeat itself. He had been 23 years old when his mother had died, and he had a terrible sense that Tyler was about to lose his father, at the same age.

Now, sat on the side of the pool with his legs dangling in the cool water, Charlie looked up at the sky, at the last wisps of clouds as they began to dissolve in the morning sun, and he remembered the terrible pain of losing his mother. He often thought of that day, his 23rd birthday, and of all the sad and shocking things that happened that day, there was one image that always came to mind; he would see himself, smartly dressed in a navy suit, holding a small bouquet of pink tulips, stood in the rain, unable to move. And he remembered that feeling, that sense that if he just stood still, nothing bad would happen.

He remembered that young man so well. He remembered how simple and unburdened his life was, and even after losing his mother, he remembered how much hope he had about his future, and how bright he thought that future was going to be. And that, for Charlie, was the saddest part of that memory; that young man in a suit, holding flowers, in the rain, didn't have a clue just how cruel the years ahead would be.

There was a noise from the side of the villa, the gate being opened and someone, a man, calling, 'Anyone home?'. Charlie turned and saw Alan walking into the courtyard, and immediately, his heart skipped a beat. He was dressed in his usual outfit, a billowing short-sleeved shirt with baggy knee-length shorts and sandals. Charlie had noticed Alan's clothes always seemed oversized as if they were for someone who was very overweight and not for Alan's skinny frame and long limbs.

'Ah, there you are,' Alan said. 'Hope you don't mind me dropping in unannounced?'

'No, of course I don't.' Charlie was quietly thrilled by Alan's unexpected arrival but knew he had to act cool and not be overly familiar in case his actions betrayed his feelings. 'I was about to make some breakfast, if you fancy it. Cup of tea and poached eggs?'

'That sounds great. As long as I'm not putting you out.'

Charlie pulled his legs from the water and stood. Collecting his towel to dry himself, he could feel himself growing a little excited at being almost naked in front of Alan, and so he repeated in his head, that Alan was just a friend, and nothing more. He slipped on his sandals and a short-sleeved polo shirt that was hanging on the back of one of the chairs and led Alan into his kitchen. It was one of the largest rooms in the house, open plan, with a large kitchen area, breakfast bar, and dining table and chairs. It was Charlie's favourite room in the villa, and he often worked there when it was too hot to work outside.

'Did you want to see me about something, or are you just dropping by?' Charlie asked as he busied himself at the counter, getting all the items together that he would need to make breakfast.

'Well, I was just a bit worried about you, to be honest,' Alan said, sitting on one of the stools at the breakfast bar. 'You left quite early, you and your brother. I just wanted to check in, see if you were OK.'

'Oh. Yes, sorry. I hope we didn't appear rude.'

'Not rude at all. But are you alright?'

Charlie stopped what he was doing and came round to sit next to Alan, 'We had a call last night. Tyler and me. Our dad's in hospital again. It doesn't sound good, to be honest.'

'I'm sorry to hear that. Anything I can do?'

'To be honest, Alan, I have no relationship with my dad. Nothing at all. I haven't seen him in years or spoken to him. But Tyler's in a different place to me and I was just a bit worried about him last night. I thought perhaps we should have an early one.'

Alan looked thoughtful, 'I remember you telling me about your dad, why he was in prison,' he said. 'I can understand why you feel the way you do. It's lovely that you are looking after your brother, but you need to look after yourself too, Charlie. If you ever need to talk to anyone, I'm here for you.' Unexpectedly, Alan leaned forward, put his arms around Charlie and pulled him into a tight embrace.

Surprised, Charlie did not immediately reciprocate and sat awkwardly for a few seconds with his hands on his lap, trying not to get aroused. But the urge to hold Alan was too great, and so he leaned into the embrace, put his arms around his friend, and gently buried his face in his shoulder. Moments passed, and Charlie stayed like that, elated by the physical contact, until finally Alan released him, sat back, and looked directly into his eyes.

Charlie wasn't sure what was happening. It felt strange, like it was a 'moment' that perhaps something was about to occur, but before either of them could speak, Charlie heard Tyler's voice calling from outside.

Charlie, flushed and feeling awkward, cleared his throat and called back. 'We're in the kitchen,' he said. The moment Tyler walked through the door, his eyes filled with tears, Charlie knew what had happened, why he had returned home so early.

'Mum called,' he said. 'She'd been trying to get hold of you.'

Charlie stood and walked to his brother. 'My phone's charging in the bedroom,' he said softly, 'I didn't hear it.'

Tyler took a deep breath and then said, 'Dad passed away this morning,' his voice breaking. Then, he looked to the floor and began to cry. Charlie wrapped his arms around him and could feel him shaking as he sobbed. He remembered that feeling, the overwhelming pain of losing a parent. But that was as close as Charlie could get to Tyler's great sorrow, a memory of it because the news of Peter's death had left Charlie feeling nothing at all.

Alan stood and asked Charlie to contact him if he needed any help, and then he quietly left, not wishing to intrude on a moment of private grief. Soon the two brothers were sat at the table outside, by the pool, Tyler still tearful but able to talk.

'She's asked us to go home,' he said. 'Mum. She's asked if we can fly home as soon as possible.'

And that was when Charlie realised Peter's death was going to present him with a serious dilemma. Because he had absolutely no wish to return to the UK.

CHAPTER 42

Tyler could tell, from the moment Angel's friends arrived at The Lodge, that his father's funeral was not going to run smoothly. They clustered at the front of the house, more than a dozen of them, all wearing dark clothes, but none of them, apart from Angel, actually in black. The Fletchers took refuge at the back of the house, all in black suits and dresses, quietly biding their time. The moment the funeral cars arrived, the hearse carrying Peter's body and two gleaming black limousines, Angel and her friends swarmed across the gravel driveway and filled all the seats.

Tyler was the first member of the family to reach the front door, and he realised immediately what had happened, that the funeral cars had been commandeered by Angel and her unpleasant group of friends. But he knew that, apart from his mum, none of the family had the energy or the will for an argument, so he swiftly made alternative travel arrangements.

'Mum can drive Lizzie and me,' he said as the family joined him in the hall. 'Billy, can you take Emma, Vicki and Jack?' And without any fuss, the Fletchers got into their own cars and followed behind the funeral procession.

At the chapel, Angel and her friends formed into a tight group behind Peter's coffin, and so the family were the last to enter. By the time they had managed to pass through the large wooden doors, the front three rows on both sides of the aisle had been filled.

Tyler knew his mother would consider that beyond the pale. He watched as she set about her business, marching down the aisle, pushing a few stragglers out of her way as she went. And then she started loudly telling the strangers sat in the front seats they needed to move. 'Peter's children are sitting here,' she told them, with a clear aggression in her voice.

'Sorry,' someone replied, a middle-aged man in a shiny blue suit, and what looked like the early stages of gin blossoms on his face. 'Angel specifically wanted all of Peter's friends to sit up front.'

Carol glanced across the aisle to the seats on the other side, where Angel was sat at the front, dabbing her cheeks with a handkerchief, perhaps using it to hide a smirk. And then she returned her attention to the man who had spoken to her. 'You listen, mate. Me and the kids have stumped up the money to cover the cost of this funeral. And if I am paying for this gig, I expect a front-row seat.'

No one moved. They simply looked at Carol as if she had no right to even speak to them, and with that single act of contempt, Carol no longer felt the need to hold her tongue. 'Move!' she yelled.

Immediately, the front two rows cleared, and Carol gestured to the Fletchers to claim their seats. 'These are ours,' she said, and then she turned to Angel and mouthed a single word, one that anyone with even the slightest ability to read lips could easily decipher. Angel's eyes widened with surprise as if she had never been called that before.

Once the Fletchers had taken their seats, the chapel fell quiet. Tyler looked to his knees and began to wonder why he didn't have a greater sense of loss. Once he had overcome the initial shock of Peter's death, he had found his grief to be not as cutting or deep as he had expected. He did have some fond memories of his dad, mostly from his childhood, some fun times, when Peter had occasionally visited him at Carol's house.

But in truth, he had seen far more of Susan than Peter during those years, and at times, it had felt more like he had two mums rather than a mum and a dad. In the years after his Auntie Susan's death, Peter's reliance on alcohol had become more prominent and Tyler had seen even less of him. And then, after the accident, prison stole his dad away entirely.

Tyler had started to write to him at least once a month, but he eventually stopped when he did not get a single letter in response. For many years, Peter became just a name, someone the family would occasionally talk about, swapping notes on prison visits or Peter's repeated failures to persuade the parole board to release him early.

The man who returned to The Lodge all those years later was not his father. The boyish charm and movie-star good looks were gone. The man who left prison was old and ill, bitter, rude and relentlessly self-

212

pitying. He surrounded himself with people no one in the family really knew, Angel and her strange circle of friends. And he spent the final few months of his life aggressively drinking himself into an early grave, as though that was what he wanted.

Tyler wondered if, perhaps, Peter's horrible behaviour had been a blessing in disguise, that it had lessened the blow of his death. Vicki, usually so emotional, had hardly cried at all and Lizzie, only fifteen years old, had appeared more preoccupied by what she was going to wear to the funeral. And then there was Billy, whose immense capacity for forgiveness had been tested to the limits by Peter's awful conduct. In all the days that had passed since Tyler had returned home, he hadn't seen anything in Billy's behaviour that suggested he was grieving. Instead, Billy seemed relieved, not that Peter was dead, but that the family had a chance to reset and move forward with their lives.

And then Tyler thought of Charlie, and he found himself wishing he was there. He understood entirely why he wasn't, why his brother simply could not face their father's funeral. But when Tyler had caught the plane home, Charlie had told him he would follow, that he would be there, at some point, to be with the family. And even though Charlie had lived abroad for many years, Tyler suddenly felt the Fletcher family was painfully incomplete without him.

The funeral celebrant appeared, a middle-aged man in a smart suit, and he made a point of stopping to quietly console Angel before taking to the small podium at the front of the chapel. As he began to speak, it became clear that all the notes and special memories the Fletchers had shared with him had been left out of the service.

There was no mention of Peter's parents or siblings, or of Susan, or any of his children, or his grandson Jack. The celebrant did little but speak about Angel and the extraordinary love she had shared with Peter, and her selfless commitment to him throughout his years of incarceration.

And then he read a short poem that Angel had written especially for Peter: 'You captured a beautiful bird, but you didn't put her in a cage. You showed her love, and you let her fly, free. As free as a bird. You understood that bird was not yours to own, but you loved her anyway.

213

And that bird loved you back. I am that bird, Peter. And I will always fly free, with your love in my heart.'

When he had finished speaking, all of Angel's friends applauded, but the Fletchers just exchanged puzzled expressions, apart from Vicki, who had to cover her face with a handkerchief because she was giggling so much. The service ended with a recording of Whitney Houston's 'I Will Always Love You', and as it played, Carol ushered the family from the chapel and back to their cars.

'Mum, is something wrong?' Tyler asked, 'I know that was awful, but it's still dad's funeral. Shouldn't we stay to the end?'

'I just don't trust that woman. I want us to get back to The Lodge.' Carol looked at Vicki and Billy and they both nodded, understanding her concerns.

'Yeah, let's go,' Billy said, despondently. 'Angel can stay and do all the handshaking. It's not as if we know anyone here.' And with that, the Fletchers got into their cars and drove away from Peter's funeral.

As they approached the house, Tyler realised his mother's concerns had been justified. Parked on the kerb outside The Lodge was a small van with the words 'Johnston Locksmiths 24-Hour service' emblazoned on the side. Carol didn't even pull onto the drive. She simply parked behind the van and hurried to the house, and Tyler quickly followed her.

There was a woman dressed in dark clothes, standing at the front door, someone Tyler recognised from the chapel, one of Angel's friends. He recalled seeing her sat alone at the back of the chapel, just inside the entrance. She was watching over a man in blue overalls who was drilling the lock on the front door. When she looked up and saw Carol storming towards her, she very obviously flinched.

'You can't come in,' the woman said nervously. 'Angel's changing the locks.'

'That woman has no fucking right to change anything!' Carol shouted back. 'Oy you, with the drill!' she yelled, and stomped up to the locksmith and prodded him on the shoulder. 'You need to stop doing that. It's criminal damage. I will phone the police.'

The man did as he was told and raised his hands, innocently. 'I'm just doing a job,' he said. 'I'm not here for any trouble.' He looked over

214

Carol's shoulder and could see a group of young people forming behind her, none of whom looked happy to see him. 'Look, look… I've only just started. I can put it back exactly as it was, if you want,' he said. 'No charge.'

'You do that,' Carol said, and went to walk into the house, but Angel's friend blocked her route. 'You can't come in,' she said again, still clearly very nervous.

Carol glared at her, then spoke quietly but very clearly, 'I swear to god, woman, if you do not get out of my fucking way, Peter won't be the only person leaving this house today in a box.'

The woman quickly stepped aside, and Carol and the rest of the family walked into the house.

'What was that all about?' Tyler asked, as they all gathered in the kitchen. 'Why's Angel changing the locks?'

Instinctively, Carol started to unpack the sandwiches and rolls from the fridge and laid them out on the breakfast bar. 'We're not going to talk about it,' she said. 'We will sit it out until everyone's gone, and then I will talk to Angel.' Exasperated, Carol stopped what she was doing and looked at them all. 'Let's be honest,' she said, a defeated tone to her voice. 'Peter made a complete mess of his life, but he still deserves some dignity in death. Even if you don't think we owe it to him, we do owe it to Susan. We need to make sure Peter gets a respectable send-off, and that his funeral reception runs smoothly. Everything else can wait.'

There seemed to be a shift in the atmosphere, and suddenly, everyone was in motion. Billy and Emma joined Carol in the kitchen, helping her to set out the food, bottles of wine, and a pile of plates interspersed with paper napkins. Tyler and Lizzie started to lay out some of the food, crockery and glasses on the large dining table while Vicki and Jack opened the doors to the garden to organise the patio furniture for the many smokers in Angel's circle of friends.

For Tyler, everything felt very familiar again, the Fletcher family preparing The Lodge for guests. His only unease was that Angel might not realise that she was one of the guests.

215

CHAPTER 43

By the time Angel and her friends began to arrive back at The Lodge, Peter's funeral reception was all prepared, and it was soon obvious it was going to be a funeral reception in two halves. An imaginary boundary formed where the breakfast bar split the kitchen and the dining area. The Fletchers sat together at the dining table and on the couch and chairs inside the French doors while Angel and her friends remained in the large kitchen area. Two tribes keeping firmly to their territories.

Carol, sat with Tyler and Lizzie, had positioned herself at the top of the dining table, where she could see into the kitchen and carefully monitor Angel's conduct. From the moment Angel had stridden into the room emanating obvious disapproval, it was clear she was furious that her plan to change the locks had failed. Carol wanted to keep an eye on her, to check she wasn't up to any further mischief. But no one said anything about the locksmith. None of Angel's friends approached the Fletchers, and the Fletchers ignored Angel and her friends with equal vigour.

For a while, the atmosphere remained cordial, with quiet chatter and some laughter too. But as the reception continued into its second hour, it occurred to Carol that no one was leaving. It was as if the people standing in the kitchen were waiting for the Fletcher family to vacate the house just as much as Carol was waiting for Angel's friends to leave, so she could speak to Angel alone.

The chatter and laughter from Angel's friends suddenly died down. Carol glanced over to see why, and she saw that everyone in the kitchen was staring towards the kitchen door. Someone had arrived.

The group shifted slightly, to clear a path through the centre of the room, and then Charlie appeared, smartly dressed in a back suit and tie. He passed through the kitchen, ignoring all the people he did not know and, without saying a word, walked directly to Carol who stood and embraced him.

'I cannot imagine how hard this is for you,' she whispered, 'but I am so pleased you're home.'

216

Charlie didn't say anything, but as he stepped back, he smiled at her, warmly, and she could tell he was trying his hardest to hold himself together, and not cry. Then everyone else stood, the whole family on their feet, hugging Charlie and kissing him, not a loud or excessive show of emotion, just a family quietly and happily welcoming home one of their own.

Their reunion was interrupted by the loud 'clink' of a glass being firmly set down on the breakfast bar. Angel strode forward to meet the new arrival. 'Charlie,' she said, rather theatrically, as though performing for her friends. 'What on earth are you doing here?'

Charlie paused for a moment to gather his thoughts, then coolly turned to face her. 'With the greatest of respect, Abigail, it's really none of your business why I am here.'

Angel raised an eyebrow, and then made a show of looking incredulously at her friends, some of whom were shaking their heads, as though unbelieving of Charlie's audacity. 'Well Charlie, *with the greatest of respect*, I wanted *all* of my stepchildren at my husband's funeral. Peter was your father, and whatever issues you may have had with him, they're in the past. If you couldn't show enough respect to him to attend the service, then I am deeply unhappy that you think it's OK to attend the reception.'

Someone in the kitchen said, 'Hear, hear,' and there followed a grumble of support from Angel's friends.

Charlie stared hard at Angel, and then he gestured towards her friends, all stood with glasses of wine and plates piled high with food. 'Considering my family and I paid for Dad's funeral, including the reception, I would say again, Abigail, that it's none of your business who attends. So, when your friends are stuffing their faces with food and guzzling back glasses of wine, perhaps they should all take into account that Peter's grieving widow couldn't be bothered to cough up a single penny for your own husband's funeral.' He swept a look over her friends, many paused mid-mouthful. 'You're welcome,' he said, contemptuously.

Charlie then noticed something, a woman, a stranger, stood towards the back of the kitchen, holding the antique music box from the sitting room. He stepped forward. 'What's she doing with that?' he demanded.

The woman, confused at first, looked down at the music box and back to Charlie. 'Angel gave it to me. As a gift.'

Charlie gritted his teeth and calmly addressed Angel, 'Your friend needs to put that back in the sitting room.'

'No, she doesn't,' Angel replied, offended. 'I've started to clear the house, Charlie. I know Peter would love nothing more than to see some of these old things being shared with his friends. Friends who were there for him, when he needed them.'

'Well, you can give away any of *Dad*'s stuff, Abigail. But there are very few things in this house that he owned. That antique music box, for instance, belongs to Vicki.'

At the mention of her name, Vicki quickly walked to Charlie and stood at his side. 'She's got my music box?' She glared through the throng at the woman who was holding it. 'Yeah, sweetheart, you want to put that back really quickly. It's mine.'

Angel now had a confused expression on her face. 'Nothing in this house is yours, Vicki. I own everything in this house now,' she said, loudly, 'and I can give it away as I please.'

'Story of her life,' Carol muttered, under her breath.

Charlie and Vicki looked at each other, both bewildered by Angel's behaviour. They both knew their father had led a confusing life, his relationships filled with affection and deceit in equal measure. But they still could not understand why Angel was acting with such inexplicable entitlement.

'Perhaps I can explain,' Vicki said, addressing Angel's friends. 'Peter's first wife, our mum, was called Susan. They were married for twenty-three years, and they had four children together. I thought I should mention this, because even though my mum was the single most important person in Dad's life, your friend Angel appears to have decided that she didn't deserve even a passing mention at his funeral.'

Charlie flinched, very obviously. 'What?' he asked. 'Mum wasn't even mentioned?'

Solemnly, Vicki shook her head, 'Sorry Charlie. We weren't mentioned either.'

218

Angel scowled at them, 'I am Peter's widow. When he died, I was all the family he had. Perhaps you Fletchers need to remember that.' There was a clear inflection in her tone when she spoke their surname, a spite and an anger, that had clearly built up against Peter's family over the years.

Vicki clenched her fists, trying her best to suppress her rising anger, 'When Mum discovered she was dying, she was worried that, once she was gone, Dad would go through this house and just start selling stuff, to make some quick money. Which, as we all know, is exactly what he would have done.

'To stop him from doing that, Mum left a long and very detailed will. A list of all her possessions, and who she was leaving each possession to. That antique music box was left to me. It is my legal property. If your friend doesn't get her grubby little mitts off it and tries to take it with her when she leaves, she'll be stealing it. And I will very happily have her arrested for theft.'

There was an obvious pause in the conversation, a stand-off, as both sides waited for someone to act. And then the impasse ended abruptly. Frustrated, Angel stormed through the kitchen to her friend. She whispered something to her, and the woman nodded and handed the music box over. Angel stomped back and handed it to Vicki. 'There's just a lot of old toot in this house,' she said, sneering. 'I just need to get rid of it.'

Vicki was completely baffled by her conduct. She knew the music box was not 'old toot' and that it was worth more than a thousand pounds. But she did not want to diminish its true value by talking about money. 'Well, this is an antique and it's been in our family for five generations,' she said. 'There's a whole story behind it, which I won't bother you with. But to be clear, Mum listed about a hundred items in her will, and if any of them is missing from this house, we will phone the police. So, keep your grubby mitts off our stuff.'

Angel span round and looked at her friends as though building up to some sort of finale, checking they were all still there to witness it. She turned back to the Fletchers, her expression happy and content. 'Well,' she said, 'I was hoping I wouldn't have to do this. Today of all days. We

219

have just cremated my husband, for god's sake. But as you know, Peter died without a will. And I just needed to know what that meant for me, his widow. Just to give myself some piece of mind. So, I've been to a solicitor to get some legal advice.

'He said, as Peter's widow, I am his next of kin and so I will inherit his estate. And obviously, that includes The Lodge. And I am really sorry to do this today… today of all days. But when you go, I want you to leave your house keys on the table. All of you. I need to have some time alone in my house, to think about my future, what I might do next, now that I've lost Peter. So please, don't make a fuss. Just go and leave your keys behind.'

CHAPTER 44

Charlie did not like talking about family business in front of strangers; he felt it was undignified as if he were washing dirty laundry in public. He knew neither his mother nor his grandmother would have tolerated it, so he decided to take the conversation offline, away from the crowd. 'Perhaps we should go into the sitting room,' he said, 'so we can resolve this in private.'

But Angel was frustrated and clearly irritated that none of the Fletchers had responded to her demand for their house keys. And she seemed to be enjoying being the centre of attention, performing in front of her friends, people Charlie considered little more than stragglers and hangers-on.

'Look,' Angel said. 'I am trying to be kind, I really am. I am a kind person, just ask any of my friends. But when I spoke to my solicitor, he advised me that I needed to have some... *clarity* about who is coming and going into my house, just while Peter's estate is settled. I really am just following his legal advice. This is nothing personal.'

'Quite right too,' came a voice from the kitchen.

'So,' Angel continued, 'I would like you all to leave my house. And, again, I want you to all leave your keys behind.'

As the words tumbled from her mouth, her demeanour somewhere between the pretence of grief and genuine spite, it began to dawn on Charlie how truly deceitful his father had been. Throughout his life, Peter seemed to have a compulsion to lie to people who loved him. And that compulsion, Charlie realised, had stayed with Peter to the bitter end – including in his relationship with his second wife.

'I am really sorry, Abigail,' Charlie said. 'But we are not giving you the keys to our family home, and I do not understand why you think we would.'

Angel laughed as though she were the only intelligent person in the conversation, trying to explain something to a simpleton. 'But Charlie,

221

that's the point. This isn't your family home, not anymore. Peter and I were married. I'm his widow. I get the house. And I want you all out.'

Charlie noticed that some of the men in the kitchen had moved forward, closer to Angel, perhaps as an attempt to intimidate the Fletchers, but he and Vicki were completely unphased and stood their ground.

'There's a good chance I might sell,' Angel continued, with a slightly more conciliatory tone, 'but if I do, obviously, I am going to give some of the proceeds to my stepchildren. I thought, perhaps, five thousand pounds each.'

From the kitchen, a couple of voices could be heard.

'Oh, Angel, that's so generous.'

'Oh, you really are an angel.'

Charlie smiled, 'Goodness. So that would be twenty-five thousand in all from the sale of a house that's worth more than two million.'

Angel grimaced, unhappy that her gracious offer was being presented as anything less than generous. 'You don't have to take a penny, if you don't want it,' she replied, curtly.

Charlie sighed and decided it was time to draw the bizarre conversation to an end. 'Abigail,' he said, 'I was widowed myself, a few years ago. And even though my husband *did* leave a will, I still had to go through a whole legal process, and I learned a lot about probate. So, I am struggling to believe you have spoken to any sort of a solicitor, because nothing you have said is even remotely correct.'

Angel threw her head back and let out a loud groan, confused as to why any of the Fletcher family were still there.

'That said,' Charlie continued, 'it's all rather academic, I'm afraid because Peter cannot leave you something that he didn't own. And he did not own The Lodge.'

Angel was so certain of her inheritance that she failed to properly listen to Charlie's words. She looked him in the eyes and spoke as though she still had the upper hand. 'Well, Charlie,' she said, trying to sound a little bored, 'I think we should just let our solicitors sort out any questions or objections. But I still want you all out. And leave your keys.'

222

She held out her hand, expecting every member of the Fletcher family to follow her instructions. The men behind her moved forward a little more, looming towards Charlie and Vicki, a clear attempt to add to the growing pressure in the situation.

'Abigail,' Charlie said firmly, trying his hardest not to sound like he was enjoying the conversation. 'You aren't listening. Dad did not own this house. He didn't own any properties. He had no life insurance, no savings or investments, no private pensions. He spent every penny he earned, and mostly, he spent it on alcohol. He has nothing to leave you but what's in his bedroom. His clothes, possibly a watch, a toothbrush. A bottle of cologne, maybe. I don't know what's up there. But that, Abigail, that is your inheritance. And I imagine it will all fit into a cardboard box.'

Finally, Angel began to listen, and she began to have a terrible feeling that Peter had been lying to her for all those years, from the very first time they had met at The Bell pub, when he had been so drunk, bragging about his big house and all his money. 'But this house, The Lodge. Peter owned The Lodge,' she said, and for the first time, her words were expressed with far less conviction, more as a question.

'He didn't,' Charlie replied.

'It's rented?' Angel asked, appalled at the idea.

'No, this is our family home,' Charlie replied. '*We* own it. Me and my brothers and sisters. Vicki, Billy, Tyler and Lizzie. The five of us. We own The Lodge.'

Angel stared at them, at all of them, and shook her head in disbelief. 'That's not true,' she cried loudly, desperately, and for a moment, the words echoed around the room, her great plan crumbling before her.

Charlie took a step forward and spoke to Angel in a hushed tone, 'When I was a baby, my grandparents – that's my mum's parents, Dorothy and Stanley – were worried that Dad wouldn't amount to anything. They were worried he wouldn't provide for Mum and me, and we would end up moving from one bedsit to another, year after year. And as much as they disliked Dad, they wanted to look after their daughter and grandson.

223

'Nan had just inherited this house from her brother, William. He died young without a wife or children. So, Nan and Granddad let us move in here, rent-free. The idea was that Dad would get a stable job, save up for a couple of years and then he and Mum would have a down payment to buy a house of their own.'

The room was silent, everyone listening to Charlie's story. Carol and his siblings knew it well, a sad tale of entitlement and loss. But for Angel and her friends, it was a very different story, one that was about to rob Angel of everything she thought she deserved after investing years of her life in a relationship with Peter.

'Of course, Dad being Dad, he couldn't see the point of wasting money on mortgage payments,' Charlie continued. 'He thought that if he and Mum just sat it out for long enough, eventually Nan and Granddad would pass away and they would inherit The Lodge. The one thing Dad didn't consider is that his mother-in-law might outlive his wife. When Mum died, Nan changed her will to leave The Lodge to her four grandchildren. When Nan passed away, and we inherited the house, we changed the deeds to add Tyler's name so he would have an equal share.'

Angel was stood, her arms folded, tears forming in her eyes, either from anger or from grief, the grief of seeing a future of unbridled privilege so cruelly snatched from her in front of her friends. 'But he lived here, all these years,' she said, 'even when all you kids were gone, when you all moved away and got your own places. After he came out of prison. You let him live here. You let us live here. I don't understand how this *isn't* Peter's house.'

Vicki stepped forward, took Charlie's hand and gave it a little squeeze. 'Mum wrote us a letter,' she said. 'The solicitor gave it to us after she had died. Mum knew what Nan was planning to do, that she was going to change her will. And Mum was worried that when we inherited The Lodge, we might just sell it, and Dad would end up homeless.

'So, in that letter, she asked us to make a promise. That, no matter what happened, we would keep the house and let Dad live here for the rest of his life. And we kept our word. Even after everything that happened, the car accident, Dad going to jail. We kept the house so it would be here for him, when he eventually came home. Just like we promised Mum. But I am sorry, Angel. Charlie's telling you the truth. Now that Dad's gone, there's nothing for you here.'

For the first time, both groups were on the same page, the Fletchers and Angel's friends. They all waited silently in anticipation, to see what Angel would say or do. And after a few moments had passed, Angel exploded with rage.

'Good for you. Good for all of you,' she screamed. 'Stealing from me. Stealing my inheritance from me. You know what, you're scum. All of you. Cheating, thieving scum. You have stolen my house. You have stolen my money. Everything. You are scum.' And then she focussed solely on Charlie, and pointed her finger at him. 'And especially you,' she said, her voice deep and filled with contempt. 'You, Charlie Fletcher, with your smugness, and all your properties abroad. But that wasn't enough for you, was it? You had to come and take what was supposed to be mine. You wouldn't come to your own father's funeral, but you were happy to jump on a plane to steal my rightful inheritance from me. You make me sick.'

Charlie listened to Angel's outburst without a care in the world, happy in the knowledge that she would soon be gone from their house and their lives, for good, and that she would take her awful friends with her.

But Tyler, sat at the table, just behind him, was having none of it. Charlie held a special place in Tyler's heart, the older sibling who once swept him up onto his lap, gave him a hug, and told him, 'Just call me your brother.' And Tyler was not going to stand by and watch Charlie being abused in his own home.

'That's enough,' he said, his deep voice booming. He stood, and then stormed forward and fronted up to the men stood behind Angel, each of them much taller than he, yet Tyler, young and muscular and brimming with anger, unnerved each of them. Surprised, they stepped back from him, and did not even object when he began to manhandle them, pushing and turning each of them back towards the kitchen.

225

'All of you, out!' Tyler shouted. 'I've had enough of the lot of you. A group of drunken, scrounging losers. Clinging to your fake friendship with my dad. The only reason you're here is because you thought he had money. Well, he didn't. So, plates down. Glasses down. Get out!'

The other people in the kitchen did as they were told, realising Angel's power had been completely demolished and that none of them had any right to remain. Tyler was joined by Billy and Emma, using their outstretched arms to guide Angel's friends from the kitchen to the hallway and then to the front door.

'And if anything is missing from this house, one single thing, you'll be seeing the police,' Billy said.

'Go on, all of you,' Emma said, loudly, brightly, clearly enjoying the process of clearing the dregs from the house. 'Show's over. Get out!'

And in just a few hectic, loud moments, everyone was gone. Everyone, apart from Angel, stood suddenly alone, bereft, left with nothing at all.

'Abigail,' Charlie said, softly, the hint of a smile on his face. 'I'm sure Dad appreciated everything you did for him. All those years, all those visits to see him in prison. And I am sure Dad knew exactly how you really felt about him. I mean, it's not as if you did all of that, for all those years, just because you thought he owned a big house.'

Angel had anger and hatred etched across her face. Without saying another word, she lifted her head, turned, and followed her friends from The Lodge.

Vicki called after her cheerfully, 'Don't worry, Angel, we'll pack up all the stuff in Dad's bedroom for you. You know, his estate. I think it probably will all fit in a cardboard box.'

Once the family heard the reassuring slam of the front door, Tyler, Billy and Emma re-entered the kitchen, having remained in the hall to ensure Angel and her friends were truly gone.

'Goodness me, Tyler,' Charlie said, and patted his brother on the back. 'I thought you were going to punch one of those blokes. That was a little unexpected. I don't think I have ever seen you lose your temper before. Not even once.'

226

'It doesn't happen very often, Charlie,' Carol said, still sitting at the table, 'but when it does, you don't want to be on the wrong side of him.' And then she stood up. 'Right, kids,' she continued, 'first things first. Let's get that list of all your mum's stuff. We'll go through the house and, I swear to god, if so much as one fucking thing is missing, I'll drag Angel to the police station myself, by her fake red hair.'

CHAPTER 45

In the days that followed Peter's funeral, all the Fletchers gravitated to The Lodge, and Charlie delayed his return to Gran Canaria so that he could spend time with his family. Each morning, Vicki would arrive with Jack and Carol with Lizzie, and they would stay for the whole day, often late into the evening. Everyone took turns preparing meals, and mostly, the family sat around drinking tea or wine and singing along to Carole King songs, which always seemed to be playing in the background.

They talked, all of them, about so many things, so many memories they had of that house, happy memories of Christmas Days, sunny barbecues, and the posh evening soirees when all the kids knew they had to be on their best behaviour. And although it was not spoken out loud, it was clear they were all saying goodbye to the house. With their father gone and the promise to their mother fulfilled, it was time to move on.

As the days drifted by, and Charlie's return to Gran Canaria approached, he began to notice something odd about Carol's behaviour. She kept arranging opportunities for them to be alone, as though she had something important to tell him or ask him. But whenever those opportunities arose, she would instead talk about everyday things, such as the weather or the general election.

Charlie had always felt that he and Carol had an open and straightforward relationship, and it was strange to feel that she might be keeping something from him or felt unable to talk to him. And so, he suggested it might be nice if he took her for lunch, just the two of them, and Carol accepted.

He purposely booked a table at an American-style diner in Southchurch Village because he knew the seating included booths, which would offer some level of privacy if Carol did indeed want to speak to him about something personal. For the first part of their meal, the conversation was **unremarkable**. Charlie spoke about his business and the way Tyler had transformed the outside space at his villa, and Carol elaborated on all the plans she had for her upcoming retirement.

228

The waiter dutifully kept their wine glasses topped up, and as they began to consume their meals, Charlie knew he had to create an environment where Carol could open up about whatever it was that she wanted to discuss with him, so he began to talk about the sale of The Lodge and what it would mean for everyone in the family.

'Vicki can pay off her mortgage and have money set aside to send Jack to university', he said. 'Billy and Emma can finally have the fancy wedding they had been saving for and have more than enough left to buy a place of their own. And it's going to give Lizzie and Tyler an amazing start to their adult lives.'

Charlie knew all the kids had agreed to give Carol a lump sum too, to clear her mortgage and make sure she had enough money to make life a little easier in retirement. But that was a conversation Tyler and Lizzie were going to have with her, at a later date.

'And what about you?' Carol asked. 'What are you going to do with your money? Because it's a great chance for you to slow down a bit, Charlie. Take care of yourself.'

Charlie agreed. 'I'm going to clear almost all my outstanding loans,' he said. 'Finally, I will be able to make a proper profit from my little empire of holiday homes. And it feels different this time, too. The money, I mean. The inheritance.'

'What do you mean?' Carol asked.

Charlie took another sip of wine, and then placed the glass onto the table. 'The money I've inherited over the years, from Jason and then from nan. It always felt like sad money, something I should put to practical use but could never actually enjoy. But this money, it feels different. It's not coming with any emotional baggage. It's like a gift. A happy gift, from nan and granddad. And from mum. It's like they're giving me this opportunity to really move on with my life.'

Carol was smiling at him, and then they both raised their glasses, a silent toast. But then, on Carol's face, that expression again, the same expression Charlie had noticed so many times over the previous few days; pensive and awkward, as though she wanted to tell him something, but couldn't bring herself to say it. This time, Charlie was going to make certain she said it out loud. 'I'm heading back to Maspalomas soon,' he said. 'I'm just trying to make sure everything... everyone is OK before I head off.'

Carol nodded, but didn't speak.

'Sooo... if there's anything you want to talk to me about, now's a really good time.'

Almost immediately, the expression on Carol's face darkened and Charlie could feel the atmosphere change, a strange sensation that took him by surprise. 'Carol?'

She shook her head. 'I'm sorry to unload this onto you, Charlie. So soon after your dad's funeral. But you see, there's this letter.'

'Letter?'

'A few days before your mum passed away, she wrote a letter to Lizzie. She asked me to keep it until Lizzie's 23rd birthday. And every year that passes, the older Lizzie gets, it's like a bloody countdown.'

'Why 23?' Charlie asked, puzzled by what appeared to be a rather randomly chosen number.

Carol shrugged. 'She didn't tell me, but her instructions were very clear. I was to give it to Lizzie on her 23rd birthday and no one, including me, was allowed to open it beforehand.'

'Well, I can't believe mum would have written anything unpleasant, or salacious,' Charlie said, puzzled as to why a letter would cause such distress.

Carol slumped down slightly and appeared a little panicked, and Charlie began to find her demeanour unnerving. He had always considered Carol to be tough, to completely own her emotions. He had never seen her like this before, suffering an uncharacteristic bout of anxiety.

'Your mum was expecting Peter to have a conversation with you, Charlie,' Carol said. 'To explain a few things to you. Things she thought it was important that you understood. So, when she wrote that letter, she thought it would all be old news by the time Lizzie was 23.'

'And what was dad supposed to tell me?' Charlie asked, worried he was blundering into a private part of his parents' marriage that he had no business knowing about.

Carol sat up slightly, and placed her hands on her lap, as though preparing to tell him a story. 'You see, you've never asked,' she said. 'About me and your dad. And Tyler. None of you have, none of you kids. Even Tyler's never asked.'

'Well, we know you and dad had... some sort of... fling,' Charlie said. 'I just don't think any of us felt comfortable asking for details. We know it happened. We know Mum was cool with it. That's all we needed to know.'

Carol began to shake her head. 'Oh, Charlie, I just don't know what to do. Above all else, I want to respect Susan's wishes, but I've always wondered if she changed her mind, at the end. Perhaps she thought it best if you didn't know everything. And perhaps there's nothing in the letter, and I'm panicking for no good reason.'

Charlie began to relive the final conversation he'd had with his mum, on that rainy day in March so many years earlier. And as her words began to repeat in his mind, he recalled something she had said, right at the end, before she had fallen asleep. Something Charlie had forgotten about, for all those years, because he had been too preoccupied with the shocking news of his father's infidelity and the truth about Tyler.

'I remember, now,' he said, almost as a whisper. 'She asked if Dad had spoken to me, and I said that he hadn't. So, she told me about Tyler, and about the arrangements for Lizzie, coming to live with you. But then she said there was more, that she was going to tell me everything. But she was so weak by then, so tired. She went to sleep, asked me to stay, said we would talk more when she woke up. But she didn't. She didn't wake up.'

His words appeared to have a calming effect on Carol, who relaxed noticeably, appearing far less anxious. 'She was going to tell you? Everything?'

Charlie nodded. 'Yes,' he replied. 'Carol, whatever it is, you and I have been through enough together over the years, that you must know, there's no judgement here. This is a safe space. Whatever you have to tell me, it will be fine. And, honestly, whatever it is, Mum *was* going to tell me. She just didn't get the chance.'

It was as though Carol finally had permission to tell her story, but not from Charlie. She had permission from Susan. She paused to gather her thoughts, and then she began to speak. 'The first thing you need to understand, Charlie, is that I was never in a relationship with Peter. I tolerated him. I suppose I grew fond of him, over time, but I never loved him. We were never together.'

'I think you were,' Charlie replied. 'I think Tyler's proof of that.'

'No, Charlie. What I mean is that Peter and I were never a couple,' Carol insisted. And then she drew a deep breath and continued to speak. 'It was your mum, Charlie. Susan and I were together for almost 15 years, right up until the day she died. I loved your mother with all my heart. I still do.'

CHAPTER 46

Charlie could feel the air rush from his lungs, as a loud and unexpected gasp escaped his lips. For the next few moments, he sat with his mouth open and all he could hear was his own heartbeat, thumping in his ears, as he tried to understand, to acknowledge, what Carol had just revealed to him. Astonished and wide-eyed, he just looked at her, unable to speak.

'It's OK, Charlie,' she said. 'It's a shock, but I want you to know the whole story. I don't want to leave you with the wrong idea. Again.'

Charlie tried to reply, but he could only manage to mumble a few 'erms' and then gave up trying.

'Why don't I just fill in the blanks for you?' Carol suggested, and then she reached across the table and gently, with the tip of her finger, pushed his mouth closed. Then, Charlie nodded, and so Carol told him the whole story. And once she had begun to speak, it was as if she couldn't stop. There were no filters, no moments when it appeared she was leaving out some of the more intimate details to save his blushes. After so many years, she was finally able to talk about the great love she had shared with Susan Fletcher, and she wanted Charlie to know all of it.

She spoke of how they had first met, working shifts together at a local plastics factory, and how their friendship had gradually blossomed into something more. She told Charlie of the first time they had shared a kiss, at a boozy New Year's Eve party at The Lodge. Peter had passed out by ten o'clock but Susan, who was more than a little tipsy herself, had still wanted someone to kiss at midnight, and so had asked Carol. It had all felt like a joke, at first, a silly drunken moment that would mean nothing. But the kiss was a little too intimate and afterwards, their eyes had lingered, for just a little too long. And that was all it took.

Carol explained about the years that had followed, of secretly pursuing a passionate affair, mostly enabled by Peter's regular trips away, for work. And then she reached the part of her tale which explained how Tyler had come into the world, and that was the part Charlie found the most shocking of all.

233

'You, Vicki and Billy were visiting your nan for the weekend, and Peter was working up in Norfolk. So, Susan and I had The Lodge to ourselves,' she said, slowing the delivery of her words, an attempt to give the moment some appropriate gravitas.

'Norfolk,' Charlie said, quietly, the word rattling something at the back of his mind, a memory, something his father had once said. 'Dad mentioned Norfolk, didn't he, once?' he said, desperately trying to recall exactly when, and why. There was a sound that went with that memory, and Charlie seemed to think it was a loud slap, and that was all it took for him to remember; his father drunk, at a bar, saying something out of spite, about a night he returned home from Norfolk, a story Carol had quickly put an end too.

'It was late, a Friday night,' Carol said, 'and we were in bed, Susan and I, naked. We'd shared a spliff and were laughing and giggling.'

'Wait, what?' Charlie interceded. 'Mum was smoking? Marijuana?'

Carol rolled her eyes. 'Seriously, Charlie. Everything I'm telling you, and that's the bit you're shocked by? That Susan occasionally rolled a joint.'

'Mum knew how to roll a joint?'

Carol threw her hands in the air. 'Charlie, seriously. That's not the focus of this story. I want to explain to you, about Peter. And Tyler.'

Charlie agreed. 'Yes, yes, of course. Sorry.'

Carol took a moment to remember what part of her story she had reached, and then she continued. 'So, we were just lying there, when all of a sudden, there was a creak, from the landing. We both looked at the door, which was open, and there was Peter, just stood there, staring at us. He'd come home for the weekend, without phoning ahead. I was horrified. I grabbed the sheets and covered myself. But your mum... she just lay there, quite happy to be naked in front of him. It was like she didn't care at all that he had caught us, in bed together.

'At first, Peter didn't say or do anything, and I noticed he was swaying from side to side, a little, and I realised he had taken a detour to the pub before coming home. And then Susan just... she just burst out laughing. Loud, hysterical laughter. She leaned over to me, and whispered into my ear, 'Shall we invite him to join in?''

234

'Oh god!' Charlie blurted out, before he was able to stop himself. He knew, instantly, how disapproving he had sounded, and he didn't want Carol to think he was judging her, or his mother. He covered his mouth with his hand, and softly apologised.

'You need to know the truth,' Carol said.

Charlie rested his hands onto the table and tried his best to remain calm, unflustered.

'Well, your dad, back then, as you know, was good looking, and quite a charmer. And your mum had told me many stories about... well... what he was like, in the bedroom, if you know what I mean.' Carol, now completely comfortable telling her story to Charlie, smirked and then flashed her eyebrows at him. 'And to be honest, I was high as a fucking kite. So, I just said, 'why not?'. Your mum held out her hand to Peter, and then I pulled back the covers, and I held out my hand too. And, honestly Charlie, you've never seen anyone get undressed so quickly. He jumped onto the bed, right in between us. And the three of us... spent the night together.'

'And that's the night you conceived Tyler?'

'Yes,' Carol said.

Although still deeply shocked, Charlie could feel that familiar urge niggling at the back of his head, the need to know more, to understand how everything had played out. 'And so, you and Mum and Dad. You were like a... what's it called? A throuple?'

Carol chuckled and shook her head. 'No,' she said. 'It was only the once.'

'OK. But then, what about you and mum? I mean, you were both, what, bisexual?'

Carol tutted and shook her head. 'Charlie, we never put labels on what we had,' she replied. 'I just... fell in love. And it just happened that the person I fell in love with was Susan. It was the same for her.'

'But you kept seeing each other, after that night, even though dad knew? Didn't he have something to say about it?'

Sighing, Carol leaned forward and rested her chin on her hands. 'You know what your dad was like, Charlie. He avoided any conversations that might be uncomfortable. He carried on like nothing had happened, everything the same. Obviously, nine months later, there was Tyler, living proof that it hadn't been some drunken fantasy. And he always accepted that Tyler was his, there was never any nonsense about that. But after that night, Peter seemed to take a step back, almost like he was keeping out of the way, letting it happen. But that was Peter. He spent his entire life with his head buried in the sand.'

It was a description of his father that Charlie could fully appreciate. His father's life had been defined not by the conversations he'd had, but by the conversations he'd avoided. Charlie had always been different to Peter, with a need to ask questions and understand things. And Carol's story had left him with plenty more questions.

'But, later, when mum was pregnant with Lizzie. How did you feel about that? Because obviously that meant she was being intimate with Dad.'

'Charlie, I know it all sounds really weird to you,' Carol replied. 'But it just worked. Your mum shared most of her life with me, but there were still some parts she shared with Peter. That was just the norm for us. For all three of us.' Carol appeared satisfied, pleased the truth was finally known, that her relationship with Susan could finally be acknowledged.

Charlie, however, wasn't sure how he felt. He didn't speak for a while, his entire understanding of his family having been flipped upside down. But as he aligned his memories of his parents with Carol's story, it all began to make sense, every word of it. Susan and Peter's mismatched relationship finally made sense.

'He never said a thing,' Charlie reflected. 'For all those years after Mum died, Dad let us all think that he was the one who'd had an affair. That it was Mum who'd been betrayed.'

'He almost told you, I think, a couple of times when he was drunk or angry,' Carol said. 'But perhaps it was easier for him to be the bad guy. Perhaps it was easier than admitting that his wife had been in a 15-year relationship with someone else. Or, perhaps, he loved your mum that much, that he didn't want anyone to think less of her. I never really understood, to be honest, why he kept it a secret. Because it might have

236

helped his relationship with you kids, and with you in particular, Charlie, if you'd known what he'd had to put up with, for all those years.'

There was no place in Charlie's heart for a single kind thought for his father, but he was able to acknowledge the point, and wondered how differently things might have played out, if Peter had summoned the courage to tell him the truth.

'I remember Mum's funeral,' he said, his voice filled with great affection. 'I saw you, so many times that day, as though you were about to cry, but each time, you stopped yourself. Mum was your partner, the love of your life, and you couldn't even properly grieve for her.'

Carol offered him a warm smile. 'Oh, I cried,' she said. 'I promise you, I cried, and I cried. Just not in front of you.'

Charlie reached across the table and held Carol's hand. 'I'm glad I finally know the truth,' he said. 'How do you feel?'

She grinned broadly. 'Free,' she said. 'Like there's a whole part of my life that I can finally talk about.' Her expression changed, becoming more serious again. 'And now, we need to decide what to do next.'

Charlie agreed, although at first, he could only worry about how everyone might react. In particular, he wondered how Tyler would feel when he learned the truth about how he came into the world, and whether he would take it in his stride or struggle with the idea he was the result of a drunken threesome.

But then, Charlie's mind shifted to a different perspective, and all he could think about was his mum, and how she must have wanted the family to know the truth about her life. And that was all that mattered.

'I'll talk to Vicki and Billy, before I go back to Maspalomas,' he said. 'Perhaps you can talk to Tyler. And you can make a judgement call on whether Lizzie should know yet. How does that sound?'

'Yes,' Carol replied. 'I'll talk to Tyler. Lizzie, I think, I will leave for a while. She's a bit young to understand all this stuff.'

'And just so I don't put my foot in it, how much do you actually want me to share with them?'

'Everything,' Carol replied immediately. 'No more secrets, Charlie. What happened, happened.' Carol reached across the table to Charlie and stroked the side of his face. 'You've all got your mum in you, you

237

know, all the Fletcher kids. Every now and again, one of you will say something, or look at me with a particular expression, and I think "oh, that was *so* Susan". And it makes me happy.'

Charlie leaned into her hand and smiled. 'I think we need another bottle of wine, don't we?' he said.

'Oh, fuck yes,' Carol replied. 'Maybe two.'

CHAPTER 47

It had been a long time since Vicki had felt so nervous and many years since she had allowed a single social worker to have any authority over her. But she kept reminding herself that things were different now, that she was on a far more even footing with the social services team, and that the next few hours could see the beginning of an exciting new chapter in her life.

She looked around the waiting room, a gloomy space with uncomfortable plastic chairs and a machine that delivered bitter-tasting coffee in paper cups, and realised just how grateful she was that Debbie and Kim were both there, to offer their support. Kim had guessed there would be a delay and so had taken the trouble to bring a plastic bag filled with chocolate digestives, although Debbie had not been impressed when she saw just how many biscuits were in the bag.

'You planning to feed the five thousand with that?' she asked.

'We could be here all day, you know what they're like,' Kim replied, popping a biscuit into her mouth.

Vicki checked her watch. 'I should have been in 25 minutes ago. Do you think there's a problem?'

Debbie shook her head. 'Not at all. They always run late.'

The door next to them opened and a man stepped out, short with dark grey hair, spectacles and in a smart grey suit. He clasped his hands together and smiled at the group. 'Victoria Fletcher?' he enquired.

Vicki stood. 'That's me, and please call me Vicki.'

Gently, he shook her hand. 'I'm David Munroe, the chair of the panel today. Please accept my apologies for keeping you waiting. We've just been reading through your forms, and we always forget just how many forms there are to read.' He glanced behind her at Debbie and Kim sat on the chairs, looking at him. 'And, well, I certainly know these two,' he said as he stepped forward to greet them. 'What a lovely surprise. How are you both? I don't suppose you're coming out of retirement, are you?'

With great affection, Kim and Debbie laughed and stood to clasp his outstretched hand in turn.

'Oh, no, no, sorry David,' Debbie said. 'We're enjoying the peace and quiet too much. But we're very happy to be here today to support this young lady's application.'

'We've submitted a letter,' Kim added, 'but we're happy to come in and talk to the panel if that helps.'

'I don't think that will be necessary,' David said pleasantly, an off-the-cuff comment but one from which Vicki immediately gleaned some reassurance. 'We've already read your letter, which was extremely helpful. But it is lovely to see you both.' He turned to Vicki and gestured towards the open door. 'Shall we? And please don't be nervous. This really is more like a chat, I promise you.'

Vicki glanced one final time at Debbie and Kim, hoping their calm and casual mood might help ease her nerves, and then, hesitantly, she walked through the door. Inside, there were five people sat around a large table, each with a pile of paperwork in front of them. They all smiled and said hello, all so friendly and happy to see her, and she could quickly feel her nerves beginning to fall away.

David closed the door behind them and gestured towards a chair. Once they were both seated, he introduced himself as a retired children's charity CFO, and made a point of saying he was independent of the local authority. He went on to introduce the others: a social worker, a foster carer, a teacher, a young woman who had grown up in foster care, and the panel's advisor. They all appeared reassuringly pleased to meet her.

'We're going to ask you a few questions about the rather long and arduous process that you've been through over the past year to get you to this point,' David said. 'Such as how you found the training and what you found most useful. But also, a little bit about your son, Jack, and how he feels about potentially sharing his home with children and young people in foster care.'

'Yes, of course.' Vicki nodded.

David flicked through the top few papers in front of him and looked to Vicki. 'We'll start with the rather obvious question as to why you have chosen to become a foster carer,' he said, 'but, also, if I may, I would like to ask this: over the years, I have known many children and young people who have grown up in foster care and who, as adults, found social work – or indeed, foster care itself – to be their vocation. But, for me, at least, this is the first time I have seen an application from someone whose experience of fostering has been as a parent whose own child was taken into foster care. I wonder if you could talk us through how that experience led you here today?'

Vicki had been expecting a question about why she wanted to be a foster carer, a version of the 'What attracted you to this position?' question asked at pretty much every job interview. She had prepared a straightforward answer about wanting to make a difference, about the number of kids taken into care each year, and how she felt she had the resilience and compassion to offer children and young people a stable home, either short or long term. But the panel's chair had given the question an entirely different context, and that threw her off balance. She paused, taking a moment to think before replying. She wanted to give an honest answer, but she realised now she had never before put into words how Jack being taken into care had affected her.

'I guess,' she started, her voice quiet, suddenly nervous again, 'I guess, when Jack went to live with Debbie and Kim, his foster parents, all I wanted was to have him back home with me. I couldn't understand why anyone would think he would be happy or be able to... flourish as a child, unless he was with his mum. But then, as I got to know Debbie and Kim, I began to see this wonderful life they were giving him. And to be honest, for a long time, I was jealous of them. Perhaps even a bit angry.'

'Why angry?' David asked.

Vicki sighed. 'I think I blamed them, partly at least, for Jack staying in foster care so long. They made him happy, gave him a home that was safe and stable. He was doing well at school, he had lots of friends. I just kept wondering how I could possibly get custody when he was living with these two... superwomen. But over the years, I grew to appreciate what they were doing for Jack, and also what they were doing for me. They really went out of their way to make it easy for me to see Jack or talk to him over the phone. They helped me be an important part of his

241

life, even though he wasn't living with me. Eventually, I learned to be grateful to them, for giving Jack such a great home, when I couldn't. That's a tough thing for a mother to admit and, honestly, it's even tougher to say it out loud. But I am grateful to them.'

David looked around the table at the other members of the panel. 'Debbie and Kim retired from fostering last year,' he informed the group, 'and we have already read their letter in support of Miss Fletcher's application, at appendix seven.'

David looked at Vicki. 'And they are here today, as well, outside in the waiting room, to support you in person. And I understand, from their letter, that after Jack returned to live with you, you chose to maintain his relationship with them.'

'Oh, yes,' Vicki said, a little breathless, hoping she was saying the right things. 'Jack lived with them for six years, a big part of his childhood. He had made a very real attachment with them, and it really wouldn't have been good for him if I'd tried to end that. But, also, for me. They had become good friends. And over the years, I've seen them look after lots of other kids and it made me think, what if there weren't people like Debbie and Kim in the world? What would have happened to all those children and young people? What would have happened to Jack? He would have ended up in some sort of children's home, or institution. Debbie and Kim made me appreciate the importance of foster carers, and I began to have a really strong feeling that it was something that I could do. Something that I *should* do. I hope that doesn't sound silly.'

Everyone in the room shook their heads, and Vicki could see them all smiling. She hoped that being honest about her feelings, perhaps fully honest for the first time, to a room of strangers had been the right thing to do.

'It doesn't sound silly at all,' David said. 'So, we have a few more questions for you. Let's move on to those.'

CHAPTER 48

Tyler was kneeling in the mud, holding a trowel and trying to focus on the job at hand, saving plants from his Auntie Susan's garden before The Lodge was sold. Transplanting was a tricky business, and he knew he had to get everything just right, or none of the flowers would survive the move to their new homes. But even by Fletcher family standards, the bombshell news his mother had dropped the day before had been confounding, and he was finding it hard to concentrate.

He wasn't sure which part of the story he had found most surprising, that his long-held suspicions about a relationship between his mum and Auntie Susan had proven correct or his mother's overly detailed description of his conception. He had spoken to Vicki and Billy, both of whom seemed to have accepted the news with astonishing ease. But he wasn't entirely sure he trusted their reactions and wondered if they were more upset than they had let on. After all, it was *his* conception they had all been told about, so perhaps his siblings simply didn't want him to know how appalled they were by the whole story.

'I'd offer to help but, to be honest, me and gardening aren't a good mix. Just ask any plant.'

Tyler relaxed back onto his calves at the sound of Charlie's voice and looked up. 'Taking into account that I have seen you successfully kill artificial turf,' he said, 'I will accept your offer *not* to help.'

Charlie was in jeans and an old t-shirt that had a faded slogan printed on the front, something about Y2K, but Tyler couldn't make out the rest. 'I hear you're heading off soon,' Tyler said.

Charlie found a clear patch of grass and knelt next to Tyler. 'Tomorrow,' he replied. 'The gang have been keeping an eye on my rentals, but they all have busy lives and jobs, and I don't feel I can burden them longer. But I've been trying to spend time with everyone here before I go. I went to see a show at the Palace Theatre with Carol and Lizzie, and then Emma took me to a Charles Dickens festival at the library because Billy was performing sections from various Dickens novels.

'I honestly thought it would be a bit stuffy, and hardly anyone would turn up, just Emma and me, a few librarians pretending to be members of the public, you know, to fill the seats. But it was absolutely rammed. People had to stand because there weren't enough chairs. Loads of women and quite a few gay guys. Clapping and cheering. Screaming at one point. It was like a rock concert more than a book reading.'

'Oh, he's got quite a fan following in Essex,' Tyler said. 'Thousands of followers on social media. Lizzie manages his Facebook and Twitter for him. I think he has Instagram too. That's why he gets offered things like that, at the library. They know he'll pull in the punters. And his amateur dramatics group has changed their next show to Joseph and the Technicolour Dreamcoat, just so they can give Billy the lead. Although I have to say there's a lusty old woman who runs the group and I think she just wants and excuse to get Billy in a loin cloth.'

Charlie grinned, remembering Billy as a young man and his penchant for middle-aged women. 'And I spent a day down the seafront with Vicki and Jack,' he continued. 'He's a smart boy, isn't he? He's already thinking about university.'

'He might be the first Fletcher kid to go,' Tyler said, and then he frowned, and added, 'I hate to say it, but the best thing that ever happened to Jack was his dad doing a bunk. I can't think how different his life might have been if Nate was still hanging around.'

Charlie didn't reply and Tyler could tell he was distracted, only half paying attention. He guessed his brother had come to speak to him about something, and he assumed he knew what it was about, and so he decided to help by nudging the conversation in the right direction. 'Were you surprised, about my mum and your mum?' he asked.

'Oh, bloody hell, yes,' Charlie gasped. 'I thought I had that whole part of the Fletcher family history neatly tied up and filed away. Turns out I was completely wrong.' Charlie shuffled about for a moment, and then rocked backwards and lay on the grass, propped up by his elbows, his legs outstretched in front of him, settling in for a longer chat. 'Carol said mum used to come round your house a lot.'

Tyler put the trowel onto the ground, and realised his brother's enquiring mind was still trying to put all the pieces of the story together.

244

'It was like a had two mums, most of the time,' he said. 'Dad didn't visit that often, and even when he did come to see me, he never really seemed to be in the room. But Auntie Susan was there a lot, reading me stories or flicking through gardening magazines with me.'

'Did you ever... suspect anything?'

Tyler shook his head. 'Not when I was a kid. But when I was older, there were things that I began to question.'

'Like?'

Tyler shrugged. 'The way Auntie Susan was with me. I mean, I was her husband's illegitimate son, but she always treated me like I was one of her own. After she died, whenever Mum spoke about her, there was something there. It was more than just reminiscing about a friend she'd lost. I could tell her heart was genuinely broken.' Tyler turned his attention to Charlie. 'How do you feel about all of this?' he asked.

Charlie leaned his head back, slightly, and allowed the sunlight to fall onto his face. 'I like it,' he said, with a casual tone that surprised Tyler. 'Dad was selfish. He only showed affection when it suited him. I'm glad Mum had Carol. I'm glad she was loved. Properly loved.'

Tyler settled back onto his bum, stretched his legs out and leaned back, mirroring Charlie, the sunshine on his face. 'And how did you feel when mum told you about *that* night?' he asked and glanced sideways to gauge his brother's reaction.

Charlie, squinting slightly, cocked his head in Tyler's direction. 'We got you out of it, bruv,' he said. 'That's all that matters.' He smiled and then turned and looked at the sky again, and Tyler realised that was the one part of the story where Charlie's thirst for detail appeared to have been satisfied.

'How's the transplanting going?' Charlie asked. 'Have you decided what you're going to save?'

'I thought the hardy geraniums, the anniversary rose and the aquilegia. Mum's getting some for her garden, and Vicki's asked if I can plant some in your garden, for when she moves in.'

'Why did you pick those? Are they the most likely to survive being moved?'

245

'Well, that. But also, I helped Auntie Susan plant them, when I was a kid. They just mean a lot to me, and I'd like to see them flourishing somewhere else.'

'Mum loved you,' Charlie said, fondly. 'None of us were in the least bit interested in gardening, but she had you, her little helper. Always out here, digging holes or pruning or... you know... whatever else gardeners do.'

Tyler chuckled. 'Auntie Susan's the whole reason I got into gardening,' he said, 'which led to my job with the parks team at the council. It all started here, in her garden. When I've finished travelling, wherever I end up, I'm going to make sure I have a garden of my own.'

'And... have you decided what you are going to do?' Charlie asked. 'I mean, are you staying here or...?'

And then Tyler understood the purpose of Charlie's visit. It hadn't been to ask him about Carol and Susan's grand affair. It was to reassure himself, that his kid brother was going to return to Gran Canaria with him. And Tyler felt quite flattered, that he meant that much to Charlie. 'I have a few things to sort out here,' he replied, 'and then, if it's OK with you, I would really like to go back to Gran Canaria, stay with you at the villa. I spoke to Martin and Peggy yesterday. They both still have work for me.'

He saw a broad smile appear on Charlie's face, either happiness or relief, or both.

'Oh, that's great,' Charlie said. 'And, just to say it again, you can stay as long as you like. Mi casa es tu casa.'

For a while, the two brothers remained where they were, lying flat on the grass, side by side, happily silent, just enjoying the time they had left, in Susan's garden. But then, Tyler's mischievous nature got the better of him.

'What's going on between you and Alan?' he asked. He didn't have to wait for a reaction. Instantly, Charlie sat up, and stared at him, seeming a little alarmed.

'What? Me and Alan? What do you mean? Nothing. What?'

Smirking, Tyler propped himself up on his elbows. 'Come on Charlie. Your face lights up every time you see him. And I'm almost

246

certain I interrupted something, that morning, when I got the news about Dad. Something was definitely going on in that kitchen.'

Charlie screwed up his face and shook his head. 'No. You've got the wrong end of the stick, there. I mean, Alan's a great bloke, but he's not even gay. So, it's not as if anything could even happen.'

Tyler raised his brow. 'Well, according to Mum, she and Auntie Susan weren't gay either, but that still happened.' He pushed himself off his elbows and sat upright. 'Charlie, whatever is or isn't going on, just remember he's quite a bit older than you. And by his own admission, he's flat broke. And you're not. There are just a few things you need to think about.'

Charlie didn't say anything, but nodded cordially, as though taking on board his brother's well-meant advice. But Tyler could tell it was too little, too late. Charlie was clearly besotted, and he wondered what might happen over the coming few days, with Charlie back at the villa on his own, before Tyler was able to rejoin him.

CHAPTER 49

For a moment, it felt as though everything was back to normal and Charlie was able to breathe again. As the afternoon unfolded and the wine flowed, his gang of friends told him everything that had happened while he had been in England. They had booked a table at his favourite restaurant, on the third floor of the Yumbo Centre, which had a great view across the huge open, grassy area in the middle of the centre.

With great excitement, Martin revealed that he was going to appear on an episode of a travel show that was to be filmed on the island, where he would give some advice to a couple from Yorkshire who were planning to buy a house in Maspalomas. Peggy told a story of how she had been forced to evict a man from her caravan park who'd been caught on security cameras peeping through the windows of the other caravans at night. Blanche had received a marriage proposal from a nice businessman from Germany, but she had declined, deciding she was too old for yet another divorce, which, she said, would be inevitable.

Throughout the afternoon, everyone kept touching Charlie, holding his hand or squeezing his shoulder, all so pleased to have him home, to see him looking well and relaxed. The only person who seemed a little distant was Alan. He had given Charlie a friendly hug when they had all arrived for their meal, but he had then chosen to sit at the opposite end of the table and seemed to take an oddly passive role in the conversation, listening and occasionally commenting but, unusually, not saying much.

Mostly, Charlie was lost in the moment, just enjoying the ambience and the conversation. But he desperately wanted something from Alan, to hold his gaze for a few moments, to exchange a knowing smile or even just a simple cheeky wink. But throughout the whole meal, it felt as if Alan was trying not to directly interact with him, and that concerned Charlie. He began to worry that he had done something wrong, something to offend him.

The meal came to an end, and after a few moments of hugs and goodbyes, they all went on their way. Charlie noticed that Alan seemed keen to be the first to leave. Feeling deflated, Charlie began a lonely walk

248

back to his villa, taking some comfort in the knowledge that his brother would be arriving in the next few days to join him.

'Charlie, wait,' came a familiar voice from behind him.

Stood at the entrance to an alleyway, Charlie turned, and his heart skipped a beat as he saw Alan trotting towards him.

'I thought you had some business to attend to,' Charlie said.

Alan did not reply immediately. He stopped just inches from Charlie and was staring into his eyes again, just as he had that morning at the villa, a moment that had ended before Charlie had known how it might develop. And now, his heart beating so fast, Charlie hoped that he had not been wrong and that perhaps Alan felt something for him, too.

Alan breathed loudly, and then he said, 'Charlie, I hope I haven't misjudged this.' And then he cupped Charlie's face in his hand, drew him forward, and kissed him. Quickly, the kiss developed, their mouths open, the embrace tighter, stronger. Charlie could feel Alan's hands slide down his back, squeezing his behind.

'Is this OK?' Alan whispered.

'Yes, yes,' Charlie replied, a little breathless. 'Bit of a surprise. But absolutely OK.'

And then it stopped. Alan released Charlie and took a step back, his face flushed. 'I've been wanting to do that for a long time.'

'I've been wanting you to do that for a long time,' Charlie replied, knowing he was desperate for things to continue. 'You don't have to stop.'

'Well, erm… how do you want to proceed?' Alan asked, his eyebrows raised.

Charlie realised he was being offered more than just a kiss. After being alone for so many years, he had almost begun to believe intimacy was no longer a part of his life. But now Alan was stood in front of him, tall and sort of handsome, but also clever and funny and kind, a man Charlie trusted. And Charlie had the most incredible urge, a need, to take him to bed.

'My place,' Charlie said, and with great haste, the two made their way back to the villa. The journey was not without incident. Whenever they passed through a shaded or empty part of the walkway, Alan would pull

249

Charlie to him, and the two would kiss, and push tightly against each other, and then they would stop, and laugh, and begin their walk again.

Once inside the grounds to the villa, Charlie sent Alan ahead to his bedroom, and then quickly locked up, and headed after him. He arrived to find Alan was already naked, stood by the window, closing the curtains. And for the first time, Charlie could see that Alan was not skinny and lanky. He was tall and muscular, everything very much in proportion. This wasn't a fantasy, this was real; he was about to have sex with Alan.

And then Charlie froze.

He stood with his fingers touching the collar of his shirt, as though he were about to pull it over his head, but he couldn't move. He just looked at Alan, at his toned physique, at his size, so comfortable being naked, and Charlie simply didn't know what to do next.

'Everything OK, Charlie? You do still want to do this?'

For a moment, words failed Charlie. He knew, he most definitely knew, he wanted Alan, he wanted him then and there, on his bed. But there was something blocking him, something that was stopping him from taking his clothes off. But then he looked at the expression on Alan's face, and it made him feel safe, and cared for, and he was finally able to find the words.

'I haven't been with anyone. In six years. Jason was the last person I was with. He was also the only person I've ever been with.'

Alan gave Charlie a look of concern, 'I didn't know that. I'm sorry, I feel like I've rushed this. I've rushed you.'

But Charlie still wanted him, so badly, and was not about to let the moment drift away. 'No, you haven't. Not at all.' He walked to Alan and put his hands on his waist. He looked him up and down, his tall, muscular, completely naked friend, and he knew it was time, it was finally time to be intimate again. 'But you might need to remind me where everything goes. I might have forgotten.'

Alan chuckled and reached for Charlie's shirt. He gently slipped it over his head and dropped it to the floor. He kissed Charlie on the neck, and lowered himself, and Charlie could feel Alan gently removing his

250

shoes, and then his trousers and underwear. And then Charlie was naked too.

Alan stood and placed his hands on Charlie's shoulders, 'You ready?'

Charlie nodded. 'Oh, yes,' he replied, a very definite tone to his voice, and so Alan led him over to the bed.

CHAPTER 50

Tyler and Carol sat quietly and watched as Lizzie leaned across the table and counted all the tea sandwiches and mini rolls on the three-tier silver stand that had just been delivered to their table. She gently rotated the stand so she could see each side and counted under her breath. Tyler, a little embarrassed, glanced around the room, an elegant restaurant in one of the large seafront hotels, and hoped no one was watching.

'Right,' Lizzie said, and sat back in her chair, satisfied that she had solved a terrible dilemma that had been causing her great anxiety. 'There are four sandwiches each and two rolls.' She lifted her plate and began to help herself. It was obvious that she was taking the sandwiches and rolls that had the most filling, the rolls stuffed with grated cheese and pickle, and the tea sandwiches thick with chicken salad.

'Put all that back, right now,' Carol said, glaring at her. 'Right now, Lizzie.'

Lizzie stopped what she was doing, and stared at Carol, as though completely bewildered by the instruction. 'I'm just taking what's mine,' she said. 'I counted.'

'That's not how you eat in a restaurant like this,' Carol replied. 'You take one sandwich at a time, and you try all the different sandwiches.'

'But these are the only ones I like,' Lizzie said, a whine to her voice.

'Rubbish,' Carol said. 'You eat beef, and cream cheese and cucumber, and egg mayonnaise. Put everything back and have one at a time.'

With a face like thunder, Lizzie did as she was told, keeping a single cheese roll on her plate.

The waiter returned to the table and brought a pot of tea for Tyler and a glass of prosecco for Carol. For Lizzie he delivered a large glass mug filled with hot chocolate under a thick layer of whipped cream, topped with sprinkles and chunks of milk chocolate, with a giant chocolate cookie on the side. Lizzie looked at it, smiling, content. But Carol was furious.

'Excuse me,' Carol said to the waiter. 'Is that the hot chocolate?'

252

'No, madam, that's the chocolate dream supreme,' the waiter replied, 'from the dessert menu. It's what your daughter ordered.'

Carol stared at Lizzie and recalled how she had asked if she could have a hot chocolate with her lunch, and then partly whispered her order to the waiter so that neither Carol nor Tyler could hear her. 'You ordered a dessert?'

'I didn't know,' Lizzie squealed, panicked at having been caught out, her eyes wide and already close to tears.

'I said you could have a hot chocolate. I did not say you could order a dessert.'

'I didn't know,' Lizzie said again, 'I didn't know.'

'I'm sorry,' Carol said, sternly addressing the waiter once more, 'but you'll have to take that back. Lizzie will have a pot of tea. I'll pay for the dessert, of course, but just a tea.'

Lizzie watched with dismay as her dessert was removed from the table.

'I just don't understand you, Lizzie, I really don't,' Carol said, quietly but crossly. 'We've got all these sandwiches, and we've got the cakes and scones to come. And you still ordered a dessert for yourself.'

'I didn't know that's what it was,' Lizzie said, tearfully.

'Yes, you did,' Carol said, 'and I've had enough of it. When we get home, we're going to sort this out for good.'

With that, Lizzie jumped to her feet, her face flushed and tears streaming down her cheeks as she rushed away from the table towards the bathroom. Carol pursed her lips, resisting the temptation to yell across the restaurant and order Lizzie back to her seat. And then she looked at her son, sat quietly watching the drama unfold.

'Bit harsh, mum,' Tyler said. 'You could have just talked to her about it when we got home.'

Carol groaned and slumped back in her seat. 'I am so sorry sweetheart,' she said. 'I've just ruined our special lunch, haven't I?'

'Mum, Lizzie will be back at the table in a few minutes,' he replied. 'She'll apologise, you'll apologise, and we'll have a lovely time. Don't worry about it.'

Carol sat forward, elbows on the table, and nodded.

253

'But we do have to sort this out,' Tyler said, softly, persuasively. 'I mean, Lizzie and food. It can't go on like this. Mum, she's already as tall as me, but I would guess she is a good three stones heavier. And if this continues, she's just going to get bigger and bigger. People come in all shapes and sizes, and there are lots of people who are heavy who lead happy and healthy lives, but Lizzie's not one of them. She's miserable, Mum.'

Carol sighed. 'I suppose everyone thinks this is my fault,' she said, morosely.

'No one is blaming anyone,' Tyler replied. 'But you've seen all of Lizzie's girlfriends. They're all tiny, always in pretty clothes. Lizzie hides under big, baggy black jumpers and trousers. She's only got another year at school, and then she's off to sixth form. I just think it's the right time to help her get... healthy.'

Carol nodded. 'No more diet clubs, though,' she said. 'We've done the lot over the years, and they never work.'

'That's fine. There are other things we can do. I could set you both up with a health and fitness app on your mobile phones, and I'll get you both a fitness tracker? You know, that you wear like a watch. So, you can count your calories each day, and count your steps. Lizzie might really enjoy that.'

'OK. But you are right. We should talk about it when we get home.' Carol reached over and brushed her hand through Tyler's thick blonde hair. 'I still can't get used to it being this short. Funny, isn't it? Peter had five kids and you're the only one that looks like him, blonde hair and blue eyes.'

Tyler laughed. 'I'm also the only short-arse in the family. Even Lizzie's going to be taller than me soon!'

Carol clasped her hands together and stared at him. 'How long will you be gone?'

Tyler shrugged. 'I can't say, Mum. I think I'll just know when it's time to come home.'

'You'll have the money from the sale of the house soon,' Carol said. 'You could buy your own place. Get back to work. Settle down. I know for a fact your boss at the council would have you back like a shot.'

254

Tyler shook his head. 'Mum,' he said, quietly, 'you keep asking why I don't have a girlfriend or a boyfriend, when am I going to buy a house, get a job.'

'I'm sorry, sweetheart. You've got this amazing inheritance coming to you, and I just don't want to see it all…'

'Wasted?'

'I don't mean that. I just don't want you to end up like your dad. He was almost seventy when he died, and he had nothing. He had no house, no savings. He was completely reliant on you kids to put a roof over his head. I just don't want you to make decisions now that you'll regret when you're older.'

Tyler reached out and squeezed his mother's hand. 'Look, I'm not going to touch the money from The Lodge. I'm going to invest it,' he reassured her. 'I saved up all the money I need to cover the cost of me travelling, and I'll be working as I go. But you need to accept that I'm not like Charlie or Vicki or Billy. I'm only 23 and I'm not looking for a long-term relationship, or kids, or a house, or a full-time job. The thought of all that, it just hurts my head. I just want to have some freedom. Maybe in 10 years' time, I might feel differently, but right now, I'm really happy with my life, really excited about what happens next. And I want you, and everyone else, to stop projecting their expectations onto me.'

Carol smiled. 'It's funny,' she said, 'you and Charlie, getting on so well. But you really are polar opposites. By the time Charlie was a teenager, he was having panic attacks about house prices and whether he'd ever get on the housing ladder. He couldn't do what you're doing.'

'But, to be fair,' Tyler said, 'I couldn't have done what he's done.'

The conversation ended as Lizzie returned to the table, the tears wiped from her face, but her cheeks still flushed. 'Sorry,' she said, timidly. Carol reached over and took Lizzie's hand.

'Me too, sweetheart,' she said. 'Listen, let's just enjoy our posh lunch. It's the last time we're going to see Tyler for a while.'

Tyler reached over the table and held Lizzie's other hand. 'It's all going to be OK, sis,' he said. 'We've got a plan.'

255

CHAPTER 51

Charlie couldn't remember the last time he had felt so fulfilled; for hours, Alan had taken him from moments of quiet tenderness to vigorous, loud lovemaking and then back again. There had been moments when Charlie had felt a little overwhelmed by Alan's physical presence, his size and strength and his dexterity, and Charlie wasn't always sure he was doing enough in return. But Alan seemed to enjoy being in charge, moving and sometimes literally throwing Charlie around the bed, making good use of the contents of Charlie's bedside table, which Tyler had packed with packets of condoms and lubricant, just in case Charlie ever 'got lucky'. Eventually, everything seemed to just fall into place and, for once in his life, Charlie simply enjoyed giving up his power and being told what to do.

During a few moments of quiet and stillness, Charlie lay on the side of the bed, the curtains moving gently in the night breeze, and he wondered what time it was, how long they had been making love. He could hear Alan breathing next to him, and he wondered if he had fallen asleep. Charlie wouldn't blame him, especially after the exertions of the previous few hours. He rolled onto his back and saw that Alan's eyes were open.

'You OK?' Charlie asked.

Alan grinned, broadly, and then rolled to his side to look at Charlie's happy face. 'I'm very lucky I met you, Charlie. And I don't want you thinking this was something that just happened out of the blue. I've had feelings for you for a long time. Probably since the first day we met. I just never found the right moment to talk to you.'

'I've had my barriers up, for a long time,' Charlie said. 'To be honest, I didn't think you batted for my team. It was quite a surprise.'

Alan smiled. 'Yeah, my wife and kids were quite surprised too.'

Charlie propped himself up, on his elbows. 'So, the ex-wife and the kids... they're real?' he asked.

'Yes, of course,' Alan replied. 'Pretty much everything I've told you is true.' He put his arm around Charlie and pulled him to his side of the bed, where they lay next to each other, their legs entwined. 'It's just that there was a bit more to my divorce, than me and the wife realising we wanted different things.'

'Surely the problem was that you both wanted the *same* thing.'

Alan laughed, 'Well, yes, I suppose you could look at it that way. But I didn't cheat on her, not once, the whole time we were married. And I did love her, genuinely. But the older I got, the more I realised it just wasn't working. I couldn't pretend anymore. And, frankly, I knew I was being unfair to her. When I eventually told her the truth, I think it was a relief for both of us. It was like all the pressure in our marriage just vanished.'

Charlie rested his head on Alan's chest, his arm wrapped around his waist. 'Do you ever speak to her?' he asked.

'Every day, pretty much,' Alan replied. 'Sometimes we talk about the kids, sometimes we just check in, to see how we're both doing. She's happy now. She's got a new fella, sounds like a good bloke. The kids like him too.'

Charlie lifted his head and looked into Alan's eyes, 'I had the impression your divorce had been pretty brutal.'

'I just say that. It stops people asking too many questions. But almost everything else I said is true.'

Charlie noticed that was the second time Alan had alluded to some level of dishonesty about his life and his divorce, but he was so happy, just lying there, with Alan's muscular arms around him, that he didn't care.

'Charlie, what I wanted to say,' Alan continued, his deep voice soft, intimate, 'is that I don't want this to be a one-off. I know it's all new and might feel sudden, but I have very deep feelings for you. And I would really like to see where this could go.'

For so many years, Charlie had felt there was no room in his life for a man. He had his villa, his business, and his friends and family. He had carried his fears and his grief with great conviction, and was convinced that his situation was just too complicated to involve anyone else. But now here he was, in bed with a man he had secretly harboured feelings for, and he liked the idea that he and Alan could take some time, to explore their relationship.

'Sounds good,' he said, and began to stroke Alan's flat, hairless stomach. 'Tyler's back soon,' he said. 'So, we might need to spend a few nights at your place. I'm sure it's not as bad as you make out.'

Alan closed his eyes and exhaled loudly. He pulled away from Charlie, swung his legs around, and sat upright on the side of the bed, his head in his hands. 'Oh, I'm such an idiot,' he grumbled under his breath.

Charlie moved across the bed, knelt behind Alan and put his arms around him. 'Sorry. I've upset you.'

'It's not you,' Alan said, 'You've done nothing wrong, Charlie. It's just me being a bloody stupid old fool.' He turned to look directly at Charlie. 'We should get dressed,' he said. 'Take a walk. I need to show you something.'

'OK,' Charlie replied, a little puzzled. 'But, just to be clear, are we OK? Because I felt like we are OK.'

Alan wrapped his arms around Charlie and kissed him on the cheek, 'Yes, we are definitely OK.'

If Charlie knew one thing, in that moment, it was that he trusted Alan. Even though he did not understand what was going on, or why Alan was acting so strangely, he knew there must be a good reason for it, and he wanted to know what it was. 'Where do you want to go?'

Charlie could not help but watch as Alan walked around the room, collecting his clothes. It had been a long time since he had truly felt lust, and as he enjoyed Alan's naked body, he had an overwhelming urge to ask if they could delay their walk and have sex again. But Alan was quickly dressed, and it appeared there was an urgency in whatever it was that he wanted to do.

As Charlie got dressed, he noticed Alan was on his phone, texting someone, and then he slipped his phone back into his trousers and held out his hand. 'Ready?' he asked.

They left the villa and walked towards the sea. Alan took Charlie onto the wide, tiled pathway that separated the beach from the large beachfront houses, hidden behind high walls covered with bougainvillea.

258

To fill the time, Charlie shared a few stories from his trip home, of saying goodbye to The Lodge, and the rather unfortunate incident involving Angel and her misguided belief that she had inherited a small fortune. Alan listened and interacted but did not share anything about the purpose of their walk.

Alan came to a halt, and Charlie looked over the seawall at the beach and, beyond that, the rolling waves of the sea and wondered if Alan was about to suggest they went for a swim. 'Well, we're here,' Charlie said, his eyebrows raised, still clueless as to what was going on. 'Are you going to explain, now?'

Alan nodded and stepped towards a large metal gate that led to one of the seafront properties. 'Come with me,' he said and pushed the gate open and walked through.

'Wait,' Charlie called after him, a loud stage whisper. 'You can't just walk into someone else's house.' But Alan did not return, and so Charlie followed cautiously, hoping no one was at home. Alan met him on the other side and closed the gate behind them as Charlie surveyed the grounds. They were stood in a charming, beautifully tended garden with a large outdoor seating area beside a gently lit swimming pool. Behind that was a three-storey house, modern and black, the exterior walls mostly darkened glass, with the rooms on the upper floor leading to large balconies.

'Goodness,' Charlie said. 'This must be worth millions.' He gestured towards the gate. 'But perhaps we should head off. They might have CCTV and call the police.'

Alan, with a pensive expression on his face, shook his head, took Charlie's hand and led him past the swimming pool and towards the house. As they approached the entrance, Charlie noticed that the wall to the kitchen was made of bi-fold doors, all of which were pushed back so the downstairs of the house opened directly onto the seating area and pool. He then noticed a man, stood in the kitchen, arms behind his back. He was older, perhaps in his sixties, Charlie guessed, with dark hair and olive skin. He was smartly dressed in a white shirt and black trousers and, to Charlie's surprise, did not react at the sight of two strangers walking towards him.

259

'Good evening, Mr Evans,' he said, and Charlie was instantly confused as to how the man knew Alan and why he wasn't on the phone to the police. 'I have made a pitcher of agua de valència and provided you with some snacks,' the man said, gesturing to the table at the centre of the seating area. There was a large crystal pitcher filled with ice and a bright orange liquid, two glass tumblers, and a plate of stuffed olives and squares of cheese. 'Is there anything else I can do?'

'No thank you, Mateo,' Alan said. 'Please turn in for the evening.'

'Very well, sir, thank you. I will see you in the morning.' Mateo nodded respectfully towards Charlie, before walking into the house and disappearing from view.

Charlie let go of Alan's hand. He stepped away from him, his mind able to offer only a single explanation for what was happening, the one logical explanation based on everything he knew about Alan. 'You rented this place, for us, for the weekend?' he asked, smiling at the thought of poor Alan, without a penny to his name, maxing out a credit card to make a grand romantic gesture. 'And it comes with a... servant?'

Alan shook his head. 'I haven't rented it. Charlie, this is my home. Mateo is my housekeeper.'

The smile quickly disappeared from Charlie's face. He looked at Alan, suddenly a stranger, stood in the grounds of a millionaire's house, and everything he thought he knew about Alan began to melt away. 'I don't understand. You live in a shithole. You told me. A flat above a restaurant.'

Alan sensed that Charlie's mood had changed, and he was worried that he might just walk away, leave before there was a chance to properly explain. So he gently took his arm and led him to the seats next to the pool. They sat down together, and Alan began to speak. 'Please give me a moment to explain,' he said, and to his great relief, Charlie nodded.

'When I first got divorced,' he said, his usually strong voice now strangely soft, uneasy, 'I went on quite a few dates, and I finally met a guy I really liked, and I thought he really liked me too. I threw myself into that relationship, heart and soul. And then I found out he had been buying loads of stuff, online, using my credit card. Tens of thousands of pounds in just a few weeks, all delivered to his flat. And when I

260

confronted him, well, it turned out he didn't like me at all. He was just in it for the money. He even said he felt disgusted every time we went to bed together. It left me a bit shattered, to be honest. A few months later, I tried again and, pretty much the same thing happened. The second guy wasn't quite so… cruel, but I realised that if I didn't have money, he wouldn't be dating me.'

Charlie was still perplexed, his emotions all over the place, but he hated the idea of anyone being so unkind, so brutally unkind, to Alan. He leaned forward and clasped Alan's hands in his own. 'I'm really sorry that happened.'

Alan stared into Charlie's eyes. It felt as though the tension was beginning to ease, and he hoped that feeling was correct because all he wanted was Charlie to forgive him, and to stay. 'I moved here, fresh start and all that, and my ex-wife suggested I tell everyone I was broke,' he said, 'so if I made new friends, or if I were to meet someone special, I would know they had good intentions. So, I did. But then I made some really great friends, and I met you of course, and the longer I left it, the harder it was to tell you the truth. I felt like I had dug myself into this big hole, and I didn't know how to get out of it.'

In his mind, Charlie could see his image of Alan beginning to come back into focus, and even with all the money Alan appeared to have, the image felt essentially the same. If anything, it made more sense Alan being wealthy; a clever, hardworking and extremely confident man like that would have been successful. And in a way, Charlie understood Alan's predicament. Once entangled in a lie or a secret, Charlie knew it could sometimes feel impossible to break free of it. 'So, why tell me now?' he asked.

'Because I'm in love with you,' Alan said.

Charlie's mouth dropped open in surprise. He hadn't been prepared to hear Alan say he was in love. The only other man to have ever said that to Charlie had been Jason, and it was oddly disconcerting to hear those words coming from someone else's lips.

'I'm not asking you to say it back, honestly,' Alan said. 'That's not what this is about. But if we are to start a relationship, I cannot do it with a lie. I want you to know everything about me.'

261

Charlie felt a little ashamed. In his heart, he knew one of the reasons he was struggling with Alan's revelation was that he had liked the idea of being the benevolent one, the man entering a relationship without caring that his partner had almost no money. But now, the situation felt reversed, and it seemed as though Alan was being benevolent, and Charlie, by comparison, was now the penniless boyfriend.

'You're very quiet,' Alan said. 'Any chance you can let me know how I'm doing here because, frankly, I'm shitting myself right now.'

Charlie exhaled loudly. 'It's just a lot to take in.'

'I am sorry I lied to you for all these years. I am really sorry.'

After a long pause, Charlie replied, 'It's not really a lie. You just kept something private. I think that's different to a lie. And I think I understand why you did.' Charlie leaned forward and kissed Alan tenderly on the lips. 'Anything else I need to know? You didn't make your fortune as a drugs baron, did you? Or trading illegal weapons?'

'No,' Alan chuckled, so relieved that he and Charlie seemed to be back on course. 'Clinical supplies, actually. PPE, medical equipment, uniforms. A one-stop shop for any health service. We design it, develop it, test it, and then sell it.'

'And this is your home?'

'Yes.'

Charlie was still a little unsure how he felt, but one thing he knew with certainty was that he had deep feelings for Alan. And, when all was said and done, there were worse secrets a partner could reveal than being a multi-millionaire businessperson with a luxury house on a Spanish island. Charlie settled back into his seat and nodded to the glasses and the pitcher. 'You going to pour that drink, then?' he grinned.

Charlie recalled how concerned Tyler had been about the possibility of Charlie entering into a relationship with an older man, someone they all believed to be flat broke. And he hoped it would offer his little brother some reassurance about Alan, because Charlie had a strong feeling he was at the beginning of something very special.

262

CHAPTER 52

Eight years later

Her heart pounding with anticipation and dread, Lizzie locked herself in the bathroom, removed her dressing gown, and nudged the weighing scales with her foot until the digital screen lit up. She placed her mobile phone on the windowsill, stepped onto the scales and looked to the ceiling as she waited for the sound of a little chime, a signal which meant her weight had been measured and recorded. As she heard that sound, she stepped from the scales and quickly shrugged on her dressing gown again.

Nervously, she lifted her phone to check her weight-loss app, and to see where a two-week holiday in Gran Canaria had left her. Her previous weight, a day before travelling, had been 16 stone and three pounds and, in her head, she had convinced herself she had probably gained enough weight to put her above seventeen stone once more. And that would be heartbreaking, undoing months of hard work.

Anxiously, she looked at her phone and read the number on the screen: *sixteen stone, five and a half pounds.* Her heart skipped a beat with joy. 'Oh my god,' she said aloud. 'Two and a half pounds. I've only put on two and a half pounds.' She had been so prepared for a much bigger number that it felt like a gift. Excitedly, she turned to the mirror above the sink and studied her reflection. Lizzie had grown very fond of this mirror because she believed it was the only mirror in the house that liked her. All the others seemed to exaggerate the parts of her body that she hated.

'Right,' she said to herself. 'Straight back on it. Calorie counting and steps. I'll get rid of the holiday weight in one week.' She ran a comb through her short brown hair, washed, brushed her teeth and went back to the bedroom to get dressed. During her weight loss journey, she had been taken on plenty of shopping trips by Vicki and Emma, who had both persuaded her to try different clothes and not just the black, baggy jumpers and trousers that had become a staple part of her wardrobe. For the first time, she had begun to enjoy clothes shopping and now her wardrobe was filled with outfits that were fitted and colourful. On that happy day, she chose a rainbow tie-dye T-shirt and slim-fitting blue jeans.

Relieved and excited, she hurried through her apartment to the kitchen, where she made herself a bowl of porridge using skimmed milk, sprinkled with sweetener rather than sugar, and poured herself a black coffee. She sat at her two-seater breakfast table, texting the good news to her loved ones and watching as the responses flowed back.

Charlie: Oh, great news sweetie, although you did so much walking this holiday, I honestly thought you'd LOSE weight. My feet are still recovering! Thanks for coming to visit. I'm so glad I got to spend your birthday with you. It was really lovely. Alan sends his love too. C xx

Mum: GOOD FOR YOU!! I knew you'd keep it off with all that fucking walking! You need to remember I'm an old woman now. I can't keep up! Love you and SO proud of you xx

Tyler: You've already lost more than five stone and you looked beautiful all holiday, Lizzie. I hope you know that. But I know how important your weight loss journey is for you, so really pleased xxx

Jack: Good for you, Auntie Lizzie! ☺

Emma: Told you! You really need to stop worrying so much and just enjoy your holidays. You've already retrained your brain, so you're leading a much healthier life without even thinking about it (even when you're having a massive Maspalomas birthday piss-up with Charlie and Alan!!!) And start to enjoy your curves. I love mine. And Billy sends his love – see you on Monday x

Lizzie was thrilled that everyone had been so positive with their responses. Ever since she had started her weight loss programme, the whole family had been incredibly supportive and excited for her. But it was her boyfriend's approval she sought the most, and was relieved when, eventually, she saw a response appear on her phone from him.

> **Stuart**: I don't understand. Did you lose weight or gain weight?
> **Lizzie**: I put on 2.5lbs but thought it might be worse after two weeks away. I'm really relieved and pleased.
> **Stuart**: But you GAINED weight?
> **Lizzie**: Yes, but a lot less than I was expecting. I'm happy ☺
> **Stuart**: You're happy that you put weight on?
> **Lizzie**: I am happy I **only** put on 2.5lbs.

Stuart finished the text exchange with an emoji of a man shrugging, and then did not text again. Lizzie placed her phone onto the table, all her joy sucked away. She wondered if she should text again, something casual and routine like '*Look forward to seeing you tonight xx*'. Perhaps he would reply with something funny, or witty, reassuring, to let her know he wasn't annoyed, that everything was OK. But she also knew he might make a passive-aggressive point of not responding at all, and that would leave her fretting all day, so she decided to leave it as it was.

Stuart was Lizzie's first boyfriend, and she was still learning how to manage life as part of a couple. In many ways, Lizzie thought Stuart was the perfect man for her, someone who had brought much joy into her life. He could be funny and romantic, supportive, sometimes even a bit sexy, and he had a way of making Lizzie feel good about herself.

But he also had a way of making Lizzie feel terrible, and mostly that was about her weight. No matter how much she lost, it never seemed to be enough, and there were regular pressure points Stuart would just explode. Lizzie had tried to understand what caused those pressure points so she could diminish them by keeping Stuart happy. But whenever he maintained a communications blackout, she knew it was the warning sign of another explosion waiting to happen.

She heard her phone chiming and quickly picked it up, hoping it would be Stuart, calling to say he was regretting his abrupt reaction to her news. But as she looked at the screen, she saw Vicki's name.

'I'm in the high street,' Vicki said, cheerfully. 'I thought I might pop in for a cup of tea.'

'I was just about to go out for a walk. We could grab a coffee at the usual. Are you on your own?'

'Oh yes. I just dropped Blake at school, so I have the whole day. OK. Let's try and get a table overlooking the sea.'

'Great, I'm on my way.'

Quickly, Lizzie finished her breakfast, put the bowl and spoon into the dishwasher, and hurried into her front room to collect her bag and purse. But the view from her window, the estuary glistening in the morning sunlight, brought her to a momentary stop. It evoked a wonderful sense of freedom, as she knew she could just grab her stuff, walk out the front door, and see people again, face to face, with no social distancing or masks.

She had bought the apartment five years earlier, shortly after her eighteenth birthday. Carol and Charlie had persuaded her to use her money from the sale of The Lodge to buy her own place, before house prices went any higher. She had always loved the parade at Clifton Terrace, each property had a view across the water and grand steps up from the street to the front door. She had waited patiently for one to become available and was quick to move when a first-floor apartment went up for sale.

For the first couple of years, having her own space had been a dream come true, a busy whirl of decorating, buying furniture, and having friends and family over for dinner. But then there had been the pandemic, and lockdown, and living alone stopped being fun. Her mother had been terrified that Lizzie's weight had made her particularly vulnerable and had begged her to remain isolated. And Lizzie had been so frightened by the daily news of infections and deaths, that she had done exactly that. She stayed home. She didn't join anyone's bubble, and only spoke to family and friends online, through video chats and WhatsApp exchanges.

She soon realised she didn't want to live like that, to be too frightened to see people, because she felt her weight had made her vulnerable. And that was when she made a change. She stopped having

266

certain foods delivered to the house, such as cheese and bread and wine, and she used the internet to seek out new ways of cooking and preparing food, filling her plate with vegetables and proteins. She spent her days at home walking around her flat, recording her steps with the activity tracker Tyler had bought for her.

And now Lizzie was back in the real world, more than sixty pounds lighter, wearing jeans and a funky top, about to grab a coffee with her sister, and she could not be happier. Before she left her apartment, she checked her phone once more to see if there had been any message from Stuart, and she felt a pang of anxiety when she saw he hadn't sent one.

CHAPTER 53

Sat at a table on the outside terrace of the seafront café, wrapped in coats and scarfs, a cold breeze blowing in from the estuary, Lizzie was drinking an americano and Vicki had a latte. Vicki had a pair of reading glasses perched on the end of her nose, they were happily looking through photographs on Vicki's phone. They were pictures of Jack, in his cap and gown, smiling his way through his graduation as his proud mother obsessively took countless pictures.

Lizzie loved her coffee mornings with Vicki, her big sister. She liked people seeing them together because she knew they looked so much alike, both with the family's dark eyes and brown hair, and she liked the idea that people would know they were sisters just by looking at them. Sometimes when she looked at Vicki, she caught a glimpse of what she might look like one day, if she lost more weight: the cheekbones and the slim waist. And that was all she wanted, to look even more like her sister.

'This is Jack before the ceremony. Oh, bless he got quite nervous,' Vicki said. 'And this is him with some of his classmates, afterwards. And here's the obligatory picture of them throwing their caps into the air.'

There were other pictures, of Vicki with Jack, and Jack with Debbie and Kim too. 'We were only supposed to have two tickets for the graduation ceremony,' Vicki said, 'but I wrote a letter to the university, pleading for a special case, and they just wrote back and said "fine", so all three of us were there. Kim cheered so loudly, I thought she was going to burst.'

'When's he coming home?'

'Oh no, he's not.' Vicki put her phone and reading glasses into her bag and cupped her latte in both hands. 'I think I have to accept that I've lost him to Manchester. He and one of his uni mates have found a flat they're going to rent, and he's scouting for some work up there. I'm a bit worried because there seem to be a lot of young people with degrees who are unemployed at the moment. Although there's always someone who needs accountants and finance people, so thank god he was good with numbers.'

268

That was so typically Vicki, Lizzie thought, to speak with such understated pride about Jack's achievements, whilst simultaneously worrying what he was going to do for work. She looked at her sister's pretty face, the delicate lines of a hard life beginning to show around her eyes, and she wished she had some of Vicki's hardness, that ability to deal more resiliently with people and situations. She knew how easily Vicki could turn to tears, but she also knew her sister had an amazing ability to tough things out, and Lizzie wished she had just a fraction of that tenacity.

'And he was the first Fletcher to go to university,' Lizzie added. 'I hope you know that we're all very proud of him. I name-drop him regularly. My nephew with the degree.'

'Well, you've not done so bad for yourself either, Lizzie,' Vicki replied, brightly. 'We're all incredibly proud of what you did during lockdown. I'm glad you got promoted. It was well deserved.'

Lizzie's job had been one of the few things to offer her some respite from the loneliness of all those months isolating. As Southend Council's digital communications officer, she had worked long hours, constantly reworking and updating information on the Council's website and social media, explaining the rules, the restrictions, the different zones and tiers and where and when people could travel. Her dedication and creativity had been noticed, and as the lockdown finished, she had been promoted to Digital Manager.

'You know Tyler was a bit of a star at the Council,' Lizzie said, grinning. 'When I first started, everyone kept referring to me as 'Tyler's sister'. Not anymore.'

At first, Vicki smiled, but then she frowned, and her face told a less happy story. 'Seems like all the boys in the family leave,' she said, downheartedly. 'Charlie and Tyler abroad. Jack up north. At least Billy and Emma bought a house in Southend.'

'Oh, Billy's not going anywhere,' Lizzie said, confidently.

Vicki drained her cup and placed it back onto the table. 'And to be honest, I think it's probably for the best that Jack's far away from here.'

'Why?'

269

Vicki appeared reluctant to speak further, but then she leaned forward, and in a quieter voice began to explain. 'Ever since his dad did a runner, there have been quite a few unsavoury characters trying to find out where he went. Sounds like he owes a lot of money to a lot of people. And, on top of that, it turns out Nate has other kids. A boy and a girl, a bit younger than Jack.'

'How much younger?' Lizzie asked and watched as Vicki rolled her eyes.

'Well, yes, that's a bit of a sore point. Unfortunately, they're not young enough. Nate definitely had them while we were still together. Anyway, they contacted Jack on Facebook and have been trying to get him to send them money. They seem to think we're all millionaires.'

'What have you said to him?'

Vicki shook her head. 'Nothing. Officially, I don't know any of this. Jack confided in Debbie and Kim. He does that sometimes. He'll try something with them before he tells me, to see what sort of reaction he might get. But they were so worried they decided to tell me.'

'And do you know what he's doing?'

Vicki nodded. 'Thankfully, Debbie and Kim took a really tough line with him and told him to block them. They told him that if the first thing these kids did was ask him for money, then what did he think his relationship was going to be like with them in the future. So, apparently, he unfriended them and hopefully they'll leave him alone.'

The sound of an electronic bleep immediately drew Lizzie's attention away from their conversation and to her phone. Furtively, she checked to see if there had been any further message from Stuart, but there was nothing, just a text message reminding her of an upcoming optician's appointment. And she could feel her anxiety beginning to swell, wondering why he hadn't been in touch since she had sent him the news about her weight. For a moment, she forgot where she was, and she held her phone in both hands and just stared at the screen, the WhatsApp icon showing no updates.

'All OK?' Vicki asked.

Lizzie looked up. 'Sorry?'

'Is everything OK? Are you waiting for a phone call?'

270

'Oh no, no,' Lizzie said, embarrassed, and slipped her phone back into her pocket.

Vicki sighed. 'Lovers' tiff?'

'Oh, just something silly,' Lizzie replied, casually. She didn't want to extend that part of the conversation, as she had always suspected her sister was not particularly fond of Stuart, although she was not entirely certain why. And so, she suppressed an urge to explain to Vicki why she was so anxious, because she knew it would never be just a private discussion. She knew it would lead to other things, possibly even a conversation between Vicki and Stuart, and she doubted that would end well.

'Well, if you ever need to talk about it, I've had a few difficult relationships over the years,' Vicki said. 'Sometimes, I think Nate wasn't even necessarily the worst.'

Lizzie knew her sister hadn't had many boyfriends over the years. After Nate, there had only been a couple that she knew of, but each had lasted much longer than they should have. And Lizzie had seen the pattern, the same type of men, who always seemed to gain far more from being in a relationship with her sister than any benefits Vicki had received in return.

And she had seen her sister manage so many confrontations and arguments, whilst just carrying on with her life as though nothing had happened. And that had always bewildered Lizzie. How, she wondered, could Vicki have a terrible row with her partner in the morning, and not allow it to ruin her entire day? How do people just carry on about their business, without being overwhelmed by anxiety or stress about what might happen next?

But she did not want to dwell on the matter, and so moved the conversation on. 'How are things going with Blake?' she asked and hoped the change of topic would not be too obvious.

A smile immediately crossed Vicki's face. 'Oh, really good,' she said, with great fondness in her voice. 'He's really settled in, at home and at school. I'm having none of the behaviours that his other foster carers had. I've got him into a really tight routine that I never deviate from, even at weekends. And he seems really happy. His social worker is happy with how things are going too.'

'He's such a cute kid,' Lizzie said, picturing the little lad in her head, just six years old, red hair and big glasses. 'Do you think he might stay with you?'

Vicki exhaled loudly. 'Well, technically, they are still looking for a family to adopt him. But because he is doing so well with me, they've said if they don't find anyone in the next few months, they're going to remove him from the adoption register and long-term link him with me instead.'

'And you would be up for that?'

'Oh god, yes,' Vicki said. 'I'd love to keep him.'

Lizzie remembered so many of the children and young people who'd lived with her sister over the years; more than twenty in all, she supposed, a broad range of youngsters from teenagers who seemed to do little else but abscond, to much younger children who'd arrived with all manner of behavioural issues. Vicki had managed it all calmly and with good humour, but there was something else going on with Blake, a very different dynamic that Lizzie hadn't seen before. Her sister seemed to have fallen in love with the little lad, and Lizzie wasn't sure if that was a good thing.

CHAPTER 54

Billy tried to remember everything his agent had told him; a call-back was good. It meant they already liked you, what you did, how you looked. So, don't reinvent the wheel. Do the same again. Read the script the same way. Wear the same clothes. Be prepared for there to be more people in the room, other people involved in the production, perhaps even other actors. But don't be intimidated by the other actors. And don't forget to enjoy it.

As he sat in the lobby of the theatre, waiting to be called to one of the rehearsal rooms for his read-through, Billy scrolled through his phone and looked at all the funny, reassuring messages Emma had sent him. He had decided to keep the audition secret from everyone else because he hadn't wanted to jinx it. During years of amateur dramatics and small walk-on parts in professional theatre and television, Billy had learned all sorts of superstitions, and one, in particular, was to keep auditions secret from everyone apart from his wife until he knew for sure whether he had the part.

He hadn't been certain about the role when his agent had first floated it to him: Brick Pollitt in a production of 'Cat on a Hot Tin Roof'. Billy had convinced himself he was too old to play the character, but his agent had pointed out that Paul Newman had also been in his thirties when he had played the role, and so Billy had been persuaded.

Since his first audition, he had heard the role of Maggie had been cast, but he didn't know who, and he had also heard the production team were trying to get a name to play Big Daddy. He was not sure what sort of big-name actors would be interested in a touring production, but he hoped it wouldn't end up being someone from a soap.

'Billy? Billy Fletcher?'

Instinctively, Billy stood, expecting to see one of the theatre runners, someone young and excited, smiling, to take him to his audition. But instead, stood in front of him was a woman, in her late fifties or early sixties, he guessed, wearing a raincoat and carrying bags of shopping. She appeared to have stepped into the lobby from the street outside.

273

'I am,' he replied, his mind desperately trying to place the woman, so as not to appear rude if it became obvious that he had not recognised her.

The woman lowered her shopping bags to the floor, and stared at him, her faced etched with weariness, but Billy could see there was something else there, in her expression, something which suggested resentment, and he began to feel uncomfortable.

'Don't worry,' she said, 'we've never met. But I do know you, Billy. My whole family knows you.'

Billy shrugged and shook his head slightly. 'I really don't know what you mean.'

For a moment, the woman did not respond, and it seemed as though she was having second thoughts about speaking to him, that perhaps she had acted too impulsively by rushing into the theatre after seeing him from outside. But then her expression changed, darkened, and she began to speak, her voice low and filled with contempt. 'After everything you did, the lies you told. You ruined our lives.'

Billy wondered if this was part of the audition process, and if perhaps there was a secret camera somewhere in the lobby, so the director could see how he would react to something unexpected. But the woman seemed genuinely troubled, her anger too authentic to be a part of a casting. 'I honestly don't know what you are talking about.'

The woman took a single step forward. 'Oh, of course you don't. I imagine you've betrayed countless people over the years, haven't you? People who tried to help you. You've really no idea how much pain you caused, just to get your name in the papers. You make me sick.'

Billy was at a loss. Over the years, he had enjoyed a considerable amount of very favourable publicity in the local newspapers, but he did not recall any that would have impacted negatively on another person. Indeed, he could not imagine a situation where he would have allowed a PR opportunity to go ahead if he thought for a moment someone else would get hurt.

'I'm Belinda Croker,' the woman said, then fell silent, as though Billy was supposed to know who she was. But he didn't, he still did not have a clue who Belinda was or why she was speaking to him with such obvious contempt.

'Sorry,' he said, at a loss.

'Belinda Croker,' she reiterated. 'I'm Neil Croker's wife.'

It was a name Billy had not heard of, or thought about, in years. A former boss at the supermarket when Billy had been 19, who had used all sorts of tricks and misdirection to try to persuade Billy to send him sexual content. Suddenly the comment about 'getting his name in the papers' made sense too.

He remembered the story, the first of many; a full page of the paper, emblazoned with pictures of both him and of Neil. Neil had been portrayed as a perverted, predatory older man, trying to take advantage of an ambitious, handsome young colleague. The article hadn't been particularly kind to Billy either, suggesting he had been willing to do almost anything to become a star. But Billy knew there was a name, now, for what Neil Croker had done all those years ago, and he felt quite justified saying it out loud.

'Your husband tried to catfish me. He was caught, he got fired. And you think I owe you an apology?'

'He did no such thing, and you know it," Belinda snapped. 'I just need to understand it, Billy. I just need to know why you told such terrible lies about my husband. A good man, a kind man. He tried to help you and your acting career. Why would you do such a horrible thing?'

Billy could tell there would be no reasoning with Belinda. He could see she had spent years with Neil, listening to his lies, his excuses, buying into an utterly false version of events, a version where her husband had been the innocent victim of circumstance whilst Billy was a ruthless, publicity-seeking villain. But he also knew how damaging those videos could have been if he had fallen for Neil's tricks, if he had made them and sent them. All these years later, those films would still exist. And Billy wondered what would have happened if Neil had shared them, and they'd ended up easily accessible on the internet, or if Neil had fallen on hard times and decided to use the videos to try and extort money from him.

275

'I had nothing to do with the story being in the paper,' Billy said. 'I am sorry that happened. I found the whole thing completely humiliating, and I can only imagine what it was like for you and your family. But you need to remember, Mrs Croker, that I could have gone to the police. I was given the option of making a criminal complaint against your husband. We had all the evidence. He would have gone to jail.'

'Oh, and out of the kindness of your heart, you didn't, is that what you are saying? Or maybe, the truth is, there was no evidence. Because you made the whole thing up, and that's why you couldn't go to the police.'

'No. It wasn't out of the kindness of my heart. The truth is, what your husband did to me, or tried to do to me, was degrading. Not just because of what he tried to get me to do on camera for him, but because he clearly thought I was stupid enough to fall for it. And you know what, if it hadn't been for my sister, I probably would have fallen for it. And I didn't want people to know that. I didn't want people to know how stupid I had been.'

As Billy spoke, he watched as Belinda grimaced and looked to the ceiling, not willing to listen to a word of it, to engage with Billy's version of events in any way.

'Well, it doesn't matter now, does it?' Belinda replied, each word delivered with pure spite. 'Because, guess what? You won. You beat us. You beat Neil. He's dead. Did you know that, Billy? My husband's dead.'

The news rendered Billy speechless. He had no words, nothing to respond with. He could feel a cold wave of anxiety sweep across his body, suddenly faced with a possibility that he might, in some way, be responsible for another person's death.

'He couldn't leave the house, for months, after that story in the paper,' Belinda said. 'And then he couldn't get a job, at least not a good one, one that he deserved. He ended up buying a van and being a delivery driver. And he hated it. He hated everything about his life. We couldn't keep up on our mortgage payments, so we had to sell our house and move into a small flat. And every year, he thought things might change. That he might get back on track with his career. But that story, that was on the internet, it was there for life. And all of that was because of you.

276

Because of what you did to him. So last year, he went for a walk in Hockley Woods, and he hung himself. And do you want to know what he wrote in his suicide letter? He wrote 'Tell Billy I forgive him'. That's how good a man he was. He even found it in his heart to forgive you.'

At first, Billy said nothing. He was overcome by too many emotions to be able to form a sentence. But even in the middle of such a terrible and confusing moment, he was able to make sense of one thing; Belinda Croker was clinging to her husband's lies, the idea that he had been a kind and loving husband and father, a decent man, who'd been the victim of conspiracies and ruthless opportunists. And Billy could see she *needed* to cling to those lies, because if she accepted the truth, she would have to also accept that her entire marriage had been a sham, and that she had spent all those years with a man she didn't really know at all.

'I think we are done,' Billy said, forcing the words from his lips, just wanting Belinda to go away, and take her accusations and fantasies with her.

Belinda pursed her lips, content that she had said what she wanted to say, and happy that Billy had said nothing to persuade her that she had been wrong. She nodded, turned, picked up her shopping bags and left. For a moment, the lobby was filled with the noise from outside, people talking and cars roaring past. But then the thick glass door clicked shut, and the room fell silent once more.

Billy retook his seat, completely bewildered by what had just happened, not even thinking about the audition he was waiting for. He thought, over and over, as to whether he could have handled things differently, all those years ago, when Vicki had first told him of her suspicions of what Neil might be up to. Should he have just tried to resolve it with Neil, face to face, rather than allowing an entire undercover operation between HR and IT? But then he remembered what Vicki had told him, that Neil was a sexual predator, and if Billy didn't take action to stop him, then there might be other young men working at that superstore that Neil might target instead. He pulled his mobile phone from his pocket and sent a text message to Vicki.

Billy: I just met Neil Croker's wife. Did you know he was dead?

A few moments passed, then his phone bleeped.

Vicki: No, I didn't. Are you OK? What did she say to you? How did he die?

Billy: Wasn't a great conversation. She said suicide. Said it was all my fault. She thinks I lied about the catfishing to get publicity.

Vicki: We both know that's a pile of crap. Give me a sec. I'm at my laptop. Going to Google him.

Billy could see Vicki was writing something, and he waited patiently for her response.

Vicki: OK. So, the Echo website has a story from last year, from the inquest into his death. It was suicide.

Vicki: It says a couple of days before he died, he was questioned by the police.

Vicki: Looks like Neil was a member of a chatroom where the members catfished other men and then shared the videos with each other.

Vicki: I am guessing his wife chose not to mention that.

Vicki: But that's why he killed himself. He got caught again, and that time the police were involved. Nothing to do with you. Ignore his wife. She's living in cloud cuckoo land if she thinks she can blame you. Everything bad that happened to that family was entirely down to Neil.

Vicki: You OK? Do you want me to call?

Billy: No, I'm good. Thank you for that. Let's talk later. Love you xx

Vicki: Love you too xx

It was unpleasant information, a disturbing tale of a man's life spiralling out of control, a man possessed by all sorts of urges and needs, obsessed with catfishing and pornography. Billy was able to take some small comfort from it, though, knowing that Neil's complicated life had been filled with cruel lies and dark secrets. Even in the very last thing he

278

ever wrote, his farewell to the world, he still hadn't been able to tell the truth and admit what he had done.

'Billy Fletcher?'

Billy looked up and was relieved to see a young man smiling at him, clipboard in hand. 'Yes, that's me,' he replied, and stood. His nerves were frayed, and he was unsure he was in the best place to audition, but he knew he had no choice and would just have to muddle through as best he could.

'Great, please come with me,' the young man said, 'They're all very excited to see you, so please don't be nervous.'

The young man guided Billy through the foyer to the stairs, which led to one of the rehearsal rooms on the first floor.

'That's good to hear,' Billy said, and then he took a deep breath and tried his very hardest to focus on the audition and nothing else.

CHAPTER 55

Vicki stood, a glass of red wine in her hand, and watched from the door as Lizzie skilfully navigated her small kitchen, preparing a three-course meal for five people. Pots were steaming on the hob, her oven filled with trays of food which had each been inserted to a perfectly observed timetable, and the slow cooker had been positioned on the breakfast table, the only spare work surface available.

Stuart's presence in the kitchen puzzled Vicki. He wasn't helping with the food. Instead, he repeatedly lifted the lids on each saucepan, shaking his head or shrugging before muttering sentences like, 'I don't understand' or 'Oh for goodness' sake'.

Vicki had never warmed to Stuart. From the moment she had met him, she had felt her sister could do better. Everything about him was average: average height, average build, average intelligence. He had a part-time job working in a call centre for a power company and rented a one-bed flat over a pub near the town's central train station. The only thing of interest about him was his thick, brown beard, which, Vicki suspected, was probably hiding a weak chin.

'It all smells lovely,' Vicki said, wanting to enthuse to mitigate whatever it was that Stuart was complaining about.

Stuart stared at her, then huffed, 'I thought we were having a nice, light, healthy meal. I don't understand why there are all these thick sauces. Why's everything being cooked in all this fat?'

'They're all from mum's personal recipe box,' Vicki replied, 'There's not a healthy meal in there. Believe me, we've all looked.'

'Well, I just thought we were having a nice, light, healthy meal,' Stuart muttered.

'Everything is healthy if you have it in moderation,' Lizzie replied. 'Now if you're not going to help in the kitchen, please go and lay the table so it's ready for when Billy and Emma get here.'

Stuart stood upright, eyebrows raised, unhappy to have been dismissed. It appeared he was about to say something, but then he looked to his side, and saw that Vicki was observing him from the

280

doorway, and he didn't say anything. Instead, he huffed loudly as he walked towards her. Vicki did not step out of the way. Instead, she made a point of staying exactly where she was, clearly waiting for him to politely ask her to move. For a few seconds, they just stood, looking at each other.

'Everything alright, Stuart?' Vicki asked, as though puzzled.

'I need to get by,' he replied, curtly.

'Oh, I didn't realise,' Vicki said. 'Most people usually say, "*excuse me*" or something like that.' She sipped her wine and stayed exactly where she was.

Stuart's eyes narrowed, and Vicki could sense he wanted to say something unpleasant or rude to her. There was a part of her that wished he would, because she was desperate to tell him exactly what she thought of him, so she was left a little disappointed when he did as she had suggested, and politely asked if he could get by.

'Of course, you may,' she replied, stepping aside.

'I have a bottle of champagne in the fridge. Not prosecco, proper champagne. I thought we could open it when Billy and Emma get here. To celebrate,' Lizzie said, completely unaware of the minor drama that had just played out behind her. 'I still can't believe it. Billy's going to be starring in a show, with people off the telly.'

Vicki smiled broadly at the thought of her kid brother finally realising his lifelong ambition of starring in a professional show.

Lizzie continued preparing the food, checking what she was doing against Susan's detailed recipe instructions, adding chopped herbs to one pot, a splash of white wine to another. 'It's lovely, isn't it?' she said. 'You grew up with this food. You, Charlie and Billy. Tyler too, I guess. And all these years later, we're all still using the same recipes.'

Vicki sat at the breakfast table, just next to the slow cooker. 'All I can say is this smells exactly like mum's kitchen,' she said, fondly. For a moment, she closed her eyes, and just enjoyed the heady sensation of the aromas dancing merrily through the air, the same delicious smells she had enjoyed as a child, sat at the table in the old kitchen at The Lodge, while Susan prepared for one of her amazing dinner parties. 'Nice for you too,' she said, and opened her eyes. 'A part of Mum for you to enjoy, even though she's not here.'

Lizzie stopped for a moment and turned to Vicki. 'It means a lot, honestly, to have these recipes. It's lovely hearing stories about her and seeing the old family photographs. But I know that if I follow her recipes exactly, then when we sit down for dinner, we'll be eating the same meals, the exact same meals, that she would have dished up. And it feels like a really genuine connection, between her and me. And that really does mean a lot.'

Vicki smiled at her sister and raised her glass. 'To Mum's recipes.'

Lizzie hadn't poured herself a glass and so, with a big smile on her face, she lifted the bottle of wine she was using for the sauce. 'To Mum's recipes,' she said. Vicki sipped from her glass and Lizzie took a large swig of wine from the bottle, then they both started laughing.

Stuart re-entered the kitchen, an expression on his face that made it clear he was still unhappy. 'I don't know what cutlery you want me to use. And were you just drinking wine out of the bottle?'

The smile immediately vanished from Lizzie's face, and she stood awkwardly, the wine bottle still in her hand. She appeared to be at a loss for something to say.

'We were just toasting our mother, Stuart,' Vicki interceded. 'She died a few days after Lizzie was born, but these recipes—'

'Yes, yes, I know the sad story about your mother,' Stuart replied, dismissively. 'But I don't understand why my girlfriend is drinking wine straight from the bottle.'

'Oh, that's simple,' Vicki replied, sternly. 'It's because my sister is a grown woman, standing in her own kitchen, and she decided to drink straight from a bottle of wine that she paid for with her own money. There. I think I've cleared up that little mystery for you, Stuart.'

'Goodness, you're grumpy this evening, Stuart,' Lizzie said, lightly and quickly placed the bottle of wine onto the kitchen counter.

Stuart looked at her, his expression sullen.

'You'll find the cutlery in the blue dresser,' she continued. 'Second drawer. The napkins are there too. Now, Billy and Emma will be here any minute, and we're going to be toasting Billy's new play with

282

champagne. So, if you could bring the flutes in too, that would be great.'
Lizzie maintained a tone that was light and airy and, without responding,
Stuart left the room.

Vicki remained unimpressed. She could tell her little sister was doing
all she could to keep the atmosphere cordial, but increasingly, it seemed
as though Lizzie had fallen into a pattern, of trying to manage Stuart and
his moods.

CHAPTER 56

Stuart sat at the head of the table, silently sipping his wine as the Fletchers excitedly caught up with each other. He had made a point of barely touching his starter, a small portion of salmon penne in a tomato and vodka sauce. Instead, he had pushed the food around his bowl a number of times before placing his spoon back onto the table. He watched as Lizzie and her guests happily shared their updates, often talking over each other, swapping topics mid-sentence, and all whilst eating and drinking and laughing.

Billy regaled them all with the story of his call-back audition and the round of applause he received on performing his monologue. Emma explained her plans to expand her barbershop, and Vicki spoke of an upcoming meeting at Blake's school where she hoped it would be confirmed she was to be long-term linked with him.

Throughout, Vicki and Billy kept stopping to congratulate Lizzie on the pasta and praise how exactly it tasted like Susan's original. Emma, sat beside Stuart, continued to try and include him in the conversation, even though he seemed reluctant to engage with the evening. She had only met him a couple of times, briefly on both occasions, and had assumed his unsociable behaviour was a sign of shyness, and that he might need a bit of friendly coaxing to bring him out of his shell.

After a while, Lizzie stood and began to collect the plates. She asked Stuart to replenish the drinks and hurried to the kitchen to serve the main course. 'I hope you've left plenty of space,' she said as she left the dining room. 'Slow-cooked chicken in white wine sauce.'

Billy chuckled. 'Has anyone noticed that all of Mum's recipes seem to have booze in them?'

Vicki and Emma laughed, Stuart did not.

'I seem to recall you telling me her dinner parties were always a great success,' Emma said. 'Perhaps that's why.'

Stuart stood and made his way around the table, refilling all the glasses with the appropriate wine. 'I don't think it's going to be anything

284

heavy, the main course,' he said. 'Lizzie's really working hard on her diet. I'm sure she doesn't want to ruin it.'

'Oh, and hasn't she done well,' Emma said, enthusiastically. 'Most people put weight on during lockdown. I think Lizzie's the only person I know who lost weight. And doesn't she look beautiful?'

'And one meal won't ruin her diet,' Vicki said, her tone a little sharper.

'I just want to help her keep on track,' Stuart replied, and retook his seat.

'I am sure my sister is fine as she is,' Vicki replied, not prepared to allow any space for Stuart's opinion on her sister's weight. 'She'd already lost about five stone before she even met you, Stuart, so it's pretty obvious she knows what she's doing.'

Stuart shrugged and did not reply, and Vicki was satisfied she had made her point. She turned away from him and quickly lost herself in a conversation with Billy about his tour, which towns and cities he would be visiting, and how long he would be away.

'So, how are things going with you and Lizzie?' Emma asked, desperately trying to think of a topic that Stuart could actually engage with. 'Must be quite a few months now.'

'Well, it's just very challenging at the moment, to be honest,' he replied, crossly.

'Challenging? How so?'

Stuart turned and looked Emma directly in the face and spoke to her quietly but sternly. 'I don't like being undermined, particularly not when I am trying to be a supportive boyfriend to Lizzie,' he said. 'She's just got back from holiday. She's put on a tonne of weight, and the last thing she needs is an evening like this. I thought you all would have cancelled, or at least postponed.'

'Oh, I see,' Emma said, and placed her glass of wine onto the table. 'Look, Stuart, she didn't put on a *tonne of weight*, at all,' she replied, calmly, 'and the last thing any woman needs is a man obsessing about her size. We obsess about it more than enough ourselves. We don't need any help. And these dinner parties are an important Fletcher family tradition. They

285

lost their mother when they were all very young, and it's a way for them to keep her memory alive.'

'Well, I'm putting a stop to them. For Lizzie at least. The rest of you can do what you want. But Lizzie won't be taking part again.'

Emma frowned, pivoting towards him and returning his stare. 'I beg your pardon?' she asked, keeping her voice low, so as not to escalate their conversation by drawing Vicki or Billy's attention. 'That is not your decision to make, Stuart.'

'Actually, it is,' he said. 'Because I am moving in, and this will be my house. And when that happens, I am putting a stop to all this nonsense so Lizzie can focus solely on her diet.'

'Oh no, no,' Emma replied, taking her voice almost to a whisper. 'If Lizzie wants you to move in, that's up to her, Stuart. But she owns this flat. This is her space. And you will not be telling her what she can do in her own space.'

'Wrong,' Stuart said, abruptly. 'This will be my house. Lizzie's already told me she's putting my name on the deeds. And I won't have people, including Lizzie's family, disrespecting me in my own house.'

Emma sat back in her seat, and gazed at Stuart, a man she barely knew, and she tried to make sense of him, of what he was saying, of how he was speaking to her. But mostly, she was trying to work out his relationship with Lizzie, and the financial implications of what he was saying about her sister-in-law. 'Stuart, you've only known Lizzie for a few months,' she said, puzzled and concerned. 'Are you actually going to allow her to sign half her house over to you? Do you think that's appropriate? She's a young woman, a woman who owns her own flat with no mortgage. And you're going to allow her to just give you half of it?'

Emma knew Lizzie was new to dating and had guessed that Stuart was probably her first-ever boyfriend. But Emma still struggled to believe Lizzie was so inexperienced, so desperate to keep Stuart, that she had been the one to suggest she add Stuart's name to the deeds of her home. Emma was greatly concerned the suggestion had originated from Stuart himself.

Stuart leaned forward and prodded his finger on the table. 'Let me be clear,' he said, his voice stern but quiet, 'In future, when you Fletchers come into *my* house, I expect you all to respect my decisions. If I say no, to one of these dinner parties, that's the end of the matter. And when you visit my house in future, Emma, I expect you to do as I say. Is that clear? Is there anything I have said that I need to explain again?'

His words, the way he spoke, sent a chill down Emma's spine, and she realised Lizzie was vulnerable, far more vulnerable than anyone in the family knew. She realised they all should have done more to protect her from a man like Stuart. Before Emma could determine the best way to reply, the door opened and Lizzie walked in, skilfully carrying three plates of food. 'Voila!' she said, proudly, and Vicki and Billy both stopped talking and applauded as she placed their meals in front of them.

'Slow-cooked chicken in white wine sauce with dauphinoise potatoes and green beans. Enjoy.' She served a plate to Vicki, Billy and Emma, and then smiled hopefully at Stuart, wishing for a positive reaction. 'I'll just get yours, darling,' she said to him, but he did not reply.

'This looks amazing,' Billy said, then he glanced down the table to his wife, and for the first time, he noticed the blank expression on her face, barely registering anything that was happening around her, or even acknowledging the plate of food that had just been laid on the table in front of her. 'Everything all right, you two?' he asked, directing his question to both Emma and Stuart.

'Getting on like a house on fire,' Stuart replied, flashing a smile in Billy's direction. But Billy noticed a slight inflexion in Stuart's voice, possibly sarcasm, and it was just enough to cause him concern. The odd exchange drew Vicki's attention, too, and she placed her wine glass onto the table and stared across at Stuart. Lizzie paused and waited for the conversation to continue so she could go and collect the final two plates from her kitchen, relaxed in the knowledge everyone was getting on and that everyone — in particular Stuart — was happy and having fun.

'Babe,' Billy said, 'is everything OK?'

Emma looked down for a moment at the exquisite meal her young sister-in-law had just given her. She took a deep breath and then, with a great sadness on her face, she looked to her husband. 'No, I'm not OK,

Billy,' she said. 'I am deeply unhappy with how Stuart has just spoken to me.'

Immediately, Lizzie could feel herself growing anxious. With those few words, it felt as though Emma had announced the end of the evening and that all her hard work to bring Stuart into the fold was about to explode. 'I'm sure he didn't mean anything, Emma,' Lizzie said. 'He has a terrible sense of humour.'

Emma paused, then she shook her head. 'Billy, can you get my coat? We're going to leave.'

'Oh, no, no, Emma, please,' Lizzie cried, a cold rush of panic sweeping through her body. 'I'm sure he didn't mean anything.' She glanced at Stuart, who was glaring at her, shaking his head, as though unhappy with Lizzie, at what she was saying, how she was reacting to the situation. And she knew, immediately, that the evening was over. Once Stuart had lost his temper, she knew he would make no further effort to be polite or tolerate the other guests. And Lizzie knew it was best if everyone left.

Without saying a word, Billy stood and went to the hallway to collect Emma's coat. Emma walked around the table to speak to Lizzie. 'I'm very sorry, Lizzie,' she said, 'but I will not be spoken to like that. And if that is any indication as to how this man speaks to you, then you shouldn't be with him.'

Lizzie's mind was racing. She wanted the last three minutes back. She wished she had called Stuart into the kitchen to help her serve up the main course. She wished she could undo whatever conversation had taken place that had caused such great offence to Emma. But none of that was possible, and as Emma embraced her then walked from the room, she could feel a terrible coldness inside of her, a sickening panic that nothing would ever be the same with her family again.

Billy re-entered the room, wearing his jacket, and put his arms around Lizzie. 'I will call you tomorrow,' he said and then, to give her some reassurance, he added, 'We'll sort this out, together.' And then he and Emma left.

Lizzie glanced back to the table where Vicki, clearly furious, had fixed Stuart with a firm glare. 'Do you want me to stay, Lizzie?' she asked.

But Lizzie knew Stuart was in no mood to have anyone else in the flat and was frightened he would say things to Vicki that would make matters even worse. 'No, it's fine,' she said. 'I'm sorry. This isn't how I wanted the evening to play out, obviously.'

As Vicki stood and embraced her sister, she could feel her, trembling, trying not to cry, so she gave her a tight squeeze. 'Coffee tomorrow morning. 10am. Usual place,' she said. And then, without saying a word to Stuart, she left the room.

The moment they heard the sound of the front door close, Lizzie went to clear the plates, each meal completely untouched.

'That's it, is it?' Stuart said. 'That's the end of the evening? You're going to let your family treat me like that, and then you just say goodbye and make coffee plans with them?'

Lizzie put the plates back onto the table and stared at him. 'I just don't understand what happened.'

'You know exactly what happened, Lizzie. I was just attacked and bullied by your family, and you stood and watched them do it. You did nothing to stick up for me. Not a thing.'

'No, no, that's not it,' Lizzie replied, her mind spinning, trying to think of a way to calm everything down.

'They're not setting foot in this house again until they've all apologised to me. And you need to tell them that.'

Lizzie exhaled loudly. 'Look, let's just put this evening behind us.'

'Oh, you'd like that wouldn't you?' Stuart replied, his voice beginning to gain volume. 'Well, that's not what's going to happen. You're going to write a letter to Emma and Billy, and a letter to Vicki. And you are going to tell them how angry you are. Not me, you. How angry *you* are at how they treated me and that you don't want them back in this house until they've apologised to me. Do you understand?'

'I can't do that,' Lizzie said. 'Look, I'll talk to Vicki tomorrow. I am sure this has all just been a misunderstanding.'

'No!' Stuart shouted. Then quieter, his voice more persuasive, 'You won't be having coffee with Vicki tomorrow. You are going to write and post those letters. You are going to stick up for me, for once, and make it clear that you are not happy with how your family treated me tonight. And that's the end of the matter.'

CHAPTER 57

Charlie could hear raised voices. He closed the gate behind him and walked towards the gleaming, three-storey house he now called home. He was in no mood for visitors, particularly if they were rowing with his fiancée. He'd had a busy day, was tired and had yet another headache, and just wanted to have a shower and lay on his bed for a while.

He could see Alan sitting at the table under the veranda, gesturing assertively at a young woman sat opposite him. She had short blonde hair, oversized sunglasses and wore a dark blouse. Her arms were folded, clearly unimpressed with whatever Alan was saying.

As Charlie approached, he was able to get a better view, and could see it was Alan's daughter, Jill, although Charlie was not aware she was due to visit. He'd been able to develop a mostly positive relationship with Jill and her brother Kieran during the previous few years. Both were younger than Charlie, much closer to Tyler's age, and both were smart and had inherited Alan's strong work ethic.

Occasionally, Charlie could sense there were tensions, and he was never entirely sure what the cause of them might be. They had been both told the circumstances of his relationship with their father, and so were aware he was not with Alan for his money, and he thought both accepted that. Even their mother, on meeting Charlie, had made it clear she approved of him.

But sometimes, Kieran would make a disparaging comment about the age gap, or Jill would seem less pleased to see him, and it would put Charlie on the backfoot, not sure what he might have done to upset them. As he drew closer, he heard his name said out loud, once by Alan and once by Jill, and it occurred to him that he was the subject of the disagreement.

'Everything OK?' he asked casually. Immediately the conversation stopped, and Alan and Jill looked like a couple of naughty children caught red-handed doing something they shouldn't. 'Jill. Nice to see you. Alan forgot to mention you were visiting.'

291

'Good to see you, Charlie,' Jill said, a little breathless, frustrated. 'My trip was last minute. Apologies for just landing on you.'

He noticed a suitcase on the floor, just next to Jill, and it became clear that she must have started to row with her father from the moment she had arrived at the house.

Charlie was exhausted. Over the previous few months, the planning for his and Alan's wedding had added to his already busy work life, and he had found himself tired more and more often. Most frustrating of all, he had found his ability to multitask had become diminished, often finding he could lose his way halfway through a conversation. But he knew he could not go for a laydown without knowing what was going on and why his name had been repeatedly mentioned.

'I am quite certain I heard my name in the middle of all that shouting.,' he said. 'Have I done something to upset you both?'

Alan immediately stood, strode forward, and embraced Charlie. 'No, no, we were just having a bit of a disagreement about something. We're fine.'

Charlie knew the embrace was Alan's way of trying to quickly defuse difficult situations, but it was a technique Charlie had grown very familiar with. Gently, he pushed Alan away. 'I heard my name, Alan. What are you arguing about?'

'It's nothing I can't handle. Now please drop it.'

Charlie groaned, and then pointedly sat down at the table. "Jill, perhaps you'd be kind enough to tell me,' he said.

She glanced up to Alan, as though looking to him for permission, father and daughter both suddenly on the same page, and Charlie did not like being made to feel like an outsider in his own home.

'You are both *really* fucking me off,' he said, brusquely.

'Charlie?' Jill replied, shocked by both his tone and his language.

'Oy, come on Charlie,' Alan said, and sat down next to him, a hand on his shoulder, a placatory gesture. 'There's no need for that.'

'I am less than two weeks from my wedding,' Charlie said, crossly, 'and I hear my name mentioned repeatedly in the middle of a row and then I'm told it is none of my fucking business. You'd better tell me what's going on.'

Charlie could see Alan staring at him, a puzzled expression, as though not recognising him, and he wondered what he had done to cause such a reaction. He relaxed onto the chair back and exhaled loudly. 'I'm tired,' he said. 'My apologies if I am not as sparkling and charming as I usually am. But we've had to postpone our wedding twice, Alan, because of the pandemic. Hopefully, this is third time lucky. But it's not going to be a great start to our married life together if you're already keeping secrets from me.'

Finally, Alan appeared to concede, and then he glanced to Jill who nodded, agreeing that Charlie should be told, and Alan returned his gaze to Charlie and prepared to speak. But Charlie wanted his bed and so interceded to hurry the conversation along.

'It's the inheritance, isn't it, Jill? You and Kieran. You're both wondering what happens to your inheritance once your dad gets remarried.'

Jill's mouth dropped open slightly, surprised and a little embarrassed, and Charlie heard Alan mutter, 'Fuck's sake,' under his breath.

'Charlie, it isn't about you,' Jill said. 'I really want to make that clear. We're all very fond of you. Even Mum likes you, and she doesn't particularly like anyone. But I've been speaking to Kieran, and we both need clarity about what happens next. After the wedding.'

Charlie shrugged. 'That's perfectly reasonable,' he replied, matter-of-factly. 'I don't understand why it turned into a row.'

'Charlie,' Alan said, 'I've told my kids its none of their business, but—'

'Yes, it is,' Charlie said, interrupting the moment the words escaped from Alan's lips. 'It absolutely *is* their business. Their inheritance is their business.'

Jill's demeanour changed, immediately. She seemed to relax, physically, as it appeared she had an unexpected ally in the conversation. 'Charlie, we see it as a family business,' she said. 'Everything mum and dad built together. It was always something that Kieran and I would take over one day.'

'And then, your dad met me,' Charlie said, 'and you and your brother have spent all these years wondering what that meant for your

293

inheritance. For goodness' sake, Jill, I wish you had spoken to me about this before now.'

'I'm know, and I'm so, so sorry,' Jill said, genuine regret obvious in her voice. 'It just never felt like the right time. And the few occasions when it did feel like the right time, Dad kept refusing to talk about it. But Kieran and I, we just want to know where we stand, that's all.'

Charlie looked at Alan whose face was flushed, either embarrassed or angered by the whole situation, and he realised his husband-to-be was genuinely just trying to look out for him. And he loved him for that. 'To be fair, Jill,' he said, 'Alan and I have never spoken about it either. Perhaps we should have done.'

'I don't see there's anything to talk about,' Alan said. 'Charlie, when we first met, I told you I didn't have a penny to my name, but you were willing to share everything you had with me. This isn't about money, it's about us being equal partners in our marriage, me sharing everything I have with you.'

'I understand that sweetheart,' Charlie replied, 'but I don't have kids. You do. And that does make your situation different to mine. And, to be fair, it's not like they're a couple of ungrateful freeloaders. They both work bloody hard, for you, for your company.'

As he spoke, Charlie had a clear sense that, left to their own devices, Alan and his daughter were not going to resolve the issue. They were too alike, too stubborn and opinionated. It was a disagreement that would just sit there, forever, in the background of their relationship, an unhappiness and a mistrust that would poison everything. And Charlie knew how that would play out. He'd lived it, with his sister. He remembered the years at The Lodge, when he and Vicki had been estranged, and he could not regret more that period of his life, and all that lost time. He did not want the same to happen between Alan and his children.

'I've been through probate quite a few times,' he said. 'It's always horrendous, trying to grieve for someone you loved whilst having to deal with a mass of paperwork and legal stuff.' He turned from Alan to look directly at Jill. 'Has your father ever told you about my first husband, Jason?'

294

For the first time, Jill uncrossed her arms and removed her sunglasses. She put them on the table and leaned forward, her barriers finally down. 'A little,' she said. 'I know about the accident and your dad going to prison.'

'Well, there's more to that story. You see, Jason came from a very chaotic household. Both his parents were heavy drinkers, and they had an extremely volatile marriage. Their house was always filled with other people and the neighbours were constantly complaining to the council or calling the police. As a kid growing up, Jason spent most of his time at my house, and to be honest, my mum was more of a parent to him than his own.

'When he was 18, and he left to go to university, he wrote to his parents to tell them he was disowning them and that they were not going to be a part of his life after that. And, true to his word, he didn't ever see or speak to them again. After the accident, I had to get in touch with them, so they didn't find out about his death by reading the local paper.

'Neither of them asked to come to his funeral. They didn't even send flowers. And I was left with the impression that I wouldn't hear from them. But then, completely out of the blue, a few months later, I received a letter from a solicitor asking when they could expect their share of their son's estate.'

'Oh my god,' Jill blurted. 'What did they think they were going to get?'

Charlie shrugged. 'Well, the letter suggested they'd had a rough estimate made as to the value of my house. They also wanted full disclosure of any other properties we owned at the time of Jason's death, plus any savings, investments, insurance pay-outs. And, whatever all that added up to, they wanted half.'

'That's horrible,' she said, then looked to her father. 'You've never told me this before.'

Alan frowned. 'It never came up,' he replied, a clear insinuation he did not consider it any of her business.

Jill sighed and shook her head, despairing at his attitude. 'Sorry, Charlie, please go on. What happened next?'

'Oh, nothing really. It was all over very quickly,' Charlie continued. 'Jason and I were in a civil partnership, and he had also added an exclusion clause into his will to make it clear that, no matter what, he did not want either of his parents to inherit from him. But they genuinely thought I should sell everything and give them half.'

'I'm really sorry, Charlie,' Jill said, quietly. 'I had no idea any of this happened. That's awful. But thank goodness he had made all those arrangements.'

Charlie smiled a little. 'And that is the point I am trying to make,' he said. 'Even though Jason was a young man, he felt it important to make sure that if the very worst thing happened, there was absolute clarity, for me, for everyone else, as to what should happen to his estate. He felt that no matter how big or small your estate, it's important the people you leave behind feel everything was done fairly, and that their legacy was protected.'

Charlie turned to Alan. 'Your legacy needs to go to your kids,' he said, 'and your kids need to have the security of knowing that's what is going to happen.'

Alan was not impressed and did not agree. 'I don't know,' he replied, unhappily. 'Charlie, I'm a lot older than you. I need to know you're going to be OK if anything happens to me.'

Charlie tutted, loudly. 'You're not a *lot* older than me,' he said, 'I'm 46 and you're 58. We're practically the same age. And, Alan, its lovely that you worry about things like that, but I've got my own stuff, sweetheart. Whatever happens, I'll be fine. And I don't want to start married life knowing there are people in your family who are stressed about this.'

Alan exhaled. 'Fine. What do you suggest?'

Charlie sat back, addressing both of them. 'Your legal guy. What's his name? Ted? Let's get him on the line and draft new wills. Both of us.'

Charlie knew the look on Alan's face, a man unable to conceal his feelings. He had an annoyed expression that suggested the matter was far from over, but, for the time being, Alan would concede that Charlie had come up with a credible way forward.

'I'll give Ted a call,' Alan said. 'But we need to sort out the details. I'm not happy about this. You're going to be my husband, Charlie. I want to make sure you're looked after too. That's important to me.'

Charlie smiled at Alan, then glanced at Jill. 'Does this sound OK to you?'

'Yes,' she replied, relief etched on her face. 'But Dad's right. This isn't about you ending up with nothing, Charlie. That's not what we've been asking for.'

The matter seemingly resolved, Charlie stood. 'That's all fine, then,' he said. 'Now, if you'll both excuse me, I have a stonking headache and so I am going to have a shower and then a quick siesta. Jill, are you joining us for dinner?'

'If that's OK,' she replied.

'Your dad can book somewhere,' he said. And then he kissed Alan on the cheek and walked into the house.

Alan and Jill didn't speak until Charlie was out of earshot, and then Jill asked, 'Is Charlie OK, Dad? I don't think I've ever heard him swear before.'

Before Alan could reply, a sudden noise brought their attention to the house; a loud bang, followed by a thumping sound, as though something was being repeatedly knocked.

'What was that?' Jill asked, but Alan was already on his feet, rushing forward, concerned. He called Charlie's name and disappeared inside. Jill stood, and began to follow her father, but then heard him yelling at her.

'Jill, get an ambulance,' he shouted. 'He's having a seizure. Charlie's having a seizure. Call a fucking ambulance.'

CHAPTER 58

Billy sat quietly in the waiting room, wondering if he was doing the right thing. Emma's description of her exchange with Stuart at the dinner party, of what he had said and the way he had spoken to her, had deeply troubled him. It felt as though Stuart had attempted to lever some control over Emma over what she was allowed to say and do. And if Stuart felt empowered to behave like that towards Emma, Billy wondered what that meant for Lizzie.

And then, the letter. It arrived a couple of days after the dinner party, signed by Lizzie. Vicki had received one too, almost identical. But Billy could not believe a single word of it had come from his little sister. He had no doubt that every angry, spiteful word had come from Stuart, a brazen attempt to isolate Lizzie from her family. Emma had even suggested the letter was a way for Stuart to buy himself time, by keeping Lizzie's family at bay until his name was on the deeds to her flat.

And that was the moment Billy knew he had to take action, to do something quickly, his one and only opportunity to expose Stuart for what he was. He had told Emma and Vicki what he was planning to do, and both had fully supported him.

'Mr Fletcher?'

Instinctively, Billy stood and looked to see who had called his name. In front of him was a young woman in a police uniform. *'William* Fletcher?' she said.

'Billy,' he replied, 'Please call me Billy.' Suddenly, what he was about to do felt very definite and real, and he had an unpleasant sensation in the pit of his stomach, a worry that perhaps he had overreacted. What if involving the police was exactly what Stuart wanted, to drive a wedge between Lizzie and her family?

'Thank you for coming in,' the police officer said, and shook his hand. 'I'm Detective Constable Grayson. I will be dealing with your complaint.'

'Complaint?' Billy asked anxiously, keen for the language to be softer, less formal.

298

'I will be listening to your concerns,' the police officer replied, gesturing to the doorway she had just walked through. 'I have a room booked, so please come with me.'

Billy followed her through a series of corridors, then up a flight of stairs amidst the continuous background noise of conversations and phones bleeping. They settled in a small room with a desk and two chairs overlooking the car park at the rear of the station.

'May I get you anything to drink?' DC Grayson asked and produced a tablet from the desk drawer and took a seat.

'No, no, I'm fine. Thank you,' Billy replied, seating himself on the opposite side of the desk.

'I am the officer you spoke to on the phone yesterday, so I do have an idea of what your concerns are. But today, I just want to go through them in a bit more detail, and I will be taking notes on this tablet as we speak. Is that OK, Billy?'

Billy swallowed hard and nodded.

'You told me yesterday that you are concerned for the wellbeing and safety of your sister, Elizabeth Fletcher. Lizzie.'

'Yes.'

'And this is in relation to the behaviour of her partner, Stuart Clarke.'

'Yes.'

'So, can you talk me through their relationship? When you first began to have concerns, and what your current concerns are.'

Nervously, slowly at first, Billy began to detail Lizzie's relationship with Stuart: how they had met, and Stuart's first introductions to various family members. And how, initially, it had all seemed very ordinary and happy and pleasant. But then Billy began to explain how things changed when various family members began to notice things, small things at first, about Stuart's behaviour, which they shared with everyone apart from Lizzie. And his words began to flow more quickly.

Carol hadn't liked how he had repeatedly mentioned Lizzie's weight in front of her. Vicki found him moody, rude and had not liked how he kept directing Lizzie to agree with his opinions. And Tyler, calling from Gran Canaria, had raised concerns following some FaceTime he'd had with Lizzie, where she had cried for almost the whole call. She had

299

shared a story with him, of how Stuart had bought her new clothes; every item obviously far too small. But he had insisted she try all of them on in front of him, only to tell her, when none of the clothes fitted, that she needed to lose much more weight, and much more quickly.

Then, the dinner party, and the way Stuart had spoken to Emma, and what he had said to her. And then the letters from Lizzie, a few days later, that simply could not have been her words. And then, the flat, and a man with no money, and barely a job, demanding his name go on the deeds.

As he spoke out loud, and listed every concern, every conversation, every terrible word from Stuart's mouth, Billy began to feel more confident he had done the right thing. His anxiety began to wane, and he hoped Lizzie would understand he was just trying to protect her from an abuser, in the same way Vicki had protected him from an abuser, all those years earlier.

After he had finished speaking, DC Grayson placed her tablet onto the desk and smiled at him, kindly. 'I know that was very difficult for you, Billy,' she said. 'Many people who report these issues, they are conflicted, they don't know if they are doing the right thing. But you are clearly concerned for your sister. And after everything you have told me, I just want to say that you made the right choice coming in today to speak with me. Domestic abuse covers a range of different behaviours, including coercive or controlling behaviour and financial abuse.'

'Thank you,' Billy said. 'I was worried. But I know this isn't right. And I know if Lizzie stays with Stuart, we'll lose her. And she'll lose everything.'

DC Grayson leaned forward onto the desk and clasped her hands together. 'Have you heard of the Domestic Abuse Disclosure Scheme? It's also known as Clare's Law.'

'No, I haven't.'

'It's a piece of legislation which means that if you are in a relationship with someone and you are concerned about their behaviour towards you, then you can make an application, through Clare's Law, for the police to disclose relevant information they have about your partner's past. But importantly, close friends or family members can also make an application, if they are concerned about the wellbeing of a loved one.'

'And what would that show, about Stuart?' Billy asked.

'If he has convictions, relating to domestic abuse, or other convictions, for example, if he had assaulted a complete stranger. But it isn't just convictions that are disclosed. It can be non-convictions and domestic-related allegations, such as harassment.'

'What's a non-conviction?'

'Well, a non-convictions could mean that someone was arrested for domestic assault, but not charged.'

Billy understood what that meant, that a victim might be persuaded by their partner to retract a complaint, to make another go of the relationship, to remain trapped in a cycle of abuse, fake apologies and misplaced blame. He wanted to save Lizzie from that.

"Then, please may I make an application?' he asked. And he wondered what sort of a life Stuart had led, and what information the police might have on him.

CHAPTER 59

As Vicki walked through the school gates, she could hear the joyful sounds of children playing. The noise echoed through the air from the playground on the other side of the building, and it pleased her to think that Blake was one of the kids making those happy sounds, now able to play with other children without losing his temper or breaking into a fight. She had made great progress with him over the previous six months, a little boy who had been through three foster care placements in a very short period of time, each one breaking down because he struggled to live with other children.

When he had arrived at Vicki's house, where there were no other kids, she had quickly gotten him into a strict routine, something Blake had reacted well to. But she had also filled his time with creative activities; they read together, they drew pictures, he helped her in the garden, and they baked cakes. And throughout all those months she and his social worker and the school staff had worked as a team to develop his skills with other children. And now he could play without there being any unpleasant consequences.

Everyone had commented on how happy and settled he was with Vicki, from the teachers at school to his own social worker. And despite her best efforts, Vicki knew she had fallen in love with the little boy and was waiting for confirmation that the adoption team was no longer searching for Blake's 'forever home' so she could be long-term linked with him instead.

'Hi, I'm here for a PEP meeting,' she said, as she entered the reception.

The woman behind the desk pushed a clipboard towards her with several sheets of paper attached to it. 'Yes, of course, for Blake,' she said. 'Can you sign in please? A few others have already arrived. I've buzzed them through.'

Vicki was given a pen, and she began to write her details onto the check-in form. She noticed Blake's social worker had already signed in, as had Donna, a straight-talking woman who chaired the meetings about

Blake's education. And then, another name she recognised, Sally. Vicki had only met her once, a few days after Blake had arrived. She was from the adoption team and had visited Vicki's house to remind Blake they were still looking for a family to adopt him. She hadn't visited since, and Vicki could only imagine Sally was attending the meeting to finally confirm they were closing their work so Blake could stay where he was.

Suddenly excited, Vicki asked to be buzzed through. Once the door lock was released, she walked briskly to the meeting room, just a few paces from reception. The room was small, snug, with the table and chairs almost filling the entire space. As she entered, she could immediately feel a positive vibe, with the teaching staff and social workers all chatting happily. And as the meeting began, the upbeat tone continued; Blake's reading age had improved, his maths and concentration skills were up, his behaviour in class was now polite and appropriate, and his interactions with other children were mostly good. A teacher described how happy Blake was when he spoke of his homelife with Vicki, and all the fun and creative things they did together. The school's SENCo discussed how Blake had clearly formed an attachment with Vicki and how he spoke of the other members of Vicki's family as if they were his family too.

Throughout the meeting, Vicki kept glancing across the table at Sally, expecting her to speak up and confirm the adoption process for Blake was at an end. But Sally appeared to take an oddly passive role in the meeting, not speaking and hardly reacting to any of the comments being made by the other professionals in the room. It was only as Donna began to bring the meeting to a conclusion that Sally finally spoke.

'Before we finish, just also to mention,' she said, 'that I will need to visit Blake in the next few days and begin the work to transition him to his new home.'

The room fell silent, and at first Vicki thought she had misheard what Sally had said. 'I'm sorry. What was that?' she asked.

'The adoption,' Sally replied, matter-of-factly. 'We need to start to prepare Blake for an introduction meeting with his adoptive family.'

303

Immediately overwhelmed by a terrible wave of loss and grief, Vicki just sat, her face pale, unable to speak. Blake wasn't staying. They were going to take him away from her, to be someone else's little boy.

'I was not made aware of this prior to this meeting,' Donna said, and looked to her social work colleagues for input, but the news had taken everyone in the room by surprise. Annoyed, Donna fixed Sally with a hard stare. 'This is quite extraordinary,' she said. 'Sally, we have spent this entire meeting working on a personal education plan for Blake, where the basis of our entire conversation, and our plans for Blake going forward, was that he would continue to live with Vicki and continue to attend this school.'

'No, he won't be continuing at this school,' Sally said, maintaining her matter-of-fact tone, completely oblivious to the upset she had caused. 'His new family live in Colchester, so he will have to move.'

Donna shook her head. 'Sally, this is completely unacceptable,' she said. 'How long have you known about this?'

Sally paused before answering, a crease forming on her brow as it began to dawn on her that everyone in the room was deeply unhappy. 'We started working with them five months ago,' she said. 'They are an absolutely perfect match for him.'

Donna looked to Vicki. 'Were you told about this?'

Close to tears, Vicki allowed her hand to partially cover her mouth, and she shook her head. 'No,' she said, quietly, and then she gasped for breath before continuing. 'I was told that if they hadn't found anyone to adopt Blake by now, then they were going to close down the adoption process and he would stay with me.'

As tears began to tumble from her eyes, she looked at Sally and felt nothing for her but contempt. 'You didn't tell me,' she said. 'You've known for five months, and you didn't mention it to me once.'

Embarrassed, Sally flipped open a folder she had brought with her. 'You should have been told,' she said, and began to read through some of the pages, as though trying to locate evidence of a paper trail, to prove Vicki had known all along.

'And how often have you visited Blake over the past five months?' Donna asked.

304

Sally fell silent and closed her folder.

'I would expect you to visit him at least once a month,' Donna said, 'to ensure he was aware you were still looking for an adoptive family for him. Because it is important it is not too much of a shock when you arrive to tell him that you have found a family.'

Sally nodded, as though agreeing with the point Donna had just made. 'Yes, so we need to plan for that, too, because obviously I have not been able to see Blake since he moved in with Vicki, and—'

'What do you mean you haven't been able to see him?' Donna snapped, clearly very angry. And then she glanced at Vicki and could see how distressed she was by the unexpected news. 'I think we will need to pause this meeting,' she said. 'If everyone would like to go and grab a coffee. But not you, Sally. You can stay. We need to discuss a few things before the meeting reconvenes.'

Looking suddenly like a naughty pupil being kept behind for detention, Sally remained in her seat as everyone apart from Donna left the room.

Vicki did not go for a coffee. She could not face the other people who had been in the meeting. The news she was losing Blake was too great, too devastating. She had allowed herself to fall in love with a little boy who was going to be taken away from her, and she just needed to get away from everyone and find somewhere she could breathe again.

305

CHAPTER 60

Vicki knew she couldn't just leave the school grounds. She had no intention of rejoining the meeting, but it had been arranged for the end of the day so she could meet Blake at the school gate, and they could walk home together, as they did every day. She knew she had to pull herself together; she could not let him know something was wrong. That was the only thing Sally had managed to get right, that they would need to plan a way to tell Blake so it wasn't too much of a shock for him.

She found an empty classroom, an art room with children's paintings pinned to the walls and a large butler sink in the corner. She closed the door behind her and used the water from the cold tap to wash her face. She patted it dry with a hand towel folded across the front of the sink and sank down onto one of the few adult-sized chairs in the room. She closed her eyes.

'It's Victoria, isn't it?' came a voice, a woman, Irish, familiar.

Vicki opened her eyes and saw an older woman had entered the room. She was attractive, smartly dressed, with short grey hair and a pair of designer spectacles. 'It is, isn't? Victoria Fletcher.'

Vicki nodded and tried to think where she knew the woman from, but her nerves were so fraught in that moment that she had barely recognised her own name.

The woman walked over and pulled a chair to be close to her. 'I don't blame you for not recognising me,' she said and sat down. 'My hair's gone grey, and I need glasses now too.'

Vicki stared at her. She knew her, she definitely knew her, but just could not put a name to her.

The woman reached over and held Vicki's hands. 'It's Louise,' she said. 'I was the manager at your grandmother's retirement village. Goodness, it's been many years since I've seen you. But you've hardly changed a bit.'

The memories immediately spilled into Vicki's head, and she recalled how fond all the Fletcher kids had been of Louise, and the

306

compassionate but no-nonsense way she had dealt with their domineering grandmother.

'I'm sorry, it took me a moment,' Vicki said. 'It's lovely to see you.'

'Well, it looks like you've not had a great day.' Louise reached into her handbag and produced a packet of paper tissues. She handed them to Vicki. 'Here. I never leave home without them.'

Vicki thanked her and padded her eyes with the tissues. 'This is quite a shock, to see you here,' she said.

'Oh, well, I'm retired now. My husband passed a few years ago, so I'm filling my time as productively as I can. I'm a school governor here, and I'm a non-executive director at the hospital. I work with a couple of charities too. Busy, busy, busy. Otherwise, my daughter would have me babysitting twenty-four-seven. Now don't get me wrong, I love my grandchildren, but I like to see them for just a few hours every now and again, and then hand them back.'

Vicki could tell Louise was trying to lighten her mood and appreciated the effort. 'I'm very sorry to hear about your husband,' she said. 'He must have been young.'

Louise sighed. 'Sixty-six,' she said. 'You know, we followed all the advice as best we could, but that Covid was a tricky little bugger. He was one of the first people in Southend to die from it. It's the reason I work with the hospital now. My little way of giving back for everything they did to try and save him.' She focussed back on Lizzie and squeezed her hands. 'Would you like to tell me what has upset you so much?'

'I've been stupid,' Vicki said.

Louise released Vicki's hands and sat back in her seat. 'I'm sure that's not the case, Victoria,' she replied.

'I'm a foster carer.'

'Oh, that's marvellous. What a lovely thing to be doing.'

'I've been so careful not to get too emotionally involved,' Vicki continued, her voice quiet, frail. 'There are all sorts of reasons why a placement might not last. But then I had this little boy, and he was such a little sod at first. But I worked so hard, and all his bad behaviours just began to go away. And I got to see the real him, and what an absolute sweetheart he is. And I forgot myself. I just adore him. I thought he was staying with me, but I've just been told he's going to be adopted.'

Vicki dipped her head and could feel tears forming in her eyes once more. She took the tissues Louise had given her and wiped her eyes with them. 'I should be happy for him,' she said, 'but I'm just too upset.'

Louise was silent for a moment, her memories of a young Vicki gradually returning. She recalled a great sadness that had come over the Fletcher family when Vicki's own son had been taken into care. And she wondered if that had led to Vicki's attachment to this other boy, a chance to experience the years she had missed with her own child.

'I know it won't help you feel any better now,' Louise said, 'but perhaps this was your part in this little boy's life. To get him ready, so that he could be adopted. Perhaps if it hadn't been for you, and all the love and attention you've given him, he wouldn't be a child they could even consider for adoption. And that is something to be proud of. And something this little lad will always remember, I'm sure.'

Tearfully, Vicki nodded, then lifted her face to look at Louise.

'Oh, I forgot how much you look like your grandmother,' Louise said, fondly, and gently stroked the tears from Vicki's cheek.

'It's times like this I wish I was more like her,' Vicki said. 'I'm always the first to cry. But nothing ever bothered Nan. She was so tough.'

Louise smiled, remembering all the years she had cared for Vicki's grandmother. 'Let me tell you something about Dorothy Morgan,' she said. 'Your grandmother spent her entire life pretending nothing affected her. But I promise you, Dorothy had a big heart, and she felt happiness and loss just as deeply as you. You are much more like your grandmother than you realise. You just need to give yourself a bit more credit.'

Their conversation was interrupted by the sound of a bell ringing across the school.

'Home time,' Louise said.

'And I need to be at the school gate to meet Blake,' Vicki replied.

They both stood, and Vicki brushed herself down. 'How do I look?' she asked.

'He's never going to know you were crying,' Louise replied, then put her arms around Vicki. 'Your grandmother would be very proud of you, Victoria. I hope you know that.'

And for a moment, at the back of her mind, Vicki could hear Dorothy's voice. 'You're a good girl, Victoria. A good girl.'

Vicki said her goodbyes to Louise and made her way towards the front of the building. She decided to let the family know straight away about Blake, but she was going to do her best to put a positive spin on the message. She hoped that if she could persuade her family she was truly happy for Blake, she might be able to convince herself too. She took her phone from her bag and scrolled through to find her family's WhatsApp group, but before she could post anything, she noticed a notification that made her heart skip a beat.

Lizzie left the group.

CHAPTER 61

As hard as she tried, Lizzie could not work out a way to create enough additional storage in her bedroom for Stuart. The wardrobe was barely big enough for her own clothes; likewise, the chest of drawers was full. The only option she could think of was to turn the dining room back into a spare room, and both she and Stuart would then have a walk-in wardrobe they could use at any time. Dolefully, she had accepted the dining room would likely be a redundant space for quite a while, and so it would make better use of it.

She made the bed and tidied up, then made her way to the kitchen and put the kettle on. Everything in her head, her entire focus, was on Stuart moving in. She knew everything would be good the moment he was in the apartment with all his possessions ready to be unpacked, his feet up and a glass of wine in his hand. They could relax, and just lose themselves in their boxsets and their silly in-jokes.

She had suffered some testing times with him over the previous few weeks. She still suffered an anxiety attack whenever she thought of the dinner party, and that horrible, gut-wrenching moment when Emma had stated she was not happy with how Stuart had spoken to her, and that she was leaving. In the 24-hours which had followed, Lizzie had found herself increasingly desperate to make peace with Stuart and prove to him how much she cared for him. She had written the letters he had wanted her to write, practically word for word, and then she had left the family WhatsApp group at his request. And after that, everything had seemed immediately better, and Stuart had returned to the kind and funny man she had fallen in love with.

And once he felt settled, once the flat was *their* home, not just Lizzie's, she knew the tough times would be gone, and the more difficult parts of Stuart's character would fade. And then she hoped, at some point in the future, she might be able to build some bridges with the rest of the family.

Before she had the chance to pour herself a cup of coffee, she heard the doorbell. She hurried back through the flat to the front door. On the other side was a police officer, in full uniform, a folder tucked under her arm. Lizzie had had quite a few visits from the police over the previous few years, asking if she had heard or seen anything after some altercation near her home, so she assumed the visit was something similar to that. It took her by surprise when the police officer said her name.

'Hello miss. I'm DC Grayson from Southend Police. Are you Elizabeth Fletcher? Lizzie?'

Lizzie frowned, her mind racing through various different scenarios that might have brought a police officer to her door. Not a single one of the scenarios involved Stuart. 'Yes, that's me. May I help you with something?'

'Are you at home alone?'

'Yes, I am.'

'Are you expecting anyone?''

Puzzled, Lizzie shook her head. 'No. Not until later. My boyfriend's coming over tonight. But that's all.'

The police officer smiled, reassuringly. 'Nothing to be overly concerned about,' she said, 'but may I come in? I have some things I need to discuss with you.'

'Erm, yes, of course.' Lizzie closed the door behind DC Grayson and led her to the front room, where they both took a seat, the police officer with the folder flat on her lap.

'I was about to make a coffee,' Lizzie said. 'May I get you a drink?'

DC Grayson declined the offer. 'I understand you are in a relationship with a man named Stuart Clarke. Is that correct?'

'Yes. But he's at work. Should I call him?

'No, it is you I came to speak to, Lizzie.'

'OK.'

DC Grayson leaned forward slightly. 'The reason I am here, Lizzie, is because we have had some concerns raised with us about Mr Clarke's conduct and, in particular, his conduct towards you' she said. 'Quite serious concerns relating to your safety and wellbeing. May I ask, if you can think why someone might have such concerns?'

Lizzie didn't want this. On a day when everything seemed so calm, so happy, she didn't want the police in her home talking about Stuart.

311

Feeling a little panicked, she wondered what would happen if Stuart found out that someone had spoken to the police about him. She knew he would explode with rage and might even blame her. 'No idea,' she replied.

'How would you describe your relationship with Mr Clarke?'

'We've been seeing each other for about six months,' Lizzie replied, trying to be as factual as possible, but she could hear her voice wavering, and knew the police officer would be able to tell she was nervous. 'He's in the process of moving in. He's just waiting for the lease to be up on his own flat.'

'I see,' DC Grayson replied, thoughtfully. 'And how is your relationship, would you say?'

'Good,' Lizzie replied, and then more brusquely added, 'I don't understand what this is about.'

DC Grayson took a more formal position. She sat upright and knitted her fingers together. She explained about Clare's Law, and then asked; 'Can you think of an example where someone might feel Stuart was exhibiting some sort of abusive behaviour toward you, Lizzie. Controlling behaviour, for instance?'

Immediately defensive, Lizzie threw her hands in the air and shook her head. "No,' she replied, the word projected a little louder than she had intended. 'He gets a bit moody if he doesn't get his own way.' And then she added a chuckle, in the hope it would conceal her growing anxiety, worried that Stuart might surprise her by arriving hours early. 'But then a lot of men are like that, aren't they?'

'And can you give me an example of that, Lizzie? Of when Stuart got his own way?'

Lizzie wanted to draw the matter to a swift conclusion, and so tried to fob DC Grayson off with talk about small things, things she hoped would sound mundane, every day; how irritated Stuart would get whenever they ran out of milk because Lizzie had forgotten to buy an extra carton. Or how annoyed he would get if he wanted a bath, but found Lizzie hadn't put the hot water on because she was trying to keep her energy bill down.

As she spoke and began to share some quiet insight into her relationship with Stuart, DC Grayson offered no judgement, but carefully and skilfully prompted Lizzie to continue sharing and to scrutinise the parts of their relationship she was unhappy with; how Stuart often made her feel anxious or worried, and the distance that now existed between Lizzie and the people she loved.

Lizzie remained defensive of Stuart and tried to present their problems as teething issues, with Lizzie placing much blame on her own inexperience in relationships. But then they examined Stuart's plan to move in, and DC Grayson pushed for clarity as to who had suggested his name be added to the property deeds. And that was the moment when Lizzie really had to think, because she was certain it had come from her. But as she repeated the various conversations they'd had about the apartment, she began to realise it had all come from Stuart. He had brought her round to his point of view, and made it seem as though Lizzie had come up with the idea herself.

'Lizzie, there are different types of domestic abuse,' DC Grayson said. 'It does not always involve violence.'

Lizzie said nothing. The police officer had used the phrase 'domestic abuse' earlier in their conversation, but it still did not connect with her. It was like she and DC Grayson were talking about different things.

'This can cover emotional abuse, controlling behaviour,' DC Grayson continued. 'A victim of domestic abuse is often persuaded that everything is their fault, that they are entirely to blame for the behaviour of the abuser. And an abuser may try to isolate their partner from friends and family.'

Lizzie said nothing.

'It can also cover financial abuse,' DC Grayson continued. 'An example of financial abuse is when your partner might put you under pressure regarding your money or your property. Such as this apartment.'

Still, Lizzie said nothing.

'Can you see why someone might be worried about this, Lizzie? You have been dating a man for just a few months, and he has persuaded you to sign half your property over to him. What would happen if, in the future, if you were to separate? Do you think he would sign it back over

313

to you, or would he want you to sell so he could take his half of the money?'

Lizzie shrugged. 'You don't go into a relationship thinking about breaking up,' she replied.

DC Grayson raised her eyebrows. 'True,' she said. 'But it's also important not to be persuaded to make life-changing decisions too early in a relationship.'

A few moments passed, and Lizzie found herself unable to speak. She wasn't sure how the conversation could progress, what more there was to say, but then DC Grayson began to share information about Stuart's past, and the happy life of domestic bliss that Lizzie had been fantasising about, quickly began to fade away.

'Stuart has been arrested a number of times for issues related to domestic abuse,' DC Grayson said. 'He was never charged, but as well as the arrests, there have been numerous complaints. This all relates to two women he was previously in relationships with. Former partners. Both now have an injunction preventing Mr Clarke from making any contact with them. They're both young, like yourself, quite inexperienced when they first started dating him.

'During both relationships, Mr Clarke made great efforts to isolate them from their loved ones. He orchestrated arguments with their friends and family, and then demanded his partner take his side. He made them delete their social media accounts; Facebook, Twitter, TikTok. He insisted they hand over their phones to him, multiple times a day, so he could check their messages. He took control of their bank accounts and transferred their salary payments to his own account. They would have to ask him for money whenever they needed to pay for something.

'This didn't happen all at once, Lizzie. It happened over a period of time. He would gain a little bit of power, and then he would wait, and then he would gain a little more. He normalised his behaviour by saying he had been cheated on in the past, and had trust issues, and that they needed to prove to him that they could be trusted.'

Lizzie buried her face in her hands, the stories, all so familiar, had begun to leave her lightheaded. She had already allowed herself to be isolated from her family, an argument instigated by Stuart. More recently, he had started to obsess about her mobile phone, quizzing her whenever a text message was received and asking why anyone would need to contact her at the weekend or in the evening. He didn't like her being on social media, he had made that abundantly clear. And he had floated the idea of a joint bank account, where their salaries would be paid, and which he could oversee.

'Lizzie, are you OK? Would you like me to get you a glass of water?'

Lizzie exhaled loudly, and then sat up, feeling overwhelmed by so many conflicting emotions; shame and anger, and regret. And amid her turmoil, she could also feel a sense of guilt, for how she was talking about Stuart, how she was allowing him to be spoken about. 'Nope, I'm fine,' she replied. 'I just needed a moment.'

Once Lizzie appeared to have caught her breath, DC Grayson continued. 'One of the young women was involved with him for almost two years, the other about a year. For both, it was the intervention of their families which brought the matter to a head, by involving us. Both are still very traumatised by their experience.'

Sat quietly, with her hands on her lap, Lizzie found herself unable to know for sure how she felt. So much of what the police officer had said was sickeningly familiar, but there was so much about Stuart that hadn't been spoken about; his kindness, his sense of humour, the intimate moments when he made her feel beautiful, and sexy.

'Lizzie,' DC Grayson said, softly, 'what are you thinking?'

'It's so hard,' Lizzie said, tears forming in her eyes. 'I just love him so much. He's so lovely to me, most of the time. He's funny and caring. I know sometimes he makes me so unhappy, and sometimes worried and anxious. But there's such a lovely side to him, too. I just wish it was easier.'

'I understand that Lizzie, I honestly do,' DC Grayson said. 'But think about everything we know about Stuart Clarke. Think about the concerns that have been raised with the police about his behaviour towards you, the experience two other young women had when they were in a relationship with him, and the fact that you are already isolated from your friends and family. I am greatly concerned things will not get

315

better, and that his behaviour towards you will get even more controlling, because that's the pattern we saw in his past relationships.'

Lizzie looked down, unable to even think about taking the conversation further, or making any sort of decision. But she knew what the police officer was leading her to, a decision to end things with Stuart.

'Would you like me to call someone?' DC Grayson asked. 'A friend, or one of your siblings? To come and sit with you?'

Lizzie refused.

'What I am going to do, Lizzie, is leave you with some information which I hope you will read through. It includes information about support services you can access. And also, my contact details. I appreciate I am leaving you with a lot to think about. But please remember, I am here because people are genuinely concerned for your wellbeing.'

DC Grayson opened the folder on her lap and handed Lizzie several leaflets and sheets of paper with information printed on them, and Lizzie's first thought was about where in her home she could hide them from Stuart. And then DC Grayson left, asking Lizzie to call her the next day, so they could arrange to meet again.

Alone, Lizzie had a terrible sense of dread about seeing Stuart. She was worried he would be able to tell something had happened, or he might find some of the papers and leaflets, no matter how well she tried to hide them. And so she sent him a text, told him she wasn't feeling well, that she was going to bed early and so not to visit. He responded quickly and repeatedly, asking what exactly the illness was, what the symptoms were, what had she been eating or drinking, and why he shouldn't come over regardless. Eventually, Lizzie sent a message saying she was going to bed and would send him a message the next day, then she abruptly logged out of WhatsApp and put her phone away.

She decided to go for a walk, just to one of the benches overlooking the estuary, a short distance from her front door. She put on her jacket and left the flat. The sky was grey, the tide was out, and there was a freshness to the air that made Lizzie think it might rain. But it didn't matter. She just needed to be outside for a moment. She sat on the bench, hands in her pockets, staring at the view without taking it in. She wondered what she should do, how to fix everything, how to keep everyone happy. Was it even possible to keep everyone happy with such toxic relations between Stuart and her family and friends?

She mulled over everything the police officer had told her about Stuart about what he had done to those other girls, so similar to what she was experiencing with him. She wondered if that was where their relationship would end up if he did move in. Would she be pressured to delete her social media accounts, to let him check her phone each day, and hand over her salary each month.

She heard a man's voice calling out a name, and then a dog was jumping up at her, a Border Collie, licking her face, so happy, delighted, to meet her.

'Oh, my lord I am so sorry, miss,' the man said, rushing towards her as quickly as he could, an elderly gentleman in casual clothes, wearing a cap, a lead in his hand. 'Casper. Casper! You stop that.'

Surprised at first, Lizzie quickly found great comfort in the dog's enormous affection and pulled her hands from her pockets to stroke him. 'He's absolutely fine,' she said, 'honestly.'

The man, wheezing slightly, quickly got his dog back on his lead and then sat next to Lizzie to catch his breath. 'He's very picky,' he said. 'He doesn't run up to just anyone.'

'Well, I am very flattered,' she said, ruffling the fur on Casper's head. 'He's absolutely beautiful. How old is he?'

'He's almost three,' the man replied. 'A present from my brother. He thought it might help if I had some company, with lockdown and everything. And, you know, he's been an absolute lifesaver. I honestly mean that. This little chap, he just means the world to me now. Gave me a reason to get out of bed every day when we were all stuck at home.'

'I know what you mean. I live alone too. Perhaps I should have thought about getting a dog.'

The man's expression changed, and he suddenly looked concerned. 'Oh goodness, that's so rude of me,' he said. Then he held out his hand. 'I forgot my manners. I'm Colin.'

Lizzie smiled and shook his hand. 'I'm Lizzie. It's very nice to meet you, Colin. And Casper.'

317

They both rested back onto the bench and took in the view. 'It's been a terrible few years, hasn't it?' Colin said. 'I think sometimes, it's like we've got collective amnesia. Like we've all chosen to forget just how bad it was. The isolation, the rules, all those poor people who died. It still feels strange for me, being out and about, not wearing a mask. This, right now, just being able to sit on a park bench next to someone, and chat to them. It all feels very strange.'

Lizzie petted the Collie again. 'You say your brother gave you Casper?'

'Oh yes. About six months into lockdown. He could tell I was struggling. You see, my wife passed away in 2017, and we were never blessed with children. But living alone was never a problem before, because I was always out and about, seeing my friends or my brothers and sisters, nieces and nephews. We're a big family, and most of them live locally. But then we were ordered to stay at home, and everything was different. So, one day, there was a knock at the door. I thought it was my supermarket delivery. But there was my brother and my sister-in-law, both wearing masks, stood a few metres back from the front door, with this little fellow, just a puppy at the time, in a cardboard box, on my doormat. And they didn't even need to say anything. I just knew, straight away, that he was mine. And I know this sounds daft, but I just started crying. I was so happy. I was like a kid at Christmas.'

'I don't think that sounds daft at all. Are you all close, you and your siblings?'

'Yes. I'm very lucky like that. We all get along. But it's more than that. We all like each other. And that's a real blessing, in a family, isn't it? Just liking each other.' He paused for a moment, then cocked his head slightly to one side. 'You?'

Instantly, Lizzie began to gush about her family, of how close they were, how lucky she was to have them. She spoke of how proud she was of each of them, and how they had all helped her over the years with great advice or support. But then, suddenly, she stopped speaking, all her words were gone. She remembered the letters she had written, and the great distance that now existed between her and her siblings.

'Is everything alright?' Colin asked.

318

Lizzie frowned, and momentarily dipped her face, as she realised what she had lost. She looked at Colin, who seemed such a sweet man, and she sighed. 'I've had a bad few weeks,' she said. 'To be honest, I'm a bit stuck. I have to make a decision, but I am really struggling. Sorry, I know this isn't any of your concern. But that's the whole reason I came to sit here. I just needed to have a think.'

'Well, that explains it,' Colin said, and Lizzie looked at him quizzically. 'Why Casper chose you,' he continued. 'You may not believe this, but he's a very perceptive animal. He can tell when someone needs a bit of love. That's why he ran up to you.'

Lizzie grinned, and stroked Casper's silky ears, his happy eyes fixed on her, his paw on her knee. 'Well, thank you Casper,' she said.

Colin patted her on the arm. 'Would you mind taking a bit of advice, from a silly old man?'

'Right now, I would love nothing more.'

Colin's expression changed, and Lizzie could see a little sadness etched in the corners of his eyes, the lines of a man who had known great sorrow. 'In my experience,' he said, 'when we are stuck with a difficult choice, the truth is, it isn't the choice that's difficult. Because most of the time, we already know what we should do. The difficult bit is convincing ourselves to make that change. Because that's the bit that we know is going to hurt. It's not the choice, it's the change.'

Lizzie didn't reply, not straight away. She knew Colin's words carried so much truth, because everything in her head, every single sensible, logical, factual thought in her head, was telling her that Stuart had to go, that she would lose everything she loved and cared for if he stayed. But she knew it was that last bit that was going to hurt so much: ending it.

They stayed on that bench for another hour, chatting about other things, happier things, and Colin shared fun stories of his family. As Lizzie listened, and sometimes laughed, she knew she was a little envious of him. To be in his seventies, and to still be so close to his brothers and sisters, to still enjoy their company almost every day. That, she thought, was such a blessing, and that is what Lizzie wanted too. To be an old woman, still throwing dinner parties for her siblings.

CHAPTER 62

Tyler had grown accustomed to the villa being noisy and filled with people; the busyness of having guests, using the pool, singing drunkenly late into the evening or asking for directions to somewhere or other. But he'd had to plan some downtime into his booking schedule, to close the villa for a few weeks, so he could return to the UK for Charlie and Alan's wedding. He was stood with a beer in his hand, alone in the courtyard, shirtless, his long blond hair moving slightly in the cool evening breeze, and he realised he did not like the peace and quiet at all.

Over the previous few years, he had transformed it from a neat and pleasant outside space to a beautiful private retreat, with bougainvillea tumbling over every wall, and lemon trees planted strategically to shield the pool from prying eyes. There was now a small bar area, an elevated deck for sunbathing, a hot tub, and plenty of hidden lighting to give the area a magical feel in the evenings. He had refurbished the inside of the villa too, with each bedroom now offering facilities more suitable for paying guests. The large kitchen had also been converted into a self-service breakfast area. He had taken great pride in his work, and an enormous amount of enjoyment in living his life away from the city of Southend-on-Sea.

He walked around the pool and took a seat at the bar. For a moment, he allowed himself the luxury of remembering the years he had spent working his way around Europe, all the places he had temporarily called home, and the people he had temporarily called friends. He knew how fortunate he had been, ending his travels when he did. If he had left it much later, he would have suffered the consequences of Brexit, and found himself living a half-life, travelling in equal parts between his happy sunny life in Maspalomas and his unhappy existence back in the UK.

'May I come in?' Charlie's voice echoed through the courtyard.

'Of course,' Tyler replied, laughter in his voice, so pleased to have a visitor. 'It's your fucking villa.'

'Yes, but are you naked?'

'I am *half* naked,' Tyler replied. 'I'm telling you no more than that. You'll just have to take your chances.'

Charlie appeared cautiously, his hand partially covering his eyes. 'I never quite know what to expect,' he said. He removed his hand and saw that his brother was fully clothed from the waist down, in a pair of white linen trousers and sandals. 'Well, you do like to show off that six-pack.'

'Come on. Beer,' Tyler said and gestured for his brother to join him. He swiftly manoeuvred to the outdoor refrigerator under the bar and produced another bottle of beer, which, with expert speed, he had de-capped by the time Charlie joined him.

'The last time I was here, there were boobs and willies flapping about all over the place,' Charlie said as he took his seat. 'I didn't know where to look.'

Tyler handed him his bottle. 'Those boobs and willies belonged to paying guests. So please show a bit more respect to those boobs and willies.'

Charlie laughed and held his bottle up slightly. 'To willies.'

Tyler laughed. 'To willies *and* boobs.' They clinked their bottles in a toast.

'It really is lovely here,' Charlie said. 'It's like you've created this little private wonderland where people can come, and relax, and just be themselves. And that's truly beautiful.'

'It is a bit strange, though, the villa being empty like this,' Tyler said. 'I used to love it when I first came here, the peace and quiet, the solitude. But now, it just feels wrong. It feels like this place should be filled with noise and people, the smell of food, music playing, people jumping in the pool at midnight.'

Charlie sipped his beer but did not reply, and Tyler had the strangest sensation his brother hadn't heard a single word he'd said. 'So,' he continued, and gently nudged his knee against Charlie's, just to make sure he was listening, 'three days until the big day. You all packed?'

'All packed,' he said, 'suits and everything.' And then he added; 'I never had an attachment to this place.' He said it quizzically, as though only having just realised it himself, and the comment left Tyler feeling puzzled, not entirely sure where the conversation was going.

'It was my first home, after Jason died. And I knew it was lovely. I absolutely knew it was lovely. But it never felt like home. It just felt like somewhere I was going to live, until I found where I was really supposed to be.'

Tyler had been expecting a few moments of silly banter before they left for dinner, and was not sure what to say in response, and so he simply asked; 'Everything OK, Charlie?'

His brother's demeanour changed, the smile suddenly gone, replaced with a more pensive expression. 'I've not been sleeping that well,' he said, quietly.

Tyler did not like this for Charlie, that he appeared so worried, so introspective, just days before what should be the happiest day of his life. 'It's OK to have wedding jitters,' he said, and then he reached across and firmly held Charlie's hand, and that made Charlie look at him, and really focus on him. 'It's going to be a great day,' Tyler said, reassuringly. And with that, it was as if Charlie snapped back into the room.

'Yes, it will be,' he replied, smiling. He paused for a moment, gathering his thoughts, and then he said. 'Look, Tyler, I need to tell you this. Alan and I have had some tough conversations over the past week, and we've both written new wills. It's a bit of a story that I won't go into, but I need to explain to you about a few decisions I've made.'

Tyler just sat and listened and continued to feel somewhat bemused by the strange conversation.

'I'm leaving the business to Vicki, Billy and Lizzie,' Charlie said. 'The apartments, I mean. The villa was never part of the business. It's a separate enterprise, so I've made separate arrangements for this place.'

'Oh,' Tyler said, feeling some disappointing news was about to be shared. 'Are you selling up?'

Charlie shook his head. 'Oh, no,' he replied. 'I'm signing it over to you. Now. You've made a home here, Tyler, and you made this a successful business. It should be yours.'

Shocked, Tyler almost fell off his bar stool, but quickly, Charlie grabbed his arm and managed to help manoeuvre him back onto his seat. 'What?' Tyler asked, a little dazed by Charlie's announcement. 'What?'

322

'Tyler, for whatever reason, and perhaps for the same reasons as me, you have decided to make Maspalomas your home,' Charlie said. 'Single-handed, you turned the villa into a thriving business, and I want it to be yours. Please just say yes.'

Tyler, still shocked, raised his hands, his mouth opening and closing, but no words coming out. 'That's too much,' he eventually managed to blurt out. 'Charlie, that's too much.'

'Well,' Charlie replied, 'I recall saying to you many, many years ago, in this family, we don't do things by half.'

And there it was. That memory. On one of the saddest days of Charlie's life, he swept a little boy into his arms and embraced him as his brother. And Tyler had never forgotten that moment.

'It… it just feels…,' Tyler said, trying to articulate his feelings but still too stunned to manage full sentences.

'Tyler, I'm about to start the rest of my life. And, without wishing to sound crass, I'm not going to want for anything. Alan's made that very clear. I want to keep running the apartments because, ultimately, I don't want to give up work. Not unless I have to. But I really don't have anything to do with the villa anymore, and I would love to just hand it over to you.'

Charlie could see Tyler was still unsure, a little overwhelmed by the offer, so he decided to appeal to his brother's business head. 'You've taken so much pride in this place. You've been a caretaker, and manager, and cleaner, and gardener, and host. You've done all the bookings, and marketing, all the customer service. And, if you had done that as an employee, well, you would have been paid a lot of money each month. So, I basically owe you five years' salary. This is just me offering appropriate remuneration for five years of hard work.'

'But I haven't done all of this for free. You've given me a share of the profits, and I live here rent-free. I have a very comfortable life.'

'Tyler, it just feels like this is the right thing to do, and the right time to do it.'

Tyler took a deep breath. For a moment, he closed his eyes, to focus on the conversation and put his thoughts and feelings into a sensible order. He could clearly envisage what the years ahead might hold if he said yes. He could imagine regular lunches with Charlie at the Yumbo Centre, and coffee mornings with Peggy, and late-night wine with Martin and Blanche, and dinner parties at Alan's house, and visits from other members of the family, and perhaps the occasional romance. And he realised that he absolutely loved the thought of every second of it.

However, the offer was just too much, too generous, and his mind was overflowing with so many different and conflicting opinions and responses. But in the middle of all that noise, he suddenly felt a sense of calm. He knew how Charlie's mind worked, how neat and tidy he needed everything to be. And for some reason, handing the villa over to Tyler was a way for Charlie to tidy up that part of his life.

'I've never told you this, Charlie,' he said, and opened his eyes again. 'I really loved my travels around Europe. All of it. But when I was living in Athens, for some reason, it was the one city I was never able to connect with. For months, I couldn't settle in a job, and I struggled to find people to hang around with. I'm used to being alone. I like my own company. But Athens was the first place where I felt lonely.

'One afternoon, I was sat at a table outside a cafe, drinking an americano and looking through some local job listings. And a song came on the radio, one of Auntie Susan's favourites, *Where You Lead I Will Follow*. And I instantly realised it was time to go home. Only, it wasn't Southend calling. It was here. It was the villa, and all my silly jobs, sweeping the floor at 'Hair by Martin' and fixing the water fountains at Peggy's caravan park and doing the occasional shift at one of Blanche's bars. And the late evenings, sat with you and Alan and the gang at Ricky's, enjoying the cabaret.

'And I would very much love to make it my home, for good. But I cannot just *take* it from you, Charlie. I honestly can't. So how about this? You get it valued, properly valued, and then take off whatever salary you think I am owed, and I will pay you the rest out of the money I've got saved up from the sale of The Lodge.'

Charlie appeared content they had reached a sensible compromise. 'Fine, deal,' he said. 'Right, you need to get a shirt on for dinner,' Charlie said.

'Oh yeah, my fifth anniversary.' Tyler began to walk toward the villa.

324

'It's rushed by, hasn't it? Five years since you finished your travels around Europe and moved here permanently.'

'Who's going to be there?' Tyler asked, disappearing through the doors into his bedroom.

Charlie shrugged casually. 'Usual gang. Me, you and Alan, Peggy, Blanche and Martin,' he said, his voice carrying through the warm night air. 'Oh, and Alan's daughter Jill. You'll like her, I think. A bit frosty at times, but perfectly nice. Good sense of humour when she gets going.'

'And how old is she?'

Charlie sniggered. 'Far too old for you.'

'Well, how old's that?'

'She's exactly your age,' Charlie replied, and began to laugh.

Tyler poked his head around the door and pretended to grimace at Charlie. 'Oy!' he said. 'You're making me sound like a cliché.'

'You are,' Charlie said, laughing. 'Everyone you date is at least 10 years younger than you.'

'I'm almost certain that's not true,' Tyler replied, and disappeared back into his bedroom.

'Fine, but I don't want you hitting on Jill just to make a point,' Charlie said.

'I'm not promising anything,' Tyler replied, and as he got dressed, he thought about Charlie's offer, the villa, and he had a strong sense that something was wrong, that there was something Charlie wasn't telling him. He wondered what it was, and why his brother appeared to have a sudden need to get his affairs in order.

CHAPTER 63

Vicki stood at her kitchen window, watching Blake running around in her small back garden, a little boy with red hair and bright blue eyes, wielding a cardboard tube as a lightsabre as he fought an imaginary group of stormtroopers. She loved to watch him play, his amazing ability to conjure up almost any scenario in his mind and then completely lose himself in it.

'We watched Star Wars last night,' Vicki said. 'He thinks he's Luke Skywalker now.'

Lizzie, a hot mug of tea clasped in her hands, joined her at the window. 'Oh, my lord, don't tell Tyler that. Once he starts talking about Star Wars, you won't be able to shut him up.'

Blake saw them both looking at him through the window, and rather than wave, he performed a number of dramatic actions with his cardboard tube. He ran off and hid behind the cabin, before pouncing back onto the lawn, a surprise ambush against his invisible adversaries.

'Do you know how much longer you have him for?' Lizzie asked.

'This weekend,' Vicki replied, attempting to sound upbeat, even though the thought of Blake leaving still hurt so much. 'They're a nice couple. Young. Sporty. Out on their bikes all the time. No other kids. I think he's going to be very happy with them. They've met him quite a few times now. They came one evening and did his bedtime routine with me. And I've taken him for lunch at their house in Colchester. And this Saturday, they'll be collecting him.'

'And is that the last time you will see him?'

'No. The adoption team is keen I maintain contact with him, so he doesn't feel rejected. But I imagine, at some point in the future, it might feel appropriate to draw a line under it. Let him just be their son.'

Lizzie put her mug down and stroked Vicki's arm. 'I am really sorry. I honestly thought he would be staying with you. I think you're being very brave.'

'I have to. I've had to be really positive about the adoption for Blake to make it sound really exciting and wonderful for him. And, I guess, that's exactly what it is. It is a good thing. I just let my guard down, that's all. Fell in love with a little boy who wasn't mine.' She placed her hand over Lizzie's and gave it a little squeeze. 'And you?' she asked. 'How are you coping?'

'I'm okay,' Lizzie replied, a little despondently. 'I still have my moments, and there are times when I just panic and wonder if I did the right thing. But I have the injunction now, and I have mostly been able to accept that I won't be seeing Stuart again.' Then her tone changed, and there was suddenly a terseness in her voice. 'I just don't understand how it happened. How I let him take so much control, to a point that I was writing shitty letters to my own family and blocking my best friend on social media.'

Vicki recognised that tone, and the expression on her sister's face, because she had lived it herself, when she had left Jack's father. She remembered the weeks that followed, whole days lost to a swirl of conflicting emotions, days that had been so confusing that she often wasn't certain how she truly felt. There had been the fear that she may have acted rashly, and sometimes the guilt at leaving Nate homeless. There was the grief at the loss of a relationship with a man she had loved, but also, there had been so much anger, as she had finally been able to see everything Nate had cost her.

She knew the weeks and months ahead would be dangerous times for Lizzie, because as resolute as her sister appeared to be in that moment, Vicki knew all too well there would be many times when Lizzie would want nothing else but to see Stuart again. Her little sister would be tempted to reach out, test the waters, to see if there was anything that could be used to build a new relationship with him, under the illusion that he could change.

'I finally plucked up the courage to speak to Billy and Emma,' Lizzie said. 'I was just so mortified. That horrible dinner party. That letter I sent them. But they were lovely. Emma gave me a big hug, and then we just sat there crying.'

Vicki chuckled. 'Lizzie, no one blames you for this. We were all just worried for you. Frightened, to be honest. We could all see Stuart for exactly what he was, what he was doing. We're all just so relieved you're safe now.'

Lizzie smiled, but only for a moment, and then sipped her tea, leaving Vicki with a terrible feeling that she didn't believe her, that on some level Lizzie felt the rest of the family was secretly angry with her and thought she had brought the situation on herself. Vicki remembered feeling like that too.

'I spoke to your mum,' Vicki said. 'I think I've managed to persuade her not to take a hit out on him.'

'That's the last thing I need right now.'

'But I haven't spoken to Charlie or Tyler. I didn't know if they knew anything about this?'

Lizzie shook her head. 'Tyler knew Stuart had upset me a few times, but he doesn't know anything more than that. And I've not mentioned anything to Charlie. It didn't feel right, what with the wedding coming up. I asked Mum and Billy to do the same.'

Blake ran by the window, yelling at the top of his voice that he was going to destroy the Death Star, and then he chased up the garden, and stood swinging his cardboard tube from side to side, making a whooshing sound with his mouth. Behind him, covering the fence panels, was a beautiful rose bush, overflowing with bright pink flowers. Lizzie had never seen it in full bloom before, and asked Vicki how long it had taken to grow.

'Actually, it was Tyler who planted it for me,' Vicki replied. 'It's one of mum's. He transplanted it from her garden at The Lodge, just before we sold it. For years, I didn't have much success with it. I mean, it grew, and I managed to train it across the fence. But flowers were few and far between, and whenever I did get flowers, they never really looked particularly healthy. Nothing like the way they blossomed in mum's garden. But Tyler kept telling me to keep the faith, look after it, that it might just be the stress of being moved from one location to another.

'And then, about a year into the pandemic, I was stuck at home on my own. Jack was up in Manchester, and I was only seeing people every now and again. Everyone was social distancing, no one was hugging. We were all wearing masks. And I just had a bit of a wobble. I panicked, thinking that was the new normal and it was always going to be like that. We'd never have a family barbecue again. I'd never go to the cinema. We'd all basically be stuck at home, on our own, forever.

'And I was stood here, at my kitchen window, looking at my back garden, which was completely covered in snow, and I was having a panic attack. A real proper panic attack. But then I noticed there was this one tiny bit of colour, this little flash of pink. And I had no idea what it was. So, I put on my boots and went to see. And there was a single rose, blossoming, in the middle of all that snow. A healthy, beautiful pink rose. On a freezing winter's day, just one flower. And somehow, it just reassured me, that life would get back to normal and that we would all be able to see each other again.'

There was a brief lull in the conversation, and then Lizzie picked up her mug and went to sit at the kitchen table. 'There's something I need to talk to you about,' she said. 'I just need your opinion on something.'

Vicki joined her at the table. 'OK,' she said, brightly, happy to offer her sister a bit of advice.

'Carol gave me a letter,' Lizzie said.

Those words immediately concerned Vicki, because she had never heard Lizzie refer to Carol by name. She had been raised as Carol's daughter and had always, always referred to her as 'Mum'. She wondered if the two had fallen out, and it was a passive-aggressive way for Lizzie to show her annoyance at whatever it was that Carol had done.

'Carol?' Vicki enquired.

'Well… Mum,' Lizzie said. 'But in this context, just this once. Carol.'

Bemused, Vicki shrugged. 'OK,' she said. 'What letter?'

Lizzie paused before answering, then said; 'It's from Mum. Susan, I mean. She wrote it just after I was born, a couple of days before she died. She asked Carol to keep it until I was 23.'

'Mum wrote you a letter?' That, in itself, did not surprise Vicki. Her mother had left a number of letters, but they had all been delivered as part of the estate being settled. 'Why 23?'

'I don't know. But Carol said it was made really clear to her that I had to be 23. So, she gave it to me back in March, on my birthday, but I just… I just haven't had the courage to open it yet. And with everything

329

that was going on with Stuart. I just put it into a drawer and left it there. I'm a bit anxious about it, to be honest. I'm not sure what to expect.'

Vicki chuckled. 'Lizzie, Mum won't have written anything bad, I can promise you that.'

'I know, I know. But everything I know about Mum, I know from all of you. This is the only time I've actually had something from her directly to me. And I... well... I wondered... I would like to open it when we were all together. Perhaps after Charlie and Alan's wedding? We'll be down in Kent for a few days. Perhaps we could open it then, read it together?'

Vicki wasn't sure that was the right thing to do. It felt as though they might all be intruding on something private her mother had written all those years ago. 'Oh, Lizzie, sweetheart, I don't know. It feels like that would be breaking Mum's trust. She wrote the letter for you.'

'Yes, but you're all going to see it anyway, at some point. Please, Vicki. I really want to enjoy hearing Mum's words, and I'm only really going to feel relaxed enough to enjoy it if you are all there with me.'

Still unsure, Vicki sighed. 'Look, have a think about it and if by the time we get to Charlie's wedding, you still haven't opened it, then I guess it would be OK for us all to do it together. But if you want to read it on your own, or with us, either is fine. We'll be there for you regardless.'

Lizzie was obviously relieved, and quite content with her sister's suggestion. But although Vicki mostly believed the advice she had given her sister, in her mind she had already begun to speculate about the content of their mother's letter. The Fletcher family appeared to have an abundance of secrets, and she wondered if there might be one more that their mother wanted to reveal.

CHAPTER 64

It was raining on Charlie's wedding day, but he didn't mind at all. Living on a hot, dry Spanish island, he often missed the seasons, and in particular, he missed the rain. The weather made no difference to the ceremony or reception, as the entire event was being held inside. He and Alan had already decided not to take any chances with a British summer and so had chosen against an outdoor wedding or a marquee.

Charlie, in navy cotton pyjamas, was sat in a beautifully carved wooden four-poster bed, having spent the night alone in the grand wedding suite, a room filled with plush fabrics, panelled walls and elegant furniture. He and Alan had bowed to tradition and spent the night apart.

He was eating his breakfast from a silver tray, and was attempting to enjoy the view of the gloriously dark skies outside his window. In a typically thoughtful gesture, Alan had alerted the kitchen that Charlie was always an early riser, and so at 7am on the dot, his favourite breakfast was delivered to the suite: poached eggs with buttered granary toast, a side of marmite in a small ramekin, a large pot of tea, and a jug of skimmed milk. Alan had included a single red rose from the grounds.

As he finished his breakfast, he pushed the tray to the empty side of the bed and climbed from under the covers. He walked in his pyjamas to the large window overlooking the gardens and watched the trees bending from side to side as the wind whipped around the grounds, stealing petals from the flower beds and swirling them around in the air.

He had wanted to enjoy the day, to relish every second of it, the day when he and Alan were finally able to get married. But he was anxious about the days and weeks ahead, with so many things now uncertain, things that could define the rest of his life far more than his marriage to Alan. And he hated being back in the country. There were so many things, so many memories, that he had left behind, all those years ago, things he never wanted to think about, ever again.

But whenever he was in England, it all came flooding back to him, filling him with a clawing sense of panic. His reoccurring dream had become persistent, haunting him almost every night; Charlie stood in the

331

rain, in his best suit, holding a small bunch of flowers, decayed and crumbling in his hand. In front of him, a dark and empty building, and behind him, a noise, someone breathing cold air onto his neck, and whispering or hissing something, but too quietly to be understood.

Charlie was never able to walk or run away. In every dream, he was unable to move his feet, and he was always too terrified to turn his head, to see who, or what, was behind him. But each morning, as he roused and passed through that otherworldly place, halfway between sleep and consciousness, he knew who it was, the frightening presence stood behind him, and he understood why their visits were so regular, so angry.

He closed his eyes, rested his head against the cold glass of the window, and tried to lose himself in the happy memories of the previous day, when the Fletcher family had assembled at Alan's manor house, stood grandly in the middle of the Kent countryside. Carol had arrived with Lizzie, whilst Billy and Emma had travelled with Tyler. Vicki and Jack had brought Debbie and Kim. And it was only as each group had arrived, open-mouthed and eyes wide, that it had occurred to Charlie that he had never properly explained to any of them just how wealthy his husband-to-be was.

Clearly, each had their own idea of it, from small details Charlie had shared over the years, and their holidays at Alan's large, modern house on Gran Canaria with its perfect views of the Atlantic Ocean from the top floor. And they all knew Alan had a house in Kent because he would occasionally reference it in conversation, but only ever in passing.

None of them had been expecting that his English residence would be a listed building, dating back to the seventeenth century, with more than 20 rooms including eight-bedroom suites, and two small cottages, set in more than six acres of perfectly tended gardens. And Charlie had taken some pleasure in their reactions, each a little overwhelmed by the sudden realisation that, by marrying Alan, Charlie was about to become a multimillionaire.

Kieran, Alan's son, ran the house as an exclusive hotel, retreat and wedding venue. And for that weekend, the couple getting married were the owner and his partner. It had not been lost on Charlie that Kieran had changed the name of the manor's Wi-Fi to *Charlie46*, and the password to *Alan58*. And he wondered if this had been done with good humour, or if it was a passive-aggressive gesture, proof that despite the many and significant concessions Charlie had made to keep the peace, Alan's children remained unhappy at their father's decision to remarry. But it was not of great concern to Charlie that day, and he assumed Alan would have any conversations with his children that he felt were necessary.

A knock at the door focused Charlie's thoughts back into the room. He slipped on his dressing gown, hanging over the footboard, and asked who was at his door, worried Alan was going to risk bad luck by seeing Charlie before the wedding.

'Uncle Charlie, have you got a minute?'

Charlie opened the door and his nephew was stood on the other side, dressed casually, waiting for permission to enter.

'Oh, of course,' Charlie replied cheerfully. He closed the door behind Jack, and they sat down, two leather bound armchairs next to each other, and a little awkwardly, Jack said, 'This might sound a bit odd, but I was lying in bed this morning. And I really needed to ask you, if you were thinking about Uncle Jason at all?'

'Oh,' Charlie gasped, at the unexpected question.

'I didn't mean to upset you.'

'No, no, not at all. I'm just surprised that you asked. Do you remember Jason?'

'Of course,' Jack replied. 'The thing is, when he died, I remember something Mum said to me. She said you were always going to be sad. It just wouldn't always be obvious. And I was lying in bed this morning, worried that you might have felt sad, secretly, and I just wanted to check that you were OK.'

Charlie was a little overwhelmed by Jack's comment. Of all the family, his nephew was the one he felt he knew the least, because there was so much of his life that Charlie had missed. There had been all the years that Jack had spent in foster care and then, just as Vicki had regained custody and brought him home, Charlie's life had fallen to pieces, and he had fled to his Spanish island to hide himself away.

Vicki and Jack had holidayed at Charlie's villa each year, and so Charlie had seen Jack grow from a child to a teenager and then a young man. But their interactions had never been significant, and he felt as though he was almost underserving of his nephew's concern. But a question had been asked, and Charlie felt it might be a nice way to grow their relationship by giving Jack an honest answer.

'I think of Jason every day,' he said. 'One way or another, he's always there, in my head. It took a long time, though, Jack. Years and years, before I could think about him without it hurting. But now, he's a happy part of my life. I think about him, I talk about him. Sometimes, when I'm alone, I talk *to* him. I just feel very lucky to have had all those years with him. So, yes, I have been thinking about him. But I'm not sad. Those memories make me happy.'

Jack seemed content with Charlie's answer, but there was something else that was on his mind, something he had been wanting to talk to Charlie about for a long time, and he simply hadn't been able to find a moment when they were both alone together. 'Since we're talking,' he began, cautiously, 'may I also ask you about my dad?'

Nate was not a good topic for Charlie, and he immediately felt himself tense up, as he wondered what sort of information his nephew wanted to know. Jack had inherited most of his looks from the Fletcher family, particularly his dark colourings. But occasionally, Charlie would catch him at a certain angle, perhaps just out of the corner of his eye, and it unnerved him, because in those fleeting moments, all he could see was Jack's father. 'I'm not the best person to speak to about him.'

'Oh, I know you didn't like him,' Jack said, but not rudely or accusingly, just as a statement of fact. 'I don't think anyone in the family has anything good to say about him. Mum won't talk about him. Neither will Debbie and Kim.'

Charlie found the whole conversation unnerving. It was not a topic he wanted to be involved in, and so he stood and began to busy himself around the room, moving his breakfast tray onto the serving trolly, and tidying the bed. He hoped if it looked as though he was distracted, the conversation might reach a natural conclusion. But undeterred, Jack continued to speak.

334

'I think I was about eight, the last time I saw him. And to be honest, I only saw him a few times before that. I don't think he was ever that interested in being a dad. Or that interested in me.'

Charlie suddenly felt rather wretched. The thought of Jack as a little boy, so easily discarded and ignored by his selfish father, made Charlie feel unkind for trying to avoid the topic. Jack was a young man, smart and hardworking, reaching out for some details, something to colour in the patchy image he had of his dad. And he had come to the conclusion that his Uncle Charlie was the only person in the family who might help.

'Look, I know he was a bit of a shady character,' Jack continued. 'But I just want to know more about him. And why he might have run off the way he did.'

After pausing for thought, to gather together what he could tell Jack and what he could not, Charlie retook his seat. 'How honest do you want me to be?

Without pausing, Jack replied, 'Completely. Honestly, Uncle Charlie. I'm not looking for a rose-tinted version of what happened. I just want someone to tell me the truth. I'm 22 years old, a grown man, a university graduate. I'm not a kid anymore. And I just want someone to tell me the truth about my dad.'

Charlie, nervous and unsure, clasped his hands together. 'Your mum will be very cross with me.'

'If it comes to that, I'll talk with Mum. She's had plenty of opportunities to tell me about Dad, but she just won't. She closes the conversation down like it's none of my business. But it is my business. And what if he shows up one day and says he wants to get to know me? Isn't it better I know exactly what I might be getting myself into?'

Charlie had to concede Jack had made a good point, even if it were somewhat redundant. He felt strongly that his nephew had a right to know the truth about Nate, but he also knew Vicki would be furious he had taken it upon himself to discuss the matter without her permission. And so, he had to accept he would simply have to face her ire at whatever point she found out.

'Jack, I would love to tell you that your dad was a complex man, that he was troubled or battled personal demons that led him down a difficult path. But that would be a lie. The truth is, Nate was lazy, selfish and entitled. He always put himself first. Before you. Before Vicki. He simply didn't care that the way he led his life had truly awful repercussions on the people around him.'

Over the next few minutes, Charlie filled in the gaps for his nephew. He spoke about the night-time police raids at The Lodge that led to Vicki, Nate and Jack moving out. He explained about the drugs and stolen goods found during further police raids at Vicki's flat. He detailed the genuine danger social services believed Jack was in, living within such a criminal environment, and the eventual decision to take him into care. But then he described the courage Vicki had shown to walk away from Nate, from everything, and to fight for the custody of her son as a single parent, knowing it was only way she stood a chance of getting him back.

Throughout, Jack remained silent, occasionally nodding or making a noise in his throat that indicated he agreed with something his uncle had said. And there was no moment when Charlie felt he had revealed anything which had truly shocked Jack. It was as though his nephew already knew the truth about his father would be dark, he just had not been certain *how* dark.

'Why do you think he ran away?' Jack asked, as Charlie's tale came to a conclusion.

'Your father had a tendency to make enemies out of friends. And when most of your friends are criminals, that's not a clever way to live your life. I would imagine he got on the wrong side of the wrong person, and simply had to disappear.'

'Do you remember the last time you saw him?'

Charlie did not reply immediately. His expression darkened, and it seemed to Jack that his uncle was lost in an unpleasant memory. 'I do,' Charlie replied. 'I remember it was pouring with rain, and he just appeared, at the house. Started telling me all these stories, about how he and your mum were going to get back together again. All lies, of course. Vicki had moved on, properly moved on. There was no way she was going to risk your custody. But I think he was just desperate, and he saw your mum as... well... his meal ticket.'

'What did you say to him?' Jack asked.

336

Charlie paused for a moment, as though concerned that his answer might upset Jack. And then he said, 'I made it clear his relationship with Vicki was over, and she wasn't going to do anything that might risk losing custody of you. And I told him that I didn't want to see his face again. Ever.'

'And he left?'

'I didn't speak to him ever again.'

The room fell silent, save for the gentle howl of the wind around the manor. Charlie did not like the way he had finished his story, and so added, 'Jack, whenever you think of that time in your life, and all of those events, please take into account that your mother was only 17 when she met your father. He was already 30 years old, and he was very experienced in normalising behaviour that Vicki should never have had to put up with. He lied to her, cheated on her, stole from her, blamed everyone else for things that were completely his fault. It took a lot for your mum to pick herself up after all of that, and finally walk away. But she did. I hope you remember that.'

Jack had learned more about his father in the previous few minutes than he had over his entire life. So much made sense now, especially why his mother had been urging him to delete Nate's other children as friends on Facebook. 'I don't blame Mum for any of it,' he said. 'Honestly, I don't. I'm just grateful that I finally know what happened. Thank you for telling me the truth, at last.'

They stood and embraced and then Jack, suffused with a sense of contentment that his uncle had provided what he had come for, returned to his room. Charlie remained, alone, looking through the windows at the rainswept gardens. And he wondered if he would ever have the courage to share with his nephew the parts of the story he had left out.

CHAPTER 65

As more than a hundred guests arrived at the manor for Charlie and Alan's wedding, the rain grew heavier, and it was quite a spectacle as a team of valets swept across the drive wearing deep blue cloaks and holding large black umbrellas aloft, to protect the guests from the storm. But the weather did not dampen anyone's spirits. Instead, it seemed to invigorate the wedding, giving all the guests something exciting to speak about as they enjoyed a glass of champagne and shared stories of their journeys through the narrow, rainswept roads of the Kent countryside.

Debbie and Kim felt a little out of sorts with the rest of the guests, all of whom seemed glamourous and moneyed, and so they had sought refuge at the bar where they had been quickly recognised by the group from Gran Canaria and were soon immersed in all sorts of conversations about the Fletcher family.

Eventually, all the guests were led to the great hall, where Alan and Kieran, neatly dressed in matching burgundy suits, were introduced to each of them. The hall had been simply decorated with summer flowers, all from the grounds, and there were rows of seats filling most of the room, a wide aisle through the middle. There was a raised section at the front for the wedding service, and an area to the side where a small live band was playing gentle ballads from the seventies.

Beyond the hall, in the private areas kept aside for the wedding party itself, the Fletcher family was together, excitedly putting the finishing touches to their wedding outfits, all dressed in various hues of navy blue. Charlie and Carol, in matching three-piece suits, stood at the edge of the room, contentedly watching the family, all so happy and relaxed with each other, and for a few moments, Charlie felt at ease with everything. He knew that whatever happened over the coming months, they would all be fine. They would have each other.

The room was littered with glasses of champagne, some full and some half empty. Everyone had been careful to only drink a little, as they knew they had an entire ceremony to get through.

338

Vicki was fussing with Jack's tie whilst Billy and Tyler were lost in a happy conversation, reliving some of their favourite moments from the years they had spent together at The Lodge. Emma was helping Lizzie with some last-minute adjustments to her hair.

Everyone had made a point of telling Lizzie how lovely she looked, in a deep blue gown with a plunging neckline. Charlie knew she had recently broken up with her boyfriend. He didn't know the details, and no one seemed particularly keen to speak about Stuart, but he had noticed how tenderly the family had treated her, how supportive they all were being, and he wondered if there was more of a story to Lizzie's heartbreak than he knew.

There was a knock at the door, and a member of hotel staff appeared. 'Just to let you know, it's two minutes, if you would like to get into position,' she said.

Immediately, and with great excitement, everyone in the room stood and began to file out of the door, but Charlie gestured for Carol to stay, and once they were alone, he said, 'There's just something I wanted to give you.' He reached into his pocket and produced a small black box. 'This is for you.'

'Oh,' Carol said, immediately feeling a little emotional. 'Charlie, you really didn't need to.' And then she quietly took the box and opened it. Inside, something familiar, from many years ago, a sapphire and diamond leaf pin brooch, sparkling and delicate, an antique passed down through Susan's family. Carol had not seen it many times, as it was not one of Susan's standards, rather it was something she had only worn on special occasions.

'This was your mum's,' Carol said, quietly.

'And before that, it belonged to Dorothy, and to her mother before that.'

Carol shook her head and closed the box. 'Charlie, it's a lovely thought, but I can't accept this. It's a family heirloom.'

'Well, that's rather the point,' he said. He took the box from Carol's hand and placed it onto the windowsill. Then, he removed the brooch, and gently pinned it to her lapel. 'We all wanted to make sure it stays in the family.'

339

Carol looked down at her lapel and fondly touched the brooch. 'Thank you, it's beautiful. I'll treasure it.'

The rain began to tap a little harder on the windows next to them, and Carol had the strangest feeling that Susan was there with her, just in that moment, trying to let her know that she approved of Charlie's gift. Carol let out a little laugh, and then tears began to fall down her cheeks. 'Oh, Charlie,' she said, 'I think I've just ruined my make-up.'

'No, you're fine,' Charlie said.

'Even so,' Carol replied, and produced a pair of black sunglasses from her pocket. 'Thank goodness we're wearing these.'

'Oh yes!' Charlie said, cheerfully, and produced a matching pair. 'I almost forgot.'

They both slipped the glasses on, and smiled at each other.

'Oh, my god, I hope this doesn't turn out to be an absolute shit show,' Carol said.

'We'll be fine,' Charlie said, and then held up his arm. 'May I?'

Carol nodded and slipped her arm through his. 'You may,' she said, and then the pair left the room.

340

CHAPTER 66

Suffering an uncharacteristic bout of nerves, Alan was stood with his son just in front of the registrar, as more than 100 guests settled into place and quietened down. The band fell silent apart from the pianist who began to play *Jesu, Joy of Man's Desiring* and everyone turned their heads to look to the back of the hall, as the Fletcher family began to enter. In pairs, they walked down the aisle slowly, in time with the music, first Tyler and Jack, and then Lizzie and Emma, and then Billy and Vicki.

Kim took out her phone and managed to grab a cheeky photograph of Jack, at the front of the procession, but was quietly scolded by Debbie. Martin, Blanche and Peggy exchanged happy smiles at the sight of Tyler, looking so dashing in his navy suit. At the front, Alan could feel himself beginning to relax at the sight of all the smiling faces before him, all of Charlie's family, people he had grown very fond of over the years. After so many postponements, his wedding day had finally arrived.

But then, suddenly, everything stopped. The music cut off, leaving the Fletchers stood still, looking around the room, as though confused as to what had happened. And then a woman's voice filled the room. 'Sorry, everyone, but this is wrong. This needs to stop.'

At first, there was confusion as all the guests looked around to see who had spoken. Alan scanned the chairs in the front row to see if his daughter had been the one to speak up. But she was the same as everyone else, looking around the room with confusion. And then all eyes fell on the singer, speaking into her microphone. 'This just isn't right.'

Alan stared at her, wondering why on earth a wedding singer had sought to stop his wedding, worried this was some sort of homophobic intervention. But then she smiled, and Alan noticed the Fletchers' confusion appeared a little forced, as though they were all just play-acting at being surprised.

'This isn't the sort of wedding where we should be playing *Bach*,' the singer continued. 'This is the sort of wedding where we should be playing something with a bit of rock and roll. Don't you agree?'

The Fletchers all cheered together, 'Yes!'

The singer then looked to the rest of the guests. 'Come on, don't you agree. We need some rock and roll.'

Some of the guests mumbled 'yes', awkward, embarrassed, and there was a gentle ripple of laughter. But then Martin sprang to his feet and threw his arms into the air. 'This is definitely a wedding that needs rock and roll.' And then Blanche and Peggy jumped and shouted 'Yes!' before howling with laughter. And then Kim and Debbie, too. And then other guests, braving the moment, stood and shouted, 'Yes', realising this was going to be anything but a dull ceremony.

'Right then,' the singer said, and she turned to her pianist. 'Mr Piano Player. Do you have something with a bit of rock and roll?'

All the guests retook their seats as the pianist pretended to think for a moment and then said, 'I think I have just the song.' He started playing the opening chords of a tune, fast and loud. The drummer and guitarist joined him, and then the singer. And with the first few words from her lips, Alan realised it was a song Charlie's mother would have loved, an old Carole King number, *I Feel the Earth Move*.

He looked back to the Fletchers, and found they were all suddenly wearing black sunglasses, and were already dancing in time with the music, and in time with each other, clicking their fingers, swaying their hips, stepping forward and backwards in perfect harmony. Realising he had been duped, Alan roared with laughter and began to clap along in time with the song, his son next to him, looking mortified.

'You'd better crack a fucking smile at some point today,' Alan said to him, grinning, so none of the guests would realise they were having cross words. And, as instructed, his son immediately forced a smile and began to clap along to the music too.

The band had reached a musical bridge, and the Fletchers continued their tightly choreographed routine, each of them having a spotlight moment at the front of the family group, with all the guests now clapping along to the music, enjoying the spectacle. And then, one at a time, each of the Fletchers span around to face the back of the hall and pointed. And there were Charlie and Carol, in matching suits, both also wearing black sunglasses and clicking their fingers in time with the music.

Some of the guests screamed and cheered and jumped to their feet, applauding. The routine continued as Charlie and Carol joined the rest of the family. Charlie kissed Carol on the cheek, then danced through the centre of the aisle, his family around him, on either side, each taking a moment to kiss him, or squeeze his shoulder. And then he was at the front, dancing along to the music, one of his mother's favourites, swinging his hips and shaking his arms with his siblings behind him, in perfect synch, and Carol behind them, just waving her arms in time with the music, having been unable to learn the routine.

As the song reached its musical crescendo, Charlie's family picked him up and elevated him onto the platform, directly next to Alan. And as the song finished, all the guests jumped to their feet and applauded, merrily laughing at the unexpected treat. Alan, a huge smile on his face, threw his arms around Charlie and held him tight. 'God, I love you, Charlie Fletcher,' he whispered into Charlie's ear.

'I love you too,' Charlie replied.

The stormy weather continued throughout the rest of the day and into the evening, but no one at the wedding seemed to notice. The reception passed without incident; the food and wine were enthusiastically consumed, the speeches were warm and funny, with even Kieran managing to find the right balance between roasting his father and welcoming Charlie into the fold. The band, who had won great affection from all the guests with their comical involvement in the Fletcher family's surprise dance routine, performed into the night, and were received with enormous enthusiasm by everyone in the hall.

Carol and Martin barely left the dance floor whilst the rest of Charlie's family mingled, danced, and caught up with each other and their friends. Alan, with great pride, introduced his new husband to his colleagues, friends and business contacts, and Charlie easily charmed them all with his knowledge of their hobbies and children.

And as the evening gradually came to an end, the valets returned the guests to their cars, and everyone else retired to their rooms, the manor fell silent. Each member of the Fletcher family wanted to get a good night's sleep as they knew they had an important task to undertake the following day: the reading of Susan's letter.

CHAPTER 67

The following day, at just before twelve, the family gathered, all casually dressed in jeans and t-shirts. A shower of rain was still visiting the manor offering a gentle layer of sound that seemed an appropriate backdrop for what was to come. After the joy and excitement of the previous day, the family's mood was a little muted, as they each wondered what Susan could possibly have written all those years ago, and why she had insisted Carol wait 23 years before giving the letter to Lizzie.

Alan tried to excuse himself, saying he had guests who had stayed the night that he needed to attend to before they departed. Charlie knew his husband simply didn't feel he deserved to be in the room, as though he would be some sort of impostor, intruding on a private family moment. But Charlie insisted Alan be there and, after much persuading, he finally agreed.

They had arranged to use the library, a large room with lots of comfortable seating and a good view of the gardens. No one had been in the mood for breakfast, and so Alan arranged for there to be tea and coffee and pastries in the room, and as the family assembled, they each helped themselves, and then found a place to sit.

Emma was the last to enter the room, having been asked by Lizzie to open and read the letter. She closed the door behind her, and then found a place to stand where she felt she had an even view of everyone in the room. 'This is a letter that Susan Fletcher wrote for Lizzie,' she said, holding the sealed envelope in her hand. 'Susan wrote it a few days before she died, shortly after Lizzie was born. And she asked that it not be opened until Lizzie was 23 years old. Lizzie has asked we all be here, with her, to hear what Susan wrote, all those years ago.'

Vicki laughed nervously. 'Just to be clear,' she said, 'I will start crying almost immediately, so please be ready for that.' And then, before she had even finished her sentence, a tear trickled down her cheek.

345

Everyone smiled at her, but no one said anything, each of them preoccupied with their own memories of Susan, and their own ideas and hopes of what the letter might contain.

Charlie was sat by a window, listening to the faint tapping of the rain against the glass, and remembered that awful day, his birthday, when he had stood outside his mother's hospice, wishing he could hold time in its place. Billy felt bereft, lost in his memory of the day his mother passed away, and how he had missed seeing her one last time, her death coming so much more quickly than anyone had expected. And Lizzie's nerves had not abated. She had heard so much about Susan over the years, mostly from Carol, who had acted as though it was her personal responsibility to keep Susan's memory alive. But for Lizzie, it felt as though Susan was about to speak to her for the very first time, and she had no idea what to expect. Carol, oddly quiet, sat on one of the couches, occasionally looking to Charlie for reassurance.

'Right, is everyone ready?' Emma asked, and nervously, they all nodded. Hands trembling slightly, she opened the envelope, unfolded the letter and began to read.

CHAPTER 68

10th March 2000

My darling Lizzie.

My heart is filled with both joy and sadness. The past 24 hours have been so joyful, with the birth of my healthy, beautiful baby girl. But there is also much sadness, because I know I will not be there for you, as you grow up. I wish so much that I could be, but I have known for many months that I do not have much time left and I have learned to accept this.

I am writing this letter for you to have on your 23rd birthday. When I have finished writing, I am going to seal the envelope and ask Carol to promise that no one will open or read it until then. I know this may sound silly, but with these words unseen and unread until that moment, I feel like I will be there with you, as though this letter is a small part of me, living on, into the future.

You may be wondering why I want you to wait so long before reading it. Well, 23 was an important age for me. I became a mother for the first time, and I got married – and to the dismay of my parents, I did it in that order. Your father and I also moved into The Lodge, which has been our home for many years, a place where we have raised our children and lived our lives. And, mostly, our lives have been filled with happiness and laughter.

The first thing I want to tell you, Lizzie, is that you are a very lucky girl. Because although you don't have me, I know how excited your father has been since the moment I told him that we had another baby Fletcher on the way. And you will have a wonderful mother in Carol. I cannot begin to tell you how much she means to me. I love her with all my heart, and I know she will love you, as her own.

You have been born into a big, loud, colourful family, and you have the most wonderful siblings who I know will love you and take care of you.

Charlie would fix the whole world if he could. He worries about everything and everyone, right down to the tiniest of details. And I love him so much for that, for his desire for everyone to be happy, and safe. He's my eldest and I can already see the man he will become. I know how hard he will work to look after you, to look after all of you. I hope he is happy, and I hope he has found someone to love him, someone to take the weight of the world off his shoulders. Because I know he has so much love to give, and whoever he shares his life with, I hope Charlie knows he has my blessing.

Your sister Vicki is very like me. She inherited a lot from her mother and, I would say, from her grandmother too. She can walk into a room of complete strangers, and within moments she will have struck up a conversation and put everyone at ease. I know she will succeed in whatever she puts her mind to. I love her so much, and I love that she wears her heart on her sleeve. It is always very obvious when she is happy, or sad, or cross. But she is also tough, much tougher than she knows. She has the strength to endure all the ups and downs of life. And that toughness is something us Fletcher girls have, Lizzie, and I promise you will have it too. You just need to find it.

Billy has the biggest heart of anyone I have ever known. He always gives people the benefit of the doubt, an open opportunity for them to be the best person they can be. I know the world isn't filled with good people and I am sure, over the years, there have been many who have let Billy down. But I hope he never loses that optimism, because Billy has an unusual gift, to make other people want to be better. And I think that's a beautiful quality to have in this difficult world. I love him so much for that, and I hope you share that quality with him, Lizzie.

And then there is Tyler, my little helper. You are going to grow up with him, and I know the two of you will be very close. I love that little lad so much, and I have loved all the days I have spent with him, sharing the things I have learned about how to make a garden flourish. I would love to think that he is still kneeling in the soil every day, because we gardeners are special. We make things grow. And I think that's what I see in Tyler, a boy who will take the ordinary and make it beautiful.

And then there is you, Lizzie, my little baby girl. And this is the hardest thing, because you won't know me in the way your siblings will. You won't remember me.

348

But I hope you know, I hope you believe, that I will always be with you. Just look for me, or listen for me, and you will know I'm there.

I might be an unexpected shower of rain, that falls in the middle of a dry, summer's day. Perhaps I will be a whisper at the back of your mind, reminding you to be brave and strong. Or the colour in a winter garden, a lone flower that blossoms out of season. Perhaps you will find me in the kind words of a stranger, who helps you when you are feeling lost. Or perhaps I'll be a song on the radio, to remind you that you are never alone.

I promise I will be all these things. Because I will always be with you all.

I love you.

Mum

CHAPTER 69

The moments which followed the reading of Susan's letter were loud and animated, a family lost in excited conversations, focussing on different moments from the letter, different parts which had offered them particular comfort or joy. It was clear no one wanted to leave the room, everyone had settled where they were, chatting and catching up. Emma opened the door to the library, and the group were soon joined by Martin, Blanche and Peggy who brought Debbie and Kim with them.

Alan then texted his children, and insisted they socialise with their new in-laws, and so Jill and Kieron joined too, hoping to ingratiate themselves with the Fletchers by bringing a serving trolly filled with champagne flutes and bottles of sparkling wine. And soon, corks were popping, and everyone was drinking.

There weren't quite enough seats, but no one cared. Some stood, some perched on the arms of the furniture. All that mattered was that everyone was together. Charlie was on the couch, Alan next to him, holding his hand. He watched quietly from the sidelines, at all the silliness, and happiness, and laughter. His gaze wandered from one person to the next, and he found himself wondering what the future would hold for each of them.

He imagined Vicki, her home full and noisy with children and young people, all so lucky to have his amazing sister looking after them. He knew there would be hard times for Vicki though. She had already learned the life of a foster carer can be difficult, sometimes even heartbreaking. But he knew she had exactly the sort of toughness she would need to meet all the challenges that lay ahead. He wasn't certain he could see a man in her future. She appeared to have settled into a happy, busy and fulfilling life surrounded by friends, family and kids. But he wondered if perhaps, just perhaps, she still had a bit of romance left in her, and that one day she might meet someone special.

Charlie suspected it would not be long before Billy and Emma announced a baby was on the way. And he could imagine they would have many children. He'd always thought Billy would make the most wonderful dad. And having seen him perform, he had great faith his brother's first national tour would lead to even greater opportunities. He truly loved them both, the couple who had somehow become the natural heart of the family, and who brought so much happiness to everyone else.

Charlie could clearly picture Tyler, running the villa, many years into the future, still looking cool, and only dating people in their twenties. To some degree he envied his brother's ability to just enjoy life, without all the trappings. And even though he appeared to have rooted himself to the same spot, Charlie suspected Tyler would go travelling every now and again. And that would be his life; the man who always wanted to travel, happily staying in the same place, except when he didn't.

And then there was Lizzie, the baby of the family, Susan's final gift to the world. Charlie wished he knew more about what had happened with her boyfriend, and why everyone seemed so reluctant to talk about him. And he worried that his little sister often seemed so fragile, so exposed in a world where there were plenty of unpleasant people. But he knew she had a small group of very good friends, young women she had known since school, who all seemed very protective of her. And even though Charlie felt, to some degree, that he had stolen Tyler away from her, he knew how close she was with Vicki and Jack, and with Billy and Emma too. She was, if nothing else, surrounded by love. And he was reassured by that, because he knew that sometimes simply being loved was all a person needed to be happy.

Charlie looked at the others in the room, all drinking and animated, laughing and chatting. He looked at his nephew Jack, happily catching up with Debbie and Kim, the first Fletcher kid to get a degree, so clever and hardworking, building such a great life for himself in Manchester. And if there was just one wish Charlie had for Jack's future, it was that his nephew would have the good sense to keep away from anyone in Nate's family. Charlie knew nothing good could possibly come from them.

Carol was regaling Alan's kids with a particularly entertaining tale. Even though Charlie could not hear what she was saying, he guessed it was one of her more colourful stories, as it had rendered both Jill and

Kieran wide-eyed and speechless. But they'd had a firm instruction from their father to be polite and to fit in, and both appeared to be doing their best to remain charming and unruffled.

For someone who's entire life had centred on being busy, constantly rushed off her feet, Charlie was surprised how much Carol had embraced retirement. Plans were afoot for her 75th birthday the following year, and he knew how important that celebration would be for everyone in the family. Because he knew how important Carol was for everyone in the family.

Then there was Alan, a man he genuinely adored, a man he would have married regardless, even if he had been the penniless divorcee he had originally claimed to be. And Charlie tried to imagine a happy future for them, falling into a very comfortable and happy routine, reducing their work commitments over time, and just enjoying their life together, with their friends and their family. He thought of his mother, and he wondered what she would make of Alan. Susan had never cared whether someone had money and treated everyone with the same good manners and respect. Charlie wondered how Alan might fair under his mother's critical gaze, stripped of his power and wealth, and judged purely on his character. He found himself smiling, knowing Susan would approve of his new husband, but that she would also take great delight quietly pricking Alan's ego if he ever appeared to get a little pompous.

He watched as his wonderful friends from Gran Canaria gleefully worked the room, catching up with everyone, knowing they would soon be stealing Charlie and Alan and taking them home with them. And the idea of that, of them, his friends, of the lunches at the Yumbo Centre, and the drag cabaret, and meeting up for a coffee in the morning, the whole idea of it filled Charlie with hope.

In the midst of such a happy moment, he knew how easy it could be to believe a new era was dawning for the Fletcher family, one promising happiness and good fortune for everyone. But whilst the wedding had been a happy distraction for him, Charlie was now left with the cruel realisation that the coming weeks were going to be difficult and perhaps even frightening. He would need Alan to be strong for him because his old soul had been tainted by too many dark days, and he no longer believed in such a thing as a happy ending or a bright new beginning.

Gradually, the room began to empty. Everyone had made plans for the afternoon, some downtime before they all met up again for dinner, their final night together. And before long, the library was almost empty, apart from Charlie, who stood alone at the window, looking out across the grounds.

'Some of us are heading into the village to look around. Do you want to come?'

Charlie turned at the sound of Vicki's voice and found her in the doorway, a coat folded over one arm. And he knew it was time. He had to tell her what was going to happen next. Because the whole family was expecting Alan and Charlie to head off for their honeymoon, but they weren't, and he needed his sister to know why.

CHAPTER 70

Tyler knocked on the door to Lizzie's suite and waited to be invited in. Once he had heard her voice, he gently pushed the door open and stepped inside. He found his sister reclined in a chair just in front of a window, re-reading the letter, a content smile on her face.

'Even her handwriting's perfect,' Lizzie said. 'Everything about this letter is so beautiful.'

Tyler closed the door behind him and sat on the edge of the bed. 'It was a pretty special moment, wasn't it?' he said, pleased to see his little sister so elated. 'I can't say I'm surprised though,' he added. 'One thing I remember about Auntie Susan, she was pure class. In every way.'

Lizzie re-read the section about Tyler: 'I would love to think that he is still kneeling in the soil every day because we gardeners are special. We make things grow. And I think that's what I see in Tyler, a boy who will take the ordinary and make it beautiful.' Placing the letter onto her lap, she smiled at her brother. 'She was clearly very fond of you.'

It felt as though that passage had proven Tyler's point. 'She always treated me as family. Like I said. Class act.'

'And she was right,' Lizzie continued. 'You create the most beautiful things, Tyler. I still have people at work send me pictures of the things you created across the parks in Southend, when you worked there. That enormous meadow you planted. It was just gorgeous. And everything you've done at Charlie's villa. It's like you've created a little oasis. Wherever you go, you create beautiful things.'

'Thanks sis. And what about you?' Tyler asked. 'Anything in the letter particularly resonate with you?'

Lizzie shrugged. 'All of it,' she replied. But then she glanced down at the paper, and the beautifully written words, and her eyes focussed on one of her mother's promises, and she read it out loud. *'Perhaps you will find me in the kind words of a stranger, who helps you when you are feeling lost.'* And with great fondness, she recalled Colin and his dog Casper, and the time they had spent together, chatting, on a bench overlooking the estuary.

354

Tyler shuffled slightly on the bed, waiting for a little more detail. When Lizzie didn't elaborate, he attempted to prompt her for a bit more information. 'Was this something to do with you breaking up with Stuart?' he asked, feeling there was a whole story that he knew only parts of.

Lizzie nodded, but she didn't want to burden Tyler with the details. She knew he would soon be flying home, and she didn't think it fair to leave him worrying about her. She was a grown-up now, 23 years old. She had to let her brother live his own life, and not stick around to look after her. 'He really wasn't the right man for me,' she said, choosing her words carefully.

'And are you OK now?'

Lizzie paused, knowing that she wasn't, not completely. She was better, and stronger, but there were moments when she was filled with rage, and other moments when she felt stupid and cried, worried she had let so many people down. And there were still moments, the moments that scared her the most, when she missed Stuart and wished things could have worked out differently. 'I'm getting there,' she said. 'I check in with the girls every day, Vicki and Emma, and my friends. They help me if I ever have a wobble.'

Tyler leaned forward and squeezed her hand. 'And listen, anytime you need to talk, please call me. Skype me. Whatever. Or just jump on a plane and come and stay with me. If there's one thing I've learned about being a Fletcher, it's that none of us ever needs to be alone.'

CHAPTER 71

Vicki was trying her hardest not to be angry. It was the day after her brother's wedding, and she didn't want to spoil the event. But Charlie had crossed a line, taking it upon himself to talk to her son about Nate, about things she had always kept secret, to protect Jack from ever knowing the awful truth about his father.

But she had found it a little too easy to fall into old habits, to start blaming Charlie. And that wasn't a person that Vicki wanted to be again. She didn't want to find herself finding fault with her brother, as a matter of course. And she knew how persuasive Jack could be and had no doubt he had placed Charlie in an awkward position. She could imagine that Charlie, being Charlie, had probably just tried to do what he thought was the right thing. And so, Vicki tried to keep it bright and breezy as she crossed the room to stand with her brother.

'Have you spoken to Jack?' he asked.

With those words, Vicki realised her attempt at 'bright and breezy' had failed and that she was evidently emitting some kind of negative energy which Charlie had sensed. Rather than dismiss the subject, she decided it was best if the two of them addressed it. 'He said you talked to him about Nate.'

'In my defence, I was in a very difficult situation,' Charlie said, his entire demeanour that of a man wracked with guilt. 'But I am sorry. It wasn't my place.'

Vicki stared at him for a moment and could feel all her animosity drain away, and she smiled a little. 'Oh, it's not your fault,' she conceded. 'To be honest, I don't know why I became so tight-lipped with Jack. I just had this barrier, something that stopped me ever talking about his dad.'

'You had a very difficult life with Nate,' he said. 'You lost an awful lot during those years. I can understand why it's hard to talk about him.'

Vicki agreed. 'To be honest, if Nate ever shows up again, I guess it is for the best that Jack knows who he's dealing with.' And then she noticed her brother swaying slightly, about to lose his balance, and he

356

suddenly grabbed sideways, for the wall, to help him stay on his feet. Vicki dropped her coat to the floor and jumped forward. 'Charlie!' she yelled. She held him tightly, pushed against him just hard enough to help him remain upright. 'It's OK. I've got you. I've got you.' A few seconds later, he was balanced again, rubbing his eyes, a little sheepish.

'Sorry, sorry. My fault,' he said. 'Lost my footing.'

'You better sit down,' Vicki said, her heart beating a little faster, worried that she and Jack may have added an entire layer of stress to her brother's busy weekend.

'No, no, I'm fine,' Charlie replied. 'It was just for a moment. Just a bit dizzy,' he replied.

Vicki picked up her coat and threw it onto a nearby chair, and when she turned back to Charlie, she noticed he was avoiding any eye contact with her. She recognised this version of him, the one who was keeping a secret.

'At least you've got your honeymoon coming up,' she said. 'Time to relax.' She reached across, and gently nudged his chin upwards, with her finger, so he would have to look at her.

'We've had to postpone,' he said. 'We're staying in the UK for a bit longer.'

As he spoke, Vicki noticed something in his tone, exasperation perhaps, or defeat. But whatever it was, it left her with the impression he was about to share something he would have preferred to keep secret. 'Why have you postponed?'

'We're going to London for a few days. I'm having some tests.'

'What sort of tests?' Vicki folded her arms and, all at once, she began to notice things that she hadn't noticed before; Charlie's face, suddenly old, tired, and how lethargic he appeared, how resistant to her questions. 'Charlie, what sort of tests?' she asked again.

'Well,' he replied, his voice uncharacteristically nervous. 'Not dissimilar to the tests mum had, at the end.'

The room silent, Vicki's head suddenly filled with noise and images, memories of their mother, all jumbled up, the final few months of her life, and one word repeated, again and again. 'Cancer?' she said.

Charlie nodded. 'Different to mum's. Melanoma.'

357

Her heart pounding, Vicki found herself desperate for reassurance, for Charlie to say something positive, that they'd caught it early, that it was just a growth he needed to have whipped off. 'Oh, skin cancer,' she said, attempting to sound nonchalant. 'That's fine. Millions of people get over that. Is it a mole?'

'Yes. On my side. Not somewhere you'd notice it.'

'But they can just cut it out, can't they?'

She hoped by saying those words out loud, with such obvious indifference, that she could guide the rest of the conversation and that Charlie would agree with her, and tell her everything was going to be fine. But there was a long pause after she had spoken, and Charlie's expression, trying so hard to be brave, made her want to cry.

'I have symptoms that suggest it may have spread. To my brain. Melanoma particularly likes the brain, apparently.'

Vicki went to speak, to say something kind, hopeful, about the wonders of modern medicine, of all the new treatments that were available, of the top private clinics Alan could easily afford. But it was as if Charlie knew what she was going to say, and needed to intervene, to stop those words from being said out loud.

'Vicki, you need to understand that, if it has spread to my brain, things get much more difficult straight away. I just need you to be ready for that, for whatever news the doctors give me.'

Tears welled up in Vicki's eyes and trickled down her cheeks, and she could feel herself trembling, her whole body aching at the thought of what might happen to her brother. 'Alan knows?' she asked.

'He's been amazing. Really strong. The only other person who knows is Jill. She was there when I had my first seizure.'

Vicki's face crumpled, and she reached over and held Charlie's hand. 'You had a seizure?' she said, quietly, her heart breaking at the thought of it. And then she leaned forward, and embraced him, and she could feel his arms around her, holding her tightly, and she realised how frightened he was, her big brother, not knowing what was going to happen to him.

'What's wrong?'

The interruption brought their embrace to an end. Vicki tried to wipe the tears from her cheeks, to pretend she hadn't been crying, and they turned to see Billy at the door, a concerned expression on his face.

'Oh, we're just having a moment,' Charlie replied, casually. 'All good. Are you heading off to the village too?'

Billy did not respond, and Vicki could tell he was trying to get a sense of what was really going on in the room. But she had to take her lead from Charlie, and it appeared he did not want to share his news with Billy, at least not just yet. She noticed Billy was holding something, a small silver tablet, and so she gestured to it.

'What you got there?'

Billy glanced down, and seeing the tablet seemed to remind him of the reason he had entered the library. 'Oh, yes. I have something to show you both.' He walked over to them, a puzzled expression on his face. 'You OK?' he asked Vicki, her eyes red, glistening.

'Oh, we were just talking about Mum's letter, and it set me off,' she said. She could tell Billy did not entirely believe her, and so she attempted to hurry the conversation on. 'What do you want to show us?'

Billy lifted the tablet and began to touch the screen. 'The marketing team have just emailed me a PDF of the programme for the show,' he said. 'I wanted you to see it.' He manoeuvred between the two of them so they could both see the display, and tapped to open the document.

And there he was, Vicki's kid brother, his handsome face adorning the cover, solemn, looking to the distance, an attractive woman with him, her head rested on his shoulder, and the title of the play emblazoned across the top of the image. Billy flicked through the rest of the pages, with information about the show, and Tennessee Williams, and two pages of cast biographies.

'Billy, it looks amazing,' Charlie said, enthusiastically. 'All your years of hard work, it's finally paying off.'

Billy turned slightly, towards his brother. 'There is something else,' he said. 'I hope you don't mind, but we're doing some shows in Southend, at the Cliffs Pavilion, and I asked the marketing team if they would produce a special programme for those shows. I had them add in a dedication.' Billy stroked his finger quickly across the screen, until he

359

reached a page that was mostly blank apart from a single paragraph of text. He used his fingers to expand the image and then read the inscription.

'This performance of Cat on a Hot Tin Roof is lovingly dedicated to the memory of Jason Day, who helped countless Southend families find a home. He'll be in the front row, cheering the loudest.'

'Oh, that's lovely,' Vicki said. She glanced at Charlie, and she could see his attempt to be strong, to control his emotions, was finally unravelling, his lip quivering, his eyes glistening.

'You see,' Billy said, 'we never forget him, Charlie. None of us does.' He put his arm around Charlie's shoulders and gave him a hug. Charlie, his voice quiet and strained, managed to whisper, 'Thank you', and then Vicki could see he was about to start sobbing, and so she moved forward to embrace them both.

'Group hug,' she said. 'This is definitely a group hug moment.' As she held onto them, her brothers, she closed her eyes and tried to think positive thoughts. She had believed the next few months were going to be calm and happy, with so many good things to look forward to. Now, the path ahead seemed less clear, perhaps even dark. But even though Charlie had asked her to be prepared for the worst, Vicki had no intention of believing her brother's situation was without hope. Because that was something Vicki had always had in abundance. Hope.

CHAPTER 72

18 September 2023

It wasn't the twenty-third birthday Vicki had wanted for her son. It began with a text message to say her package had been delayed and wouldn't be delivered to him until the following day. And then she and Jack had managed only a brief video chat, with Jack in the street, rushing to catch a bus to work, and barely enough signal for his mother to sing Happy Birthday. She could tell he was distracted, asking after his Uncle Charlie, hoping for some change in the news.

In the three months since the wedding, there had been a terrible sense of history repeating for Vicki, moments of hope being snatched away so quickly, so completely, time and time again. Sometimes, she felt as though the whole family was on pause, none of them able to really focus on life whilst Charlie's health continued to decline. She had set up an additional WhatsApp group called Charlie's Gang, with Billy and Emma, Tyler, Lizzie, Carol and herself. It was a chance for them to touch base with each other, and make sure everyone was in the loop about what was going on with their brother.

Tyler would send regular updates from Maspalomas, whenever Charlie and Alan were back home. His messages were always filled with joy and sunshine, of life continuing as normal, of meals at the Yumbo Centre with their friends, and early morning coffee at the villa. But sometimes, there were other things he would mention, things that were less sunny, of Charlie saying something out of character, or forgetting where he was, or being simply too exhausted to get out of bed.

Billy messaged every day from his touring show. She knew how well the production was doing, with sell out performances across the country and great reviews, with Billy regularly singled out as one to watch. Billy's fame was quickly growing, his social media followers surging into the hundreds of thousands. But poor Billy, she thought, so worried, often expressing how useless he felt, so far away, unable to enjoy any part of

361

his success. The only comfort Billy could find was with Emma, who he knew was supporting the family in his absence.

Vicki had been very impressed with Lizzie, of how she had turned her life around, but she was worried her little sister was spending too much time online, seeking miracle cures. At least once a week, Lizzie would post something into Charlie's Gang, a link to a story about a new treatment or a drug trial, and it made Vicki worried that, of all the family, Lizzie was still the farthest from accepting that Charlie did not have long to live.

And then there was Carol, who'd reacted to the news of Charlie's prognosis with what could only be described as anger, and she had remained angry ever since. Vicki understood why because Carol had always behaved as though she had a duty of care for all the Fletcher kids. If anything bad happened to any of them, Vicki knew Carol would feel as though she had failed Susan.

Alan had shown great strength, keeping everything organised and everyone up to date with what was going on. The moment he had heard Charlie's diagnosis, he had offered to spend a small fortune on his treatment. But her brother, so stubborn, had insisted he be treated by the NHS. At first, Alan had wanted to do everything, to be the only person helping Charlie. But he had soon realised there was an entire family who wanted, perhaps even needed, to have a role, and so there were occasions when he stepped aside and let one of the Fletchers take the lead.

That morning, Vicki was to collect Charlie from the hospital and then drive him to a seafront apartment Alan was renting for whenever he and Charlie were in Southend. And she knew how devastating it would be to see her brother again because each time he returned to the country for treatment, it seemed there was less of him there, the man she had known all her life, his body failing him, and his character quietly vanishing before her eyes.

She busied herself around the house for a few hours, some of the chores she had forgotten to do. And then she went to the cabin in her garden, which she had turned into her office space, and began to catch up on her fostering notes. Vicki was in between placements but knew

362

that wouldn't last, so was attempting to make the most of her downtime before her home was noisy and busy once more.

And then, at 11.30am, she left for the hospital. She always liked to leave earlier than needed, just in case the car park was busy. Sometimes, just trying to find a space could add half an hour onto her journey. But that day, she was fortunate and managed to park almost as soon as she arrived, and so made her way to the ward.

She had learned the route, which lift to take, and which floor she needed to reach and could now get there without looking at a single sign along the way. Some of the clinical staff on the ward, the nurses and doctors, had become familiar faces and many recognised her when she arrived. There was a nurse, José, who she particularly liked. He treated family members as people who needed care and attention too. He understood how stressful the process was for relatives, how anxious they could be, of any bad news or sudden changes.

As she entered the reception area, José was there, in his neatly ironed dark blue uniform. He saw her arrive and approached her straight away, a cheerful smile on his face, which immediately put Vicki at ease.

'Hello, Miss Fletcher,' he said. And then, in a quieter voice, he added; 'Your brother is having a lay down in one of the private rooms. He had a reaction to his treatment this morning. Nothing to worry about. It's not unusual. But he felt quite nauseous, so we thought he should have a bit of recovery time before he went home with you.'

'But that's normal?'

'Yes, yes. Not unusual at all. Also, I know Dr Ghosh wants to see him. Just to go through his latest results. So, if you could just stay until then. I don't think she will be long.'

Vicki resisted the urge to ask José if he knew anything about the test results, partly because she was too frightened to ask, but also because she knew Charlie had to be told first. He led her to one of the private rooms, opened the door for her, and then he said he would try to find the doctor and left.

The room was small, with just enough space for a bed, a side table and a couple of chairs. Charlie was lying on his side, his back to the door, gazing at the window. Outside, a glorious view over the city, but from

363

his position, Vicki knew Charlie would only be able to see the sky. She walked to the other side of the bed, pulled up a chair and then sat down. She stared at her brother's face, so pale and slim, his eyes tired and lined. She felt as though he could just fade away in front of her. He moved his head to look at her and, unusually, didn't smile as he saw her. Instead, he looked pensive, something on his mind.

'Heard you were a bit sick,' she said, and held his hand. 'You OK now?'

He shuffled about on the bed and managed to sit up. 'I feel better,' he said. 'But I don't think we can go yet. The doctor wants to talk to me. Is that alright with you?'

'Of course, of course,' Vicki said. 'I've got all day. Jack sends his love. He said thank you for the birthday money. He's putting it towards a new laptop.'

Charlie stared at her, blankly, and Vicki could tell he didn't have a clue what she was talking about. But she didn't want to dwell on it, because she knew how frustrating it would be for him, that he had forgotten it was his nephew's birthday.

'Alan's at the apartment all day, so he'll be there when-'

'Vicki, I need to talk to you about something,' Charlie said, interrupting. 'I've been putting this off for... so long. But I must tell you.'

His voice, so frail, so lethargic, and yet Vicki could clearly hear something else as he spoke. Charlie was frightened. He was really frightened.

'You can tell me anything,' she said, to try and reassure him. At the age of 46, her brother was reaching the end of his life, and she could not imagine that anything could possibly be worse than that. 'After everything we've been through Charlie, I promise, it will be OK.'

Charlie closed his eyes as though trying to gather some strength, and then he spoke. 'It won't be OK,' he said. 'I've kept this for so many years. But I have to tell you what I did. Because I'm going to make a statement to the police, and you need to hear this from me, before I do that.'

He opened his eyes again, and glanced to the window, at the rolling grey clouds above the hospital. And in that moment, that pause in the conversation, Vicki wondered if she should call for assistance, concerned

Charlie was confused, or had become delirious. There was nothing, she thought, nothing he could possibly have done that could involve the police. 'Charlie, are you alright? Do you need me to call for help?'

He moved his head, to look at her, his eyes, so dark, focusing on her's. 'I can't risk it. Not being here, in the future, and the police finding out. They might think someone else was involved. And I won't be here to tell them the truth. So, I have to tell them now. While I still can.'

Vicki began to stand. 'Charlie sweetheart, I think I should get-'

'I know where Nate is.'

The words, so unexpected, stopped Vicki in her tracks. She was stood, with her back slightly turned on Charlie, ready to walk from the room to seek medical assistance, her brother so confused. But it didn't feel as though those words, those bizarre, inexplicable words, were the symptom of delirium. She had a feeling, a strange feeling in the pit of her stomach, that Charlie might actually know something.

Slowly, she returned to her seat, and then she leaned forward, and with great tenderness, she took her brother's hand once more. 'Charlie, it's been more than a decade,' she said, her voice quiet, gentle. 'No one's seen him since 2009. The police have been looking for him all this time. How could you have tracked him down? Why would you even want to?'

Charlie shook his head as though frustrated that Vicki didn't understand what he was trying to tell her. 'I haven't tracked him down. I've always known where he is,' he said, flatly.

Nothing Charlie was saying made sense to Vicki, but she needed him to keep talking, so that she could be certain whether or not he was simply confused, or if he genuinely did have some information about what Nate had been up to for all those years. 'Then where is he, Charlie?' she asked.

Charlie paused, offering his sister a final moment of normality before he shared what he knew. 'He's in your back garden,' he said.

Vicki, words failing her, could only offer him a shrug, unable to understand what he was talking about. She waited, for Charlie to say more, but when he did finally speak, Vicki's world was changed forever.

'I buried him under the cabin.'

365

CHAPTER 73

Vicki wondered how she got there; by a window, so high up, a chair overturned on the floor in front of her, and a man sitting up on a bed, his hand held out to her. Her heart was pounding so hard in her chest that she almost screamed out for help. But something stopped her, something prevented her from drawing attention to whatever was going on in that room.

As she gasped, caught her breath, she looked at the man, and she could see it was Charlie, so thin, his expression one of shock. And suddenly she remembered what he had said, so casually, just seconds before; *'I buried him under the cabin.'*

'It's OK,' Charlie said, calmly, 'I understand. But I have to explain to you what happened.'

Vicki knew he was telling the truth; somehow, she just knew. Nate was dead. He had been dead all that time, buried in her back garden. Her son's father, rotting in the ground, and her brother had known it, all along. 'How?' she cried, her voice louder than she had intended.

'Please, please, come and sit down,' Charlie said, breathlessly. 'This is a horrible shock, I know. But I must tell you what happened. All of it. You have to hear it all.'

Vicki couldn't move, at first. Frozen to the spot, she stared at her brother, a stranger suddenly, a man who had done something terrible, gruesome. And she realised she was frightened of him. But he was right, she knew that at least. She had to know everything. Slowly, she moved towards him. She picked the chair up from the floor and set it back on its feet. And then she sat, her hands on her lap, and said; 'Tell me what you did to Nate.'

Charlie began to share his story. He described a terrible rainstorm, thunder and lightning, his house in darkness. He spoke of a hooded intruder, trying to break in, believing the house to be empty, and of his shock when he realised who the intruder was. He described their conversation; Nate's pretence that he knew the house belonged to Charlie, his claim that he and Vicki were to reconcile, and how he joked

366

about what had happened to Jason. And the whole time, Charlie had stood, a large kitchen knife in his hand, wishing Nate dead.

But the story did not progress in the way Vicki feared it might. Instead, it ended abruptly; Nate simply left, and Charlie went back into the house. 'I sat there, for a long time, in the dark', he said, 'so angry at what he'd said. I thought about calling the police, but I was too tired by then, and probably a bit drunk. So, I just went to bed. I was going to call them in the morning.'

He fell silent, as though the story was over, but Vicki knew there was much more he had yet to tell. 'Charlie, what did you do to Nate?' she asked.

He exhaled, his dark eyes filled with sorrow, so frightened to say out loud what had happened, all those years earlier. 'In the morning, I got dressed and went outside, to tidy up after the storm. There was stuff all over the garden. Tree branches, part of someone's fence panel. And the ground was sodden, completely waterlogged. But the main problem was this long trench Jason had dug for his koi pond. You remember? It was wide and long, about six feet deep.

'Jason had covered it with a sheet of tarpaulin that he'd weighed down at each corner with these heavy cement slabs. But the rain had been so heavy that part of the trench had collapsed in on itself and taken one of the slabs with it, and the tarpaulin was all tangled up in the hole. I tried to pull it out, so at the very least I could cover over the trench again, until I could decide what to do with it. But it was really heavy and seemed to be stuck on something.'

Vicki could feel her insides tightening and her blood running cold, as she realised what her brother was about to tell her. 'Oh god,' she whispered.

'And then, I gave it one really hard tug, and something just... appeared, down in the hole. It just sort of raised up, out of the mud and the water. I couldn't work out what it was, or how it got there. So, I leaned over to have a closer look, and I realised it was an arm. Someone was down there, a dead body, in my back garden.

'Out of pure fright, I stumbled backwards, and without realising, I pulled the tarpaulin again, and then more of the body came to the

367

surface. It was right next to where the cement slab had dropped down, into the hole. I could see a shoulder and the face. And even though it was all muddy, I could see it was Nate, a large gash at the side of his head.

'And that's when I realised, that's why he'd been calling my name. He must have stumbled across the trench and fallen in. He'd gotten all tangled up in the plastic sheeting, too. I guess he was panicking, trying to climb out. But the ground was so wet that, I think, as he grabbed at the mud, it must have all just collapsed on top of him and brought the cement slab down onto his head. I think either that killed him, or maybe it knocked him out and then he suffocated under the mud.'

Amid all the disturbing images her brother was evoking, Vicki's tormented heart was suddenly lost to a deep sense of anguish. She knew Nate had been a bad man, and she knew the dark path he had chosen to follow throughout his life. But there were moments, occasionally, when she remembered the man she had fallen in love with; funny and caring, that cheeky smile, full of optimism. And for some strange reason, that was the version of Nate she pictured in that hole, and the cold and lonely death he must have endured. He would have been so frightened at the end, she thought, in the dark, and the rain, trapped, with no one to help him. And Charlie had left him there, in that hole, for all those years, alone and lost to the world.

'Why didn't you call the police?' she asked. 'If it was just an accident, why not call the police?'

Charlie, unflinching, replied. 'I tried,' he said. 'I went inside, and I picked up my phone, and I went to dial. But then I just stopped. And I thought, who the hell is going to believe me? Who's going to believe this enormous coincidence, that of all the thousands and thousands of houses in Southend, Nate just happened to pick mine.'

Vicki knew she had never shared the address with Nate. There was never a reason he would need to have it. The only reason he could have been at Charlie's house that night, was for exactly the reason Charlie had said; a coincidence. But what a truly enormous coincidence, she thought, one any police officer would have been very suspicious of.

368

'And everyone knew I hated him,' Charlie continued. 'A man I hated died in my back garden. No witnesses. Just me and him. And I started to panic. It was like I could envision the police turning up, and the look on their faces, and the disbelief, and then the questioning. I could feel it, inside me, this... knowing. That once I made that phone call, everything that happened afterwards, it would be set. Unchangeable. I'd be charged, and then prison. And all because Nate tried to burgle my house.'

'And so you just... filled the hole? Left him down there?'

Charlie nodded, and then leaned forward slightly, sitting upright on the bed, and he gazed into his sister's eyes. 'You do believe me, don't you?' he asked. 'You know what I'm saying is true?'

Vicki could tell that was when Charlie was the most frightened; the idea that his sister might think he was lying. But she knew Charlie too well. He rarely ever told lies, and when he did, he was terrible at it. And, as he had told his gruesome story, there hadn't been a single word that Vicki thought might not be true. Nate's death had been a horrific accident, just as Charlie had described it.

'I know you're telling the truth,' she said, solemnly. 'But I just don't know what to say. This is horrible. It's Jack's father we're talking about. He's been dead for fourteen years, and you knew it, all along. You even let me buy your house, knowing he's buried in the garden.'

Charlie rested back against the pillows once more, and glanced downwards, ashamed. 'I know, I know,' he said, quietly. 'It just felt safer at the time. That the house would stay in the family. No one coming in to dig everything up.'

Vicki still couldn't believe the conversation they were having, that her brother, her own brother, had kept such a horrific secret for so many years. But now, his strength depleted, and so ready for his own ending, Charlie finally wanted to do the right thing and confess to the police.

'They might believe you,' she said. 'The police. Nate was a serial burglar. He robbed dozens of homes. Some of them in the town centre. It's not inconceivable that he might have stumbled across your house by accident. And we all knew about the pond. You and I even spoke about it a few times, after Jason died, what you were going to do with it.'

369

Charlie smiled at his sister. 'I think you are trying to convince yourself,' he said. 'But it doesn't really matter. Whether or not the police believe me. I don't have much time left and I just need to make sure no one else is implicated.'

'And Alan? What has he said?' Vicki watched as the smile faded from Charlie's face, replaced with an expression of sadness.

'I should never have gotten involved with him,' he said. 'I should have kept my barriers up. But when I was home, on Gran Canaria, it all began to feel so far away, and so long ago. Like a bad dream. I fooled myself into thinking I could just put it to the back of my mind, forget about it.'

Vicki leaned forward in her chair. 'But what has he said about this?'

Charlie shrugged. 'I've only told you,' he said. 'I'm going to tell Alan tonight, at the flat. And I'm going to divorce him, if I can. It wouldn't be fair on him, to make him stay with me, after all this comes out.'

The conversation was interrupted by a knock at the door, and then a doctor stepped into the room, a middle-aged woman in a white coat, a clipboard under her arm. 'Mr Fletcher,' she said, softly. 'I would like to talk you through your treatment. Are you feeling well enough?'

It wasn't until that interruption that Vicki realised how desperately she needed to be out of that room, away from Charlie. She immediately stood and said, 'I'll get a coffee. I'll leave you to it.' As she hurried from the room, she could feel Charlie's eyes on her, and knew he was trying to assess how she might be feeling, and what she might do.

Still trembling, she realised her legs weren't going to carry her far, and so she quickly found an empty chair in the ward's reception area, and sat down, her face in her hands. She kept having flashes of that stormy night, and Nate screaming for Charlie to help him, from deep inside that dark trench. And then she could picture Charlie, the next day, desperately shovelling soil into the hole, to bury Nate forever in the back garden. Vicki was resisting a strong urge to just run away, to pretend the whole story was fiction, a delusion, just an unpleasant symptom of her brother's condition. But she knew it was true, and she knew she had nowhere to run, because her home no longer felt like her safe space. Nate was buried in her back garden.

370

She sat up and, out of pure habit, immediately produced her mobile phone from her pocket and opened WhatsApp. On the main family group, there were birthday messages from everyone to Jack, and Jack had uploaded pictures from his office, of his desk decorated by his colleagues with banners and balloons, and a little cake with a candle on it.

Vicki lost herself in those images for a while, enjoying the happiness and normality of them. She was so proud of everything Jack had achieved, how hard he had worked and how easily he made friends. But she was so frightened of how terrible and dark the coming days and weeks would be for her son, to be told his father had been dead all those years and that the police were going to excavate his own mother's back garden, to retrieve whatever was left of the body. He was going to discover that an uncle, who he adored, was so cruelly involved, and the whole gruesome story would most likely play out in the national press.

And that frightened Vicki the most, because she had seen it all before, with Billy, and all the salacious stories that had been printed about him, and Neil Croker. The whole family had believed there would be just that one story, for one day, but that wasn't how it had played out. Billy had endured weeks of articles and exclusives, opinion pieces and photographers, a tabloid feeding frenzy; the handsome aspiring actor and his perverted, predatory boss.

She could imagine the same might happen for her son, and the terrible impact it would have on the exciting, joyful life he had created for himself in Manchester. She feared it would all be stolen away from him, that his friends and work colleagues would suddenly feel differently about him, about the sort of young man that he was, and the sort of family he came from.

And then she wondered, about that joyful life, and how things would be different, if Nate had been alive for all those years. She doubted he would have been interested in Jack as a child. He might have seen Jack, every now and again, when it suited him, but mostly Vicki could imagine Nate making all sorts of promises to their son, and then just not showing up.

371

Jack as an adult, though, that was different, she thought. Nate would most definitely show up now. She could imagine Nate, trying to insert himself into Jack's life, possibly even relocating to Manchester, moving into Jack's home, kipping on his couch, and introducing her son to all sorts of dropouts and criminals. Her son, so kind and eager to please, would slowly be drawn into Nate's dangerous world.

There had been too many people, Vicki thought, who'd involved themselves with the Fletchers, because they thought they had something to gain from them; Neil Croker, of course, who'd abused the trust of her younger brother in such a horrible way. But then she remembered the months following the car accident, and how Jason's parents had tried to exploit their own son's death to take money from Charlie.

She thought of Angel, who had plotted for so many years to steal the Fletcher family home. And even though that situation was long since resolved, for Vicki many uncomfortable questions remained unanswered; she had never been certain how ruthless Angel had been in her pursuit of The Lodge, and whether she had ably assisted Peter in drinking himself into an early grave. And then there was Stuart, who had taken such cruel advantage of her inexperienced younger sister, and who's abusive and manipulative behaviour would likely affect Lizzie for many years to come.

There had been too many people, Vicki thought, who had brought nothing but pain and heartbreak to her family, and she knew Nate had been one of the worst. And just for a moment, Vicki allowed herself to indulge a dark thought, that Jack was undeniably better off, with his father long dead.

'How are you, Miss Fletcher?'

Vicki looked up and saw José had joined her.

'Fine, fine,' she said. She gestured towards her phone. 'It's my son's birthday. But he lives in Manchester, so he's sending me pictures.' As she spoke, she wondered if she sounded normal, or if José might notice something strange about her behaviour. But he simply responded with a smile.

'Lovely,' he said. 'And have you told him the good news about your brother? What a great birthday present for him. Must be such a relief for you all. But you must make sure he keeps up with his treatment. I know Dr Ghosh has updated his plan.'

Vicki knew she was being told something important, but at first her mind couldn't quite process what José was saying. 'I didn't quite understand... about the tumour,' she said, pretending she knew what he was talking about.

José sat on the chair next to her and began to explain. 'Oh. Dr Ghosh is a wonderful doctor, but she does sometimes forget to explain things in a way patients and their families can fully understand. Very simply, immunotherapy has done a much better job at clearing the cancer cells than we had anticipated. We don't see this very often. In fact, it's very rare, but Dr Ghosh has updated your brother's prognosis.'

As José spoke, Vicki could feel her entire world changing around her. Everything she had been forced to accept as a certainty was now in doubt, and she could feel all the pressure and darkness of that terrible day beginning to dissolve. 'He's not going to die?' she asked.

José frowned. 'Well, there are no definites when it comes to cancer, Miss Fletcher, but right now, I would say things are looking positive, and there is a very good chance your brother is going to lead a long and, hopefully, healthy life. I must say again how rare this is. And I hate to use the word lucky, but your brother is a very lucky man.'

Vicki had to see Charlie. She had to see him straight away, to talk to him, to stop what he was going to do. Because everything was different now. Vicki thanked José for explaining and then she stood and started to walk away from him, briskly moving towards Charlie's room, her heart suddenly singing with joy.

He wasn't going to die. Her brother was going to live. Charlie was going to live.

EPILOGUE

Dr Ghosh was just leaving as Vicki reached the door to Charlie's room. She offered Vicki a warm and satisfied smile, a doctor who'd delivered some unexpectedly good news. Vicki hurried inside and closed the door, and she found Charlie on the bed, his face in his hands, quietly sobbing. She perched on the side of the bed and wrapped her arms around him.

'Hey, hey, no tears,' she said. 'No tears. This is wonderful. I get to keep you. We all get to keep you.' She could feel her brother trembling, overwhelmed by the whole idea that the years ahead might not have been stolen from him, after all. But she also knew the only reason he had shared his terrible secret was because he thought he was going to die, and it was too late to take it back.

Vicki gave Charlie a squeeze and then, with her hands on his shoulders, she gently manoeuvred him onto the pillows behind him and handed him a tissue from a box on the bedside table. He wiped his eyes, and then stared at her, his expression sad, not happy.

'It doesn't change anything,' he said. 'This has gone on for too long. I have to talk to the police. I have to give you all closure.'

Fondly, Vicki lifted her hand, and began to brush her fingers through Charlie's hair, trying to make it tidy. There he was, her brother, trying to do the right thing, regardless of everything it would cost him. But Vicki had come to a very different conclusion about what needed to be done, and Charlie confessing to the police was not a part of it. 'No,' she said. 'You won't be doing that.'

'I have to.'

Vicki frowned, and slowly shook her head. 'Nope. You don't. And you won't.'

Charlie went to speak, but Vicki placed her finger over his lips, and then she sat, and she told Charlie what was going to happen next.

'You are not going to tell anyone else. Not even Alan. This stays between the two of us, is that clear?'

'Vicki, no,' he replied, anxious, as though worried for her. 'I promise, this has been horrible. All these years, this secret. It will eat you up, inside. It will always be there, gnawing at you. I can't ask you to go through that, for the rest of your life.'

'But Charlie, the alternative is far, far worse,' she said. 'Because I think you're right. I think you *would* go to prison. And that's not fair, because this was all Nate's fault. He's the one who tried to break into your house in the middle of Hurricane bloody Gilbert. He's the one who fell down a great big hole and died. None of that was down to you. And I understand why you panicked. I understand why you covered it up, and kept it secret all these years.'

She could see the expression on her brother's face, so unconvinced, and even the threat of prison was no longer enough to dissuade him from what he thought he should do.

'It would ruin Jack,' she said, hoping Charlie might respond differently, if he had to think about the repercussions on the people he loved. 'This would be in all the papers, up and down the country. And they'd look for him, wouldn't they, the press? They would want to track down Nate's son. His whole life would be turned upside down.'

'But don't you think he deserves to know the truth, Vicki?'

'No, actually I don't,' she replied, matter-of-factly. 'Whenever he talks about Nate, which isn't often, but whenever he does, he always mentions that he could be dead. The longer Nate's been gone, the more Jack seems to think that's probably the case. I just can't see there's any benefit in Jack knowing that for certain. Not with everything else that would happen.

'And what about Billy? He's a rising star, Charlie. He's heading towards a million social media followers. It's only going to take one smart reporter to link Billy to this, to a dead body in a garden in Southend, and he'll be all over the newspapers again. And he'll be dropped from the show, the moment all that bad publicity headed his way.'

Charlie lowered his head and looked downwards, and Vicki began to feel her words might finally be having an effect.

'And you know Nate's family. They're all scum. They're not going to care he's dead. They're just going to care about money, who they can sue. And it won't be long before they realise who you're married to, Charlie, how much money Alan has. He's the one they'll go after.

'And then there's me. I'll have the police at my house, digging everything up. All the neighbours knowing and pointing; 'That's the house where they found a dead body in the garden'. I doubt the fostering team will ever place a child with me again.'

Charlie remained still, facing downwards, making almost no sound, apart from the gentle noise of his breathing.

'Charlie?' Vicki said, hoping he hadn't fallen asleep.

But then he looked up, and stared at her, his expression changed. He no longer appeared anxious, instead he appeared calm.

'This would impact on all of us, Charlie,' she said. 'Tyler and Lizzie and Carol and Emma too. It would affect all of them, if you went to the police. And why? Nate ruined too many lives. We can't let him ruin any more, now he's dead.'

Gently, Charlie reached towards his sister and held her hands in his. 'You need to be sure,' he said. 'You just need to be absolutely certain you can do this. Because it's a terrible secret to keep, Vicki. A man is dead.'

Vicki knew he was right. She could already feel it, a coldness, settling into her bones. It was the darkest family secret of all, and she knew she would have to carry it for the rest of her life. But she could also see the bigger picture and she knew how important it was that Nate was never found. She knew the devastation that would bring, if the truth was ever revealed, not only for Charlie, but for her son, for the whole Fletcher family. And so, she leaned forward and kissed Charlie on the forehead, and then she spoke, her decision final.

'Just you and me, bruv. This must stay just between you and me,' she said. 'Our secret.'

376

377

378

Acknowledgements

Inspector Laura Stellon, Essex Police
Dr Darrell Green, Norwich Medical School, University of East Anglia
Gemma Taylor, Oak Leaf Editing
Barnaby Edwards, Artist

Printed in Great Britain
by Amazon